THE SINS
OF THE
WOLF

Also by Anne Perry
Published by Fawcett Books

Featuring Thomas and Charlotte Pitt

The Cater Street Hangman
Callander Square
Paragon Walk
Resurrection Row
Rutland Place
Bluegate Fields
Death in the Devil's Acre
Cardington Crescent
Silence in Hanover Close
Bethlehem Road
Highgate Rise
Belgrave Square
Farrier's Lane
The Hyde Park Headsman

Featuring Inspector William Monk

The Face of a Stranger
A Dangerous Mourning
Defend and Betray
A Sudden, Fearful Death

THE SINS OF THE WOLF

Anne Perry

FAWCETT COLUMBINE
New York

To Kimberly Hovey
for her help and friendship

THE SINS
OF THE
WOLF

CHAPTER
ONE

———

Hester Latterly sat upright in the train, staring out of the window at the wide, rolling countryside of the Scottish Lowlands.

The early October sun rose through a haze above the horizon. It was a little after eight in the morning, and the stubble fields were still wreathed in mist, the great trees seeming to float rootless above it, their leaves only beginning to turn bronze on odd branches here and there. The buildings she could see were of solid gray stone, looking as if they had sprung from the land in a way the softer colors of the south never did. There were no thatched roofs here, no plaster walls pargeted in patterns, but tall chimneys smoking, crowstepped gables outlined against the sky, and broad windows winking in the early light.

She had come home when her parents had died at the close of the Crimean War, nearly a year and a half before. She would like to have stayed in Scutari until the bitter end, but the family tragedy had required her presence. Since then she had attempted to put into effect some of the new nursing practices she had learned so painfully, and even more, to reform England's old-fashioned ideas of hospital hygiene in accordance with Miss Nightingale's theories. And for her pains, she had been dismissed as opinionated and disobedient. There really was no defense against either charge. She was guilty.

Her father had died in social and financial disgrace. There was no money for her, or for her brother Charles. He would have provided for her, of course, out of his own salary, and she could have lived with him and his wife as a dependent, but that thought was intolerable. Within a short space of time she had found a position as a private nurse, and when the patient recovered, she had found another. Some were agreeable, others less so, but she had never been more than a

3

week without some remunerative employment, and so she was her own mistress.

This summer she had taken another hospital appointment briefly, at the urgent request of her friend and frequent patron Lady Callandra Daviot, when the death of Nurse Barrymore had threatened Dr. Christian Beck with arrest and prosecution. When that matter had been finally resolved she had found another private post, but that too was at an end, and she was once again seeking a place.

She had found it in the form of an advertisement in a London newspaper. A prominent Edinburgh family was seeking a young woman of good birth, and some nursing background, to accompany Mrs. Mary Farraline, an elderly lady of delicate but not critical health, who wished to make the journey to London, and back again some six days later. One of Miss Nightingale's ladies would be preferred. All travel would naturally be paid for by the family, and there would be a generous remuneration for the duties required. Applications were to be sent to Mrs. Baird McIvor, at 17 Ainslie Place, Edinburgh.

Hester had never been to Edinburgh before—indeed, she had not been to Scotland at all—and the thought of four such train journeys at this time of the year seemed most agreeable. She wrote to Mrs. McIvor stating her experience and qualifications, and her willingness to accept the position.

She received a reply four days later, and enclosed with Mrs. McIvor's acceptance of her application was a second-class train ticket for the night journey to Edinburgh on the following Tuesday, leaving London at 9:15 in the evening and arriving in Edinburgh at 8:35 the morning after. A carriage would meet her at Waverley Station and take her to the Farraline house, where she would spend the day becoming acquainted with her patient, and that evening she and Mrs. Farraline would board the train and return to London.

Hester had made some inquiries, out of interest, even though she would barely arrive in Edinburgh before she left it again, at least on the initial visit. Perhaps when she returned with Mrs. Farraline after her stay in London she would have the opportunity to remain a day or two. Her time would be her own, and she could see something of the city. She had been informed that in spite of being the capital of Scotland, it was a great deal smaller than London, a mere one hundred and seventy thousand compared with London's nearly three million. Nonetheless it was a city of great distinction, "the Athens of the North," renowned for its learning, most particularly in the fields of medicine and law.

The train rattled and lurched around a curve in the tracks, and when the air had cleared Hester could see in the distance the dark rooftops of the city, dominated by the crooked skyline of the castle perched on its massive rock, and beyond them all, the pale gleam of the sea. In spite of all common sense, she felt a thrill of excitement ripple through her as though she were at the outset of some great adventure, not a single day in a strange house before a very ordinary professional task.

The journey had been long and uncomfortable, there being no privacy in a second-class carriage, and very little room. She had naturally sat upright all night, so she was stiff, and had only the occasional snatches of sleep. She stood up and straightened her clothes, then, as discreetly as possible, redid her hair.

The train finally drew into the station amid gushing steam, clanking wheels, shouting voices and slamming doors. She seized her single piece of luggage, a soft-sided valise large enough for only a change of underclothing and her toiletries, and made her way to alight onto the platform.

The cold air struck her sharply, making her draw in her breath. Everywhere there was noise and bustle, people shouting for porters, newsboys calling out, the clatter of trollies and wagons. Cinders shot out of the funnel and a grimy stoker whistled cheerfully. Steam belched and billowed across the platform and a man swore as smuts descended on his clean shirt collar.

Hester felt wildly exhilarated, and she strode along the platform towards the stairs and the exit with most unladylike haste. A large woman in a stiff black dress and poke bonnet looked at her with disapproval and remarked ringingly to the man next to her that she did not know what young people were coming to these days. No one had any sense of what was proper anymore. Manners were quite shocking, and everyone was a deal too free with their opinions, whether they had any right to them or not. As for young women, they had every kind of unsuitable idea in their heads that one might imagine.

"Aye, m'dear," the man said absently, continuing to look for a porter to carry their very considerable baggage. "Aye, I'm sure you're right," he added as she appeared to be about to continue.

"Really, Alexander, I sometimes think you are not listening to me at all," the woman said testily.

"Oh, I am, m'dear, I am," he answered, turning his back on her and waving to a porter.

Hester smiled to herself and made her way up the steps to the exit, and after handing in her ticket, went out onto the street. It took her only a few moments to find the carriage which had come to meet her; the driver was the only one looking from person to person, but hesitating when he saw a young woman in a plain gray costume and carrying a single valise. Hester passed her and addressed the man.

"Excuse me, are you from Mrs. McIvor?" she inquired.

"Aye, miss, I am that. Would you be Miss Latterly, just come up from London to be with the mistress?"

"Yes I am."

"Well then, you'll be ready to come and sit down to a decent breakfast, I daresay. I don't suppose they serve anything on those trains, but we can do better, and that's a fact. Here, I'll take your bag for you."

She was about to protest that it was not heavy, but he took it anyway, and crossing the pavement, handed her up into the carriage and closed the door. The journey was far too short; she would have liked to see more of the city. They proceeded simply off the bridge into Princes Street, down the greater part of its length past the fine fronts of shops and houses to the right, and to the left the green slope of the gardens, Scott's monument and the castle beyond and above. They turned right up towards the new town, and after the briefest passage through Georgian streets, they were in Ainslie Place. Number seventeen was exactly like its neighbors to either side: four stories high with spacious windows decreasing in size with each floor, and perfect symmetry to its facade, proportions that were full of grace and ease and the Regency's eye for simplicity.

She was driven around the back; after all, she was more of a servant than a guest. She alighted in the yard before the coachman returned the vehicle and horse to the stables, and presented herself at the door. It opened before she had time to pull the bell, and a bootboy regarded her with interest.

"I'm Hester Latterly, the nurse to accompany Mrs. Farraline on her journey," she introduced herself.

"Oh yes, miss. If ye'll come in, I'll tell Mr. McTeer." And without waiting for her answer, he led her through the kitchen to the passageway, where he almost walked into a gaunt-faced butler with a funereal expression. The butler regarded Hester closely.

"So ye're the nurse that's come to take the mistress to London." He said it as if London were the burial ground. "Ye'd better come in. Mirren'll be bringing your case, no doubt. And I daresay ye'll be wanting a bite to eat before ye go and see Mrs. McIvor." He looked at her appraisingly. "And a wash and a chance to comb your hair."

"Thank you," she accepted self-consciously, feeling untidier than she had hitherto thought herself.

"Aye, well if ye like to go into the kitchen, the cook'll get ye breakfast, and someone'll come for ye when Mrs. McIvor's ready."

"Come on," the bootboy said cheerfully, turning on his heel to take her back. "What are them trains like, miss? I never been on one."

"You get about your business, Tommy," the butler ordered dourly. "Never mind about trains. Have you done Mr. Alastair's good boots yet?"

"Yes, Mr. McTeer, I done them all."

"Then I'll find something else for you. . . ."

Hester was given an excellent meal at a corner of the large kitchen table, then shown to a small bedroom set aside for her use, next to the nursery, where her valise had been left. She washed her face and neck, and did her hair yet again.

She had no time to wait until she was sent for and conducted by the dismal McTeer through the green baize door into a large hall with a black-and-white flagged floor like a chessboard. The walls were paneled in wood and there were half a dozen trophies of animal heads mounted and hung, most of them red deer. However, the one thing that arrested her attention and held it was a life-size portrait of a man straight ahead of her. It dominated the room, not only with its coloring, which was remarkable, but with some quality of character in the features. His head was long and narrow with large, clear blue eyes, a long slender nose, pinched at the bridge, and a broad mouth whose lines were blurred and strangely uncertain. His fair hair swept across his brow in a splash of color so startling as to draw the eyes from all the surrounding darkness of oak and gilt and the glassy stare of the long-dead stags.

The butler led her across the hall and down a passage past several doors until he came to one where he knocked briefly, then he opened it and stood back for her to pass.

"Miss Latterly, ma'am, the nurse from London."

"Thank you, McTeer. Please come in, Miss Latterly." The voice was soft, gently modulated, and only very slightly accented in the precise, very proper, rather flat Edinburgh society pitch.

The room was decorated largely in a cool mid-blue with a floral pattern of some indistinct sort upon the walls and in the carpet. The wide windows overlooked a small garden and the early light gave the room a chilly air, even though there was a fire burning in the grate. The single occupant was a slender woman in her late thirties and the moment Hester saw her she knew she must be related to the man whose portrait hung in the hall. She had the same long face, and nose and broad mouth, but in her there was no hint of indecision. Her lips were beautifully shaped, the blue eyes steady and direct. Her fair hair was dressed in the current severe fashion, but its warm color gave it a charm which would have been absent in a less glowing shade. And yet her face was not beautiful; there was a power in it which was too apparent and she took no pains to mask her intelligence.

"Please come in, Miss Latterly," she repeated. "I am Oonagh McIvor. I wrote to you on behalf of my mother, Mrs. Mary Farraline. I hope you had an agreeable journey from London?"

"Yes, thank you, Mrs. McIvor, it was quite pleasant, and that part of it which was in daylight was most enjoyable."

"I am delighted." Oonagh smiled with sudden warmth, transforming her face. "Train travel can be so weary and so terribly grubby. Now I am sure you would like to meet your patient. I must warn you, Miss Latterly, my mother appears to be in excellent health, but it is largely a charade. She tires more easily than she will admit, and her medicine is really quite vital for her well-being, indeed possibly for her life." She spoke the words quite calmly, but there was a sense of urgency in her conveying the importance of what she said. "It is not in the least difficult to administer," she continued. "A simple potion which is unpleasant to the taste, but a small confection after it will more than compensate." She looked up at Hester standing in front of her. "It is simply that my mother can forget to take it if she is feeling well, and by the time she is ill for its lack, it is too late to make up for the oversight without distress, and possible damage to her permanent well-being. I am sure you understand?" Even though she said she was sure, there was a question in her face.

"Of course," Hester said quickly. "A great many people prefer to do without medicine if they can, and misjudge their own capacity. It is easily understood."

"Excellent." Oonagh rose to her feet. She was as tall as Hester, slender without being in any way thin, and she moved with grace despite the awkwardness of wide skirts.

They crossed the hall, and Hester could not help glancing at the portrait again. The face haunted her, the ambiguities in it remained in her mind. She could not decide whether she liked it or not. Certainly she could not forget it.

Oonagh smiled and hesitated in her step.

"My father," she said, although Hester had known it must be. She heard the catch in Oonagh's voice and knew there was intense emotion behind it, carefully controlled, as she imagined such a woman would always be in front of strangers—and servants. "Hamish Farraline," Oonagh went on. "He died eight years ago. My husband has managed the firm since then."

Hester opened her mouth in surprise, then realized how inappropriate that was, and closed it.

But Oonagh had seen. She smiled and her chin lifted a fraction. "My brother Alastair is the Fiscal," she explained. "He does go to the firm as often as he is able to, but his duties keep him most of the time." She saw Hester's confusion. "The Procurator Fiscal." Her smile broadened, curling her lips. "Something like what you in England would call the Crown Prosecutor."

"Oh!" Hester was impressed in spite of herself. Her acquaintance with the law involved only Oliver Rathbone, the brilliant barrister she had met through Callandra and Monk, and about whom her feelings were so painfully mixed. But that was personal. Professionally she had for him only the profoundest admiration. "I see. You must be very proud of him."

"Yes indeed." Oonagh continued on her way to the stairs and hesitated till Hester was beside her, then began to climb them. "My younger sister's husband also works in the company. He is very skilled in all matters to do with printing. We were very fortunate that he chose to become one of us. It is always better when an old company like Farralines can remain within the family."

"What do you print?" Hester inquired.

"Books. All kinds of books."

At the top of the stairs Oonagh turned along the landing, carpeted in Turkish red, and stopped at one of the many doors. After a brief knock she opened it and entered. This was entirely different from the blue room downstairs. The colors were all warm yellows and bronzes, as if it were filled with sunlight, although in fact the sky beyond the flowered curtains was actually quite a threatening gray. There were small, gilt-framed landscape paintings on the walls, and a gold-fringed lamp, but Hester barely had time to notice them. Her attention was taken by the woman who sat facing them in one of the three large floral armchairs. She seemed tall, possibly even taller than Oonagh, and she sat with a stiff back and erect head. Her hair was almost white and her long face had an expression of intelligence and humor which was arresting. She was not especially handsome, and even in youth she could not have been a beauty—her nose was too long, her chin far too short—but her expression obliterated all such awareness.

"You must be Miss Latterly," she said with a firm, clear voice, and before Oonagh could effect any introduction. "I am Mary Farraline. Please come in and sit down. I understand you are to accompany me to London and make sure that I behave myself as my family would wish?"

A shadow crossed Oonagh's face. "Mother, we are only concerned for your welfare," she said quickly. "You do sometimes forget to take your medicine. . . ."

"Nonsense!" Mary dismissed it. "I don't forget. I simply don't always need it." She smiled at Hester. "My family fusses," she explained with humor. "Unfortunately, when you begin to lose your physical strength, people tend to think you have lost your wits as well."

Oonagh looked over at Hester and her expression was patient and conspiratorial.

"I daresay I shall be quite unnecessary," Hester said with an answering smile. "But I hope I shall at least be able to make the journey a little easier for you, even if it is only to fetch and carry, and to see that you have all you wish."

Oonagh relaxed a little, her shoulders easing as though she had been standing unconsciously at attention.

"I hardly need a Florence Nightingale nurse for that." Mary shook her head. "But I daresay you will be a great deal better company than most. Oonagh says you were in the Crimea. Is that right?"

"Yes, Mrs. Farraline."

"Well sit down. There is no need to stand there like a maidservant." She pointed to the chair opposite her and continued talking while Hester obeyed. "So you went out to nurse with the army? Why?"

Hester was too taken aback to think of an immediate reply. It was a question she had not been asked since her elder brother Charles had first demanded of her why she wanted to do such a dangerous and totally unsuitable thing. That, of course, had been before Florence Nightingale's fame had made it almost respectable. Now, eighteen months into the peace, Florence Nightingale was second only to the Queen herself in the respect and admiration of the country.

"Come now," Mary said with amusement. "You must have had a reason. Young ladies do not pack their bags and abandon all their families and friends and depart for foreign lands, and disastrous ones at that, without a very pressing reason."

"Mother, it may have been something quite personal," Oonagh protested.

Hester laughed aloud. "Oh no!" she answered them both. "It was not a love affair, or being jilted. I wished to do something more useful than sit at home sewing and painting, neither of which I do well, and I had heard of the terrible conditions from my younger brother, who served in the army there. I—I suppose it suited my nature."

"That is what I imagined." Mary nodded very slightly. "There are not many ambitions for women. Most of us sit at home and keep the lamps burning, literally and metaphorically." She looked around at Oonagh. "Thank you, my dear. It was most thoughtful of you to have found a companion for me who has a sense of passion and adventure, and has had the courage to follow it. I am sure I shall enjoy my trip to London."

"I hope so," Oonagh said quietly. "I have no doubt Miss Latterly will look after you very well and prove interesting company. Now I think I had better have Nora show her your medicine case and how the dose is prepared."

"If you really feel it is necessary. . . ." Mary shrugged. "Thank you for coming, Miss Latterly. I look forward to seeing you at luncheon, and then at dinner of course, which will have to be early. I believe our train leaves at a quarter past nine, so we shall board it at least half an hour before that. We shall have to leave here at a quarter past eight. That usually is too early to dine in any comfort, but there is no help for it tonight."

They excused themselves, and Oonagh took Hester to Mrs. Farraline's dressing room and introduced her to the lady's maid Nora, a thin, dark woman with a grave manner.

"How do you do, miss," she said, regarding Hester politely, and apparently without the slightest envy or resentment.

Oonagh left them, and for the next half hour Nora showed Hester the medicine case, which was as simple as Mary had indicated, merely a matter of a dozen small glass vials filled with liquid, one for each night and morning until she should return again. The dose was already prepared; there was no measuring to be done. All that was necessary was to pour it into a glass already provided and see that Mrs. Farraline did not accidentally spill it, or far more seriously, that she did not forget that she had taken it and repeat the dose. That, as Oonagh had pointed out, could be extremely serious, possibly even fatal.

"You are to keep the key." Nora locked the case and passed the key, tied to a small red ribbon, to Hester. "Please put it around your neck, then it cannot be lost."

"Of course." Hester obeyed, and slipped the key inside her bodice. "An excellent idea."

Hester was sitting sideways on the dressing room's single chair; Nora stood next to the wardrobes. Mary's cases were spread out where the maid had packed them. With the wealth of fabric in every single skirt, half a dozen dresses took up an enormous space. A lady who expected to change at least three times a day—from morning dress to something suitable to go out for luncheon, and then to afternoon dress, tea gown and dinner gown—could hardly travel with less than at least three large cases, if not more. Petticoats, chemises, corsetry, stockings and shoes would require one alone.

"You won't need to tend to any clothes," Nora said with proprietary pride. "I'll take care of all of that. There's a list written out of everything, and there'll be someone at Miss Griselda's to unpack. All you might have to do is dress Mrs. Farraline's hair for her in the morning. Can you do that?"

"Yes, certainly."

"Good. Then that's all I can show you." A slight frown shadowed her face.

"Is there something else?" Hester asked.

"No, no there's nothing." Nora shook her head. "I just wish she wasn't going. I don't hold wi' travel. There's no need. I know Miss Griselda's newly wed, and expecting her first child, and the poor soul worries something wretched, from all the letters she's been sending. But that's the way some folk are. She'll be all right, like as not; and either way, there's nothing the mistress can do."

"Is Miss Griselda delicate?"

"Lord no, just took it into her head to worry herself. She was all right till she married that Mr. Murdoch with his airs and graces." She bit her lip. "Oh, I shouldn't't've said that. I'm sure he's a very nice man."

"Yes, I expect so," Hester said without belief.

Nora looked at her with a faint smile.

"I daresay you'd like a cup o' tea," she offered. "It's near eleven. There'll be something in the dining room, if you want."

"Thank you. I think I will."

The only person sitting at the long oak table was a small woman Hester judged to be in her twenties. She had very dark hair, thick and shining, and a dusky complexion full of the most attractive color, as if she had just come in from an invigorating walk. It was not in the least fashionable, not in London anyway, but Hester found it a pleasant change from the much admired pallor she was accustomed to. The woman's features were neat, and at first seemed merely pretty, but on closer examination there was an intelligence and a determination which was far more individual. And perhaps she was not twenty, but in her early thirties.

"Good morning," Hester said tentatively. "Mrs. Farraline?"

The woman looked up at her as if startled by her intrusion, then she smiled and her entire bearing changed.

"Yes. Who are you?" It was not a challenge but curiosity, as if Hester's appearance were miraculous, and a delightful surprise. "Please do sit down."

"Hester Latterly. I am the nurse to accompany Mrs. Mary Farraline to London."

"Oh—I see. Would you like some tea? Or do you prefer cocoa? And oatcakes, or shortbread?"

"Tea, if you please, and the shortbread looks excellent," Hester accepted, taking a seat opposite.

The woman poured tea and passed it to Hester, then proffered the plate with the shortbread. "Mother-in-law has hers upstairs," she went on. "And of course all the men have gone to work, and Eilish is not up yet. She never is at this hour."

"Is she . . . poorly?" As soon as Hester spoke she knew she should not have. If a member of the household chose not to rise until nearly lunchtime, it was not her business to inquire the reason.

"Good gracious no! Oh dear, I did not introduce myself. How remiss of me. I am Deirdra Farraline—Alastair's wife." She looked inquiringly at Hester to see if her explanation meant anything, and saw from her face that she already knew who he was. "Then there is Oonagh," she continued. "Mrs. McIvor, who wrote to you, and then Kenneth, and Eilish—who is Mrs. Fyffe, although I never think of her like that, I don't know why—and lastly Griselda, who now lives in London."

"I see. Thank you."

Hester sipped her tea and bit into the shortbread. It tasted even better than it looked, rich and crumbly, melting on the tongue.

"Don't worry about Eilish," Deirdra went on conversationally. "She never gets up at a decent hour, but she's perfectly well. One has only to look at her to see that. A charming creature, and the loveliest woman in Edinburgh, I shouldn't wonder—but also the laziest. Don't misunderstand me, I'm very fond of her," she added quickly. "But not to deny her faults."

Hester smiled. "If we cared only for perfection, we should be very lonely."

"I quite agree. Have you been to Edinburgh before?"

"No. No, I have never even been to Scotland."

"Ah! Have you always lived in London?"

"No, I spent some time in the Crimea."

"Good gracious!" Deirdra's eyebrows shot up. "Oh. Oh, of course. The war. Yes, Oonagh said something about getting one of Miss Nightingale's nurses for Mother-in-law. I can't see why. She only wants a little dose of medicine, hardly an army nurse! Did you sail out there? It must have taken ages." She screwed up her face earnestly and took another piece of shortbread. "If only man could fly. Then one would not have to go 'round Africa at all, one could simply go straight across Europe and Asia."

"One doesn't have to go 'round Africa to the Crimea," Hester pointed out gently. "It is on the Black Sea. One goes through the Mediterranean and up the Bosphorus."

Deirdra waved away the irrelevance with a small, strong hand. "But one has to go 'round Africa to get to India, or China. It is the same principle."

Hester could think of no suitable reply, and returned to her tea.

"Don't you find this terribly ... tame ... after the Crimea?" Deirdra asked curiously.

Hester might have assumed that the remark was idle conversation, had she not seen the intensity in Deirdra's face and the obvious intelligence in her eyes. She wondered how to answer her. The chores of nursing were frequently tedious, although patients seldom were. Certainly the danger and the challenge of the Crimea were gone, as was the comradeship. But then the hunger, the cold, the fear and the terrible rage and pity were gone also. In its place had been the emotional tumult of working with Monk. She had met William Monk when he had been a police inspector investigating the Grey case, and then, through Callandra, she had assisted him with the Moidore case so shortly afterwards. But he had stormed out of the police force and been consequently forced to practice as a private agent of inquiry. She had again found herself calling for his help for Edith Sobel when General Carlyon had been murdered. And she had been the ideal person to take a position in the hospital when Nurse Barrymore's body had been found.

But the relationship with Monk was far too complicated to try to explain, and certainly not something likely to recommend her to a highly respectable family like the Farralines as a suitable companion for their mother.

Deirdra was still waiting, her eyes on Hester's face.

"Sometimes," she admitted, "I am delighted to miss the conditions, but I miss the companionship also, and that is hard."

"And the challenge?" Deirdra pressed, leaning forward over the table. "Is it not a wonderful thing to try to accomplish something immensely difficult?"

"Not when you have no chance of success, and the pain of failure is other people's suffering."

Deirdra's face fell. "No, of course not. I'm sorry, that was heartless of me. I did not mean it quite as it sounded. I was thinking of the challenge to the mind, to the inventiveness, to one's own aspirations— I . . ." She stopped as the door opened and Oonagh came in. Oonagh glanced from one to the other of them, then her face softened in a smile.

"I hope you are comfortable, Miss Latterly, and being well looked after?"

"Oh yes, indeed, thank you," Hester answered.

"I have been asking Miss Latterly about her experiences, or at least some of them," Deirdra said enthusiastically. "It sounds most stimulating."

Oonagh sat down and helped herself to tea. She looked across at Hester doubtfully.

"I imagine there are times when you must find England very restricting after the freedom of the Crimea?"

It was a curious remark, one that betrayed a far more intelligent consideration than was usual. It was no idle piece of conversation made merely for something to say.

Hester did not reply immediately, and Oonagh sought to explain herself. "I mean the weight of responsibility you must have had there, if what I have read is anywhere near the truth. You must have seen a great deal of suffering, much of it quite avoidable, had more sense been exercised. And I imagine you did not always have a senior officer to hand, either medical or military, every time some judgment had to be made."

"No—no we didn't," Hester agreed quickly, startled by Oonagh's perception. In fact, now that she sat here in this quiet dining room with its polished table and handsome carved sideboard, she realized that the trust and responsibility, and the power to act for herself, were two of the aspects of the Crimea that she missed the most profoundly. Now so many of her decisions were trivial.

It must be even more so for a woman like Oonagh McIvor, whose responsibilities were largely domestic. What should Cook serve for dinner? How should she resolve the squabble between the kitchen maid and the laundry maid? Should she invite so-and-so to dine this week with the Smiths—or next week with the Joneses? Should she wear green on Sunday, or blue? Looking at the intelligence and the resolve in Oonagh's features, Hester saw that she was not a woman to waste her energy on such things, which mattered not in the slightest, even today, never mind in the course of one's life. Was it envy she could hear in the curious timbre of Oonagh's voice?

"You have a remarkable understanding," she replied aloud, meeting Oonagh's steady gaze. "I don't think I had even phrased it to myself so well. I confess that at times I have found myself almost suffocated by the necessity of obedience, when I had been used to action, simply because there was no one else to turn to and the urgency of the situation did not allow us to delay."

Deirdra was watching her closely, her face quickened with interest, her tea forgotten.

Oonagh smiled as if the answer in some way pleased her.

"You must have seen much waste, and a fearful amount of pain," she observed. "Of course there will always be deaths, when one is occupied with medicine, but there can be nothing like the battlefield in a hospital. That aspect of it must be a relief to you. Does one get hardened to seeing so much death?"

Hester considered for several moments before replying. This was not a person who deserved, or would accept, a trite or insincere response.

"It is not that you become hardened," she said thoughtfully. "But you learn to govern your emotions, and then to ignore them. If you allowed yourself to dwell on it you would become so wretched you would cease to be any use to those who were still living. And while it is very natural to pity, it is also quite pointless in a nurse, where there is so much that is practical to do. Tears don't remove bullets or splint broken limbs."

A look of calm filled Oonagh's eyes, as though some irritating question had been resolved. She rose from the chair, ignoring the rest of her tea, and smoothed her skirts. "I am sure you are exactly the person to accompany Mother to London. She will find you most stimulating, and I have every confidence you will be ideal to care for her. Thank you for being so frank with me, Miss Latterly. You have set my mind at rest entirely." She looked at a fob watch hanging from a ribbon at her shoulder. "It is still some time until luncheon. Perhaps you would like to spend it in the library? It is quite warm in there, and you will not be disturbed, should you wish to read." She glanced at Deirdra.

"Oh yes." Deirdra stood up also, "I suppose I had better go and check through the accounts with Mrs. Lafferty."

"I've already done it," Oonagh said quietly. "But I haven't been through tomorrow's menu with Cook yet. You might do that."

If Deirdra resented her sister-in-law's assumption of household governance, there was not a shred of it in her face.

"Oh, thank you so much. I hate figures, they're always much the same, and so tedious. Yes, by all means, I'll speak to Cook." And with that she smiled charmingly at Hester and excused herself.

"Yes, I should very much like to read," Hester accepted.

It had not been precisely an invitation, but she had nothing better to do, so she permitted herself to be directed to the very gracious library, lined with books on three sides, many of them leather bound and tooled in gold. She was curious to see that several of the handsomest, as well as many bound in ordinary cloth, had been printed by Farraline & Company. They covered a very wide variety of subjects both factual and fictional. Several well-known authors were represented, both living and from the past.

She selected a book of verse and settled herself in one of the half dozen or so large armchairs and opened it to read. The room was almost silent. Through its heavy door she could not hear the sounds of the household beyond; there was only the faint crackle of a fire in the grate and the occasional tapping of a leaf as the wind caught it and sent it against the window.

She lost track of time, and was startled when she looked up to see a young woman standing in front of her. She had not heard the door opening.

"I'm sorry, I did not mean to startle you," the woman apologized. She was very slender, and quite tall, but her form was forgotten the moment one saw her face. She was one of the loveliest creatures Hester had ever seen; her features were subtle and delicate, yet full of passion. Her skin was fair with that radiance peculiar to auburn coloring, her hair thick in a wild halo around her head, the rich shades of bronzed leaves. "Miss Latterly?"

"Yes," Hester said, gathering her wits. She laid the book aside.

"I am Eilish Fyffe," the young woman introduced herself. "I came to tell you that luncheon is served. I hope you will join us?"

"Yes please." Hester rose to her feet, then turned, remembering to replace the book.

Eilish waved her hand impatiently. "Oh leave it. Jeannie will put it away. She can't read, yet, but she'll find the place it came from."

"Jeannie?"

"The maid."

"Oh! I thought she was . . ." Hester stopped.

Eilish laughed. "A child? No—at least, yes. I suppose so. She's only one of the housemaids. She's about fifteen, she thinks. But she is learning to read." She shrugged as she said it, as if to dismiss the subject. Then she smiled dazzlingly. "The children are Margaret and Catriona, and Robert."

"Mrs. McIvor's?"

"No, no. They're Alastair's. He is my eldest brother, the Fiscal." She pulled a slight face as she said it, as if she had been in awe of him until very lately. Hester knew just how she felt, thinking of her own elder brother, Charles, who had always been a trifle forbidding and had far too little sense of the absurd. "Alec and Fergus are away at school. They are Oonagh's sons. I daresay Robert will be going soon." She opened the library door into the hall. She made no mention of her own family, so Hester presumed that as yet she had none. Perhaps she had not been long married.

Luncheon was not a heavy meal, and the family present were all assembled as Eilish led Hester into the dining room and indicated the chair she was to occupy. Mary Farraline sat at the head of the table, Oonagh at the foot. On the far side were Deirdra and an elderly man who so resembled the portrait in the hall that Hester was taken aback so much she found herself staring. But it was only coloring and feature, the same fair hair, now thinning drastically, fair skin, and the refined nose and sensitive mouth. The inner man was utterly different.

He too had wounds of the spirit, but he gave Hester no sense of un-certainty as the portrait had done, no ambiguity; there was a sharp knowledge of pain which had overwhelmed him, and he had lost to it, while knowing exactly what it was. His blue eyes were sunken and he gazed ahead of him at no one in particular. He was introduced as Hec-tor Farraline, and spoken of as Uncle Hector.

Hester took her seat and the first course was served. Conversation was polite, and generally meaningless; it served the purpose for which it was intended, to convey goodwill without costing any thought or distracting from the meal. Discreetly Hester looked around at their faces, which had so much in common and which circumstance and character had stamped so differently. The only ones not born Farraline were Deirdra and Mary. Where they were slender and fair and well above average height, she was small and dark and inclined to stocki-ness. Yet there was a fierce inner concentration in her face, a sense of controlled excitement, which gave her a warmth the others lacked. She answered when civility required it, but she did not generate any remarks. Her own thoughts apparently consumed her.

Eilish spoke sporadically, as if prompted by good manners, and in between her thoughts also filled her mind. Hester found herself look-ing at Eilish repeatedly, possibly because she was so beautiful it was natural to stare, but also because of a sadness she thought she could see through the thin mask of courtesy and interest.

It was left to Oonagh and Mary to raise one agreeable, unconten-tious subject after another.

"How long does your journey take, Mother-in-law?" Deirdra asked, turning to Mary as soon as the main course was served.

"About twelve hours," Mary replied. "Although most of it I shall spend asleep, so it will feel much shorter. I think it is an excellent way to travel, don't you, Miss Latterly?"

"Indeed," Hester agreed. "Although the little I saw of Scotland on my way here, I should imagine it is very beautiful to look at, especially at this time of the year."

"You will have to go back during the day on your return next time," Mary suggested. "Then you can look out of the window all the way. If it doesn't rain, it should be really very nice."

"I don't know why you're going," Hector Farraline said, speaking for the first time. He had an excellent voice, rich in timbre, and even though a few of his words were slurred, one could tell that when he was completely sober his diction would have been beautiful—and with the faint lilt of the northern Scots, not the flatter Edinburgh accent of Mary's speech.

"Griselda needs her, Uncle Hector," Oonagh said patiently. "It's a very emotional time for a woman when she is expecting her first child. It is not unusual to feel unwell and a trifle apprehensive."

Hector seemed confused. "Apprehensive? Of what? Won't they have the best possible care for her? I thought they were well-to-do . . . socially prominent family. That's what young Connal said to me."

"Socially prominent! The Murdochs?" Mary said with sharp amusement, her silver eyebrows rising high, giving her face a startled look. "Don't be absurd, my dear. They come from Glasgow. Nobody who matters has ever heard of them."

"They've heard of them in Glasgow," Deirdra put in quickly. "Alastair says they are prominent, and certainly have a great deal of money."

Eilish flashed a smile at Hector, then lowered her eyes. "Mother said nobody who matters," she said quietly. "I rather think that excludes all of Glasgow, doesn't it, Mother?"

Mary blushed very slightly, but she did not retreat. "Most of it, perhaps not quite all. I believe there are some quite agreeable areas a little to the north."

"Just so." Eilish smiled down at the plate.

Hector frowned. "Then why doesn't she come home to have her child, where we can look after her? If there's nobody who matters in Glasgow, what is she doing in London?" After that piece of eccentric logic he turned and looked at Mary, his eyes soft, his face confused and on the verge of anger. "You should stay here, and Griselda should come home and let her child be born in Scotland. Why doesn't what's-his-name—" His face creased up. "What is his name?" He looked at Oonagh.

"Connal Murdoch," she supplied.

"Yes," he agreed. "That's right! Why doesn't Colin Murdoch—"

"Connal, Uncle Hector."

"What?" Now he was totally confounded. "What are you talking about? Why do you keep interrupting me and then repeating what I say?"

"Have a glass of water." Oonagh suited the action to the word and poured a tumbler for him, passing it across.

He ignored it and sipped at his wine again. He did not continue. Hester had the strong impression he had forgotten what he was going to say.

"Quinlan says they are going to reopen the Galbraith case," Deirdra said in the silence, then almost immediately her face tightened as if she wished she had chosen some other subject of conversation.

"Quinlan is Eilish's husband," Oonagh explained to Hester. "But he is not involved in the law, so I don't know how reliable his information may be. I daresay it is merely gossip."

Hester expected Eilish to come to his defense and insist that he was correct, or that he did not listen to, much less repeat, gossip. But she remained silent.

Hector shook his head. "Alastair'll not be pleased," he said dourly.

"No one will." Mary looked unhappy, a frown puckering her brow. "I thought that was over and done with."

"I expect it is," Oonagh said with conviction. "Don't think of it, Mother. It is just idle talk. It will die away when nothing comes of it."

Mary looked at her gravely, but did not reply.

"I still wish you weren't going to London," Hector said to no one in particular. He looked sad and aggrieved, as if it were a personal blow to him.

"It'll only be a few days," Mary replied, her face surprisingly gentle as she looked at him. "She needs reassurance, my dear. She really is very troubled, you know."

"Can't think why." Hector shook his head. "Lot of nonsense. Who are these Munros? Won't they look after her properly? Doesn't Colin Munro have a physician?"

"Murdoch—" Oonagh's lips thinned in impatience. "Connal Murdoch. Of course he has a doctor, and no doubt midwives. But it is how Griselda feels. And Mother will only be gone a week."

Hector reached for more wine and said nothing.

"Have they new evidence in the Galbraith case?" Mary asked, turning to Deirdra, a pucker between her brows.

"Alastair didn't mention it to me," Deirdra replied, looking surprised. "Or if he did, I don't remember. I thought he said there was not sufficient evidence and threw it out?"

"He did," Oonagh said firmly. "People are only talking about it because it would have been such a scandal if Galbraith had come to trial, being who he is. There will always be those who are envious of a man in his position, and whose tongues will wag, whether there is anything for them to wag about or not. The poor man has had to leave Edinburgh. That should be the end of it."

Mary glanced at her, as if to speak, then changed her mind and looked down at her plate. No one else added anything. The rest of the meal passed with only the odd remark, and after it was finished, Oonagh suggested that Hester might like to rest for a few hours before the commencement of the return journey. She might go up the main stairs to the bedroom set aside for her use, if she cared to.

Hester accepted gratefully, and was on her way up the stairs when she encountered Hector Farraline again. He was halfway up and leaning heavily on the banister, his face filled with sorrow, and beneath it a deep anger. He was staring across the checkered expanse of the floor at the portrait on the far wall.

Hester came to a stop on the stair behind him.

"It's very fine, isn't it," she said, intending it as a form of agreement.

"Fine?" he said bitterly and without turning to look at her. "Oh yes, very fine. Very handsome, was Hamish. Thought himself quite a fellow." His expression did not change, nor did he move, but stood clinging to the banister rail and leaning half over it.

"I meant it was a fine portrait," Hester corrected. "Of course I didn't know the gentleman to comment upon him."

"Hamish? My brother Hamish. Of course you didn't. Been dead these last eight years, although with that thing hanging there, I don't feel that he's dead at all—just mummified and still with us. I should build a pyramid and pile it on top of him—that's a good idea. A million tons of granite. A mountain of a tomb!" Very slowly he slid down until he was sitting on the tread, his legs sprawled across the stair, blocking her way. He smiled. "Two million! What does a million tons of rock look like, Miss—Miss—" He looked at her with wide, unfocused eyes.

"Latterly," she offered.

23

He shook his head. "What do you mean, girl, latterly? A million tons is a million tons! It's always the same. Latterly—formerly—anytime!" He blinked.

"My name is Hester Latterly," she said slowly.

"How do you do. Hector Farraline." He made as if to bow, and slid down another step, bumping against her ankles.

She retreated. "How do you do, Mr. Farraline."

"Ever seen the great pyramids of Egypt?" he asked innocently.

"No. I have never been to Egypt."

"Should go. Very interesting." He nodded several times and she was afraid he was going to slide down ever farther.

"I will do, if I should ever have the opportunity," she assured him.

"Thought Oonagh said you'd been there." He concentrated fiercely, screwing up his face. "Oonagh's never wrong, never. Most unnerving woman. Never argue with Oonagh. Read your thoughts as another man might read a book."

"I've been to the Crimea." Hester retreated another step. She did not want him to knock her over if he should lose his balance again, which he looked to be in imminent danger of doing.

"Crimea? Whatever for?"

"The war."

"Oh."

"I wonder . . ." She was about to ask him if she might pass, when she heard the discreet steps of the butler, McTeer, coming up behind her.

"Why would you go to a war?" Hector refused to let go of the puzzle. "You're a woman. You can't fight!" He began to laugh, as if the idea amused him.

"Now Mr. Farraline, sir," McTeer said firmly. "You go up to your room and lie down a while. You can't sit here all afternoon. People need the stairs."

Hector shook him off impatiently. "Go away, man. You've got a face like a chief mourner at a funeral. You couldn't look worse if it were your own."

"I'm sorry, miss." McTeer looked apologetically at Hester. "He's a bit of a nuisance, but he's no harm. He'll no bother ye, except for prattlin' on." He took hold of Hector under the arms and hauled him to his feet. "Come on now, ye don't want Miss Mary to see you behaving like a fool, do ye?"

The mention of Mary's name sobered Hector dramatically. He gave one more venomous glance at the portrait across the hall, then allowed McTeer to assist him properly to his feet and together they made their way slowly up the stairs, leaving room for Hester to follow unhindered.

Hester slept, although she had not intended to, and woke with a start to find that it was time to prepare herself for an early dinner and bring her bag down to the hall, along with her cape, ready for departure to the railway station.

Dinner was served in the dining room, but this time the table was set for ten, and it was Alastair Farraline who sat at the head. He was an imposing-looking man and Hester knew instantly who he was because the family resemblance was startling. He had the same long face with fair hair, thinning considerably towards the front, a long nose, definitely aquiline, and a broad mouth. The shape of his bones favored Mary rather than the man in the portrait, and when he spoke his voice was deep and rich, quite his most remarkable feature.

"How do you do, Miss Latterly. Please be seated." He indicated the last remaining empty chair. "I am delighted you accepted our offer to accompany Mother to London. It will set all our minds at rest concerning her welfare."

"Thank you, Mr. Farraline. I shall do my best to see she has an easy journey." She sat down, smiling at the others around the table. Mary sat at the foot, and to her left a man possibly approaching forty, who looked as utterly different from the Farralines as did Deirdra. His head was deep through from front to back, and his heavy hair, almost black, swept thickly across it with barely a wave. His eyes were set deep under dark brows, his jutting nose was straight and strong and his mouth betrayed both passion and will. It was an interesting face, unlike any other Hester could recall.

Mary caught her glance.

She introduced him with a smile of affection. "My son-in-law, Baird McIvor." Then she turned to the younger man at her left, beyond Oonagh. He was obviously a family member; his coloring was too like the others', his face had the same uncertainty, the shadow of humor and vulnerability in it. "My son Kenneth," she said. "And my other son-in-law, Quinlan Fyffe." She looked opposite to the remaining person Hester did not already know. He was also fair, but his hair was flaxen, almost silver in color, and cropped close to his head in tight curls. His face was long, his nose very straight and a trifle large for the rest of his features, his mouth small and chiseled in shape. It was a clever, meticulous face, that of a man who concealed as much as he told.

"How do you do," Hester said punctiliously. They each replied, and conversation was stilted and sporadic while the first course was served. They inquired after her journey up from London, and she replied that it had been excellent, and thanked them for their concern.

Alastair frowned and looked across at his younger brother, who seemed to be eating with remarkable haste.

"We have plenty of time, Kenneth. The train does not leave until a quarter past nine."

Kenneth continued eating and did not turn his head to look at Alastair. "I am not coming to the station. I shall say good-bye to Mother here." There was a moment's silence. Oonagh also stopped eating and turned towards him. "I am going out," he said, his voice taking on a defiant tone.

Alastair was not satisfied. "Where are you going to, that you dine here first and cannot come to the station with us to wish Mother farewell?"

"What difference does it make if I wish to say good-bye here or at the station?" Kenneth demanded. "And I am dining here so that I can see her off properly, rather than go before dinner." He smiled as if that were a most satisfactory answer.

Alastair pursed his lips, but said no more. Kenneth continued eating, still rapidly.

The next course was served, and while they were eating, Hester discreetly studied their faces. Kenneth was obviously intent upon his engagement, whatever it was. He looked neither right nor left, but ate steadily, and then sat with impatience plain in his face while he waited for the maid to clear his plate and the main course to be served. Twice he looked up sharply as if to speak, and Hester felt he would have asked for his portion to be served separately, ahead of the others, had he dared.

Hector ate very little, but emptied his wineglass twice. Before filling it the third time, McTeer glanced up and met Oonagh's eyes. She shook her head minutely, and it was only because Hester was looking directly at her that she saw it at all. McTeer removed the bottle in its basket, and Hector said nothing.

Deirdra made some mention of an important dinner which was to be held and she wished to attend.

"For which, no doubt, you will need a new gown?" Alastair said dryly.

"It would be nice," she agreed. "I only wish to do you justice, my dear. I should not like people to think that the Fiscal's wife made do from one event to another."

"Little chance of that," Quinlan remarked with a smile. "You have had at least six this year . . . that I know of." But there was no rancor in his voice, only amusement.

"As Fiscal's wife, she goes to far more of those events than most of us," Mary said soothingly. Then added, "Thank goodness," under her breath.

Baird McIvor looked at her with a smile. "You don't care for civic dinners, Mother-in-law?" He spoke as if he already knew the answer, his dark face conveyed both amusement and considerable affection.

"I do not," she agreed, her eyes bright. "A lot of people only too aware of their own importance, sitting around eating too well, and giving portentous opinions upon everything and everyone. I often have the feeling that anyone caught making a joke would be fined immediately and then dismissed."

"You exaggerate, Mother." Alastair shook his head. "Judge Campbell is a bit dour, his wife is more than a little self-important, Judge Ross tends to fall asleep, but most of them are well enough."

"Mrs. Campbell?" Mary raised silver eyebrows and her expression assumed a sour severity. "Ayv'e never heeard anything layke it in all may born days!" she said in heavily affected accent. "When aye was a geerl, we didn't . . ."

Eilish giggled and glanced at Hester. It was apparently something of a family joke.

"When she was a girl, her grandfather was selling fish on the

Leith docks and her mother was running errands for old McVeigh," Hector said with a twist of his lips.

"Never!" Oonagh was incredulous. "Mrs. Campbell?"

"Aye—Jeannie Robertson, as she was then," he assured her. "Two brown pigtails down her back, she had, and holes in her boots."

Deirdra looked at him with new appreciation. "I shall remember that, next time she looks me up and down with a sneer on her face."

"The old man was drowned," Hector went on, enjoying his audience. "Took a dram too much, and fell off the docks one night in December. Twenty-seven, I think it was. Yes, eighteen twenty-seven."

Kenneth's impatience finally overcame his caution and he told McTeer to bring his dessert ahead of the others. Mary frowned; Alastair opened his mouth as if to say something, then caught Mary's eye and changed his mind.

Oonagh made some remark about a play that was on in the city. Quinlan agreed with her, and Baird immediately contradicted him. The matter was totally trivial, and yet Hester was startled to hear in their voices an animosity which sounded acutely personal, as if the subject were one of intense importance. She glanced at Quinlan's face and saw his eyes hard, his lips tight as he stared across the table. Opposite him Baird was brooding, his brows drawn down, his hands clenched. He looked as if he nursed within himself some deep pain.

Eilish did not look at either of them, but down at her plate, her fork idle, food ignored.

No one else appeared to notice anything unusual.

Mary turned to Alastair. "Deirdra says they are going to reopen the Galbraith case. Is that true?"

Alastair raised his head very slowly, his face set in a hard, wary expression. "Gossip," he said between his teeth. He looked down the table at his wife. "It is repeating such things that gives ignorant people to start speculating, and reputations are ruined. I'm sorry you did not know better than to do such a thing."

Mary's face darkened at the insult, but she did not speak.

The color rushed up Deirdra's cheeks and the muscles in her throat tightened. "I mentioned it to no one outside this room," she said angrily. "Miss Latterly is hardly going to rush out around London telling people. They've never heard of Galbraith! Anyway, is it true? Are they going to reopen it?"

"No, of course not," Alastair said angrily. "There is no evidence. If there had been, I would not have dismissed it in the first place."

"There is no new evidence?" Mary pressed.

"There is no evidence at all, old or new," Alastair replied, meeting her gaze squarely, finality in his voice.

Kenneth rose from the table. "Excuse me. I must go, or I shall be late." He bent over and kissed his mother lightly on the cheek. "Have a good journey, Mother, and give Griselda my love. I'll come to meet you at the station when you get home again." He looked across at Hester. "Good-bye, Miss Latterly. I'm happy to have made your acquaintance, and that Mother will be in such able hands. Good night." And with a wave he went out of the room and closed the door.

"Where is he going?" Alastair said irritably. He looked around the table. "Oonagh?"

"I've no idea," Oonagh said.

"A woman, I imagine," Quinlan suggested with a shadow of a smile. "It is to be expected."

"Well why don't we know about her?" Alastair asked. "If he is courting her, we should know who she is!" He glared at his brother-in-law. "Do you know, Quin?"

Quinlan's eyes widened in surprise.

"No. Certainly not! It is merely an educated guess. Maybe I am wrong. Perhaps he is gambling, or going to a theater?"

"It's late for a theater," Baird said quickly.

"He said he was late!" Quinlan said.

"He didn't. He said he would be late if he waited for us to finish," Baird contradicted him.

"It is only ten minutes before eight," Oonagh put in. "Perhaps it is a theater close by."

"Alone?" Alastair said doubtfully.

"He may be meeting people there. Really, does it matter so much?" Eilish asked. "If he is courting someone, he'd have told us—if he is having any success."

"I want to know who it is before there is any 'success'!" Alastair glared at her. "By that time it would be too late!"

"Stop making yourself angry over something that has not happened yet," Mary said briskly. "Now—McTeer, bring in the dessert and let us have a pleasant end to the meal, before you take Miss Latterly and me to the station. It is a fine night, and we shall have an agree-able journey. Hector, my dear, would you be good enough to pass me the cream. I am sure I should like cream on it, whatever it is."

With a smile Hector obliged, and the rest of the meal was spent in inconsequential chatter, until it was eventually time to rise, bid farewell, and gather coats, baggage, and make their way out to the waiting carriage.

CHAPTER
TWO

———

"Come on, Mother." Alastair took Mary by the arm and guided her through the throng towards the London train, huge and gleaming beside its platform, the brass-knobbed doors open, the carriages with polished sides seeming to tower over them as they approached it. The engine let out another billow of steam. "Don't worry, we've half an hour yet," Alastair said quickly. "Where's Oonagh?"

"Gone to see if it is leaving on time, I think," Deirdra replied, moving a little closer to him as a porter with five cases on a trolley pushed past her.

"Evenin', miss." He made a gesture to tip his cap. "Evenin', sir, ma'am."

"Evening," they replied absently. They expected the courtesy, and yet it was an intrusion into their party. Hector stood with his coat collar turned up, as if he felt the cold, his eyes on Mary's face, even though she was half turned away from him. Eilish was walking towards the open carriage door, full of curiosity. Baird stood guarding Mary's three cases, and Quinlan was shifting from foot to foot, as if impatient to have the matter over with.

Oonagh returned, stood undecided for an instant, looking at Alastair, then at her mother, then, as if reaching some resolve, she took Mary's arm and together they moved along the platform until they reached the carriage where Mary had a reservation. Hester followed a couple of yards behind. Mary was going to be absent only a week, but even so this was not a time when a stranger, and an employee, should allow her presence to be felt. Her duties had not yet begun.

Inside, the coach was utterly different from the second-class carriage in which Hester had ridden up. It was not a large open space with hard upright seats, but a series of separate compartments, each with two single upholstered seats facing each other, either of which would quite comfortably have allowed three people to sit side by side, or, wonderful thought, one person to curl up and tuck her feet under her skirts and go to sleep in something like comfort. It would be quite private enough to feel safe from intrusion, since a glance told that it was reserved for Mrs. Mary Farraline and companion. Hester's spirits were lifted already. It would be so different from the long, exhausting journey up, during which she had managed only brief and disturbed catnaps. She found herself smiling in anticipation.

Mary merely glanced around her as she stepped in. Presumably she had been in first-class carriages before, and this one held no interest for her.

"The luggage is in the guard's van," Baird said from the doorway, his eyes on Mary's face with a directness which did not seem to be there when he spoke to anyone else. "They will unload it for you in London. You may forget about it until then." He lifted the small overnight case with toiletries and the medicine chest onto the luggage rack for her.

Alastair glanced at him irritably, then did not bother to say anything, as though it all had been said before, and had been no use then, or now, or perhaps in these circumstances was too trivial to bother with. His attention was on his mother. He looked troubled and short-tempered.

"I think you have everything you need, Mother. I hope your journey will be uneventful." He did not look at Hester, but his meaning was obvious. He bent as if to kiss Mary on the cheek, then apparently changed his mind and straightened up again. "Griselda will meet you, of course."

"We'll be here to meet you on your return, Mother," Eilish said with a quick smile.

"Hardly, my dear." Quinlan's expression indicated his feelings profoundly. "It will be half past eight in the morning. When were you ever up at that hour?"

"I can be—if someone wakes me," Eilish said defensively.

Baird opened his mouth, and closed it again without speaking.

Oonagh frowned. "Of course you can, if you wish to enough." She turned back to Mary. "Now, Mother, do you have everything you need? Are there any footwarmers here?" She looked down at the floor, and Hester's eyes followed hers. Footwarmers. What a blessed thought. On the journey up her feet had been so cold she had almost lost all sensation in them.

"Send for some," Quinlan said with raised eyebrows. "There ought to be."

"There are," Oonagh answered him, bending down to pull one of the large stone bottles forward. It was filled with hot water, and also with a chemical which was supposed, when shaken vigorously, to restore some of the heat naturally lost towards morning. "There you are, Mother, it's lovely and hot. Rest your feet on that. Where's the traveling rug, Baird?"

He handed it to her obediently, and she took it and made Mary comfortable, wrapping it around her, and folded the spare one on the other seat. No one was taking much notice of Hester, who was apparently not expected to begin her duties until they had actually departed. She arranged her valise where it was out of the way, then sat down on the seat opposite and waited.

Gradually all the good-byes were said and each of them moved back into the corridor until only Oonagh was left.

"Good-bye, Mother," she said quietly. "I shall look after everything while you are gone—and do it as you would have."

"What an odd thing to say, my dear." Mary smiled in amusement. "You look after most of the household now. And when I come to think of it, I believe you have done for some considerable time. And I assure you, it had never crossed my mind to worry."

Oonagh kissed her very lightly, then turned to Hester, her eyes direct and very clear. "Good-bye, Miss Latterly." And the next moment she was gone.

Mary settled a trifle more comfortably in her seat. She was naturally facing forward, and it was Hester who would travel always looking the way she had come.

A wry look crossed Mary's face, as though her last words in some way amused her.

"Are you worried?" Hester said quickly, wondering if there were some way she might ease her concern. Mary Farraline was not only her patient, she was also a person towards whom she felt a natural warmth.

Mary lifted her shoulders in the slightest of shrugs. "Oh no, not really. I can think of no sensible thing to worry about. Are you going to be warm enough, my dear? Please use the other rug." She indicated where Oonagh had put it. "It is brought for you. Really, they should have given us a footwarmer each." She made a little click of annoyance between her teeth. "I daresay that one will be quite sufficient for two of us. Please—move yourself to sit precisely opposite me, and place your feet on the other half of it. Don't argue with me. I cannot possibly be comfortable if I know you are sitting there shivering. I have caught trains from Edinburgh station quite often enough to be familiar with their discomforts."

"Have you traveled a great deal?" Hester inquired, moving to sit as Mary had directed, and finding the blessed relief of the footwarmer on her already chilled feet.

Outside doors were slamming and the porter was shouting out something, but his voice was lost in a belch and hiss of steam. The train clanked and lurched forward, then very slowly gathered speed and they emerged from the canopy of the station into the darkness of the countryside.

"I used to," Mary replied to the question with a reminiscent look. "All sorts of places: London, Paris, Brussels, Rome. I even went to Naples once, and Venice. Italy is so beautiful." She smiled and her face lit with memory. "Everyone should visit it once in their lives. Preferably when they are about thirty. Then they would be old enough to realize how marvelous it is, to feel something of all it has been and sense the past around them, to give depth to the present. And yet they would still be young enough for the flavor to enrich the larger portion of their lives." The train jolted hard, and then continued forward at greater speed. "I think it is a shame to have your miracles in life when you are too young, and in too much of a hurry to realize what they are. It is a terrible thing to know your blessings only in hindsight."

Hester was considering the impact of that thought so seriously she did not reply.

"But you have also traveled," Mary said, her eyes bright on Hester's face. "And far more interestingly than I—at least for the most part. Oonagh told me you were in the Crimea. If you are not pained by recalling it, I should most dearly like to hear something of your experiences. I admit, my mind is filled with questions in a manner most unbecoming. I am sure it must be ill-bred to inquire so much, but I am old enough not to care what is considered proper."

Hester had found many peoples' questions poorly framed and based on assumptions made from the peace and ignorance of England, where the vast majority knew only what newspapers told them. Although that knowledge was now increasing their ability to criticize and raise doubts, it still carried very little of the passion or the horror of reality.

"It brings back distressing memories?" Mary said quickly, apology vivid in her voice.

"No, not at all," Hester denied, more in courtesy than strict truth. Her memories were sharp and complex, but she had seldom found herself desiring to escape them. "I fear that they may become tedious for people because I felt so strongly about so much, I tend to repeat myself about the wrongs and omit the details which may make the tale more interesting."

"I should not be in the least interested in a well-considered and emotionless account that I might read in my daily newspaper." Mary shook her head vigorously. "Tell me what you felt. What surprised you most? What was best, and what was worst?" She waved a long hand dismissively. "I don't mean the suffering of the men, I shall take that for granted. I mean for yourself."

The train had settled with a steady rhythm that was almost soothing in its regularity.

"Rats," Hester answered without hesitation. "The sound of rats falling off the walls onto the floor; that, and waking up cold." The memory was sharp as she said it, blurring the present and the sense of the warm rug around her. "It wasn't so bad once you were up and moving around—and thinking of what you were doing—but when you woke up in the night and were too cold to go back to sleep again, no matter how tired you were, that's what stays with me most." She smiled. "Waking up warm, pulling the blankets close around me, hearing the sound of the rain outside, and knowing that there is nothing alive in the room except me, that's marvelous."

Mary laughed, a rich sound of pure enjoyment.

"What an unpredictable faculty memory is. The oddest things will bring back times and places we had long thought lost in the past." She leaned back in the seat, her face relaxed, her eyes on some distance of the imagination. "You know, I was born the year after the fall of the Bastille—"

"The fall of the Bastille?" Hester was confused.

Mary did not look at her, but kept her gaze on the sudden memory that was apparently woken so sharply. "The revolution in France, Louis the Sixteenth, Marie Antoinette, Robespierre . . ."

"Oh! Oh, of course."

But Mary was still lost in her own thoughts. "Those were such times. The Emperor had all Europe under his heel." Her voice sank in awe so it was barely audible above the rattle of the wheels over the ties. "He was twenty miles away across the channel, and only the navy stood between his armies and England—and then of course Scotland too." The smile on her lips broadened, and in spite of the lines in her face and her silver hair, there was in her a radiance and an innocence as though the years between had fallen away and she was a young woman momentarily caught in an old woman's body. "I remember the spirit we had then. We expected invasion every day. Everyone's eyes were turned eastward. We had lookouts on the cliff tops and beacon fires ready to light the moment the first Frenchman set foot on the shore. Right up and down the coast every man, woman and child was watching and waiting, homemade weapons ready to hand. We would have fought till the very last of us was dead before we would have let them conquer us."

Hester said nothing. England had been secure all her lifetime. She could imagine what it might have been like to fear foreign soldiers trampling through the streets, burning the houses, laying waste the fields and farms, but it was only imagination, it could never touch the reality. Even in the very worst days in the Crimea when the allied armies were losing, she had always known England itself was peaceful, impregnable, and except in small, private bereavements, untouched.

"The newspapers used to print terrible cartoons of him." Mary's smile broadened for a moment, then vanished suddenly, and she shivered, looking directly at Hester. "Mothers used to terrify their naughty children by threatening that 'Bony' would get them. They used to say that he ate little children, and there were pictures of him with a great gaping mouth, and a knife and fork in his hands, and Europe on his plate."

The train slowed almost to walking speed as it climbed a steep gradient. A man's voice shouted something indistinguishable. A whistle blew.

"And then when I had my own children in Edinburgh," Mary went on, "people used to frighten the disobedient with stories of Burke and Hare. Odd, isn't it, how much more sinister that seems now? Two Irishmen who started selling corpses to a doctor so he could teach his students anatomy, then progressing to robbing graves, and finally to murder."

The train began to pick up speed again. She looked at Hester curiously.

"Why does murder to dissect the corpses chill the blood in a way murder to rob never can? After it all came out in 1829, and Burke was hanged—Hare never was, you know! For all I can say, he's still alive now!" She shivered. "But afterwards, I remember we had a maid who left without giving notice. We never knew where she went—off with some man, in all probability—but of course all the other servants said Burke and Hare had got her, and she was cut up in pieces somewhere!"

She wrapped her shawl tighter around her, although the carriage was no colder than it had been before, and their feet were on the footwarmer and snugly wrapped in a blanket.

"Alastair was about twelve then." She bit her lip. "And Oonagh was seven, old enough to have heard the stories and understood the terror they woke. One night, it was late in the winter and there was a fearful storm, I heard the thunder and got up to see if everything was all right. I found the two of them together in Oonagh's room, sitting up in bed, huddled under the blanket with the candle lit. I knew what had happened. Alastair had had a nightmare. He had them sometimes. And he had gone into her room, ostensibly to see if she was all right, but really because he wanted the comfort of being with her himself. She was frightened too; I can still see her face in my mind, white-skinned, wide-eyed, but busy telling Alastair about Burke having been hanged and that he was quite dead." She gave a dry little laugh. "She described it in detail, she was so certain of it."

Hester could picture it. Two children sitting together, each pretending to assure the other, and whispering in hushed voices of the horrors of body snatchers, resurrectionists, secret murder in dark alleys, and the dissector's bloody table. Such memory runs deep, perhaps below the surface of consciousness, but those things shared forge a trust which excludes other, later, comers. She had no such moments with her elder brother, Charles. He had always been a little on his dignity, even from the earliest times she could recall. It had been James with whom she had had adventures and secrets. But James had been killed in the Crimea.

"I'm sorry," Mary said quietly, her voice cutting across Hester's thoughts. "I have said something that distressed you." It was not a question but an observation.

Hester was startled. She had not thought Mary was more than peripherally aware of her, certainly not enough to notice her feelings.

"Perhaps resurrectionists were not the most sensitive of subjects to raise," Mary said ruefully.

"Not at all," Hester assured her. "I was thinking of the two children together, and remembering my younger brother. My elder brother was always a little pompous, but James was fun."

"You speak of him in the past. Is he—gone?" Mary's voice was suddenly gentle, as if she knew bereavement only too well.

"Yes, in the Crimea," Hester replied.

"I'm so sorry. To say I know how you feel would be ridiculous, but I have some idea. I had a brother killed at Waterloo." She said the word carefully, rolling it off her tongue as if it held some mystic quality. To many of Hester's age that would have been incomprehensible, but she had heard too many soldiers speak of it for it not to give her a shiver through the flesh. It had been the greatest land battle in Europe, the end of an empire, the ruin of dreams, the beginning of the modern age. Men of all nations had fought to exhaustion till the fields were strewn with the wounded and the dead, the armies of Europe, as Lord Byron had said, "in one red burial blent."

She looked up and smiled at Mary, so she would know Hester understood at least something of its immensity.

"I was in Brussels then," Mary said with a wry turn of her lips. "My husband was in the army, a major in the Royal Scots Greys. . . ."

Hester did not hear the rest of what she said. The clanking of the train wheels over the tracks drowned out a word here and there, and her mind was filled with a picture of the man in the portrait, with his fair sweep of hair and the face which at once had such emotion and ambiguous power and vulnerability. It was easy to imagine him, tall, straight-backed, wildly elegant in uniform, dancing the night away in some Brussels ballroom, knowing all the while that in the morning he would ride out to a battle to decide the rise or fall of nations and from which thousands would not return and more thousands would come home blind or maimed. And then she thought of the painting she had seen of the charge of the Royal Scots Greys at Waterloo, the light on the white horses plunging through the heat of battle, manes flying, scarlet riders bent forward, the dust and gun smoke clouding the rest, darkening the scene behind them.

"He must have been a very fine man," she said impulsively.

Mary looked surprised. "Hamish?" She sighed gently. "Oh yes, yes he was. It seems like another world, so very long ago, Waterloo. I hadn't thought of it in years."

"He came through the battle all right?" Hester was not afraid to ask because she knew he had died only eight years before, and Waterloo was forty-two years in the past.

"He had a few cuts and bruises, but nothing worth calling a wound," Mary replied. "Hector had a musket ball in his shoulder and a saber cut on his leg, but he healed quickly enough."

"Hector?" Why should she be surprised? Forty-two years ago Hector Farraline might have been a very different man from the drunkard he was now.

The look in Mary's eyes was far away, sad and sweet and full of memory. "Oh yes, Hector was a captain. He was a better soldier than Hamish, but being the younger brother, his father only bought a captain's commission for him. He hadn't Hamish's grace, or his charm. And when the war was over, it was Hamish who had the imagination and the ambition. It was he who started the Farraline printing company." There was no need to add that, being the elder, he would have inherited whatever money there might have been. That was something everyone knew.

"He must have been a great loss," Hester said aloud.

The light died out of Mary's face and her expression became formal, as if receiving condolences in a long-practiced fashion. "Yes, naturally," she replied. "Thank you for saying so." She sat more uprightly in her seat. "But we have talked about the far distant past too much already. I should like to hear something of your experiences. Did you ever meet Miss Nightingale? One reads so much about her these days. I swear, she seems more revered in some quarters than the Queen herself. Is she really so very remarkable?"

For nearly half an hour Hester recalled her experiences as vividly as she could. She told Mary of pain and waste, the stupidity and the constant fear, the biting cold of winter and the hunger and exhaustion of siege. Mary listened attentively, interrupting only to ask for greater detail, often merely nodding assent. Hester described the heat and sparkle of summer, the white boats on the bay, the glamour of officers and their wives, the gold braid in the sun, the boredom, the companionship, the laughter and the times when she dared not weep or she might never stop. And then at Mary's request, with sharp memory, with laughter and anecdote she recounted much of the individual people she had admired or despised, loved or loathed, and all the time Mary sat with total attention, her clear eyes on Hester's face, while the train rattled and jolted, slowed for inclines, and then gathered speed again. They were completely islanded in a world of lamplight and rhythmic clanking and swaying through the darkness, the countryside beyond the windows invisible. They were warmly wrapped in rugs, their feet almost touching on the stone footwarmer.

Once the train stopped altogether and they both alighted into the chill night air, not so much to stretch their legs, although that was welcome, but to avail themselves of the conveniences at the station.

Back in the train again, whistle blowing, steam billowing as the engine gathered impetus, they rewrapped themselves in the rugs, and Mary requested that Hester continue her account.

Hester obliged.

She had not intended to, but she found herself now speaking with vehemence about the ideals which had burned so deeply in her when she first returned, her passion to begin reforming the outdated hospital wards in England with their closed practices.

Mary smiled wistfully. "If you tell me you succeeded, I shall begin to disbelieve you."

"And so you should. I am afraid I was dismissed for arrogance and acting without orders." She had not meant to reveal that. It was hardly conducive to confidence in a patient, but Mary was already far more than that, and the words were out before she considered it.

Mary laughed, a rich sound filled with delight.

"Bravo. If we all acted only upon orders, we should still not have invented the wheel. What have you done about it?"

"Done?"

Mary put her head a little to one side, her face full of quizzical doubt.

"Don't tell me you have simply accepted dismissal like a good girl and gone obediently on your way! Surely you are fighting the cause in some fashion or other?"

"Well—no. . . ." She saw Mary's face slowly fill with dismay. "No—because there have been other battles," she went on hastily. "For—for justice of other sorts."

Mary's eyes widened with new interest. "Oh?"

"Er—I—" Why should she be so reluctant to talk of helping Monk? There was nothing dishonorable in assisting the police. "I became acquainted with a police inspector who was investigating the murder of an army officer, and it seemed as if there was going to be a terrible miscarriage of justice. . . ."

"And you were able to prevent it?" Mary leaped to the conclusion. "But afterwards, did you not return to the question of nursing reform?"

"Well . . ." Hester found herself coloring very faintly, Monk's face with dark gray eyes and broad, high cheeks so vivid in her mind he could have been in the seat opposite her.

"Well, there were other cases . . . soon afterwards." She stumbled a little over the words. "And again there was the question of injustice. I was in a position to help. . . ."

A slow smile curled Mary's lips. "I see. At least I think I do. And no doubt after that one, another? What is he like, this policeman of yours?"

"Oh he is not mine!" Hester disclaimed instantly and with more vehemence than she had intended.

"Is he not?" Mary looked unconvinced, but there was laughter in her voice. "Are you not fond of him, my dear? Tell me, how old is he, and what does he look like?"

Hester wondered for a moment if she should tell the truth, that Monk did not know how old he was. A carriage accident had robbed him of all his memory, and his self-knowledge was returning only in fragments as the months passed into a year, and more. It was too long a story, and not truly hers to tell. "I am not quite sure," she prevaricated. "Around forty, I should think."

Mary nodded. "And his appearance, his manner?"

Hester tried to be honest and impartial, which was more difficult than she had expected. Monk always aroused emotions in her, both admiration, for his cutting intelligence, his courage and his dedication to truth; and impatience, even contempt, for his occasional bitterness towards those he suspected of crime, not towards his own colleagues if they were less quick, less agile of mind than himself, or less willing to take risks.

"He is a good height," she began tentatively. "In fact, quite tall. He stands very straight, which makes him look . . ."

"Elegant?" Mary suggested.

"No—I mean, yes, it does, but that is not what I was going to say." It was absurd to be stumbling over words this way. "I think the word I was looking for was *lithe*. He is not handsome. His features are good, but there is a directness in him, which . . . I was going to say that it approaches arrogance, but that is not true at all. It is arrogance, quite simply." She took a deep breath and continued before Mary could interrupt. "His manner is abrasive. He dresses beautifully and spends far too much money on his clothes because he is vain. He tells what he sees to be the truth without the slightest regard as to whether it is suitable or not. He has neither patience nor respect for authority, and little time for those who are less able than himself, but he cannot abide an injustice once he has seen it, and will acknowledge a truth at whatever cost to himself."

"A singular man, by your account," Mary said with interest. "And it seems you know him very well. Is he aware of it?"

"Monk?" Hester asked with surprise. "I have no idea. Yes, I suppose so. We have seldom minced words with one another."

"How interesting." There was not the slightest sarcasm in Mary's voice, only the most acute fascination. "And is he in love with you, this Monk?"

Hester's face burned. "Certainly not!" She denied it hotly, and her throat tightened as she said the words. For one idiotic moment she thought she was going to cry. It would be mortifying, and thoroughly stupid. She must clear up the misapprehension which Mary quite obviously bore. "We have been friends in certain issues, because we believed in the same causes and were both prepared to fight against what was wrong," she said firmly. "Where matters of love are concerned, he has no interest in women like me. He prefers"—she swallowed, memory sharp and peculiarly painful—"women like my sister-in-law, Imogen. She is very pretty indeed, very gentle, and knows how to be charming without clumsy flattery, but how to make one feel the desire to protect her. Not that she is ineffectual, you understand."

"I see," Mary agreed, nodding her head. "We have all known women like that at some time in our lives. They smile at a man, and instantly he feels better and handsomer, and definitely braver than before."

"Exactly!"

"So your Monk is a fool where women are concerned." It was a statement, not a question.

Hester chose not to answer that. "And I prefer someone like Oliver Rathbone," she went on, not really sure how much truth there was in her words. "He is a most distinguished barrister. . . ."

"Well-bred, no doubt," Mary said flatly. "And respectable!"

"Not especially, that I know," Hester replied defensively. "However, his father is one of the nicest people I have ever met. I feel comfortable merely to recall his face."

Mary's eyes widened. "Indeed. I misunderstood. So Mr. Rathbone is not without interest. Tell me more."

"He is also extremely clever, in a different kind of way. He is very sure of himself, and he has a dry sense of humor. He is never boring, and I admit I do not often know what he is really thinking, but I am quite certain it is not always what he says."

"And is he in love with you? Or do you not know that either?"

Hester smiled smugly, that sudden impulsive kiss coming back as sharply as if it had been a week ago instead of a year. "I think that is too strong a term, but he has given me occasion to think he finds me not unattractive," she replied.

"Oh excellent!" Mary said with evident pleasure. "And these two gentlemen dislike each other, I trust?"

"Certainly," Hester agreed with a satisfaction which surprised her.

"But I don't think it has anything to do with me—or at least, very little," she added.

"This is really most intriguing," Mary said happily. "I am sorry our acquaintance will be so short I shall not see the end of this."

Hester felt her face growing hot again. Her mind was in total confusion. She had spoken of her feelings as if it were a romance. Did she wish it were? She was embarrassed for her foolishness. She could not possibly marry Monk, even if he were to ask her, which he would not. They would quarrel all the time. There was far too much in him she really did not like. She had not mentioned it to Mary—it would be disloyal—but there was a streak of cruelty in him which appalled her; there were dark areas of his character, impulses she did not trust. She could not commit herself to such a man, not as anything more than a friend.

Or would she marry Oliver Rathbone, if he were to yield to any emotion powerful enough to make him ask her? She ought to. It would be a far better offer than most women ever received, certainly any woman at all at her age. She was nearly thirty, for heaven's sake. Only heiresses could expect marriage at that time of life. And far from being an heiress, she was obliged to earn her own living.

Then why would she not leap at the chance?

Mary was still looking at her with her eyes full of laughter.

Hester started to speak, and then had no idea what she was going to say.

The amusement died out of Mary's face. "Be very sure which one you want, my dear. If you make the wrong decision you may rue it the rest of your life."

"There is no decision to make!" Hester said far too quickly.

Mary said nothing, but the comprehension, and the disbelief, were plain in her face.

The train was slowing down again, and with a clatter it finally came to a stop. Doors opened and someone was shouting. The stationmaster passed by on the platform, calling the name of the station outside every carriage. Hester rearranged the rug more closely around their knees. Outside in the flickering darkness a hand bell rang, and a few minutes later the engine belched steam and began to move forward again.

It was almost half past ten. Hester felt the tiredness of the previous night's journey beginning to catch up with her, but Mary was obviously still wide-awake. Oonagh had said that her medicine should be given no later than eleven o'clock or, at the outside, a quarter past. Apparently Mary did not habitually retire early.

"Are you tired?" she suggested. Actually she was enjoying Mary's company, and there would be no further opportunity to talk in the morning. They would arrive shortly after nine and the time would be taken up with alighting, finding baggage and locating Griselda and Mr. Murdoch.

"No," Mary said cheerfully, although she had smothered a yawn once or twice. "No doubt Oonagh has told you I am to retire by eleven at the latest? Yes, I thought so. I think Oonagh would have made a good nurse. She is naturally intelligent and efficient, the most practical of my children; but more than that, she has the art of persuading people to do the right thing in such a way that they are convinced that it was their own idea." She pulled a slight face. "That truly is an art, you know? I have often wished I had it myself. And her judgment is excellent. I was surprised how quickly Quinlan learned to respect her. It is not often a man of his nature will have that kind of regard for a woman, especially one close to his own age, and it is genuine—I am not speaking of the kind of good manners he shows towards me."

Hester did not find it hard to believe. She had seen the strength of determination in Quinlan's face and the intelligence behind those quick, blue eyes. He would be far better served to make a friend of Oonagh than anyone else in the family. Baird obviously loathed him, Deirdra was indifferent, occupied with her own interests, and by Mary's account, Alastair relied upon Oonagh's judgment as he had done since they were children.

"Yes, I expect she would," Hester agreed. "But good judgment and the arts of diplomacy are never wasted in a large family. They may make the difference between happiness and misery."

"You're right, of course you are," Mary agreed with a nod. "But perhaps it is a fact not everyone appreciates."

Hester smiled. It would have been clumsy to acknowledge her understanding.

"Will you have a pleasant time in London?" she asked. "Will you have the opportunity to dine out and to go to the theater?"

Mary hesitated a moment before replying. "I am not entirely sure," she said thoughtfully. "I do not know Connal Murdoch or his family very well. He is rather a stiff young man, very conscious of other people's opinions. Griselda may not care to come. But if we do go to the theater, it will be to see something very unadventurous, I fear, and certainly nothing controversial."

"He may be concerned to impress you well," Hester pointed out. "After all, you are his mother-in-law, and he will care very much what your opinion of him may be."

"Oh dear." Mary sighed, biting her lip. "I stand corrected. Of course he may. I remember when Baird was newly married to Oonagh, he was so shy it was painful, and yet at that time so much in love." She took a deep breath. "Of course that kind of passion wears away as we become better acquainted; the mystery is discovered, familiarity takes away the sense of wonderment. One can only remain excited and amazed for really quite a short time."

"Surely then there comes a friendship, and a kind of warmth that . . ." Hester's voice trailed away. She sounded naive, even to herself. She felt her cheeks burning.

"One hopes so," Mary said softly. "If you are fortunate, the tenderness and the understanding never die, nor the laughter, and the memories." She looked beyond Hester as she spoke, towards something in her imagination.

Hester pictured the man in the portrait again, wondering when it had been painted, trying to see the marks of time in his face and how he might have changed, how familiarity might have stripped the glamour from him. She failed. To her there was still too much in his face which was unreachable, laughter and emotions that would always be his alone. Had Mary discovered that, and remained in love with him? Hester would never know, nor should she. Monk was like that. You would never know him well enough that he would no longer be able to surprise you, reveal some passion or belief you had not seen in him.

"Idealism is a poor bedfellow," Mary said suddenly. "Something I must tell Griselda, poor child; and most certainly tell this man she has married. It may be fairy princes with whom one walks up the aisle, but it is certainly very ordinary mortals with whom we wake up the following morning. And since we are ordinary mortals too, that is no doubt just as well."

Hester smiled in spite of herself. She prepared to stand up.

"It is growing late, Mrs. Farraline. Do you think I should take out your medicine now?"

"Should?" Mary raised her eyebrows. "Quite probably. But I am not yet ready to take it. To return to your original question, yes, I believe I shall go to the theater. I shall insist upon it. I have brought with me some gowns suitable for such occasions. Unfortunately I could not bring my favorite because it is silk, and I marked it right at the front where it shows."

"Can it not be cleaned?" Hester said sympathetically.

"Oh certainly, but there wasn't time before I left. I'm sure Nora will take care of it in my absence. But apart from the fact that I like it, unfortunately it is the only gown I have which really sets off my gray pearl pin, so I didn't bring it. It is quite beautiful, but gray pearls are not easy to wear; I really don't care for it with colors, or with anything that glitters. Still, no matter. It is only a week, and I daresay we shall have few enough formal occasions. And I am going in order to see Griselda, not to sample London's social life."

"I expect she is very excited about having her first child?"

"Not at the moment," Mary said, pulling a small face. "But she will do. I am afraid she worries about her health overmuch. There is really nothing wrong with her, you know." Mary stood up at last, and Hester rose to her feet quickly to offer her arm in assistance. "Thank you, my dear," Mary accepted. "She just worries about every little ache and pain, imagining it to be some serious fault with the child, or some irreparable defect. That is a bad habit, and one men dislike intensely, unless, of course, it is something wrong with them." She stood at the compartment entrance, slender and very straight, a smile on her lips. "I shall warn Griselda of that. And assure her that she has no cause for anxiety. Her child will be perfectly well."

The train was slowing again, and when it reached the station they both alighted to take advantage of the facilities offered. Hester found herself returned to the carriage first. She did what she could to tidy the seats, spread the rug ready for Mary and shook the footwarmer again. It really was getting very chilly now and the darkness beyond the windows was spotted with rain. She took down the medicine chest and opened it. The vials were all stacked in neat rows, the first one already used, the glass empty. She had not noticed it when she had seen it in Edinburgh, but the glass was tinted and the liquid hard to see. Nora must have used that one this morning, which was foolish. That meant they were one short. Still, possibly it was easy enough to replace, providing she warned Mary in time.

She stifled a yawn with difficulty. She really was very tired. It had been thirty-six hours since she had had a proper sleep. At least tonight she would be able to put her feet up and relax, instead of sitting upright between two other people. "Oh, you have the chest down," Mary said from the entranceway. "I suppose you are right. Morning will be here soon enough." She came in, swaying a little with the rough movement as the train jerked forward and began to pick up speed.

Hester put out her hand to steady her, and Mary sat down.

The conductor appeared at the doorway, his uniform spotless, buttons gleaming.

"Evening, ladies. Everything well wi' ye?" He touched the peak of his cap with his forefinger.

Mary had been staring out of the window at the streaming night, not that there was anything to see but the rain and the darkness. She turned around abruptly. Then her face paled for an instant, before the calm returned in a flood of relief.

"Oh, yes, thank you." She took a quick breath. "Yes, all is well."

"Right y'are, ma'am. Then I'll bid ye good night. London at a quarter past nine."

"Yes, thank you. Good night."

"Good night," Hester added as he retreated quickly, walking with a peculiar ungainliness that kept his balance perfectly.

"Are you all right?" Hester said anxiously. "Did he startle you? I think perhaps we are a little late with your medicine. I must insist you take it now. You do look rather pale."

Mary pulled the rug over herself and Hester tucked it around her.

"Yes, I am perfectly all right," Mary said firmly. "The wretched man reminded me of someone else, that long nose and brown eyes; he looked just like Archie Frazer for a moment."

"Someone you dislike?" Hester took the stopper out of the vial and poured the liquid into the little glass provided.

"I don't know the man personally." Mary's lip curled in distaste. "He was a witness in the Galbraith case, at least what should have been the Galbraith case, had it come to court. It was dismissed. Alastair said there was insufficient evidence."

Hester offered her the glass and she took it and drank, pulling a slight face. Oonagh had also packed some small sugared sweets to take away the taste, and Hester offered her one. She took it gratefully.

"Then Mr. Frazer was a public figure?" She pursued the subject to take Mary's mind off the taste of the medicine. She returned the glass to its place and closed the chest, lifting it back onto the luggage rack.

"More or less." Mary lay down and made herself as comfortable as she could, and Hester tucked the rug more closely around her.

"He visited the house one night," Mary continued. "A little weasel of a man, creeping in and out like some nocturnal creature bent on no good. That is the only time I have seen him in person. It was by lamplight, just like that wretched conductor, poor soul. I am sure I am maligning him." She smiled. "And possibly Frazer too." But still there was uncertainty in her voice. "Now please go to sleep yourself. I know perfectly well you are ready for it. They will call us well in time to rise and make ourselves respectable for London."

Hester looked at the single oil lamp which gave the soft, yellowish light in the compartment. There was no way to turn it down, but she doubted its glow would keep either of them awake.

She curled up in the seat as comfortably as possible, and was amazed that in a few minutes the rhythmic rattle of the wheels over the ties lulled her to sleep.

She woke several times, but only to try to make herself more comfortable and wish she were a little warmer. Her dreams were troubled with memories of the Crimea, of being cold and overtired and yet ready to keep awake to care for those who were immeasurably worse.

Finally she woke up with a start to find the conductor in the doorway, looking at her cheerfully.

"London in half an hour, ma'am," he said. "Morning to ye!" And he disappeared.

She was stiff and very cold. She got up slowly. Her hair had fallen down and she had lost some of the pins, but that was a small thing. She must wake Mary, who was still tucked up with her face towards the wall, just as she had left her. She seemed hardly to have moved. The rug was not in the least disturbed.

"Mrs. Farraline," she said as cheerfully as she could. "We are approaching London. Did you sleep well?"

Mary did not stir.

"Mrs. Farraline?"

Still no movement.

Hester touched her shoulder and shook her very gently. Some older people slept very deeply. "Mrs. Farraline!"

The shoulder did not yield at all; in fact, it seemed quite stiff.

Hester felt a twinge of alarm.

"Mrs. Farraline! Wake up! We are nearly in London!" she said with mounting urgency.

Still Mary did not move.

Hester pulled at her sharply and forced her over. Her eyes were closed, her face was white, and when Hester touched it the flesh was cold. Mary Farraline had been dead all night.

CHAPTER
THREE

———

Hester's first feeling was one of profound loss. Long ago she might have had an initial moment of rejecting the fact altogether, refusing to believe Mary was dead, but she had seen too much death not to recognize it, even when it was completely without warning. Last night Mary had seemed in excellent health and buoyant spirits, and yet she must have died quite early in the night. Her body was cold to the touch, and such stiffness took from four to six hours to achieve.

Hester pulled the blanket up over her, gently covering her face, and then stood back. The train was moving more slowly now, and there were houses in the gray, early morning beyond the rain-streaked windows.

Then the next emotion came: guilt. Mary had been her patient, entrusted to her care, and after only a few hours she was dead. Why? What had she done so badly? What had she bungled, or forgotten, that Mary had died without even a sound, no cry, no gasp, no struggle for breath? Or perhaps there had been, only Hester had been too soundly asleep to hear, and the clatter of the train had masked it.

She could not just continue to stand there, staring at the motionless form under the rug. She must tell the authorities, beginning with the conductor and the guard. Then of course when they reached the station there would be the stationmaster, and possibly the police. After that, infinitely worse, she would have to tell Griselda Murdoch. The thought of that made her feel a little sick.

Better begin. Standing there would not help anything, and the contemplation of it was only adding to the hurt. Feeling numb she went to the compartment entranceway, in her awkwardness banging her elbow on the wooden partition. She was cold and stiff with tension. It hurt more than it would have normally, but she had no time for pain. Which way to go? Either. It made no difference. Just do something, don't stand undecided. She went left, towards the front of the train.

"Conductor! Conductor! Where are you?"

A military man with a mustache peered around a corner and stared at her. He drew breath to speak, but she had rushed on.

"Conductor!"

A very thin woman with gray hair looked at her sharply.

"Goodness, girl, whatever is the matter? Must you make so much noise?"

"Have you seen the conductor?" Hester demanded breathlessly.

"No I haven't. But for heaven's sake lower your voice." And without further comment she withdrew into her compartment.

"Can I help you, miss?"

She spun around. It was the conductor at last, his bland face unsuspecting of the trouble she was about to impart. Perhaps he was used to hysterical female passengers. She made an effort to keep her voice calm and under some control.

"I am afraid something very serious has happened. . . ." Why was she shaking so much? She had seen hundreds of dead bodies before.

"Yes, miss. What would that be?" He was still quite unmoved, merely politely interested.

"I am afraid Mrs. Farraline, the lady with whom I was traveling, has died in the night."

"Probably just asleep, miss. Some folk sleep very deep—"

"I'm a nurse!" Hester snapped at him, her voice rising sharply. "I know death when I see it!"

This time he looked thoroughly disconcerted. "Oh dear. You quite sure? Elderly lady, is she? Heart, I suppose. Took bad, was she? Ye should'a' called me then, you know." He looked at her critically.

At another time Hester might have asked him what he could have done, but she was too distressed to argue.

"No—no, she made no sound in the night. I just found her when I went to rouse her now." Her voice was wavering again, and her lips almost too stiff to form the words. "I don't know—what happened. I suppose it was her heart. She was taking medicine for it."

"She had forgot to take it, did she?" He looked at her dubiously.

"No of course she didn't! I gave it to her myself. Hadn't you better report it to the guard?"

"All in good time, miss. Ye'd better take me to your compartment and we'll have a look. Maybe she's only poorly?" But his voice held little hope and he was only staving off the moment of acknowledgment.

Obediently Hester turned and led the way back, stopping at the entrance and allowing him to go in. He pulled the blanket back from the face and looked at Mary for only an instant before replacing it and stepping out again hastily.

"Yes, miss. Afraid you're right. Poor lady's passed over. I'll go and tell the guard. You stay 'ere, and don't touch anything, understand?"

"Yes."

"Good. Maybe you'd better sit down. We don't want you fainting or anything."

Hester was about to tell him she didn't faint, and then changed her mind. Her knees were weak and she would be very glad to sit down again.

The compartment was cold and, in spite of the rattle and jolt of the train, seemed oddly silent. Mary lay on the seat opposite, no longer in the comfortable position in which she had gone to sleep, but half turned over as Hester had left her, and the conductor had seen her upturned face. It was ridiculous to think of comfort, but Hester had to restrain herself from going and trying to ease her back to a more natural position. She had liked Mary, right from the moment they had met. She had a vitality and candor which were uniquely appealing, and had already awoken in Hester something close to affection.

Her thoughts were interrupted by the arrival of the guard. He was a small man with a heavy mustache and lugubrious eyes. There was a smudge of snuff on the front of his uniform jacket.

"Sad business," he said dolefully. "Very sad. Fine lady, no doubt. Still, nothing to be done now to 'elp 'er, poor soul. Where was you takin' 'er?"

"To meet her daughter and son-in-law," Hester replied. "They will be at the station. . . ."

"Oh dear, oh dear. Well, nothing else for it." He shook his head. "We'll let all the other passengers get orff, and we'll send for the stationmaster. No doubt 'e'll find this daughter. What's 'er name? D'ye know 'er name, miss?"

"Mrs. Griselda Murdoch. Her husband is Mr. Connal Murdoch."

"Very good. Well, I'm afraid the train is full, so I can't offer you another compartment to sit in, I'm sorry. But we'll be in London in another few moments. You just try to stay calm." He turned to the conductor. "You got something as you can give this young lady, medicinal, like?"

The conductor's bushy eyebrows shot up.

"Are you asking me if I got strong drink on me person, sir?"

"Of course I in't," the guard said smoothly. "That'd be agin company policy. But I just thought as yer might 'ave had summink medicinal on yer, against the cold, or shock, or summink. For passengers, and the like."

"Well ..." The conductor looked at Hester's wan face. "Well, I suppose I might be able to find something—like ..."

"Good. You go and look, Jake, an' if you can, you give this poor soul a nip, right?"

"Yes sir! Right!"

And he was as good as his word. Having "found" the forbidden brandy, he gave Hester a brimming capful and then left her again, muttering unintelligibly about duty. It was a further quarter of an hour, during which she was shivering cold and feeling increasingly apprehensive, before the stationmaster appeared in the compartment entranceway. He had a bland, curious face, auburn hair and, at the present moment, a severe cold in the head.

"Now then, miss," he said, and sneezed violently. "You'd better tell us exactly what happened to the poor lady. Who is she? And for that matter, who are you?"

"Her name is Mrs. Mary Farraline, from Edinburgh," Hester replied. "I am Hester Latterly, employed to accompany her from Edinburgh to London in order to give her her medicine and see that she was comfortable." It sounded hollow now, even absurd.

"I see. What was the medicine for, miss?"

"A heart ailment, I believe. I was not told any details of her condition, only that the medicine must be given to her regularly, how much, and at what time."

"And did you give it to her, miss?" He regarded her under his eyebrows. "Ye'r sure you did?"

"Yes, absolutely sure." She rose to her feet and pulled down the medicine cabinet, opened it, and showed him the empty vials.

"There's two gone," the stationmaster observed.

"That's right. I gave her one last night, at about a quarter to eleven, the other they must have used in the morning."

"But you only joined the train yesterday evenin'," the conductor pointed out, peering over the stationmaster's shoulder. " 'Ad to 'ave. It don't start till evenin'."

"I know that," Hester said patiently. "Perhaps they were short of medicine, or the maid was lazy, and this was already made up, ready to use. I don't know. But I gave her the second one, out of this vial." She pointed to the second one in its bed. "Last night."

"And how was she then, miss? Poorly?"

"No—no she seemed very well," Hester said honestly.

"I see. Well, we'd best put a guard on duty 'ere to see she in't"—he hesitated—"in't disturbed, and you'd better come and find the poor lady's daughter who's come to meet her, poor soul." The stationmaster frowned, still staring at Hester. "You sure she didn't call out in the night? You were here, I take it—all night?"

"Yes I was," Hester said stiffly.

He hesitated again, then sneezed fiercely and was obliged to blow his nose. He looked at her carefully for several minutes, regarding her straight-backed very slender figure, and making some estimate of her age, and decided she was probably telling the truth. It was not a flattering conclusion.

"I don't know Mr. and Mrs. Murdoch," Hester said quietly. "You will have to make some sort of announcement in order to find them."

"We'll take care of all that sort of thing. Now you just compose yourself, miss, and come and tell these poor souls that their mother has passed over." He looked at her narrowly. "Are you going to be able to do that, miss?"

"Yes—yes certainly I am. Thank you for your concern."

She followed after the stationmaster as he backed out of the entrance and led the way to the carriage door. He turned and assisted her to alight onto the platform. The outside air was sharp and cold on her face, smelling of steam and soot and the grime of thousands of dirty feet. A chill wind whistled along the platform, in spite of the roof overhead, and the noise of trollies, boot heels, banging doors and voices echoed up into the vast overhead span. She followed the stationmaster jostling through the thinning crowd as they reached the steps to his office.

"Are they . . . here?" she asked, suddenly finding her throat tight.

"Yes, miss. Weren't 'ard to find. Young lady and gentleman looking to that train. Only 'ad to ask."

"Has anyone told them yet?"

"No, miss. Thought it better to learn that from you, seein' as you know the family, and o' course knew the lady herself."

"Oh."

The stationmaster opened the door and stood back. Hester went straight in.

The first person she saw was a young woman with fair auburn hair, waved like Eilish's, but much duller in color, sandy rather than burning autumnal. Her face was oval, her features good, but lacking both the passion and the beauty of her sister. Compared with anyone else, she would have been handsome enough, in a quiet, very seemly sort of way, but having met Eilish, Hester could only see her as a shadow, a pale reflection. Perhaps in time, when her present condition had run its term and she was no longer plagued by anxieties, she could be more like Oonagh, have more vivacity and confidence in her.

But it was the man beside her who spoke. He was three or four inches taller than she, his face bony, with hooded eyes and a habit of pursing his lips, which drew attention to his well-shaped mouth.

"You are the nurse employed to accompany Mrs. Farraline on the train?" he demanded. "Good. Perhaps you can tell us what this is all about? Where is Mrs. Farraline? Why have we been kept waiting here?"

Hester met his eyes for a moment in acknowledgment that she had heard him, then turned to Griselda.

"I am Hester Latterly. I was employed to accompany Mrs. Farraline. I am deeply sorry to have to bring you very bad news. She was in excellent spirits last evening, and seemed to be quite well, but she passed away in her sleep, during the night. I think she could not have suffered, because she did not cry out. . . ."

Griselda stared at her as if she had not comprehended a word she had heard.

"Mother?" She shook her head. "I don't know what you are saying. She was coming down to London to tell me—I don't know what. But she said it would all be all right! She said so! She promised me." She turned helplessly to her husband.

He ignored her and stared at Hester.

"What are you saying? That is not an explanation of anything. If Mrs. Farraline was in perfect health yesterday evening, she wouldn't simply have"—he looked for the right euphemism—"have passed over—without ... For heaven's sake, I thought you were a nurse. What is the point of having a nurse to come with her if this is what happens? You are worse than useless!"

"Come now, sir," the stationmaster said reasonably. "If the good lady was getting on in years, and had a bad heart, she could have gone any time. It's something to be grateful for, she didn't suffer."

"Didn't suffer, man? She's dead!" Murdoch exploded.

Griselda covered her face and collapsed backwards onto the wooden chair behind her.

"She can't be gone," she wailed. "She was going to tell me ... I can't bear this! She promised!"

Murdoch looked at her, his face filled with confusion, anger and helplessness. He seized on the refuge offered him.

"Come now, my dear. There is some truth in what the stationmaster says. It was extraordinarily sudden, but we must be grateful that she did not suffer. At least it appears so."

Griselda looked at him with horror in her wide eyes. "But she didn't—I mean, there wasn't even a letter. It is vitally important. She would never have ... Oh this is terrible." She covered her face again and began to weep.

Murdoch looked at the stationmaster, ignoring Hester.

"You must understand, my wife was devoted to her mother. This has been a great shock to her."

"Yes sir, only natural," the stationmaster agreed. " 'Course it is. Would to anyone, especially a young lady o' sensibility."

Griselda rose to her feet suddenly. "Let me see her!" she demanded, pushing her way forward.

"Now really, my dear," Murdoch protested, grasping her shoulders.

"That would do no good at all and you must rest. Think of your condition. . . ."

"But I must!" She fought free of him and confronted Hester, her face so pale the dusting of freckles across her cheeks stood out like dirty marks. Her eyes were wild and staring. "What did she say to you?" she demanded. "She must have told you something! Something about her purpose in coming here—something about me! Didn't she?"

"Only that she was coming to reassure you that you had no cause for anxiety," Hester said gently. "She was quite definite about that. You need have no anxiety at all."

"But why?" Griselda said furiously, her hands held up as if she would grasp Hester and shake her if she had dared. "Are you sure? She might not have meant it! She could have been simply—I don't know—being kind."

"I don't think so," Hester replied quite frankly. "From what I saw of Mrs. Farraline, she did not speak idly in order to set someone's mind at rest; if what she had said was not completely true, she need not have mentioned it at all. Of course it is extremely difficult for you at such a dreadful time, but I should try to believe that you really do have no cause for concern."

"Would you?" Griselda said eagerly. "Do you think so, Miss . . ."

"Latterly. Yes I do."

"Come, my dear," Connal said soothingly. "This is really not important now. We have arrangements to make. And you must write to your family in Edinburgh. There is a great deal to take care of."

Griselda turned to him as if he had been speaking a foreign language.

"What?"

"Don't worry yourself. I shall attend to it all. I shall write this morning, a full letter with all that we know. If I post it today, it will go on the night train, and they will receive it in Edinburgh tomorrow morning. I will assume then that it was very quiet and she almost certainly felt nothing." He shook his head a little. "Now, my dear, this has been a terrible day for you. I shall take you home where Mama can care for you." His voice held a sudden relief at having thought of the ideal way of releasing himself from a situation beyond his ability. "You really must consider your . . . health, my dear. You should rest. There is nothing you can do here, I assure you."

"That's right, ma'am," the stationmaster said quickly. "You go with your husband. 'E is absolutely right, ma'am."

Griselda hesitated, shot another anguished look at Hester, then succumbed to a superior force.

Hester watched her go with relief, and a sharp, sad memory of Mary saying how unnecessarily Griselda worried. She could almost hear Mary's voice in her head, and the very humor in it. Perhaps she should have said more to comfort her. She had seemed more devastated by the lack of reassurance over her child than by her mother's death. But perhaps that was the easier of the two emotions to face. Where some people retreated into anger, and she had seen that often enough, Griselda was grasping on to fear. Being with child, especially a first, could cause all kinds of strange turmoils in the mind, feelings that would not normally be so close to the surface.

But Griselda was gone, and there was nothing she could add now. Perhaps in time Murdoch would think of the right things to say or do.

It was nearly another hour of questions and repeated futile answers before Hester was permitted to leave the station. She had recounted to every appropriate authority the exact instructions she had been given in Edinburgh, how Mary had seemed during the evening, that she had made no complaint whatever of illness, on the contrary, she had seemed in unusually good spirits. No, Hester had heard nothing unusual in the night, the sound of the wheels on the track had obliterated almost everything else anyway. Yes, without question she had given Mrs. Farraline her medicine, one vial as instructed. The other vial had already been empty.

No, she did not know the cause of Mrs. Farraline's death. She assumed it was the heart complaint from which she suffered. No, she had not been told the history of the illness. She was not nursing her, simply accompanying her and making sure she did not forget her medicine or take a double dose. Could she have done so? No, she had not opened the case herself, it was exactly where Hester had put it. Besides which, Mary was not absentminded, nor approaching senility.

At last, feeling numb with sadness, Hester was permitted to leave, and made her way to the street, where she hailed a hansom cab and gave the driver Callandra Daviot's address. She did not even consider whether it was a courteous thing to turn up in the middle of the morning, unannounced and in a state of distress. Her desire to be warm and safe, and to hear a familiar voice, was so intense it drove out normal thoughts of decorum. Not that Callandra was someone who cared much for such things, but eccentricity was not the same as lack of consideration.

It was a gray day, with gusts of rain on the wind, but she was unaware of her surroundings. Grimy streets and soot-stained walls and wet pavements gave way to more gracious squares, falling leaves and splashes of autumn color, but they did not intrude into her consciousness.

" 'Ere y'are, miss," the driver said at last, peering down at her through the peephole.

"What?" she said abruptly.

"We're 'ere, miss. Ye goin' ter get out, or d'yer wanner stay sitting in 'ere? I'll 'ave ter charge yer. I got me livin' ter make."

"No of course I don't want to stay in here," she said crossly, scrambling to open the door with one hand and grasp her bag with the other. She alighted awkwardly and, setting her bag on the pavement, paid him and bade him a good day. As the horse moved off, and the rain increased in strength, making broad puddles where the stones were uneven, she picked up the bag again and climbed the steps to the front door. Please heaven Callandra was at home, and not out engaged in one of her many interests. She had refused to think of that before, because she did not want to face the possibility, but now it seemed so likely she even hesitated on the step, and stood undecided in the rain, her feet wet, her skirts becoming sodden where they brushed the stones.

There was nothing to lose now. She pulled the bell knob and waited.

The door opened but it was a moment before the butler recognized her, then his expression changed.

"Good morning, Miss Latterly." He made as if to say something further, then thought better of it.

"Good morning. Is Lady Callandra at home?"

"Yes ma'am. If you care to come in, I shall inform her you are here." He moved aside to allow her to pass, his eyebrows slightly raised at her bedraggled appearance. He took her bag from her and set it down gingerly, then excused himself, leaving her dripping onto the polished floor.

It was Callandra herself who appeared, her curious, long-nosed
face full of concern. As always, her hair was escaping its pins as if to
take flight, and her green gown was more comfortable than elegant.
The wide skirts had become her when she was younger and slimmer;
now they no longer disguised a certain generosity of hip, but made her
seem shorter than she was. However, her carriage, as always, was excellent, and her humor and intelligence more than made up for any
lack of beauty.

"My dear, you look awful!" she said with anxiety. "Whatever has
happened? I thought you had gone to Edinburgh. Was it canceled?"
For the moment she ignored the sodden skirt and the generally crum-
pled gown, the hair as untidy as her own. "You look quite ill."

Hester smiled in sheer relief at seeing her. It filled her with a sense
of warmth far deeper than anything physical, like a homecoming after
a lonely journey.

"I did go to Edinburgh. I came home on the overnight train. My
patient died."

"Oh my dear, I'm so sorry," Callandra said quickly. "Before you got
there? How wretched. Still—oh—" She searched Hester's face. "That's
not what you mean, is it? She died in your charge?"

"Yes."

"They had no business to dispatch you with someone so ill," she
said decisively. "Poor creature, to have died away from home, and on
a train, of all things. You must feel dreadful. You certainly look it."
She took Hester's arm. "Come in and sit down. That skirt is soaking
wet. Nothing of mine will fit you, you'd step right through them.
You'll have to make do with one of the maid's dresses. They are quite
good enough until that dries out. Or you'll catch your—" She stopped
and pulled a sorrowful face.

"Death," Hester supplied for her with a ghost of a smile. "Thank
you."

"Daisy," Callandra called loudly. "Daisy, come here if you please!"

Obediently a slender dark girl with wide eyes came out of the dining room door, a duster in her hand, her lace cap a trifle crooked on
her head.

"Yes, your ladyship?"

"You are about Miss Latterly's height. Would you be good enough
to lend her a dress until hers is dried out. I have no idea what she has

been doing in it, but it is shedding a pool of water in here, and must be as cold as Christmas to wear. Oh, and you'd better find some boots and stockings for her too. Then on your way ask Cook to send some hot chocolate into the green room."

"Yes, your ladyship." She bobbed in something like a half curtsy, and with a glance at Hester to make sure she had understood the instruction, led her away to fulfill the errand.

Ten minutes later Hester was dressed in a gray stuff gown which fitted her excellently apart from being a couple of inches short at the ankle, showing her borrowed stockings and boots, and sitting beside the fire opposite Callandra.

The room was one of her favorites, decorated entirely in dark green and white, with white doors and window embrasures, directing one's eye toward the light. The furniture was warm, dark rosewood, upholstered in cream brocade, and there was a bowl of white chrysanthemums on the table. She put her hands around the cup of hot chocolate and sipped it gratefully. It was ridiculous to be so cold; it was not even winter, and certainly far from frosty outside. And yet she was shivering.

"Shock," Callandra said sympathetically. "Drink it. It will make you feel better."

Hester sipped again, and felt the hot liquid down her throat.

"She was so well the evening before," she said vehemently. "We sat up and talked about all sorts of things. She would have talked longer, only her daughter instructed me she should not stay up later than quarter past eleven at the outside."

"If she was well until the very last evening of her life, she was most fortunate," Callandra said, looking at Hester over the top of the cup. "Most people have at least some period of illness, usually weeks. Of course it is a shock, but in a little while it will seem more of a blessing."

"I expect it will," Hester said slowly. Her brain knew that what Callandra said was perfectly true, but her emotions were sharp with guilt and regret. "I liked her very much," she said aloud.

"Then be glad for her that she did not suffer."

"I felt so—inefficient, so uncaring," Hester protested. "I didn't help her in the slightest. I didn't even wake up. For any use or comfort I was to her, I could have stayed at home."

ANNE PERRY

"If she died in her sleep, my dear girl, there was no use or comfort you could have been," Callandra pointed out.

"I suppose so. . . ."

"I imagine you had to inform someone? Family?"

"Yes. Her daughter and son-in-law had come to meet her. She was very distressed."

"Of course. And sometimes sudden grief can make people very angry, and quite unreasonable. Was she unpleasant to you?"

"No—not at all. She was really very fair." Hester smiled bitterly. "She didn't blame me at all, and she could well have done. She seemed more distressed that she could not learn what her mother was going to tell her than anything else. The poor soul is with child, and it is her first. She was anxious about her health, and Mrs. Farraline had gone to reassure her. She was almost distracted that she would never know what it was that Mrs. Farraline was going to say."

"A most unfortunate situation altogether," Callandra said sympathetically. "But no one is at fault, unless it is Mrs. Farraline for having undertaken such a journey when she was in such delicate health herself. A long letter would have been much better advised. Still, we can all be clever after the event."

"I don't think that I have ever liked a patient more thoroughly or more immediately," Hester said, swallowing hard. "She was very direct, very honest. She told me about dancing the night away before the Battle of Waterloo. Everyone who was anyone in Europe was there that night, she said. It was all gaiety, laughter and beauty, with a desperate, wild kind of life, knowing what the morrow might bring." For a moment the dim lamplight of the carriage, and Mary's quick, intelligent face, seemed more real than the green room and the fire of the present.

"And then their partings in the morning," she went on. "The men in their scarlet and braid, the horses smelling the excitement and the whiff of battle, harnesses jingling, hooves never still." She finished the last of the chocolate but kept holding the empty cup. "There was a portrait of her husband in the hall. He had a remarkable face, full of emotion, and yet so much of it half hidden, only guessed at. Do you know what I mean?" She looked at Callandra questioningly. "There was passion in his mouth, but uncertainty in his eyes, as if you would always have to guess at what he was really thinking."

"A complex man," Callandra agreed. "And a clever artist to catch all that in a face, by the sound of it."

"He formed the family printing company."

"Indeed."

"He died eight years ago."

Callandra listened for another half hour while Hester told her about the Farralines, about the little she had seen of Edinburgh, and what she would do about obtaining another position. Then she rose and suggested that Hester tidy her hair, which was still lacking several pins and far from dressed, and they should consider luncheon.

"Yes—yes of course," Hester said quickly, only just realizing how much of Callandra's time she had taken. "I'm sorry. . . . I . . . should have . . ."

Callandra stopped her with a look.

"Yes," Hester said obediently. "Yes, I'll go and find some more pins. And I daresay Daisy will wish for her dress back. It was very kind of her to lend me this."

"Yours will hardly be dry yet," Callandra pointed out. "There will be plenty of time after we have eaten."

Without further argument Hester went upstairs to the spare bedroom where Daisy had put her bag, and opened it to find her comb and some additional pins. She poked her hand down the side hopefully and felt around. No comb. She tried the other side and her fingers touched it after a moment. The pins were harder. They should be in a little screw of paper, but after several minutes she still had not come across it.

Impatiently she tipped up the bag and emptied the contents out onto the bed. Still the pins were not immediately visible. She picked up her chemise that she had changed out of in Mrs. Farraline's house when she had rested. It was hard to realize that had been only yesterday. She shook it and something flew out and went onto the floor with a faint sound. It must be the screw of paper with the pins. It was the right size and weight. She went around to the far side of the bed and knelt down to find it. It was gone again. She moved her hand over the carpet, gently feeling for it.

There it was. Next to the leg of the bed. She picked it up, and instantly knew something was wrong. It was not paper, or even loose pins. It was a complicated scroll of metal. She looked at it. Then her stomach lurched and her mouth went suddenly dry. It was a jeweled pin, a hoop and scroll set with diamonds and large gray pearls. She had never seen it before, but its description was sharp in her mind. It was Mary Farraline's brooch, the one she had said was her favorite and which she had left behind because the dress it complemented was stained.

With clumsy fingers she clasped it, and, her hair still trailing out of its pins, she went back down the stairs and into the green room. Callandra looked up.

"What is it?" She had taken one look at Hester's face and knew there was something new and seriously wrong. "What has happened?"

Hester held out the pin.

"It is Mary Farraline's," she said huskily. "I just found it in my bag."

"You had better sit down," Callandra said grimly, holding out her hand for the brooch.

Hester sank into the chair gratefully. Her legs seemed to have no strength in them.

Callandra took the brooch and turned it over carefully, examining the pearls, then the hallmark on the back.

"I think it is probably worth a good deal," she said in a soft, very grave voice. "At least ninety to a hundred pounds." She looked at Hester with a frown between her brows. "I suppose you have no idea how it came to be in your bag?"

"No—none at all. Mrs. Farraline said she had not brought it with her because the dress she wears it with had been stained."

"Then it would seem that her maid did not obey instructions very well." Callandra bit her lip. "And is also . . . a great deal less than honest. It is hard to see how this could have happened by accident. Hester, there is something seriously wrong here, but try as I might, I cannot understand it. We need assistance, and I propose that you ask William . . ."

Hester froze.

". . . to give us his advice," Callandra finished. "This is not something we can deal with ourselves, nor would it be sensible to try. My dear, there is something very wrong. The poor woman is dead. It may be some kind of unfortunate error that her jewelry has found its way into your belongings, but for the life of me I cannot think what."

"But do you think . . ." Hester began, hating the thought of going to Monk for help. It seemed so ineffectual, and at the moment she felt too tired and stunned to be up to the kind of emotional battle Monk would engender.

"Yes I do," Callandra said, yielding nothing. "Or I would not have suggested it. I will not override your wishes, but I cannot urge you strongly enough to get counsel and do so without delay."

Hester stood still for several moments, thinking, trying to find an explanation so she would not have to go to Monk, and even as she was doing it, knowing it was futile. There was no explanation that made any kind of sense.

Callandra waited, knowing she had carried the argument, it was simply a matter of coming to the point of surrender.

"Yes . . ." Hester said quietly. "Yes, you are right. I shall go back upstairs and find the pins, then I'll go and see if I can find Monk."

"You may take my carriage," Callandra offered.

Hester smiled wanly. "Do you not trust me to go?" But she did not wait for an answer. They both knew it was the only course that made sense.

Monk looked at her with a frown. They were in the small sitting room she had suggested he use as a place to receive prospective clients. It would make them feel much more at ease than his rather austere office, which was far too functional and intimidating. Monk himself was unnerving enough, with his smooth, lean-boned face and unwavering eyes.

He was standing by the mantelpiece, having heard the outer door open and come in immediately. His expression on recognizing her was an extraordinary mixture of pleasure and irritation. Obviously he had been hoping for a client. Now he regarded with disfavor her plain dress, the one borrowed from Callandra's maid, her pale face and her hastily done hair.

"What's wrong? You look dreadful." It was said in a tone of pure criticism. Then a flicker of anxiety crossed his eyes. "You are not ill, are you?" There was anger in his voice. It would inconvenience him if she were ill. Or was it fear?

"No, I'm not ill," she said tartly. "I have returned from Edinburgh on the overnight train, with a patient." It was difficult to say this with the composure and the chill she wished. If only there had been some-one else to turn to who would be equally able to see the dangers and give good and practical advice.

He drew breath to make some stinging retort, then, knowing her as well as he did, realized there was something profoundly wrong. He waited, looking at her intently.

"My patient was an elderly lady of some position in Edinburgh," she went on, her voice growing quieter and losing its sharpness. "A Mrs. Mary Farraline. I was employed to give her her medicine last thing at night, that was really all I had to do. Apart from that, I think it was mainly company for her."

He did not interrupt. She smiled with a bitter amusement. A few months ago he would have. Being obliged to seek customers in order to obtain a living, instead of having them as a right, as he had when a police inspector, had taught him, if not humility, at least enlightened self-interest.

He motioned her to sit down, while he sat opposite her, still listening.

She returned her mind painfully to her reason for being there.

"She went to sleep about half past eleven," she continued. "At least she seemed to. I slept quite well myself, having been up . . . in a second-class carriage all the way from London the night before." She swallowed. "When I awoke in the morning, shortly before our arrival in London, I tried to rouse her, and discovered she was dead."

"I'm sorry," he said. There was sincerity in his voice, but also a waiting. He knew it must have disturbed her. Although it was proba-bly beyond her control, it was a kind of failure and he knew she would regard it as such. But she had never confided her failures or sadnesses to him before . . . or at least only indirectly. She would not have come simply to say this. He stood with one foot on the fender, shoulder against the mantelshelf, waiting for her to continue.

"Of course I had to inform the stationmaster, and then her daugh-ter and son-in-law, who had come to meet her. It was some time be-fore I was able to leave the station. When I did, I went to see Callandra. . . ."

He nodded. It was what he would have expected. In fact, it was what he would have done himself. Callandra was perhaps the only person in whom he would confide his emotions. He would never willingly allow Hester to see his vulnerability. Of course she had seen it a few times as Callandra never had, but that was different, and had been unintentional.

"While I was there I had occasion to go upstairs and search for some further hairpins. . . ."

His smile was sarcastic. She knew her hair was still untidy, and exactly what was passing through his mind. Her voice sharpened again.

"I put my hand into my case, and instead of pins I found a brooch . . . with diamonds and gray pearls in it. It is not mine, and I am quite sure it was Mrs. Farraline's, because she described it to me in the course of conversation about what she might do in London."

His face darkened and he moved away from the mantelpiece and sat down in the chair opposite her, waiting patiently for her to be seated also.

"So she was not wearing it on the train?" he asked.

"No. That is the point. She said she had left it at home in Edinburgh because the gown it went with had been stained!"

"It only went with one gown?" he said in surprise, but the disbelief in his voice did not carry to his eyes. Already his mind was ahead, understanding the fears.

"Gray pearls," she explained unnecessarily. "They would look wrong with most colors, rather dull." She went on talking to avoid the moment when she would have to acknowledge what it really meant. "Even black wouldn't be—"

"All right," he said. "She said she had left it behind? I don't suppose she packed her own clothes. She had a maid for that sort of thing. And her cases would be in the guard's van during the journey. Did you meet this maid? Did you quarrel with her? Was she jealous of you because she wished to come to London herself, and you were taking her place?"

"No. She didn't want to go at all. And we did not quarrel. She was perfectly agreeable."

"Then who put the brooch in your bag? You wouldn't be coming to me if you'd done it yourself."

"Don't be fatuous!" she said. "Of course I didn't do it. If I were a thief, I would hardly come and tell you about it!" Her voice was getting louder and higher with anger as fear caught hold of her and she began to see more clearly the peril of the situation.

He looked at her unhappily. "Where is the brooch now?"

"At Callandra's house."

"Since the unfortunate woman is dead, it is not a matter of simply returning it to her. And we do not know if it was lost in a genuine accident or if it is part of an attempted crime. It could become very ugly." He bit his lip doubtfully. "People in bereavement are often irrational and only too ready to retreat from grief into anger. It is easier to be angry, to feel relief at having something with which to blame someone else. The matter of returning it should be dealt with professionally, by someone retained solely to look after your interests in the case. We had better go and speak to Rathbone." And without waiting to see whether she agreed with this advice, he took his coat from the rack and his hat off the stand and advanced towards the door. "Well, don't sit there," he said tartly. "The more rapidly it is done, the better. Besides, I might lose a client if I dither around wasting time."

"You don't need to come with me," she said defensively, rising to her feet. "I can find Oliver myself and tell him what happened. Thank you for your advice." She went past him and out of the door into the entranceway. It was raining outside, and as she opened the street door the cold air chilled her, matching the fear and sense of isolation within.

He ignored her words and followed her out, closing the door behind him and beginning to walk towards the main thoroughfare, where they could find a hansom to take them from Tottenham Court Road west across the city towards the Inns of Court and Vere Street, where Oliver Rathbone had his office. She was obliged to go with him, or else start an argument which would have been totally foolish.

The traffic was heavy, carriages, cabs, wagons, carts of every description passing by, splashing the water out of the gutters, wheels hissing on the wet road, horses dripping, sodden hides dark. Drivers sat hunched with collars up and hats down in a futile attempt to keep the cold rain from running down their necks, hands clenched on the reins.

The crossing sweeper, a boy of about eight or nine years, was still busily pushing manure out of the way to make a clean path for any pedestrian who wished to reach the other side. He seemed to be one of those cheerful souls willing to make the best out of any situation. His skimpy trousers stuck to his legs, his coat was too long for him and gaped around the neck, but his enormous cap seemed to keep most of the rain off his head, except for his chin and nose. He wore the cap tilted at such an angle that the lower half of his face was visible, and his gap-toothed smile was the first thing one saw of him.

Monk had no need to cross the road, but he threw him a half-penny anyway, and Hester felt a sudden surge of hope. The boy caught it and automatically put it between his teeth to assure himself it was real, then tipped his finger to the peak of his cap, almost invisible under its folds, and called out his thanks.

Monk hailed a hansom and as it stopped, he pulled open the door for her and then followed her in, calling out Rathbone's address to the driver.

"Shouldn't I go and get the brooch first?" Hester asked. "Then I can give it to him to return to the Farralines."

"I think you should report it first," he replied, settling himself in his seat as the cab lurched forward. "For your own safety."

The chill returned. She said nothing. They rode in silence through the wet streets. All she could think of was Mary Farraline, and how much she had liked her, her stories of Europe in her youth, of Hamish as a soldier, dashing and brave, and the other men with whom she had danced the nights away before those tumultuous days. They had seemed so alive in her memory. It was hard to accept that she too was suddenly and so completely gone.

Monk did not interrupt her thoughts. Whatever he was concerned with, it apparently held him totally. Once she glanced sideways at him and saw the deep concentration in his face, eyes steadily ahead, brows drawn fractionally downward, mouth tense.

She looked away again, feeling closed out.

At Vere Street the cab stopped and Monk alighted, held the door for her long enough for her to move over and grasp it herself, then paid the driver and went across the pavement to the entrance of the offices and tugged sharply at the bellpull.

The door was opened by a white-haired clerk in winged collar and frock coat.

"Good afternoon, Mr. Monk," he said stiffly. Then he caught sight of Hester behind him. "Good afternoon, Miss Latterly. Please come in out of the rain. Fearful weather." He shook his head, standing back for them to follow him into the foyer, and then the outer office. "I am afraid Mr. Rathbone is not expecting you." He looked at them doubtfully, his pale gray eyes very steady, like a disillusioned schoolmaster. "He has a gentleman with him presently."

"We'll wait," Monk said grimly. "This is a matter of urgency."

"Of course." The clerk nodded his head and indicated a seat where they could make themselves comfortable. Monk declined and stood impatiently, staring through the glass partitions to the office where juniors in black coats copied writs and deeds in copperplate, and other more senior clerks searched in huge law books for references and precedents.

Hester sat down, and Monk sat also but almost immediately rose to his feet again, unable to keep still. One or two heads lifted as they caught sight of him out of the corner of their eyes, but no one spoke.

Minutes ticked by. Monk's face grew tighter and his impatience more obvious.

Finally the door of Rathbone's office opened and an elderly gentleman with massive side whiskers came out, turned and said something, then bowed very slightly and made his way across the office to where the clerk who had welcomed Hester and Monk left his desk and handed the gentleman his hat and cane.

Monk moved forward. No one was going to preempt him. He grasped the handle of the office door and swung it wider, coming face-to-face with Oliver Rathbone.

"Good afternoon," Monk said briskly. "Hester and I have the most urgent matter with which we require your assistance."

Rathbone did not back away. His long face with its humorous eyes and mouth registered only good-natured surprise.

"Indeed?" He looked past Monk at the clerk who had shown the previous client to the door and was now standing wondering what to do about Monk and his regrettable lapse from good manners. Rathbone met his eyes, and understanding passed between them. Monk saw it, and unaccountably it irritated him. But he was in the position of a supplicant, so it would be self-defeating to be sarcastic. He stepped back to allow Rathbone to see Hester, who was now just behind him.

Oliver Rathbone was of medium height, slender, and dressed with the immaculate ease of one who is accustomed to the best of material things and has grown to take elegance for granted. It required no effort; it was a way of life.

However, when he saw Hester's pale face and unusually grim and bedraggled appearance, his composure was shaken, and ignoring Monk, he went forward anxiously.

"My dear Hester, whatever has happened? You look quite—distressed!"

It was nearly two months since she had last seen him, and then it had been more by chance than design. She was not sure how he regarded their relationship. In any formal sense it was professional rather than personal. She did not move in his social sphere at all. Yet they were friends in a deeper sense than most acquaintances ever were. They had shared passionate beliefs in justice, spoken more frankly than perhaps either had to anyone else about certain things. On the other hand, there were whole worlds of personal emotions they had never touched on at all.

Now he was staring at her with obvious concern. In spite of his fairish hair, his eyes were very dark, and she was acutely aware of the intelligence in him.

"For goodness' sake tell him!" Monk said, waving his arm towards the office. "But not out here," he added, in case she should be absent-minded enough to be so indiscreet.

Without looking at Monk, Hester walked in front of Rathbone and into the office. Monk followed her, and Rathbone came in behind and closed the door.

Hester began straightaway. Quietly and succinctly, with as little emotion as she could manage, she told him the elements of what had transpired.

Rathbone sat listening without interruption, and although twice Monk opened his mouth to speak, on each occasion he changed his mind.

"Where is this brooch now?" Rathbone said when at last she finished.

"With Lady Callandra," she replied. Rathbone knew Callandra well enough and no introduction of her was necessary.

"But she did not see you find it? Not that it matters," he added quickly, on observing her consternation. "Could you have misunderstood Mrs. Farraline on the subject of having left this article in Edinburgh?"

"I cannot think how. She had no reason to bring it, since the dress was stained, and she said quite specifically that it went with no other." She could not restrain herself from asking, "What do you think has happened?"

"Does your bag resemble any that Mrs. Farraline had, either with her or in the guard's van? Or any that you observed in her dressing room in Edinburgh?"

Hester felt cold and there was a hard knot inside her.

"No. Mine was a very ordinary brown leather bag with soft sides. Mrs. Farraline's were yellow pigskin, with her initials monogrammed on them, and they all matched." Her voice was scratchy, her mouth dry. She was aware of Monk's growing irritation behind her. "No one could think mine was one of hers," she finished.

Rathbone spoke very quietly.

"Then I am afraid I can think of no explanation other than malice, and why anyone should do such a thing, I cannot imagine."

"But I was only there less than a day," Hester protested. "I did nothing that could possibly offend anyone!"

"You had better go and get this piece of jewelry and bring it to me immediately. I shall write to Mrs. Farraline's estate and inform them of its discovery, and that we shall return it as soon as possible. Please do not waste any time. I do not believe we can afford to wait."

Hester rose to her feet. "I don't understand," she said helplessly. "It seems so pointless."

Rathbone rose also, coming around to open the door for her. He glanced at Monk, then back at Hester.

"Probably it is some family quarrel we know nothing of, or even some malice directed at Mrs. Farraline which has tragically gone astray with her death. It hardly matters at the moment. Your part is to bring it to me, and I shall give you a receipt for it and deal with the matter as regards Mrs. Farraline's executors."

Still she hesitated, confusion welling in her mind, remembering their faces: Mary, Oonagh, Alastair at the dinner table, the beautiful Eilish, Baird and Quinlan who so obviously disliked each other, Kenneth hurrying to his appointment, absentminded Deirdra, the man whose portrait hung in the hall, and drunken, rambling Uncle Hector.

"Come," Monk said sharply, pulling abruptly at her elbow. "There is no time to waste, and certainly none to stand here trying to solve a problem for which we have no information."

"Yes—yes, I'm coming," she agreed, still uncertain. She turned to Rathbone. "Thank you."

They rode back to Callandra's house in silence, Monk apparently lost in thought, and Hester still wrestling with her memories of Edinburgh and searching for any reason at all why someone should have played such a pointless and malicious trick on her. Or was it on Mary? Or the lady's maid? Was that it? Yes, that must be it. One of the maids was jealous, and trying to get her into trouble, perhaps even usurp her position, without actually stealing the brooch.

She was about to say this to Monk when the cab pulled up and they alighted, and the thought was lost in action.

However, the butler who opened Callandra's door was pale-faced and totally unsmiling, and he led the way hastily, closing the door with a snap.

"What is it?" Monk demanded immediately.

"I am afraid, sir, that there are two persons from the police in the withdrawing room," the butler replied grimly, his expression conveying both his distaste and his apprehension. "Her ladyship is speaking with them now."

Monk strode past him across the floor and threw open the withdrawing room door. Hester followed after him, calmer and cold now that the moment had come.

Inside the room Callandra was standing in the center of the floor and she turned around as soon as she heard the door. Beside her were two men, one small and stocky with a blunt face and wide eyes, the other taller, leaner and foxy looking. If they knew Monk they gave no sign of it.

"Good afternoon, sir," the shorter one said politely, but his eyes did not widen in the slightest.

"Good afternoon, ma'am. Sergeant Daly, Metropolitan Police. You must be Miss Latterly, am I right?"

Hester swallowed. "Yes. . . ." Suddenly her voice would not stay level. "What is it you wish? Is it regarding the death of Mrs. Farraline?"

"No, miss, not at present." He came forward, polite and very formal. His taller companion was apparently junior. "Miss Latterly, I

ANNE PERRY

have authority to search your baggage, and your person if necessary, for a piece of jewelry belonging to the late Mrs. Mary Farraline, which, according to her daughter, is missing from her luggage. Perhaps you can save us the necessity for anything so unpleasant by telling us if you have such a piece?"

"Yes she has," Monk said icily. "She has already reported the matter to her legal adviser, and we came here, on his counsel, to take the pin to him so that he might return it to Mrs. Farraline's estate."

Sergeant Daly nodded. "Very wise of you, ma'am, but not sufficient, I'm afraid. Constable Jacks"—he nodded abruptly at the other man—"would you go with this gentleman and obtain the said article." He looked at Monk. "Perhaps you'd be good enough, sir? And you, Miss Latterly, I'm afraid you'll have to come with us."

"Nonsense!" Callandra stepped forward. "Miss Latterly has told you what happened. She found the piece of jewelry that was missing and made provision to return it. You do not need further explanations. She has had a long journey to Edinburgh and back again, and a most distressing experience. She is not going anywhere with you, merely in order to repeat an explanation which is quite clear to you now. You are not a fool, man, you understand exactly what has happened."

"No, I do not understand, your ladyship," he said calmly. "I don't understand at all why a respectable woman who cares for the sick should take from an old lady a piece of jewelry which belongs to her, but that's unarguably what it looks like. Theft is theft, ma'am, whoever did it and whatever for. And I'm afraid, Miss Latterly, you will have to come with us." He shook his head gently. "And don't make it harder for yourself by resisting. I'd hate to have to take you in manacles—but I will, if you force me."

For the second time that day, Hester felt shock and disbelief buffet her like a blow, and then they vanished, leaving only cold, bitter knowledge.

"I shall not make that necessary," she said in a very small voice. "I did not steal anything from Mrs. Farraline. She was my patient, and I had the highest regard for her. And I have never stolen anything from anyone." She turned to Callandra. "Thank you, but I think protest is of no value at this time." She felt herself painfully close to tears, and did not trust herself to speak anymore, least of all to Monk.

Callandra produced the brooch, which she had placed on

the mantelshelf before Hester had left, and silently gave it to the sergeant.

"Thank you, ma'am," he said as he accepted it, and wrapped it in a large clean handkerchief which he took from his coat pocket. He turned again to Hester. "Now, miss, I think it would be best if you come along. Perhaps Constable Jacks can fetch your valise for you. You'll already have everything you need in that, at least for tonight."

Hester was surprised, then she realized that of course they knew she would have them with her. They had known where to find her. Her landlady must have given them Callandra's name. It was an educated guess. She had stayed with her often enough before, between cases. The knowledge was like a door slamming, closing her in.

She had time only to glance at Monk and see the burning anger in his face. The next moment she was in the hall, a policeman on either side of her, being taken inexorably towards the open front door and the street beyond, cold and gray with driving rain.

CHAPTER
FOUR

———

Hester sat in the back of the black closed-in police van between the constable and the sergeant. She could see nothing, in fact only feel the jolt and sway of movement as they drove from Callandra's house to wherever they were taking her. Her mind was in a senseless whirl. It was as if her head were full of noise and darkness. She could not grasp hold of any thought. The moment she had it, it was whipped away from her.

How had the pearl brooch come to be in her bag? Who could have put it there? Why? Mary had left it at home, she had said so. Why would anyone have wished Hester any harm? She had not had time to make an enemy, even if she were important enough to any of them.

The van came to a stop, but she could see nothing through the closed-in sides. A horse whinnied somewhere ahead, and a man swore. They jolted forward again. Was she merely the victim of some plot, some scheme or vengeance she knew nothing about? But what scheme? How could she defend herself? How could she prove any of it?

She glanced sideways at the sergeant, and saw only his rigid profile as he stared ahead of himself at the far wall of the van. The disgust in him was so palpable she could feel it like a chill in the air. She could understand it. It was contemptible to steal from a patient, an old lady, an invalid who trusted you totally.

It was on the tip of her tongue to say again that she had not taken it, but even as she drew breath, she knew it would be futile. They would expect her to deny it. A thief would. It meant nothing.

The journey passed like a nightmare, and eventually they reached the police station, where she was taken into a quiet, drab room and formally charged with having stolen a pearl brooch belonging to her patient, Mrs. Mary Farraline, of Edinburgh, now deceased.

"I did not take it," she said quietly.

Their faces were sad and scornful. No one made any answer at all. She was taken to the cells, pushed in gently with a hand in the small of her back, and before she had time to turn around the door was closed with a heavy clang and the bolt shot home.

The cell was about ten or eleven feet square, with a cot on one side and a wooden bench with a hole in it, which obviously served the calls of nature. There was a single high, barred window above the cot, the walls were whitewashed and the floor blackened stone of some smooth, seamless nature.

But the most surprising thing was that there were already three people in it, one an elderly woman of perhaps close to sixty, her hair unnaturally yellow, her skin putty-colored and curiously lifeless. She regarded Hester expressionlessly. The second occupant was very dark, with long loose hair that hung in a knotted mass. Her narrow face was handsome in its own way. Her eyes, so shadowed as to seem almost black, looked at Hester with growing suspicion. The third occupant was a child, not more than eight or nine years old, thin, dirty, and with raggedly cut hair so it was impossible to tell at a glance whether it was a boy or a girl. Clothes were little help, being a conglomeration of adult clothes shorn down to size, patched, and tied around with a length of twine.

"Well, you look like a dying duck in a thunderstorm," the dark woman said critically. "First time, eh? What yer do? Thievin'?" Her sharp eyes took note of Hester's borrowed dress. "Dollymop? You don't look like no tail, not in that square-rigged thing!"

"What?" Hester was slow-witted, confused.

"You'll never pull no gents dressed like that," the woman said contemptuously. "No need to stand on your importance wi' us, we're all family." Her eyes narrowed again. "Which you ain't—are yer." It was an accusation, not a question.

" 'Course she ain't," the older woman said wearily. "She don't even understand yer, Doris."

"Are you . . . related?" Hester asked slowly, including the child in her remark.

"No we ain't related, yer dimwit!" The woman shook her head dismissively. "I mean we're all professionals. Which you ain't, are yer? Jus' thought you'd try yer 'and and yer got caught. Watcha do . . . nick summink?"

"No. No, but they said I did."

"Oh. Innocent, eh?" Her sneer was totally disbelieving. "In't we all! Marge 'ere didn't do no abortions, did yer, Marge? And Tilly 'ere didn't spin no top. An' o' course I don't keep no bawdy 'ouse." She put one hand on her hip. "I'm a decent, respectable woman, I am. Can I 'elp it if some o' me clients is bent?"

"What do you mean, 'spin a top'?" Hester moved farther into the small cell and sat down on the cot, about two feet from the woman named Marge.

"You simple or summink?" Doris demanded. "Spin a top," she said, and made a spiral movement with her fingers. "In't yer never played wi' a top when you was a kid? Yer must 'ave seen one, less yer blind as well as daft."

"You don't go to jail for spinning tops." Hester was beginning to get annoyed. The gratuitous insults were something she could fight against.

"Yer do if it gets in people's way," Doris said with a curl of her lip. "Don't yer, Tilly, eh? Cheeky little sod."

The child looked at her with wide eyes and nodded slowly.

"How old are you?" Hester asked her.

"Dunno," Tilly said with indifference.

"Don't be daft," Doris said again. "She can't count."

"I can so!" Tilly protested indignantly. "I know 'ow many's ten."

"Yer in't ten," Doris said, dismissing the subject. She looked back at Hester. "So what didn't you steal then, my fine lady wot got caught at it?"

"A brooch with pearls in it," Hester replied tartly. "What are you respectable ladies doing that brings you here?"

Doris smiled, showing stained teeth, strong and regular. They would have been beautiful had they been white. "Well, some of us was letting gentlemen pay for their pleasures, which is only fair, as I sees it. But there was one in me back room as was screevin', and the pigs don't like that, cos' the briefs don't like it." She watched Hester's confusion with evident complacency. "Or to put it fancy like, so your ladyship can understand it: they says I was taking money for fornication, and the geezer in the back room was writing recommendations and legal papers for people as wanted 'em but couldn't get 'em the usual way. Very good wi' a pen, is Tam. Write anything for yer ... deeds in property, wills, letters of authority, references o' character. You name it, 'e'll write it, and takes a good lawyer to know the difference."

"I see. . . ."

"Do yer? Do yer now?" Her lip curled. "I don't think yer see anything, yer stupid cow."

"I see you in here the same as I am," Hester said. "Which makes you just as stupid, except you've been here before. To do it twice takes a real art."

Doris swore. Marge smiled mirthlessly. Tilly slunk backwards and crouched by the end of the cot, expecting a fight.

"You'll get yours," Doris said sullenly. "They'll put yer somewhere like the 'Steel' down Cold Bath Fields for a few years, stitching all day till yer fingers bleed, eating slops, 'ot all summer and cold all winter, and nobody ter talk ter wi' yer fancy voice."

Marge nodded. "That's right," she said dolefully. "Keep yer in silence, they do. No talking. An' masks, too."

"Masks?" Hester did not understand her.

"Masks," Marge repeated, dragging her hand across her face. "Masks, so yer can't see nobody's phys."

"Why?"

"Dunno. Just to make you feel worse, I suppose. So yer alone. Don't learn nothing wicked from nobody else. It's the new idea."

Hester's day was taking on more and more of the proportions of a nightmare. This last piece of information lent it a quality of total unreality. Hester tried to imagine troops of women in gray dresses, silent and masked, faceless, laboring, cold, filled with hatred and despair. In such a world, how could they be anything else? And children who spun tops in the street and got in people's way. She was choked with a mixture of rage and pity, and the almost hysterical desire to escape. Her heart was beating high in her throat, and her knees were suddenly weak, even though she was sitting down. She could hardly have stood, even if she had wanted to and there had been any point.

"Sick?" Doris said with a smile. "Yer'll get used ter it. An' don't think yer 'avin' the cot, cos yer ain't. Marge is sick for real. She gets it. Any'ow she was 'ere first."

Early the following morning Hester was taken to a magistrate's court and remanded in custody. From there she was taken to the prison at Newgate and placed in a cell with two pickpockets and a prostitute. Within an hour she was sent for and told that her lawyer had come to speak with her.

She felt a wild surge of hope as if the long nightmare were over, the darkness dispelled. She shot to her feet and almost fell over in her eagerness to get through the door and along the bare stone passage to the room where Rathbone would be.

"Now, now," the wardress said sharply, her hard, blunt face tightening. "Just be'ave yerself. No call to get excited. Talk, that's all. Come wi' me, stay be'ind me and speak when yer spoken to." And she turned on her heel and marched away with Hester at her elbow.

They stopped in front of a large metal door. The wardress produced a huge key from the chain at her belt and placed it in the lock and turned it. The door swung silently under the pressure of her powerful arms. Inside was painted white, gaslit and relatively cheerful. Oliver Rathbone was standing behind the chair at the far side of the plain wooden table. There was an empty chair on the nearer side.

"Hester Latterly," the wardress said with a half smile at Rathbone. It was a sickly gesture, as if she were undecided whether to try to be charming with him or whether he was an enemy, like all the inmates. She looked at his immaculate clothes, his polished boots and neat hair, and opted for charm. Then she saw the look on his face at the sight of Hester, and something within her froze. The smile was a dead thing, fixed and horrible.

"Knock when you want to get out," she said coldly, and then as soon as Hester was inside, banged the door so the reverberations of metal on stone jarred in the head.

Hester was too close to tears to speak.

Rathbone came around the table and took both her hands in his. The warmth of his fingers was like a light in darkness, and she clung to him as tightly as she dared.

He stared into her face for only a few moments, gauging the fear in her, then as suddenly let her go and pushed her gently back into the chair closest to her.

"Sit down," he ordered. "We must not waste the time we have."

She obeyed, fumbling with her skirts to arrange them so she could pull the chair comfortably to the table.

He sat opposite her, leaning forward a little. "I have already been to see Connal Murdoch," he said gravely. "I thought I might persuade him that the whole matter is one of error, and not something in which the police should be involved at all." There was apology in his eyes. "Unfortunately I found him very rigid on the subject, and I have not been able to reason with him."

"What about Griselda, Mary's daughter?"

"She barely spoke. She was present, but seemed to defer to him in everything and, frankly, to be in a state of considerable distress." He stopped, searching her face as if to judge from it how he should continue.

"Is that a polite way of saying she was not able to apply her mind?" she asked. She could not afford euphemisms.

"Yes," he conceded. "Yes, I suppose it is. Grief takes many forms, not a few of them unattractive, but she did not seem so much grieved as frightened—at least, that is the impression I received."

"Of Murdoch?"

"I am afraid I am not receptive enough to be certain. I thought not, but then I also felt that he made her nervous . . . or anxious? I have no clear impression. I'm sorry." He frowned. "But it is all of little importance now. I failed to persuade him to dismiss the matter. I am afraid it will proceed, and my dear, you must prepare yourself for it. I will do everything I can to see that it is settled as rapidly and discreetly as possible. But you must help me by answering everything you can with the utmost clarity." He stopped. His eyes were steady and seemed to look through all her defenses as if he could see not only her thoughts but the mounting fear inside her. A day ago she would have found that intrusive; she would have been angry at his presumption. Now she clung to it as if it were the only chance of rescue in a cold quicksand that was growing deeper by the moment.

"It doesn't make any sense," she said desperately.

"It will do," he insisted with a faint smile. "It is simply that we do not have all the facts. It is my task to learn at least enough of them to prove that you have committed no crime."

No crime. Of course she had committed no crime. Perhaps she had overlooked something, and if she had not, then Mary Farraline might still be alive. But certainly she had not taken the brooch. She had never seen it before. A lift of hope brightened inside her. She met Rathbone's eyes and he smiled, but it was a small, bleak gesture, a matter of determination rather than confidence.

Beyond the bare room in which they were sitting they could hear the sounds of slamming doors, heavy and resonating, iron against stone. Someone called out, and the sound echoed, even though the words were indistinguishable.

"Tell me again precisely what happened from the time you entered the Farraline house in Edinburgh," he instructed.

"But I—" she began, then saw the gravity in his face, and obediently recounted everything she could remember from the time she had stepped into the kitchen and met the butler, McTeer.

Rathbone listened intently. It seemed to Hester as if everything else in the world became distant except the two of them sitting opposite each other, leaning across the wooden table in desperate concentration. She thought that even with her eyes closed, she would see his face as it was now, every detail of it etched on her mind, even the silver flecks in his hair where it sprang smoothly from his temples.

He interrupted her for the first time. "You rested?"

"Yes—why?"

"Apart from your time in the library, was that the first occasion in which you were alone in the house?"

She perceived his meaning immediately.

"Yes." She spoke with difficulty. "I suppose they will say I could have gone back to the dressing room and taken the brooch then."

"I doubt it. It would be an extraordinarily dangerous thing to do. Mrs. Farraline was probably in her bedroom. . . ."

"No—no, when I saw her, it was in a boudoir, a sitting room some distance from her bedroom, I think. Although I suppose I am not sure. Certainly it was some way from the dressing room."

"But the maid could have come into the dressing room," he argued. "In fact, her duties immediately prior to such a long journey would almost certainly have taken her there a number of times, checking that she had everything packed, all the necessary linen was clean, pressed, folded, placed where it should have been. Is that a time you would risk going in, if you were not supposed to be there?"

"No . . . no it isn't!" Then her spirits fell again immediately. "And when I rested in the afternoon my valise was in the room with me. No one could have put the pin into it there."

"That is not the point, Hester," he said patiently. "I am trying to think what they will say, what opportunity you had to find the pin and take it. We must ascertain where it was kept."

"Of course," she said eagerly. "She may have kept it in a jewel case in her bedroom. It would be much more sensible than having it in the dressing room." She looked at his face, and saw a gentleness in it which gave her a curious prickle of pleasure, but there was no lightness in him which corresponded to hers. Surely if Mary had kept it in her room, that was almost proof Hester could not have taken the brooch?

He looked almost guilty, like someone who must disillusion a child.

"What?" she demanded. "Isn't that good? I never went into her bedroom. And all the time except when I was in the library, or resting, I was with other people."

"At least one of whom, my dear, must be lying. Someone placed the pin in your case, and it cannot have been by accident."

She leaned forward urgently. "But it ought to be possible to show that I had no chance to take it from the bedroom, which will be where she kept her jewel case. I am almost certain it was not in the dressing room. To begin with, there was nothing for it to rest on." Her voice rose in excitement as she recalled the details of the room. She leaned closer towards him. "There were three wardrobes along one wall, a window in the second, a tallboy with drawers on the third, and also a dressing table with a stool in front of it, and three mirrors. I remember the brushes and combs and the crystal jars for pins and hair combings. There was no jewel case on it. It would have blocked the mirrors. And there was nothing on the tallboy, and it was too high to be reached."

"And the farther wall?" He smiled wryly.

"Oh . . . the door, of course. And another chair. And there was a sort of daybed."

"But no jewel case?"

"No. I am certain of it." She felt triumphant. It was such a small piece of memory and reason, but it was the first. "It has to mean something."

"It means your recollection is very clear, not a great deal more."

"But it has to," she said urgently. "If the case was not there, then I could not have taken anything from it."

"But, Hester, there is only your word that the case was not there," he said very softly, his mouth pinched with concern and sadness.

"The maid—" she began, then stopped.

"Precisely," he agreed. "The two people who would know that are the maid, who may well have been the one to place the pin in your luggage . . . and Mary herself, who is beyond our reach. Who else? The eldest daughter, Oonagh McIvor? What will she say?" There were both anger and pain in his face, though he was attempting to be as formal as his profession demanded.

She stared at him wordlessly.

He reached one hand across the table as if to touch her, then changed his mind and withdrew it.

"Hester, we cannot afford to hide from the truth," he said earnestly. "You have fallen into the midst of something we do not yet understand, and it would be foolish to imagine anyone involved in it is your friend, or will necessarily tell the truth if it is contrary to their interests. If Oonagh McIvor has to choose whether to blame someone in her own household or you, a stranger, we cannot rely upon her either wishing, or being able, to recall and repeat the exact truth."

"But . . . but if someone in her house is a thief, surely she would wish to know that?" she protested.

"Not necessarily, particularly if it is not a maid, but one of her family."

"But why? Why just one brooch? And why put it in my case?"

His face tightened, as if he were suddenly colder, and the anxiety in his eyes deepened.

"I don't know, but the only alternative I can see is to suppose that you did take it, and that is not tolerable."

The enormity of what he had said became hideously plain to her. How could she expect anyone to believe she had not seized the chance, suddenly offered, and taken the brooch . . . then when Mary was found dead, suddenly become frightened and tried to return it? She met Rathbone's eyes and knew he was thinking precisely the same thing.

Did he really believe her, in his heart? Or was he only behaving as if he did because it was his professional obligation to do so? She felt as if reality were slipping away from her and nightmare closing in, isolation and helplessness, endless confusion where nothing made sense, one moment's sanity was the next moment's chaos.

"I didn't take it," she said suddenly, her voice loud in the silence. "I never saw it before I found it in my bag. I gave it straight to Callandra. What else could I have done?"

His hands closed over hers, surprisingly warm when she was so cold.

"I know you didn't take it," he said firmly. "And I shall prove it. But it will not be easy. You will have to resign yourself to a battle."

She said nothing, struggling to keep the panic under control.

"Would you like me to inform your brother and sister—"

"No! No—please don't tell Charles." Her voice was sharp, and unconsciously she had jerked forward. "You mustn't tell Charles—or Imogen." She took a deep breath. Her hands were shaking. "It will be hard enough for him if he has to know, but if we can fight it first . . ."

He was frowning at her. "Don't you think he would wish to know? Surely he would wish to offer you some support, some comfort?"

"Of course he would wish it," she agreed with a fierce mixture of anger, pity and defensiveness. "But he wouldn't know what to believe. He would want to think I was innocent, and he would not know how to. Charles is very literal. He cannot believe something he cannot understand." She knew she sounded critical, and she had not meant to, but all her own fear and anguish was in her voice, she could hear it and it was out of control. "It would distress him, and he could do nothing to help. He would feel he ought to visit me, and that would be terrible for him."

She wanted to explain to Rathbone about her father's suicide when he was ruined by a cheat, and their mother's death shortly afterwards, and the shock it had been for Charles. He had been the only one of the three children to be in England at the time, James having died recently in the Crimea, and Hester being still out there nursing. The full weight of the disgrace and the financial ruin had fallen on Charles, and then the grief afterwards.

Of course Rathbone knew something of it, because he had defended the man charged in the resulting murder case. But if he had not known the full extent of her father's disgrace, she was not willing to tell him now, or to expose and relive her father's vulnerability. She found herself sitting silently, risking his thinking her sullen.

Rathbone smiled very slightly, a small expression of resignation, and a kind of bitter humor.

"I think you are judging him ill," he said calmly. "But it is not of great importance now. Perhaps later on we can discuss it again." He rose to his feet.

"What are you going to do?" She stood up also, too quickly, knocking herself against the table and scraping the chair legs loudly on the floor. She lost her balance clumsily and only regained it by holding on to the table. "What happens next?"

He was close to her, so close she could smell the faint odor of the wool of his coat and feel the warmth of his skin. She longed for the comfort of being held with a depth that made the blood rush up to her face in shame. She straightened and took a step backwards.

"They will keep you here," he answered, wincing. "I shall go and seek Monk and send him to learn more of the Farralines and what really happened."

"To Edinburgh?" she said with surprise.

"Of course. I doubt there is anything more we can discover in London."

"Oh."

He moved to the door and knocked. "Wardress!" He turned back to see her. "Keep heart," he said gently. "There is an answer, and we shall find it."

She forced herself to smile. She knew he was speaking only to comfort her, but even so the words themselves had some power. She clung to them, willing herself to believe.

"Of course. Thank you. . . ."

They were prevented from saying anything further by the clang of the keys in the lock and the wardress's appearing, grim-faced and implacable.

Before calling upon Monk, which Rathbone viewed with very mixed thoughts, he returned to his offices in Vere Street. He had learned little of practical value from his interview with Hester, and he felt more emotionally drained than he had foreseen. Visiting clients accused of crime was always trying. Naturally they were frightened, shocked by arrest. Even when they were guilty, capture and charge took them by surprise. When they were innocent the sense of bewilderment and having been overtaken by events out of their control was devastating.

He had seen Hester angry before, burning with injustice, frightened for other people, close to despair, but never with the fear for herself. In a sense she had always been in some control of events, her own freedom not at stake.

He took off his coat and gave it to the clerk waiting to take it from him. Hester was so impatient of fools, so fierce to charge into battle. It was a characteristic most alarming, and highly unattractive in a woman. Society would not tolerate it. He smiled as he imagined how it would be greeted by most of the respectable ladies he knew. He could visualize the expressions in their well-bred faces. And it alarmed him, as his smile broadened with self-mockery, that it was the quality in her which most appealed to him. Gentler, more conventionally behaved women he found more comfortable, less challenging, less disturbing to his well-being, his assumptions and certainly his social and professional ambitions, but they did not remain always in his memory after they had parted. He was neither troubled by them nor invigorated. Safety was beginning to cloy, for all its seeming advantages.

Absentmindedly he thanked the clerk and walked past him to his office. He closed the door behind him and sat down at his desk. He must not allow this to happen to Hester. He was one of the best barristers in England, he was the ideal person to protect her and get this absurd charge dismissed. It irritated him that he would have to use Monk to find out the truth of what had happened, or at least enough of it to prove Hester's innocence—and reasonable doubt would be far from satisfactory—but without facts he could do nothing.

It was not that he disliked Monk, not entirely. The man had an excellent mind, courage, and a kind of honor; even the fact that he was abrasive, often ill-mannered, and always arrogant was not of itself a strike against him. He was not a gentleman, for all his confidence, his elegance, his fine diction. The difference was indefinable, but it was there. There was a certain underlying aggression in him of which Rathbone was always aware. And his attitude towards Hester was intensely irritating.

Hester's welfare was the only thing that mattered at the moment. His own feelings about Monk were irrelevant. He would send a messenger to fetch him, and while he was waiting for him to arrive, prepare sufficient money to send him to Edinburgh on the night train with instructions to remain there until he could learn precisely what jealousies, pressures financial or emotional, existed in the Farraline household which had produced this ridiculous accident of circumstance.

He rang the bell for the clerk to come, and when the door opened, drew breath to speak, then saw the man's face.

"What is it, Clements? What is wrong?"

"The police, sir. Sergeant Daly is here to see you."

"Ah." Perhaps the charge had been withdrawn, and he would not need to send for Monk after all. "Ask him to come in, Clements."

Clements bit his lip, his eyes troubled, and withdrew to obey.

"Yes?" Rathbone said hopefully as Sergeant Daly appeared in the doorway looking solid and sad. Rathbone was about to ask if the charges had been dropped when something in Daly's face stopped him.

Daly closed the door behind him quietly, the latch clicking home with a snick.

"I'm sorry, Mr. Rathbone." His voice was light and very clear. In other circumstances it would have been pleasant, in spite of the London edge to the accent. "But I've got some rather unpleasant news."

The words were very mild, and yet Rathbone felt a sense of dread out of all proportion to the situation. He breathed in, and his stomach lurched. His mouth was suddenly dry.

"What is it, Sergeant?" He managed to sound almost as calm as Daly had, completely belying the fear inside him.

Daly remained standing, his blunt face filled with sorrow.

"Well sir, I'm afraid Mr. and Mrs. Murdoch weren't totally satisfied with the way poor Mrs. Farraline died, it being so unexpected like, and they called their own doctor to make an examination . . ." He left the words hanging in the air.

"You mean a postmortem?" Rathbone said sharply. Why on earth did the man not come to the point? "What of it?"

"He's not satisfied she died natural, sir."

"What?"

"He's not satisfied—"

"I heard you!" Rathbone made as if to rise from his seat but his legs betrayed him and he changed his mind. "What was . . . unnatural about it? Didn't the police surgeon say it was heart failure?"

"Yes sir, he did that," Daly agreed. "But it was a somewhat hasty examination, made with the understanding that the lady was elderly and that she suffered from a heart ailment already."

"Are you now saying that that is not true?" Rathbone's voice rose, even though he had not intended it to. He sounded shrill and he knew it. He must keep more control of himself!

"No sir, o' course I'm not," Daly said, shaking his head. "There's no question she was elderly, and apparently she'd 'ad this complaint for some time. But when Mr. Murdoch's own doctor had a closer look, like 'e was asked to, he wasn't so sure. Mr. Murdoch suggested a postmortem examination, as is Mrs. Murdoch's right, in the circumstances, what with the theft, an' all."

"What on earth do you mean, man?" Rathbone exploded. "You aren't suggesting Miss Latterly strangled her patient for a piece of jewelry, are you? And then immediately reported finding it and made every effort to return it to the family?"

"No sir, not strangled . . ." Daly said quietly.

Rathbone's throat tightened so he could hardly breathe.

"Poisoned," Daly finished. "With a double dose of her medicine, to be exact." He looked at Rathbone with deep sadness. "They found it when they cut her open an' looked inside her. Not easy to spot, affects the heart, but seein' as the lady was on the medicine, an' two vials was empty when it should'a' bin one, natural thing to look for, see? Not very pleasant, I'm afraid, but undeniable. I'm sorry, sir, but Miss Latterly is now being held on a charge of murder."

"B-but . . ." Rathbone's voice died away, choked in his throat, his lips dry.

"There weren't no one else there, sir. Mrs. Farraline were perfectly all right when she got onto the train in Edinburgh with Miss Latterly, and she was dead, poor soul, when she arrived in London. You tell me what else we're to believe."

"I don't know. But not that!" Rathbone protested. "Miss Latterly is a brave and honorable woman who served in the Crimea with Florence Nightingale. She saved dozens of lives, at great cost to herself. She gave up the comfort and safety of England to—"

"I know all that, sir," Daly interrupted firmly. "You prove as someone else killed the old lady, and I'll be the first to drop the charge against Miss Latterly. But until you do, we're holding 'er." He sighed, looking at Rathbone sadly. "I got no pleasure in it. She seems like a nice young lady, and I lost a brother in the Crimea meself. I know what some o' those women did for our men. But it's my duty, and liking 'as nothing to do with it most of the time."

"Yes—yes of course." Rathbone leaned back in the chair, feeling drained, as if he had run a great distance. "Thank you. I shall begin my duty now, to find out what did happen and prove she had no part in it."

"Yes sir. I wish you luck, sir. You'll need all you can get, and more than luck as well." And with that he turned around and opened the door, leaving Rathbone staring after him.

He had been gone only a few moments when Clements returned, his expression anxious. He poked his head around the door inquiringly.

"Mr. Rathbone, is there anything I can do, sir?"

"What?" Rathbone jerked to attention, at least physically. His thoughts were still in tumult. "What is it, Clements?"

"Is there anything I can do, sir? I take it it's bad news of some nature."

"Yes there is. Go and fetch Mr. William Monk, immediately."

"Mr. Monk, sir? The detective, do you mean?"

"Yes of course, the detective. Fetch him here."

"I shall have to give him some reason, Mr Rathbone," Clements said unhappily. "He is not the sort of gentleman to come simply because I say so."

"Tell him the Farraline case has taken a profound turn for the worse, and I need his undivided attention most urgently," Rathbone replied, his voice growing sharper and unintentionally louder.

"If I don't find him—" Clements began.

"Keep looking until you do! Don't return here without him, man."

"Yes sir. Indeed, I'm very sorry, sir."

Rathbone forced his mind to attention. "What for? You've done nothing amiss."

"No sir. I'm very sorry the Farraline case has turned for the worse. Miss Latterly is a fine young lady, and I'm sure—" He stopped. "I'll go and find Mr. Monk, sir, and fetch him back right away."

But it was two long, heavy hours before Monk pushed the office door open, without having knocked, and strode in. His face was pale, his wide, thin mouth drawn in a hard line.

"What happened?" he demanded. "What's gone wrong now? Why haven't you got in touch with the Farralines' lawyer and explained what happened." His eyebrows rose. "Surely you don't want me to take it up to Edinburgh."

The emotions that Rathbone had been fighting against since Daly first came in—the fear, the anxiety, the helplessness, the imaginings ahead that his intelligence foresaw—all burst in anger, the rawest and easiest release.

"No I do not!" he said between his teeth. "Do you think I'd send Clements 'round to fetch you simply to run errands for me? If that's the extent of your ability, I've wasted my time—and yours. I should have called someone else ... anyone else, God help me!"

Monk grew even paler. He read Rathbone's temper as if it had been a page printed large in front of him. He understood both the fear and the self-doubt, and both were like a cold slap to the face for Rathbone.

"Mary Farraline's body has been examined, postmortem," Rathbone said icily, "at the request of her daughter Griselda Murdoch. Apparently she died of an overdose of her medicine, the medicine Hester was employed to give to her. The police have accordingly charged Hester with her murder . . . presumably for the sake of the gray pearl brooch."

It was a vicious satisfaction to him to see Monk's face blanch even further and his eyes widen fractionally with shock, as if he had sustained a heavy and totally unexpected blow.

The two stood facing each other across Rathbone's desk in frozen silence for seconds. Then Monk absorbed the shock and recovered himself, far more rapidly than Rathbone had expected him to, more rapidly than he had himself.

"I presume we are agreed that Hester did not kill her?" Monk said levelly. "In spite of any evidence to the contrary?"

Rathbone smiled bleakly, remembering Monk's own fearful suspicions of himself when he had awakened in his amnesia, the struggle through the tightening webs of evidence. He saw the same memories in Monk's eyes and for an instant their understanding was as clear as the dawn light. Even great distances seemed close enough to touch. Enmity vanished.

"Of course," Rathbone agreed. "We know only a fraction of the truth. When we know it all, the story will be utterly different."

Monk smiled.

Then the moment vanished.

"And what makes you think we shall ever know it all?" Monk demanded. "Who, in God's name, ever knows all the truth about anything? Do you?"

"If I know enough about the facts to put it beyond dispute," Rathbone said coldly, "that would be sufficient. Are you willing to help in the practicalities, or do you wish to stand there arguing the nicer philosophical points of it?"

"Oh, practicalities?" Monk said sarcastically, his eyebrows high.

"What had you in mind?" His gaze swept the desk, searching for something achieved, some sign of progress, and found nothing.

Rathbone was acutely aware of his inadequacies, and what he had actually been doing between the time Daly left and Monk arrived was getting rid of all other pressing matters to leave himself free to attend to the Farraline case, but he refused to explain himself to Monk.

"There are three possibilities," he said in a hard, level voice.

"Obviously," Monk snapped back, "she might have taken an overdose herself, by accident. . . ."

"No she didn't." Rathbone contradicted him with satisfaction. "She did not take it herself at all. The only accident could be if someone else filled the vial wrongly before it left the Farraline house in Edinburgh. If she took anything herself then it was deliberate, and must have been suicide, which is physically the second possibility, but from the circumstances, and her personality as Hester described her, quite out of the question."

"And the third is murder," Monk finished. "By someone other than Hester. Presumably someone in Edinburgh who filled the medicine vial with a lethal dose and left Hester to administer it."

"Precisely."

"Accident or murder. Who prepared the dose? The doctor? An apothecary?" Monk asked.

"I don't know. That is one of a number of questions to be answered."

"What about the daughter, Griselda Murdoch?" Monk moved impatiently about the office as if he could not bear to remain still. "What do you know of her?"

"Only that she is recently married and is expecting her first child, and is apparently anxious about her health. Mrs. Farraline was coming south to reassure her."

"Reassure her? What do you mean? How could she reassure her? What could she know that Mrs. Murdoch didn't know herself?" Monk looked irritated, as if the nonsense of the answer were stupidity on Rathbone's part.

"For heaven's sake, man, I'm not a midwife. I don't know," Rathbone said waspishly, sitting down in his chair again. "Perhaps it was some childhood complaint she was worried about."

ANNE PERRY

Monk ignored his reply. "I assume there is money in the family?" he said, turning back to face Rathbone.

"It appears so, but they may be mortgaged to the hilt, for all I know. It is one of the many things to find out."

"Well, what are you doing about it? Aren't there lawyers in Scotland? There must be a man of affairs. A will?"

"I shall attend to it," Rathbone said between his teeth. "But it takes time. And whatever the answer, it will not tell us what happened in the railway carriage, nor who tampered with the medicine cabinet before they even boarded the train. The best we can hope for is some light on family affairs and the motives of the Farraline household. It may be money, but we cannot sit here waiting with our arms folded in the hope that it will be."

Monk's eyebrows shot up, and he regarded Rathbone's elegant figure, seated with his legs crossed, with intense dislike.

Curiously, Rathbone found it did not anger him. Complacency would have. Any kind of calm would have incensed him, because it would have meant Monk was not afraid, that it did not matter to him enough to reach his emotions and cut them raw. Lack of fear in Monk would not have comforted him. The danger was real; only a fool would not see it.

"I want you to go to Edinburgh," Rathbone said with a tiny smile. "I shall provide funds, of course. You are to learn everything you can about the Farraline family, all of them."

"And what are you going to do?" Monk demanded again, standing in front of the desk, feet slightly apart, hands clenched at his sides.

Rathbone looked at him icily, in part because there was so very little that was of use yet. His real skill was in the courtroom, faced with witnesses and a jury. He knew how to smell a lie, how to twist and turn words until they trapped the liar, how to uncover truth beneath the layers of deceit, the fog of ignorance and forgetfulness, how to probe like a surgeon until he extracted the damning fact. But he had no witnesses yet, except Hester herself, and she knew so desperately little.

"I am going to learn more of the medical facts," he replied. "And the legal ones you pointed out earlier. And I shall prepare for trial."

The word *trial* seemed to sober Monk out of his anger as sharply as a dash of cold water in the face. He stood still, staring at Rathbone. He made as if to say something, then changed his mind. Perhaps there was nothing that was not already known.

"I'll go and see Hester first," he said quietly. "Arrange it." His face tightened. "I have to know all she can tell me about them. We need everything we can find, even impressions, things half heard, thoughts, memories . . . anything at all. God knows how I am going to get them to admit me, let alone speak to me."

"Lie to them," Rathbone said with a twisted smile. "Don't tell me that offends you!"

Monk gave him a filthy look, but did not answer. He stood stiffly for a moment, then turned on his heel and went to the door.

"You said something about funds," he said with acute dislike. It occurred to Rathbone with a sudden flash of insight that Monk loathed having to ask. He would like to have done it without assistance, for Hester's sake.

Monk saw the understanding in Rathbone's eyes, and it infuriated him, both to be read so easily and that Rathbone should know his financial state, and perhaps even more, his care for Hester. He had not wished to know that himself. The color burned up his cheeks and his mouth tightened.

"Clements has it ready for you," Rathbone answered. "And a ticket for tonight's train to Edinburgh. It leaves at quarter past nine." He glanced at the gold watch at his waistcoat, a beautiful piece with an engraved case. "Go to your lodgings and pack whatever you will need, and I will make arrangements for you to visit the prison. Write from Edinburgh with whatever progress you make."

"Of course," Monk agreed. He hesitated for a moment, then opened the door and went out.

Monk went back to his lodgings with his mind in a daze. Hester charged with murder. It had the horrible quality of a nightmare; the brain would not accept it, and yet the gut knew it was violently and dreadfully real. It had an air of familiarity, as if he had known it all before.

He packed all the clean linen he would be likely to need, and socks, shaving brush and razor, hairbrush, toiletries, and a spare pair of boots. He could not foresee how long he would be there. So far as he knew he had not been to Edinburgh before. He had no idea how cold it would be. Probably like Northumberland. But then he could remember that only in snatches, and in pictures, not sensation. Still, that hardly mattered now.

He knew why the sinking feeling was familiar, the fear and the mixture of disbelief and complete acceptance. It was like his own experience of being both hunter and the hunted when he had first awakened in the hospital after the accident. He had not even known his own name, discovering himself piece by piece as he pursued Joscelin Grey's murderer. He still knew far from all of himself nearly two years later, and much of what he had learned, seeing it through the eyes of others, half remembered, half guessed at, was confusing to him, full of qualities he did not like.

But this was no time to think of himself. He must solve this absurd problem of the death of Mrs. Farraline, and Hester's part in it.

He closed his case and took it with him as he informed his landlady briskly and without further explanation that he was off to Edinburgh on business and did not know when he would be back.

She was used to his manner and disregarded it.

"Oh yes," she said absently. Then added, with a sharp eye to what was important to her, "And you'll be sending the rent, no doubt, if you're gone that long, Mr. Monk?"

"No doubt," he agreed tersely. "You'll keep my letters."

"That I will. Everything will be exactly as it should be. When have you ever found it different, Mr. Monk?"

"Never," he said grudgingly. "Good day to you."

"Good day, sir."

By the time he reached the prison where Hester was being held Rathbone had been as good as his word, and arrangements had been made for Monk to gain admittance, as Rathbone's assistant, and therefore, in a sense, a legal adviser to Hester.

The wardress who took him along the gray, stone-floored passageway towards the cell was broad-backed, heavily muscled and had an expression of intense dislike in her powerful face. It chilled Monk to see it and filled him with something as close to panic as he could remember in a long time. He knew why it was there. The woman knew the charge against Hester—that of having murdered an old lady who was her patient and who trusted her implicitly, for the chance to steal a piece of jewelry worth perhaps a few hundred pounds. That was enough to keep her in luxury for a year—but at the cost of a human life. She would have seen all sorts of tragedy, sin and despair pass through her cells, brutalized women who had murdered violent husbands, pimps or lovers; inadequate despairing women who had murdered their children; hungry and greedy women who had stolen; cunning women, crude or brazen women, ignorant, vicious, frightened, stupid—all manner of folly and vice. But there was little as despicable in her mind as an educated woman of good family who stooped to poison an old lady who was in her specific charge, and for gain of something she did not need.

There would be no forgiveness in her, not even the usual casual pity she showed for the thief and the prostitute caught in a sudden act of violence against a violent world. With the envy and frustration of the ignorant and oppressed, she would hate Hester for being a lady. And at the same time she would hate her also for not having lived up to the privilege with which she was born. To have been given it was bad enough, to have betrayed it was beyond excusing. Monk's fear for Hester condensed into a cold, hard sickness inside him.

The wardress kept her back to him all the way along the corridor until she came to the cell door, where she inserted the heavy key into the lock and turned it. Even now she did not look at Monk. It was a mark of her utter contempt that it extended to him. Even curiosity did not alleviate it.

Inside the cell Hester was standing. She turned slowly as she heard the bolt draw back, a look of hope lighting her face. Then she saw Monk. The hope died, and was replaced by pain, wariness and a curious flicker between expectancy and distress.

For a moment Monk was torn with emotion, familiarity, a desire to protect her, and anger with events, with Rathbone, most of all with himself.

He turned to the wardress.

"I'll call when I want you," he said coldly.

She hesitated, for the first time her curiosity caught. She saw something in Monk's face which disturbed her, an instinctive knowledge that he would fight with weapons she could not match, that he would never be afraid for his own safety.

ANNE PERRY

"Yes sir," the wardress said grimly, and slammed the door closed unnecessarily hard.

Monk looked at Hester slowly and with great care. She had nothing to do here from morning till night, and yet she looked tired. There were shadows around her eyes and no color at all in her skin. Her hair was straight and she had obviously made no effort to dress it flatteringly. Her clothes were plain. She looked as if she had given up already. She must have had her own clothes sent to her lodgings, by Callandra, probably. Why had she not chosen something less drab, more defiant? Then memory flooded back of his own despair during the Grey case, when worse horror had stared him in the face, the thought not only of prison, and hanging, but the nightmare of guilt itself. It was Hester's courage and her stinging anger which had saved him then.

How dare she give up for herself.

"You look awful," he said icily. "What in God's name is that you're wearing? You look as if you're waiting to be hanged. They haven't even tried you yet!"

Her expression darkened slowly from puzzlement to anger, but it was a quiet, cold emotion, no heat in it at all.

"It is a dress I used nursing," she said calmly. "It is warm and serviceable. I don't know why you bother to mention it. What on earth does it matter?"

He changed the subject abruptly. "I am going to Edinburgh on the train tonight. Rathbone wants me to find out all I can about the Farralines. One assumes it was one of them who murdered her. . . ."

"It is all I can think of," she said quietly, but without conviction in her voice. "But before you ask me, I don't know who or why. I can't think of any reason, and I have had nothing to do here but try to think of it."

"Did you kill her?"

"No." There was no anger in her, only quiet, black resignation.

It infuriated him. He wanted to take her physically and shake her until she was as angry as he was, until she was enraged enough to fight and go on fighting until they knew the truth, and then force everyone else to look at it, acknowledge it and admit they had been wrong. He hated the change in her; the quietness was uncharacteristic. Not that he was so fond of the way she had been. She talked far too much, and with much too much opinion, whether she was informed or not. She was quite unlike the sort of woman that appealed to him; she had not the gentleness, the feminine warmth or the grace he admired and which quickened his pulses and awoke his desire. But still, to see her like this disturbed him profoundly.

"Then someone else did," he said. "Unless you are telling me she committed suicide?"

"No of course she didn't!" Now at last she was angry too. There was a faint touch of pink in her cheeks. "If you'd known her you would not even entertain such an idea."

"Perhaps she was senile and incompetent?" he suggested. "And she killed herself by accident?"

"That's ridiculous." Her voice rose sharply. "She was no more senile than you are. If that is the best you can do, you are wasting my time! And Oliver's, if he is employing you!"

He was delighted to see her spirit returning, even if it was only in the defense of Mary Farraline; and he was thoroughly piqued by the suggestion that he was here solely at Rathbone's request, and because he was paid. He did not know why it stung so sharply, but it was a painful thought, and he reacted instantly.

"Don't be childish, Hester. There isn't time, and it's most unbecoming in a woman of your age."

Now she was really angry. He knew it was the reference to her age, which was idiotic, but then at times she was idiotic. Most women were.

Hester looked at him with intense dislike.

"If you are going to Edinburgh to see the Farralines, they are hardly likely to tell you anything other than that they employed me to accompany Mrs. Farraline to London, to give her her medicine night and morning, and see that she was comfortable. And I failed them most dismally. I don't know what else you would expect them to say?"

"Self-pity doesn't become you any better than it does most people," he said sharply. "And we haven't time."

She glared at him with loathing.

He smiled back, a twisting of the lips, but still relieved that she was angry enough to fight—not that he wished her to perceive that. "Of course they will say that," he agreed. "I will ask them a great many questions." He was formulating his plan as he spoke. "Because I shall tell them that I have come on behalf of the prosecution and wish to make sure of everything in order to have an unanswerable case. I shall pursue every detail of your stay there."

"I was only there a day," she said.

He ignored her. "Then in the course of so doing, I shall learn everything else I can about them. One of them murdered her. In some way, however slight, they will betray themselves." He said it with more certainty than he felt, but he must not allow her to know that. The least he could do was protect her from the bitterest of the truth, the odds against success. He wished desperately he could do more. It was appalling to be helpless when it mattered so intensely.

The anger drained out of her as suddenly as if someone had turned out a light. Fear overtook everything else.

"Will you?" Her voice shook.

Without thinking he reached forward and took her hand, holding it tightly.

"Yes I will. I doubt it will be easy, or quick, but I will do it." He stopped. They knew each other too well. He saw in her eyes what she was thinking, remembering—that other case they had solved together, finding the truth at last, too late—when the wrong man had been tried and hanged. "I will, Hester," he said with passion. "I'll find the truth, whatever it costs, and whoever I have to break to get it."

Her eyes filled with tears, and she looked away suddenly. For a moment she was so frightened she could hardly control herself.

He gritted his teeth.

Why was she so stupidly independent? Why could she not weep like other women? Then he could have held her, offered some kind of comfort—which would have been meaningless. And he would have hated it. He could not bear the way she was, and yet for her to change would have been even worse.

And he hated the fact that he could not dismiss it and walk away. It was not simply another case. It was Hester—and the thought of failure was unendurable.

"Tell me about them," he commanded gruffly. "Who are the Farralines? What did you think of them? What were your impressions?"

She turned and looked at him with surprise. Then slowly she mastered her emotions and replied.

"The eldest son is Alastair. He is the Procurator Fiscal—"

He cut across her. "I don't want facts. I can find them for myself, woman. I want your feelings about the man. Was he happy or miserable? Was he worried? Did he love his mother or hate her? Was he afraid of her? Was she a possessive woman, overprotective, critical, domineering? Tell me something!"

She smiled wanly.

"She seemed generous and very normal to me. . . ."

"She's been murdered, Hester. People don't commit murder without a reason even if it is a bad one. Somebody either hated her or was afraid of her. Why? Tell me more about her. And don't tell me what a charming person she was. People sometimes murder young women because they are too charming, but not old ones."

Hester's smile grew a little wider.

"Don't you think I've lain here trying to think why anyone would kill her? Alastair did seem a little anxious, but that could have been over anything. As I said, he is the Procurator Fiscal. . . ."

"What is a Procurator Fiscal?" This was not a time to stand on his pride and blunder on in ignorance.

"Something like the Crown Prosecutor, I think."

"Hmm." Possibilities arose in his mind.

"And the youngest brother, Kenneth, was bound on an appointment the family knew little of. They assumed he was courting someone and they had not met her."

"I see. What else?"

"I don't know. I really don't. Quinlan, that is Eilish's husband—"

"Who is Eilish? Did you say Eilish? What kind of a name is that?"

"I don't know. Scottish, I presume. She is the middle daughter. Oonagh is the eldest. Griselda is the youngest."

"What about Quinlan?"

"He and Baird McIvor, Oonagh's husband, seemed to dislike each other. But I don't see how any of that could lead to murder. There are always undercurrents of likes and dislikes in any family, most particularly if they all live under one roof."

"God forbid!" Monk said with feeling. The thought of living so closely with other people appalled him. He was jealous of his privacy and he did not wish to account for himself to anyone at all, least of all someone who knew him intimately.

She misunderstood him.

"No one would murder for the freedom to leave."

"Wasn't the house hers?" he asked instantly. "What about the money? No, don't bother to answer. You wouldn't know anyway. Rathbone will find that out. Tell me exactly what you did from the time you arrived at the house until you left. When were you alone? Where was the dressing room or wherever the medicine case was left?"

"I've already told Oliver all that," she protested.

"I want it from you," he said coldly. "I can't work on secondhand evidence. And I'll ask you my own questions, not his."

She complied without further argument, sitting on the edge of the cot, and carefully in exact detail, telling him all she could remember. From the ease of her words, and the fact that she did not hesitate, he knew she had rehearsed it many times. It made him acutely aware of how she must have lain in the cell in the dark, frightened, far too intelligent not to be fully aware of the magnitude of the danger, even of the possibility they might never learn the truth, or that if they did it would be too late to save her. She had seen it happen. Monk himself had failed before.

By God he would not fail this time, no matter who it cost.

"Thank you," he said at length, rising to his feet. "Now I must go. I must catch the train north."

She stood up. Her face was very white.

He wanted to say something which would ease her fear, something to give her hope—but it would be a lie, and he had never lied to her.

She drew in her breath to speak, and then changed her mind.

He could not leave without saying something—but what? What was there that would not be an insult to her courage and her intelligence?

She gave a little sniff. "You must go."

On impulse he took her hand and raised it to his lips, and then let it go and strode the three steps to the door. "I'm ready!" he shouted, and the next moment the key clanged in the lock and the door swung open. He left without looking backwards.

When Monk left the office, Oliver Rathbone hesitated only a few moments before making his decision that he would, after all, go and see Charles Latterly. Hester had begged him not to tell her family when it had been only a charge of theft, which they had both hoped would be dealt with, and dismissed, within a matter of days at the very most. But now it was murder, and the evening newspapers would carry the story. He must reach him before that, in common humanity.

He already knew the address, and it was a matter of five minutes to find a hansom cab and instruct the driver. He tried to think of some decent way to break the news. Even though his intelligence told him there was none, it was an easier problem to consider than what he would do next to prepare for Hester's defense. He could not possibly allow anyone else to conduct it, and yet the burden of such a responsibility was already heavy on him, and not twelve hours had passed yet since Daly's arrival in his office with the news.

It was ten minutes past five in the afternoon. Charles Latterly had just arrived home from his day's business. Rathbone had never met him before. He alighted from the cab, instructed the driver to wait however long was necessary until he should be ready to leave, and went up to the front door.

"Yes sir?" the butler said with polite inquiry, his skilled eye summing up Rathbone's status as a gentleman.

"Good evening," Rathbone replied briskly. "My name is Oliver Rathbone and I am Miss Hester Latterly's barrister-at-law. I require to see Mr. Latterly on a matter of business which, I regret to say, cannot wait."

"Indeed, sir? Perhaps if you would be good enough to come into the morning room, sir, I will acquaint Mr. Latterly with your arrival and the urgency of your business."

"Thank you." Rathbone stepped in, but instead of going to the morning room when the butler opened the door for him, he remained in the hall. It was a pleasant room, comfortable, but even at a casual and somewhat hasty glance, he could see the signs of wear and subtly reduced circumstances. He was reminded with a stab of pity of the ruin and suicide of Mr. Latterly senior, and the death from distress shortly afterwards of his wife. Now he had brought news of a new tragedy, even worse than the last.

Charles Latterly came out of the door to the right of the back of the hall. He was a tall, fair man in his late thirties or early forties, his hair thinning a little, his face long and, at this time, pinched with apprehension.

"Good evening, Mr. Rathbone. What can I do for you, sir? I do not recall that we are acquainted, but my butler informs me you are my sister's attorney-at-law. I was not even aware she had occasion for such a person."

"I am sorry to disturb you without warning, Mr. Latterly, but I bring most distressing news. I have no doubt whatever that Miss Latterly is totally without blame of any kind, but there has been a death—an unnatural death—of one of her patients, an elderly lady traveling by train from Edinburgh to London. I am sorry, Mr. Latterly, but Hester has been charged with murdering her."

Charles Latterly stared at him as if he did not understand the meaning of the words.

"She was neglectful?" he said, blinking his eyes. "That is not like Hester. I do not approve of her profession, if you can call it such, but I believe she is more than competent in its practice. I do not believe, sir, that she has conducted herself improperly."

"She is not charged with negligence, Mr. Latterly," Rathbone said slowly, hating having to do this. Why could the man not have understood without his having to repeat it? Why did he have to look so injured and bewildered? "She is charged with having deliberately murdered her, in order to steal a brooch."

"Hester? That's preposterous!"

"Yes, of course it is," Rathbone agreed. "And I have already employed an agent of inquiry to go to Edinburgh, tonight, in order to investigate the matter so that we can learn the truth. But I'm afraid we may not be able to prove her innocence before the whole matter comes to trial, and most likely it will be in the newspapers by tomorrow morning, if not this evening. That is why I have come to inform you so you do not discover it that way."

"The newspapers! Oh dear heaven!" Every vestige of color fled from Charles's already pallid face. "Everyone will know. My wife. Imogen must not hear of this. She could be . . ."

Rathbone felt unreasonably angry. Charles's every thought had been for his wife's feelings. He had not even asked how Hester was—or even where she was.

"I am afraid that is something from which you cannot protect her," he said a little tartly. "And she may well wish to visit Hester and take her whatever comfort she can."

"Visit?" Charles looked confused. "Where is Hester? What has happened to her? What have they done with her?"

"She is in prison, where she will be until she comes to trial, Mr. Latterly."

Charles looked as if he had been struck. His mouth hung slack, his eyes stared as disbelief turned to horror.

"Prison!" he said, aghast. "You mean . . ."

"Of course." Rathbone's tone was colder than he would have made it were his own emotions less engaged. "She is charged with murder, Mr. Latterly. There is no possibility of them allowing her free in those circumstances."

"Oh . . ." Charles turned away, his thoughts inward, his face at last showing pity. "Poor Hester. She always had courage, so much ambition to do the most extraordinary things. I used to think she must be afraid of nothing." He gave a jerky little laugh. "I used to wish she would be afraid, that it would give her a little sense of caution." He hesitated, then sighed. "I wouldn't have had it happen this way." He looked back at Rathbone, his features still touched with sorrow, but quite composed now. "Of course I will pay you whatever I can towards her defense, Mr. Rathbone. But I am afraid I have very little, and I cannot rob my wife of the support and care I owe her, you understand?" He colored unhappily. "I have some knowledge of your reputation. Perhaps in the situation in which we find ourselves, it would be better if you were to pass over the case to some less . . ." He searched for a euphemism for what he meant, and failed to find one.

Rathbone assisted him, partly because he did not enjoy seeing the man struggle—although he felt little liking for him—but mainly because he was impatient.

"Thank you for your offer, Mr. Latterly, but your financial help will not be necessary. My regard for Hester is sufficient recompense. The greatest boon you can offer her will be to go to her aid personally, comfort her, assure her of your loyalty, and above all, keep your spirits high so that she may draw strength from you. Never, in any circumstances, allow her to think you fear the worst."

"Of course," Charles said slowly. "Yes of course. Tell me where she is, and I shall go to her—that is, if they will allow me in?"

"Explain to them that you are her only family, and they will certainly allow you in," Rathbone answered. "She is in Newgate."

Charles winced. "I see. What am I permitted to take her? What might she need?"

"Perhaps your wife could find her some change of clothes and of personal linen? She will have no facilities for laundering."

"My wife? No—no, I should not permit Imogen to go. And to such a place as Newgate. I shall keep as much of this from her as I am able to. It would distress her terribly. I shall find Hester some clothes myself."

Rathbone was about to protest, but looking at Charles's face, suddenly closed over, his mouth pursed, his eyes stubborn, he knew there were subtleties in the relationship he could not guess at, depths of Charles's own character, and argument would be useless. An unwilling visit would do Hester no good, and Hester was all he really cared about.

"Very well, if that decision is final," he said coolly. "You must do what you believe to be right." He straightened his shoulders. "Again, Mr. Latterly, I am profoundly sorry to bring you such grave news, but please be assured I shall do everything that is possible to insure that Hester is cleared completely and that in the meantime she is treated as well as may be."

"Yes—yes of course. Thank you, Mr. Rathbone. It is most courteous of you to have come in person. And . . ."

Rathbone waited, half turned towards the door, his eyebrows raised.

Charles looked uncomfortable.

"Thank you for undertaking Hester's defense without fee. I—we—we are deeply grateful to you."

Rathbone bowed very slightly. "My privilege, sir. Good day to you."

"Good day, sir."

By a quarter to nine Rathbone was at the railway station. It was quite pointless. There was nothing else he could tell Monk, yet he could not help himself from being there to speak to him a last time, even to make absolutely sure he was on the train.

The platform was noisy, crowded with people and baggage carts, porters shouting, carriage doors swinging wide one moment, slamming shut the next. Travelers stood shivering, some saying their last good-byes, others glancing one way and then another looking for a familiar missing face. Rathbone made his way through them, coat collar turned up against the wind. Where was Monk? Damn the man! Why did he have to be dependent on someone he liked so little?

He ought to be able to recognize him on the platform. His stance was individual enough, and he was that fraction taller than average. Where on earth was he? For the fifth time he glanced at the station clock. Ten to nine. Perhaps he was not here yet? It was still early. The best thing would be to go through the train itself.

He traced his steps to the end closest to the buffers, pushing his way through the thickening crowd, and boarded the train, looking into every compartment to see if Monk were there. Every so often he glanced out of the window as well, and it was on one of those occasions, about halfway along the length of the train, and already seven minutes past nine, that he saw Monk's face for an instant as he passed by, outside, hurrying along the platform.

Rathbone swore in a mixture of anger and relief, and pushing past a large gentleman in black, flung open the carriage door and almost fell out.

"Monk!" he shouted loudly. "Monk!"

Monk turned. He was dressed as elegantly as if he were on the way to dine out. His coat was beautifully cut, slender and hanging without a wrinkle, his boots were polished to a satin gleam. He looked surprised to see Rathbone, but not discomforted.

"Have you found something?" he said in surprise. "Already? You can't have heard back from Edinburgh, so what is it?"

"I haven't found anything," Rathbone said, wishing passionately that he had. "I merely came to see if there was anything else upon which we should confer while there is still the opportunity."

A shadow of disappointment crossed Monk's eyes, so slight that had Rathbone been less perceptive he would have missed it altogether. He almost forgave the perfect coat.

"I know of nothing," Monk replied coldly. "I shall report to you by mail, whatever I learn of use. Impressions I shall keep until I return. It would be useful if you would do the same for me, assuming you do find anything. I shall inform you of my address as soon as I have lodgings. Now I am going to take my seat, before the train leaves without me. That would serve neither of us." And without any further form of farewell, he turned and walked towards the nearest carriage door and climbed in, slamming it behind him, leaving Rathbone standing on the platform swearing under his breath, feeling offended, inadequate, and as if there were something else he should have said.

CHAPTER
FIVE

Monk did not enjoy the journey in any respect at all. The encounter on the platform with Rathbone gave him some sense of satisfaction because it demonstrated how acutely concerned Rathbone was. It would have taken an emotional involvement of extraordinary depth to cause him to abandon his dignity sufficiently to come on such a completely pointless errand. Normally, if nothing else, his awareness of Monk's perception of it would have been enough to keep him at home.

But the comfort all that gave him very quickly wore off as the train steamed and rattled its way out of the station and through the rain-soaked darkness of the London rooftops and the occasional glimpse in gaslight of emptying streets, wet cobbles gleaming, lamps haloed in mist, here and there a hansom about to do business.

He imagined Rathbone returning to his office to sit behind his desk shuffling papers uselessly and trying to think what to do that would help, and Hester alone in the narrow cell in Newgate, frightened, huddling beneath the thin blankets, hearing the hard sound of boot heels on the stone floor and the clang of keys in the lock, seeing the hatred in the wardresses' faces. And he had no illusions about that. They thought her guilty of a despicable crime; there would be no pity. The fact that she had not yet been tried would weigh little with them.

Why couldn't Hester be like other women, and choose a more sensible occupation? What normal woman traveled all over the place, alone, to nurse people she had never even met? Why did he bother himself with her? She was bound to meet with disaster some time or other. It was only extraordinary good luck she had not encountered it already in the Crimea. And he was stupid to allow his feelings to be engaged at all. He did not like the kind of woman she was, he never had. Almost everything about her irritated him in one way or another.

But then common humanity required that he do everything he could to help. People trusted him, and so far as he knew, he had never betrayed a trust in his life. At least not intentionally. He had failed his mentor, years ago, that much he now remembered. But that was different. It was a failure through lack of ability, not in any way because he had not tried everything he could. It was not kindness; every evidence he had discovered about himself showed he was not a kind man. But he was honorable. And he had never suffered injustice.

No. He winced and smiled bitterly. That was untrue. He had never suffered legal injustice. He had certainly been unjust often enough himself—unjust to his juniors, overcritical, too quick to judge and to blame.

But however much it hurt, there was no point wallowing in the past. Nothing could change it. The future lay in his own power. He would find out who had killed Mary Farraline, and why, and he would prove it. Apart from his own pride, Hester deserved that. She was frequently foolish, almost always overbearing, acid-tongued, opinionated and arbitrary; but she was totally honest. Whatever she said about the journey from Edinburgh would be the truth. She would not even lie to herself to cover a mistake, let alone to anyone else. And this was a rare quality in anyone, man or woman.

And of course she had not killed Mary Farraline. The idea was ludicrous. She might have killed someone in outrage—she would certainly have the courage and the passion—but never for gain. And if she had killed someone she deemed to be monstrous enough to warrant such an act, she would not have done it that way. She would have done it face-to-face. She would have struck her over the head, or stabbed her with a blade, not poisoned her in her sleep. There was nothing devious in Hester. Above all else, she had courage.

Hester would survive this. She had suffered worse in the Crimea, physical hardships of a greater order, terrible cold, probably hunger too, weeks without proper sleep—and danger as well, danger of injury or disease, or both. She had been on the battlefield within sound of the guns, within range of them, for all he knew. Of course she would survive a week or two in Newgate. It was absurd to be frightened for her. She was not an ordinary woman to faint or weep in the face of hardship. She would suffer, of course, she was as susceptible as anyone else, but she would rise above it.

His part was to go to the Farraline house and learn the truth.

But as the evening lengthened into night and those around him drifted into weary sleep, the sanguine mood left him, and all he could see as he grew colder and stiffer and more tired was the difficulty of discovering anything useful from a household in mourning, closed in on itself, where one member was guilty of murder and they had the perfect scapegoat in an outsider already accused and charged.

By morning his back ached, his leg muscles were jumping with the long lack of either comfort or exercise, and he was so cold his feet had lost all sensation. His mood and his temper were equally poor.

Edinburgh was bitterly cold, but at least it was not raining. An icy wind howled down Princes Street, but Monk had no interest in either its history or its architectural beauties, so he was perfectly happy to hail the first cab he saw and give the driver the Farralines' address in Ainslie Place.

From the footpath the house was certainly imposing enough. If the Farralines owned it freehold and without mortgage, then they were, financially at least, in very good fortune indeed. It was also, in Monk's opinion, in excellent taste. Indeed, the classical simplicity of the whole square appealed to him.

But that was all incidental. He turned his attention to the matter in hand. He mounted the step and pulled the doorbell.

The door opened and a man who should have been an undertaker, from his expression, regarded him without a shred of interest.

"Yes sir?"

"Good morning," Monk said briskly. "My name is William Monk. I have come from London on a matter of importance. I should like to speak either to Mr. Farraline or to Mrs. McIvor." He produced a card.

"Indeed, sir." The man's face registered no change at all. He offered a silver tray. Monk dropped the card onto it. Apparently he was not an undertaker but the butler after all. "Thank you, sir. If you'll be good enough to wait in the hall, I'll see if Mrs. McIvor is at home."

It was exactly the same polite fiction as in London. Of course he would know whether his mistress was at home, it was simply a matter of whether she would receive Monk—or not.

He waited in the crepe-hung hall, shifting from foot to foot in impatience. He had already worked out what message he would send next if she should refuse. He hoped the fact that he had come from London might be sufficient, anything further was not for the servants to be informed.

He had not long to be in doubt. It was not the butler who returned, but a woman in her mid-thirties, slender and straight-backed. For an instant her bearing reminded him of Hester; she had the same pride and determination in the set of her shoulders and the carriage of her head. However, her face was quite different, and the sweep of fair, almost honey-colored hair was unlike any he had ever seen before. She was not quite beautiful; there was too much individuality in her features, a strength in the jaw and a coolness in the eyes which offended convention. This must be Oonagh McIvor.

"Mr. Monk." It was an acknowledgment, not a question. As soon as he heard her voice with its clarity and timbre he knew she would have mastered any but the most desperate of situations. "McTeer informs me you have come from London on some business with which you wish my assistance. Did he understand you correctly?"

"Yes, Mrs. McIvor." From Hester's description he had no doubt it was she, and no need to ask. Nor did he have the slightest qualm in lying. "I am involved in the prosecution of Miss Latterly in the matter of your late mother's death, and it is my assignment to ascertain the facts, such as are known or can be discovered, so that there will be no errors, oversights or unpleasant surprises when the matter comes to trial. The verdict will be final. We must make sure it is the right one."

"Indeed?" Her fair eyebrows rose minimally. "How very thorough. I had no idea the English prosecution—I believe it is not a Procurator Fiscal such as we have—was so diligent."

"It is an important case." He met her look squarely and without evasion or the slight tentativeness of good manners. Instinctively he felt she would despise deference and respect strength, as long as he at no time presumed, or allowed her to sense bluster in him, and never made a threat, implicit or explicit, that he could not keep. They had met only moments before, and yet already there was an awareness of each other's nature and a measuring of both intellect and resolve, one he thought not without interest on her part.

"I am pleased you are sensible of it." She allowed the slightest smile to curve her lips. "Naturally the family will give you all the assistance of which we are capable. My elder brother is the Procurator Fiscal, here in Edinburgh. We are familiar with the fact that even in cases where guilt seems beyond question the prosecution can fail to obtain a conviction, if those conducting it do not take every care in the preparation of evidence. I assume you do have a letter to this effect?" The inquiry was made courteously, but brooked no evasion.

"Naturally." He produced a very creditable forgery he had taken the care to prepare on police paper he still had. That it was from the wrong station he trusted she would not know.

"It makes my task a great deal easier that you so readily comprehend the necessity of being sure of every detail," he said as she examined the letter. "I confess, I had not thought I should be so fortunate in finding such . . ." He hesitated, allowing her to think it delicacy, in truth searching for exactly the right word that would not sound like flattery. He judged her to be a woman who would feel only contempt for anything so obvious, although he doubted she would be so open as to show it, except by the chill of a glance, the sudden fading of interest from her eyes. ". . . a grasp of reality," he finished.

This time her smile was broader, a definite warmth in all her face, and something like a flicker of curiosity in her eyes as she regarded him.

"I am grieved, of course, Mr. Monk, but it has not so destroyed my wits as to rob me of my understanding that the world must proceed, and its business be done according to the law, and with the proper procedure. Please tell me in what way, precisely, we may be of assistance. I imagine you will wish to question people, the upstairs servants in particular?"

"That would be necessary," he agreed. "But servants can be very easily frightened by such a tragedy, and then their accounts sometimes vary. It would be most helpful to speak with the members of the family as well, perhaps leave the servants until later, when their first apprehension has had time to disappear. I do not wish to give the impression that I suspect them of anything."

This time her smile was one of humor, albeit bitter.

"Don't you, Mr. Monk? No matter how convinced you are of Miss Latterly's guilt, surely it must have crossed your mind that my mother's lady's maid, at least, could conceivably have stolen the brooch?"

"Of course it has crossed my mind, Mrs. McIvor." He smiled back, without looking away from her eyes. "All sorts of other answers are possible, with a stretch of the imagination, however unlikely. And the defense—and no doubt there will be one—since it cannot prove Miss Latterly innocent, will have to endeavor to prove someone else guilty. Or at the worst for them, prove that someone else could have been guilty, by virtue of motive, means or opportunity. It is precisely that which I have come to forestall."

"Then we had better make plans to begin," she said with decision. "No doubt if you have just arrived in Edinburgh, you will wish to find yourself accommodation, and possibly rest after your journey, if you have been on the train all night. Then perhaps you would dine with us this evening, when you may meet the rest of my family?" It was an invitation formally given, and for a most businesslike reason, and yet there was interest in her which was of a sharper nature, however slight.

"That would be excellent, thank you, Mrs. McIvor," he accepted. He must not become carried away with optimism; he had barely begun and had learned nothing whatever, but at least the first barrier was crossed with surprising ease. "Thank you."

"Then we shall see you at seven," she said with an inclination of her head. "McTeer will show you out, and if he can give you any directions which may be helpful, please feel free to ask. Good day, Mr. Monk."

"Good day, Mrs. McIvor."

Monk had asked McTeer to advise him about lodgings, and the butler's grim response had stung him with its condescension. He had suggested several inns and public houses of one sort or another, all in the old part of the city. When Monk had asked if there was nothing closer to Ainslie Place, he had been informed, with raised eyebrows, that Ainslie Place was not the area where such establishments were to be found.

So at ten o'clock Monk was in a street with high tenements on either side, and known as the Grassmarket, his case in his hand, his temper still seething. He had a sharp sense of being in a foreign city. The sounds and smells were different from those in London. The air was colder and had not the grit and odor of chimneys in it, although the buildings were stained enough and the eaves dripping grimy water. The cobbles of the street were like those of London, but the narrow footpaths at the sides were barely above the level of the thoroughfare, the gutters shallow. But then the street itself was at such a pitch its surface drained down the hill anyway.

He walked slowly, staring around him, interested in spite of himself. The buildings were largely of stone, which gave them a dignity and permanence, and nearly all were four, five or six stories high, ending in a jumbled mass of steeply inclined roofs, dormers and fine crowstepped gables, like numerous flights of stairs amid the slates. On one gable he saw an iron cross, and then craning upwards to see the better, he noticed another, and another. It was certainly not a church, nor did it seem to have been a religious establishment of any sort.

Someone bumped into him sharply and he realized with a jolt that he had not stood still while gazing upwards, and was thus causing something of a hazard.

"Sorry," he apologized peremptorily.

"Aye, well watch where ye're goin' an' stop gaupin', afore ye knock some poor soul into the gutter," came the reply, in a voice so strongly accented it barely sounded like English, and yet so distinct was the diction it was understandable without effort. "Are ye lost?" The man hesitated, detecting a stranger and forgiving error because of it. Strangers were half-witted anyway, and one should not expect normal behavior from them. "Ye're in Templelands, in the Grassmarket."

"Templelands?" Monk said quickly.

"Aye. Where are you making for, do you know?" He was now disposed to be helpful, as good men are towards those they sense cannot care for themselves.

Monk was obliged to smile to himself. "I've been looking for lodgings."

"Oh, aye? Well ye'll find a good, clean room at William Forster's, down there at number twenty, and there's McEwan the baker's, next door. Innkeeper and stabler, Willie is. Ye'll see it written up on the wall. Can't miss that, if ye've eyes in yer head."

"Thank you. I'm obliged."

"Ye're welcome." He made as if to move on.

"Why Templelands?" Monk asked quickly. "What temple was there here?"

The man's face registered amusement and mild contempt. "No temple at all. The land used to belong to the Knights Templar, long ago. You know, Crusades, and the like?"

"Oh." Monk was surprised. He had not thought of Edinburgh as being of such age, or of the Templars so far north. Dim memories of history came back to him, names like Mary Queen of Scots, and the Auld Alliance with France, and the Stuart kings, battles on the moors above Culloden, Bannockburn, massacres in the snowbound steeps of Glencoe, secret murders like the death of Duncan, or of Rizzio, or perhaps Darnley right here in Edinburgh. It was in a mist of stories and impressions he could only dimly recall, but it was part of his northern heritage, and it made these streets with their towering houses more familiar. "Thank you," he added, but the man was already moving away, his duty discharged.

Monk crossed over the street and walked on until he saw WM. FORSTER, STABLER & INNKEEPER written right across the front of a large building, between the second and third stories, and the name of McEwan's Bakery at one end. It was a four-story building; the first two were of cut stone blocks, and the windows were large, indicating generous rooms. Several of the high chimney pots at the spine of the roof were smoking, a hopeful sign. Since he had no horse, he did not bother going through the archway into the yard, but knocked hastily on the front door.

It was opened almost immediately by a large woman, busy drying her hands on her apron. "Aye?"

"I'm looking for lodgings," Monk replied. "Possibly for a week or two. Have you a room?"

She glanced at him rapidly, summing him up, as was her trade.

"Aye, I have." Evidently she approved of him. If he had more clothes in his case of the same quality as those he was wearing, they alone would pay his rent for a month or more. "Come in and I'll show ye." She backed away to allow him in, and he followed gratefully.

Inside was narrow and dimly lit, but it smelled clean and the air was warm and dry. Someone was singing in the bowels of the kitchen, loudly, and every so often a little sharp, but it was a cheerful sound, and he felt it welcoming. She led him up three flights of stairs, puffing and blowing noisily and stopping on each landing to regain her breath.

"There," she said between gasps when they reached the top floor and she threw open the door to the room he was to occupy. It was clean and airy and looked out over the Grassmarket and the roofs opposite.

"Yes," he said without hesitation. "This will do very well."

"Ye up from England?" she asked conversationally.

She made it sound like a foreign land, but then strictly speaking it was.

"Yes." It was an opportunity he should not waste. There was certainly no time to spare. "Yes, I'm a legal consultant." That was something of a euphemism, but advisable, and better than suggesting he was from the police. "Preparing for a trial concerning the death of Mrs. Farraline, up at Ainslie Place."

"She dead?" the woman said with surprise. "How'd that happen? Still, she was getting on, so little wonder. Contesting the will, are they?"

There was interest in her face, and her assumption certainly caught Monk's attention.

"Well, it really isn't something I should discuss, Mrs. Forster. . . ." He took a chance, and it was not contradicted. "But I daresay you won't need me to tell you everything anyway?"

Her smile broadened knowingly. "Money ain't always a blessing, Mr. . . .?"

"Monk, William Monk," he supplied. "Lot of money, is there?"

"Well, ye'd know that, wouldn't ye?" Her eyes were bright brown and full of amusement.

"Not yet," he prevaricated. "But I have my guesses—naturally."

"Bound to be." She nodded. "All that big printing works, been there ever since the twenties, getting bigger all the time, and that fine house up the new town. Oh yes, there's a lot of money there, Mr. Monk. Well worth fighting over, I should think. And the old lady still owned a fair piece of it, or so I heard, in spite of Colonel Farraline being dead these eight or ten years."

Monk thought rapidly and took a gamble.

"Mrs. Farraline was murdered, you know? That is the case I am concerned with."

Her face was aghast.

"Ye don't say so! Murdered? Well I never! The poor old soul. Now who in the good God's name would have done a thing like that?"

"Well, there is suspicion it was the nurse who accompanied her on the train down to London. . . ." He hated saying it, even in so slight a way and without naming Hester. It was almost like an admission that the idea was possible.

"Oh. What a wicked thing to do! Whatever for?"

"A brooch," he said between his teeth. "Which she gave back, and before anyone missed it. Found it in her own baggage, by accident, or so she said."

"Oh yes?" Mrs. Forster's eyebrows rose with delicate skepticism. "And what would a woman like that be doing with the sort of brooch Mrs. Farraline would wear? We all know what nurses are like. Drunken, dirty and no better than they should be, most of them. What a terrible thing. The poor soul."

Monk felt his face burning and his jaw tightened as if he would grind the words between his teeth.

"She was one of the young ladies who went out to nurse our soldiers in the Crimea—served with Miss Nightingale." His voice was rasping and without any of the control he had sworn he would keep.

Mrs. Forster looked nonplussed. She stared at Monk, reading his face to see if he had really meant what he had said. It took her only a glance to assure herself that he did.

"Well I never," she said again. She took a deep breath, her eyes wide and troubled. "Perhaps it was not her after all. Had ye thought o' that?"

"Yes," he said with a grim smile. "I had."

She said nothing, but stared at him, waiting.

"In which case it was somebody else," he said, completing the thought for her. "And it would be most interesting to find out who."

"Aye, that it would," she agreed, and shrugged her ample shoulders. "And I'll not be envying you the task o' that. They're a powerful family, the Farralines. He's the Fiscal, you know?"

"What about the others?" It was easy and natural to ask, and her opinion might yield something.

"Oh, well I don't know anything beyond what's said, mind. But McIvor runs the printing business now, he's Miss Oonagh's husband, but he's no a Scot, he's from down south in England somewhere. No but he's a good enough sort of man, they say. Nothing really against him."

"Except that he's English?"

"Aye. And I suppose he canna help that. And then there's Mr. Fyffe. He comes frae Stirling, I've heard. Or maybe it's Dundee, but somewhere a wee bit north o' here. Clever man, word has it, gae clever."

"But not liked overmuch." Monk said what she did not.

"Oh well . . ." She was loath to put it into words, but the agreement was there in her face.

"He'd be Miss Eilish's husband," he prompted.

"Aye, he would. Now there's a great beauty, so they say. Not that I've ever seen her myself, y'understand? But they say she's the loveliest thing ever to set foot in Edinburgh."

"What else?"

"What?"

"What else do they say about her?"

"Why nothing. Isn't that enough?"

He smiled, in spite of himself. He imagined what Hester would have said to a description like that.

"What is she like, her ambitions, her ideas?"

"Oh, for certain I never heard that."

"And Mrs. Farraline herself?"

"A fine lady, so they say. Always was, for years back. Colonel Farraline was a gentleman, generous with his money, and she followed on the same. Always givin' to the city. Poor Major Farraline, that's the younger brother, now he's a different kettle of fish. Drinks like a sot, he does. Hardly ever sober. Shame that, when a gentleman with all his opportunities goes to the bottle."

"Yes it is a shame. Do you know why? Was there some tragedy?" She pursed her lips.

"Not that I ever heard. But what would I know? Just a weak man, I suppose. World's full o' them. Looks for the answer to all o' life's problems in the bottom of a bottle. You'd think after a score or so they'd realize it wasn't there—but not them."

"What about the last son, Kenneth?" Monk asked, since she seemed to have exhausted the subject of Hector.

She shrugged again. "Just a young gentleman with more time and money than sense. He'll grow out of it by and by, I expect. Pity his mother isn't here any longer to see he does, but I daresay the Fiscal will. Wouldn't want him doing something stupid and spoiling the family name. Or making a foolish marriage. He wouldn't be the first young dandy to do that."

"Does he not work at the family business?" Monk asked.

"Oh aye, so I've heard. Don't know what he does, but no doubt it would be easy enough to find out." A strange expression lightened her eyes, curiosity, disbelief and a kind of beginning of excitement. "Do you think one of them killed their own mother?" Then caution took hold again. "Never! They're very well respected people, Mr. Monk. Highly thought of. Takes a big part in city affairs, does Mr. Alastair. A lot to do with government, as well as being the Fiscal."

"Yes, I don't suppose it's likely," Monk said judiciously. "But it could have been a maid. It's possible, and I've got to look at everything."

" 'Course you have," she agreed, straightening her apron and making to move. "Well, I'd best be leaving you to get on about it then." She went to the door and turned back. "And ye'll be here for a week or two, right enough?"

"I will," he agreed with a shadow of a smile. "Thank you, Mrs. Forster."

As soon as he had unpacked the few clothes he had brought with him, he wrote a short note to Rathbone, giving his new address at 20, Grassmarket, Edinburgh, and after a brief luncheon at the inn, went to post his letter and then made his way back up towards the new town and Ainslie Place. The local public house would be a good spot at which to make inquiries about the family. In all possibility the footman or grooms would drink there. He would have to be extremely discreet, but he was used to that, it was his trade.

However, it was too early in the day now, and by dinnertime he would be at the Farraline house. He would fill in the afternoon by learning exactly which of the local tradesmen dealt with number seventeen, then tomorrow and the next day he could track down delivery boys, who in turn might know maids and bootboys, and discover more about the daily lives of the Farralines.

And of course there would be the routine tasks of questioning Mary Farraline's physician who had prescribed the medicine, finding the exact dosage normally given; and then the apothecary who had made up the prescription, and pressing him in the possibility of an error, which naturally he would deny.

And then he would have to search for all the other apothecaries in Edinburgh to prove Hester had not purchased digitalis from them, and there was always the remote hope they could identify one of the Farraline family as having done so.

Monk arrived back at Ainslie Place, faultlessly elegant, at seven o'clock, as he had been directed. He was admitted by McTeer, as lugubrious as before, but this time unquestioningly polite, and shown into the withdrawing room, where the family was awaiting the announcement of dinner.

The room was large and very formal, but he had no time to spare for looking at it. His entire attention was immediately absorbed by the people who, as one, were staring at him as he was shown in. A lesser man would have found it unnerving. Monk was too worried and inwardly angry to have any such misgivings. He faced them with head high and eyes unwavering.

Oonagh was the first to come forward. She was dressed in black, of course, as they all were. One mourned at least a full year for a relative as close as a mother. But her gown was beautifully cut, quite moderate in fashion, the hoops of her skirt not extreme, and the lamplight shown on the rich, pale gleam of her hair, making one think she might well have chosen the color, or lack of it, for effect as well as duty.

"Good evening, Mr. Monk," she said graciously. She did not smile, yet there was a warmth in her eyes and her voice which made him feel more welcome than he could have expected in the circumstances.

"Good evening, Mrs. McIvor," he replied. "It is most gracious of you to be so courteous to me. You have turned a chore into an experience I shall not forget."

She received the compliment as it was intended, a little more than a mere politeness; and then she turned to indicate the man who stood almost to the mantelshelf, in the warmest and most comfortable place in the room. He was slightly above average height, slenderly built but beginning to put on weight around the waist. His hair was as fair as hers, but thickly waved, and already sparse at the front. His features were aquiline and distinguished, perhaps not ordinarily handsome, but certainly imposing.

"This is my elder brother, Alastair Farraline, the Procurator Fiscal," she said, introducing them. Then, turning to Alastair, she added, "As I told you earlier, Mr. Monk has come up from London to make quite certain that the trial produces no unpleasant surprises through our having taken too much for granted."

Alastair surveyed Monk with cool, very blue eyes. His expression did not change except for the slightest tightening of the curves of his lips.

"How do you do, Mr. Monk," he replied. "Welcome to Edinburgh. I cannot see the necessity of your journey, myself. It seems overcautious to me. But I am glad that the prosecution in London regards the matter as of sufficient importance to dispatch someone up here to make certain of things. I have no idea what they are afraid of. There can be no defense."

Monk bit back the response that rose in him. He must never, for an instant, forget why he was here. Only the truth was important, whatever it cost to find it. "I can think of none," he agreed, his voice unexpectedly harsh. "I imagine they may well be desperate when they anticipate the prospect of facing a jury."

Alastair smiled bleakly. A flicker in his face betrayed that he had heard the edge to Monk's tone and taken it for horror at the crime. It must never occur to him that Monk's outrage was not against Hester, but on her behalf.

"I imagine it will be a formality," he said grimly. "Enough to satisfy the law that she has been represented."

Oonagh turned to a dark-haired man standing some distance back from the rest of them. His features were quite different in character, the very shape of his head broader and less angular. He could have been a member of the family only by marriage. His expression was brooding, his face full of unexpressed emotion.

"My husband, Baird McIvor," Oonagh said with a charming smile, though still looking at Monk. "He manages the family company, since my father's death. Perhaps you already knew that?" It was only a rhetorical question, to remind them all of Monk's purpose.

"How do you do, Mr. McIvor," Monk responded.

"How do you do," Baird replied. His voice was precise, a little sibilant, his diction perfect, but Monk instantly caught a shadow of regional flavor, and in a moment realized it was Yorkshire. So Baird McIvor was not only an Englishman, but from that wild and proudest of counties, almost a small country to itself. Hester had not mentioned that. Perhaps her ear had not placed the intonation. Like most women, she was more interested in relationships.

Next Oonagh turned to a man of barely average height and long face like her own, but even fairer hair which surrounded his head in an aureole of close curls. Superficially he resembled the Farralines, but the differences were easy to see, the less generous mouth with carefully chiseled lips, and the ruler-straight nose. And there was something different in his manner as well, a confidence born of intellect, not status or power. Curious how such fractional things, the angle of a head, a furrow between the brows, a hesitation, a measuring as if of a potential threat, could give away a man's origins even before he spoke.

"This is my brother-in-law, Quinlan Fyffe," Oonagh said, looking first to him and then back at Monk. "He is a master at printing, fortunately for us, and brilliant at business of every sort." She did not use the slight condescension an English gentlewoman would have towards trade; she spoke of it with admiration. But then the Farralines were not gentry—they had made their own wealth, and presumably were proud of their skills. Her father had begun the company, not merely as owner but as proprietor. She would have no false vanity about idleness and the superiority of those who could afford to spend their lives in leisure.

"How do you do, Mr. Fyffe," Monk acknowledged.

"And Quinlan's wife, my sister Eilish," Oonagh continued, smiling at the younger woman with gentleness, and then glancing back at Quinlan and touching his arm. It was an odd, familiar gesture, as if she were in some way again giving her sister to him, or perhaps reminding him of the event.

After what Mrs. Forster had said, Monk regarded Eilish with interest, and was prepared to be disappointed, even condescending. One glance at her swept away all such indifference. Her beauty was not

merely a matter of flawless features, it had a radiance, almost a lumi-
nescence, that touched the imagination, and a grace that stirred all
manner of half-forgotten dreams. Looking at her, Monk was not sure
if he even liked it; it was disturbing, self-sufficient, lacking in the vulnerability which usually appealed to him in feminine beauty. He liked
a certain imperfection—it made a woman seem fragile, attainable. But
he could not possibly dismiss her either. When one had seen Eilish
Farraline, one could not forget her.

She looked at him with very little curiosity, as if her attention
were not fully engaged. It occurred to him that perhaps she was too
absorbed in herself to occupy her thoughts with anyone else.

The moment the introductions had been effected they were interrupted by the entrance of the nominal mistress of the house. Deirdra
Farraline was small and dark with a vitality powerful enough to make
her rather scruffy black gown seem irrelevant and her lack of jewelry
an oversight of no importance. She had none of the extraordinary
beauty of her sister-in-law, but hers was a face that pleased Monk the
moment he saw her. There was warmth in her, and humor, and he felt
he might discover yet more admirable qualities in her, upon acquaintance.

"Good evening, Mr. Monk," she said as soon as she had been introduced. "I hope we shall be of assistance to you." She smiled at him,
but looked beyond him almost immediately, something else upon her
mind. "Has anyone seen Kenneth? It really is too bad of him!"

"Don't wait," Alastair said tartly. "He can catch up with us when
he arrives, or go without. His behavior these days is totally thoughtless. I shall have to speak to him." His face tightened. "One would
have thought in the circumstances he would have shown a little family loyalty. It is more than time we found out who this woman is he
is pursuing, and if she is suitable."

"Don't worry about it now, my dear," Oonagh said quietly. "You
have more than enough to attend to. I'll speak with Kenneth. I daresay he did not like to bring her here just at the moment."

He looked at her with a flash of relief, then smiled. It altered his
whole face. With a little imagination Monk could visualize the youth
he had been and see something of the closeness between brother and
sister. He glanced at Oonagh, and wondered if in fact she were the
older, in spite of appearance to the contrary.

"Very well," Deirdra said hastily. "McTeer informs me dinner is served. Let us go through to the dining room. Mr. Monk?"

"Thank you," he accepted, pleased that it was she who had asked him.

The meal was good, but not lavish, and Alastair presided at the head of a long, oak refectory table with gravity, as suited the occasion, but perfectly adequate courtesy. Kenneth did not appear, and Monk saw no sign of Hector Farraline, whom Hester had described. Perhaps he was too inebriated to attend.

"Maybe I missed the explanation," Quinlan began as the soup was cleared away and the beef served. "But what is it you have come to Edinburgh to accomplish, Mr. Monk? We know nothing of that wretched woman, beyond what she told us herself, which presumably is lies anyway."

A shudder of anger crossed Oonagh's face, but she controlled it almost immediately.

"You have no cause to say that, Quin," she reproved. "Do you really suppose I would have sent Mother with someone who had no proof of her identity or her qualifications?"

Pure malice gleamed for an instant in Quinlan's face, then he hid it beneath respect. "I am quite sure, my dear Oonagh, that you would not knowingly have sent her anywhere at all with a murderess, but it seems indisputable that you did so unknowingly."

"Oh that's beastly!" Eilish burst out, glaring at him.

He turned towards her, smiling, completely unperturbed by her anger or her disgust. Monk wondered if he was used to it, or if he was truly indifferent. Did he take some perverse pleasure in shocking her? Perhaps it was the sharpest reaction she was capable of feeling, and to arouse that was better than mere apathy. Still, the nature of their relationship was probably irrelevant to Mary Farraline's murder, and that was what mattered. All else was peripheral.

"My dear Eilish," Quinlan said with mock concern. "It is undoubtedly tragic, but it is also unarguably true. Isn't that why Mr. Monk is here? Mary was robust enough; she could have lasted for years. She was certainly not absentminded or clumsy, and anyone less suicidal I have never met."

"You are unnecessarily indelicate," Alastair said with a frown.

"Please remember you are in the presence not only of ladies, but ladies newly bereaved."

Quinlan's fair eyebrows shot up, wrinkling his brow.

"And what would be the delicate way of putting it?" he inquired.

Baird McIvor glowered at him.

"The delicate way would have been to hold your tongue altogether, but since nobody thought to tell you so, it would be too much to expect of you."

"Really—" Deirdra began, and was cut off by Oonagh's decisive interruption.

"If we must quarrel over the dinner table"—she waved a slender hand—"let it at least be over something that matters. Miss Latterly brought excellent references with her, and I have no doubt whatever that she was in the Crimea with Miss Nightingale and that as a nurse she was both skilled and diligent. I can only assume she succumbed to a momentary temptation, brought about by some circumstance in her own life of which we know nothing, and that when it was too late, she panicked. It may conceivably even have been remorse." She shot a quick glance at Monk, her eyes wide and bright. "Mr. Monk is here to make sure that the case against her is perfect and her defense counsel can spring no surprises upon us. I think it would be in all our best interests for us to assist him as we may."

"Of course it would," Alastair said quickly. "And we shall do so. Pray tell us what you wish from us, Mr. Monk. I have no idea."

"Perhaps we could begin with everyone giving as exact an account as they can of the day Miss Latterly was here," Monk answered. "That would at least define more closely the times at which she had opportunity to put the brooch in her bag, or to tamper with the medicine cabinet." As soon as he had said it he realized how he had betrayed himself. He felt his face burn and his stomach go cold.

There was a moment's silence around the table.

Alastair frowned, glanced at Oonagh, then at Monk.

"What makes you think she did either of those things here in this house, Mr. Monk?"

Everyone was watching him, Deirdra with curiosity, Eilish with anxiety, Quinlan with contempt, Baird with guarded interest, Oonagh with humor and something close to pity.

Monk's brain raced. How could he extricate himself from the trap he had sprung upon himself? He could think of no lie that would serve. They were waiting. He must say something!

"You think it was spontaneous?" he asked slowly, looking from one to another. "Which did she do first, steal the brooch or mix the poison?"

Deirdra winced.

Eilish let out a little grunt of distress.

Quinlan smiled at Monk. "You make my attempt of indelicacy look amateur," he said pleasantly.

Eilish put her hands up to her face.

Baird shot Quinlan a look of venom.

"I imagine Mr. Monk is doing it for a purpose, Quin, not simply out of malice," Deirdra said quietly.

"Quite," Monk agreed. "How do you imagine it happened?" Unconsciously he looked at Oonagh. In spite of the fact that Alastair was the head of the family, and Deirdra the mistress of the house, he felt Oonagh was the strongest, that it was she who had taken what he imagined had been Mary's place.

"I—I admit, I had not thought of it at all," she said hesitantly. "It is not something I had—wished to think of."

"Mr. Monk, is this really necessary?" Alastair's nose wrinkled in distaste for the crudity of it. "If it is, perhaps we could discuss it in my study afterwards, away from the ladies?"

Monk had no gentlemanly delusions about the emotional strength of women. In a flash of memory astoundingly vivid he recalled women he had known in the past whose courage and endurance had held families together through illness, poverty, bereavement, social disgrace and financial ruin, and who were perfectly capable of keeping a stiff lip and steady eye in the face of all human weakness and extremity. When it came to raw nature, they were much less shockable than men.

"I would prefer to discuss it with the ladies present," he said aloud, smiling around his teeth at Alastair. "It has been my experience that they are far more observant of people, especially other women, and their memories are usually excellent. I would be very surprised if they do not remember a great deal more of Miss Latterly than you do, for example."

Alastair looked at him thoughtfully.

"I daresay you are right," he conceded after several seconds. "Very well. But not this evening. I have some papers I have to read tonight. Perhaps you would care to come for luncheon on Sunday, after kirk? That would give you an opportunity to conduct whatever other inquiries you have to make in the area. I assume you will wish to see the house. And the servants, of course."

"Thank you. That is most thoughtful of you," Monk accepted. "With your permission I shall do both, perhaps tomorrow. I should also like to speak with the family physician. And I should be delighted to dine with you on Sunday. What time would be suitable?"

"A quarter to one," Alastair replied. "Now, to speak of something pleasanter. Have you been to Edinburgh before, Mr. Monk?"

Monk returned to the Grassmarket deep in thought, trying to see in the people in Ainslie Place the emotions Hester had outlined so briefly, and to build on them something darker than the very natural, prosperous trading family that they appeared. Certainly Quinlan and Baird McIvor did not like each other. It might have had some ugly cause, but it might equally easily be simply a natural antipathy of two men who had all the wrong things in common—arrogance, hasty temper and ambition—and none of the right ones—such as background, humor or tolerance.

But he was extremely tired after a poor night on the train and the shattering news of the previous day. Speculation now was pointless. He could observe them all on Sunday, time enough then to form theories. Tomorrow he would begin with the family physician, whose name Alastair had given him, and the apothecaries. After that it would be a matter of other sources for general information, the nearest public house which the male servants might occasionally frequent, errand and delivery boys, street peddlers and crossing sweepers who might have an observant eye and, for a few pence, a ready tongue.

"Aye," the physician said dubiously, regarding Monk with profound suspicion. "I treated Mrs. Farraline. A fine lady she was too. But ye'll be knowing that anything that passed between us was in confidence?"

"Of course," Monk agreed, keeping his temper with difficulty. "I merely wish to know the exact dosage of the heart medicine you prescribed for her. . . ."

"For why? What affair is it o' yours, Mr. Monk? Did ye no' say ye were to do with the prosecution o' that wretched nurse who killed her? I heard she gave her two doses, is that no' true?" He looked at Monk through narrowed eyes.

"Yes it is," Monk said very carefully, keeping his voice level. "But it needs proving beyond doubt in the court of law. All the details must be checked. Now, Dr. Crawford, will you please tell me precisely what you prescribed, was it exactly the same as usual, and who was the apothecary who made it up?"

Crawford seized a pen and paper and wrote furiously for several moments, then passed the paper across to Monk.

"There you are, young man. That is the precise prescription, which ye'll not be able to fill, because I've no signed it. And that is the name and address of the apothecary who made it up usually. I daresay they always had the same one."

"Is it unusual for a double dose of medicinal strength to be fatal?"

"Aye, there's very little in it. It must be measured exact." He held up his finger and thumb to show a hair's breadth between them. "That's why it's put in a suspension in glass vials. One vial per dose. Can't make a mistake."

Monk considered trying to elicit a little information from him about the other members of the family, and judged it would be pointless.

Crawford watched him with guarded eyes, full of both suspicion and amusement.

"Thank you," Monk said curtly, folding the slip of paper and putting it into his waistcoat pocket. "I'll call upon Mr. Landis."

"Have not known him make a mistake," Crawford said cheerfully. "And never known an apothecary who admitted to one either." He laughed with genuine amusement.

"Nor I," Monk conceded. "But someone either put two doses into one, or substituted a lethal dose for a medicinal one. He may be able to tell me something of use."

"Why wouldn't they simply have given her two of the usual doses?" Crawford said argumentatively.

"They could have." Monk smiled back. "Was she the sort of woman who would have taken two? I assume you did warn her that two would be lethal?"

The amusement vanished from Crawford's eyes.

"O' course I did!" he said. "Are you accusing me of incompetence?"

Monk looked at him with undisguised satisfaction. "I'm trying to learn if it was likely Mrs. Farraline would have taken two doses, rather than one that had been tampered with."

"Aye, well now you know! Go and see Mr. Landis. He'll no doubt tell you how it could be done. Good day to you, sir."

"Well, you could distill it." Landis screwed up his face thoughtfully. "Reduce the liquid till it was the same amount as a single dose. But you'd have to have the right equipment for that, or something that would serve. Hardly use the kitchen while the cook was busy. Be noticed. Too chancy. Not the sort of thing to have to do on the spur of the moment."

"What else?" Monk asked. "How would you do it?"

Landis looked at him sideways. "On the spur of the moment? That's hard to say. Don't think I would. I'd wait a bit until I had a better idea. Has to be instant though, doesn't it!"

"She was only there one day."

"Buy some digitalis and substitute a double-strength dose for the ordinary one. Are you sure she didn't carry digitalis with her? Woman was a nurse, wasn't she? Perhaps she had some already, against an emergency—no, that won't do. Doctor, perhaps, not a nurse. Stole it?"

"What for?"

"Ah, there you have me; unless she was waiting for a chance like this? That'd make her a cold-blooded woman all right." Landis pulled a face. "Mind, that's possible. Had a nasty poisoning with digitalis a few months ago here in Edinburgh. Man poisoned his wife. Ugly case. Terrible woman, tongue like a viper, but doesn't excuse poisoning her, of course. Would have got away with it too, if he'd just given her a little less. Not easy to trace, digitalis. Looks like ordinary heart failure, if you get the amount exactly right. The poor devil overdid it. Made them suspicious."

"I see. Thank you."

"Not been much use, have I? Sorry."

"I suppose you didn't sell any digitalis that day to a woman who could answer her description?" Monk asked, feeling suddenly a little sick. Of course Hester had not bought it, but what if someone like her had? "A little taller than average, thin, square shoulders, brown hair, intelligent face, rather strong, pronounced features, but a very good mouth."

"No," Landis said with certainty.

"You are quite sure? You could swear to it?"

"With no trouble at all. Didn't sell any that day to anyone."

"What about that week, to anyone else in the Farraline household?"

"No, not to anyone except Dr. Mangold and to old Mr. Watkins. Known them both for years. Nothing to do with the Farralines."

"Thank you," Monk said with sudden enthusiasm. "Thank you very much. Now, sir, can you tell me the names and whereabouts of all the other apothecaries within reasonable radius of Ainslie Place?"

"Of course I can," Landis agreed with a frown of puzzlement. He reached for a paper and wrote down several lines of information, then gave them to Monk, wishing him luck.

Monk thanked him profusely and strode out, leaving the door swinging on its hinges.

He received in essence the same answer from every other shop he tried. No one recognized his description of Hester, and none of them had sold digitalis to any member of the Farraline household, or indeed to anyone not known to them personally.

He pursued the other sources of information, the public house, the street peddlers and crossing sweepers, the errand and delivery boys and the news vendors, but all he learned was very general gossip that seemed to serve no purpose. The Farralines were extremely well thought of, and had long been generous to the city and the various worthy causes. Hamish had been ill for some time before his death eight years before, but his reputation was high without being unnatural. Hector was spoken of with tolerance and a pity for Mary, while respecting her that she gave him a home. Indeed, she seemed to be respected for just about everything she did, and more essentially for what she was, a lady of dignity, character and judgment.

Alastair also was held in both respect and something amounting to awe. He held high office and wielded considerable power. That he did it discreetly was to his credit. He had conducted himself with dignity during the recent case involving a Mr. John Galbraith, who had been accused of defrauding investors out of a very great deal of money, but the issue was very clouded. Those bringing the charge were of a very dubious honor. The evidence was tainted. The Fiscal had had the courage to throw the case out.

The rest was just gossip of the most ordinary sort. Quinlan Fyffe was very clever, an incomer from Stirling, or perhaps it was Dundee. Not yet a popular man. McIvor, for all his name, was English. Pity Miss Oonagh had not seen fit to marry an Edinburgh man. Miss Deirdra was very extravagant, so it was said, always getting new dresses, but absolutely no taste at all. Miss Eilish stayed in bed till all hours of the day. She might be the most beautiful woman in Scotland; she was also the laziest.

It was all quite useless, and not even very interesting. Monk thanked the various sources and gave up.

Sunday luncheon at Ainslie Place was a less formal affair than dinner had been. Monk arrived just as the family was returning from the high kirk, all dressed in black. The women were in huge skirts like up-turned bells, fur-trimmed capes hugged about them and black-ribboned bonnets narrowing vision and protecting the face from the splattering rain. The men wore tall hats and black overcoats, Alastair's with an astrakhan collar. They walked in pairs, side by side, unspeaking until they were in the hall, Monk immediately behind them. The funereal McTeer took their coats and welcomed them. He also took Alastair's hat and stick, leaving Baird, Quinlan and Kenneth to place their own in the stand or the rack appropriately.

"Good day, Mr. Monk," he said grimly, taking Monk's hat and coat. Monk had never carried a stick since the Grey case. "A verra cold day, sir, and bound to get worse. It'll be a hard winter, I'm thinking."

"Thank you," Monk acknowledged. "Good afternoon," he said, inclining his head to each member of the family. Alastair looked pinched with cold, but Deirdra's warm coloring made her vividly alive, and if she were grieving, it did not mar her vitality. Oonagh was pale, but as previously, her resolve of character more than compensated for any turmoil or misgivings within.

Eilish had obviously made the effort to get up in time to accompany the family to kirk, and nothing could dim her beauty.

The errant Kenneth was also present, an agreeable but ordinary young man with sufficient resemblance to mark him as one of the family. He seemed to be in something of a hurry, and as soon as he was relieved of his outdoor clothing, he nodded to Monk, then disappeared towards the withdrawing room.

"Do come in, Mr. Monk," Oonagh said with a curious, direct smile. "Warm yourself by the fire and perhaps take a little wine. Or maybe you would prefer whiskey?"

Monk disliked declining her invitation, but he could not afford to have his wits dulled.

"Thank you," he said. "The fire sounds excellent, and wine too, if everyone else is also partaking? It is a little early for me to enjoy whiskey." He followed where she led into the same large withdrawing room as on the first occasion. The fire was roaring in the grate with a hiss and crackle that promised heat even before he glanced at its yellow blaze. He also found himself smiling without intending to.

As each person came into the room, unconsciously he or she moved closer to the fire, the women sitting in the large chairs, the men standing. One of the footmen served goblets of mulled wine from a silver tray.

Alastair looked across the top of his at Monk.

"Are you having any success with your inquiries, Mr. Monk?" he asked with a frown. "Although I don't know what it is you think you can discover. Surely the police will do all that is necessary?"

"Pitfalls, Mr. Farraline," Monk replied easily. "We don't want the case dismissed because we have been overconfident and careless."

"No—no indeed. That would be disastrous. Well, please make any inquiries you wish of the servants." He glanced at Oonagh.

"I have already instructed them," she said gently, turning from Alastair to Monk. "They are to answer you fully and frankly." She bit her lip as if considering an apology of some sort, but then deciding against it. "You will have to excuse a little nervousness on their part." She regarded him gravely, searching his face for understanding, her eyes widening a fraction when she perceived it. "They are all anxious to excuse themselves from carelessness. Naturally each of them feels that in some way they should have been able to prevent what happened."

"That's absurd," Baird said abruptly. "If anyone is to blame, we are. We hired Miss Latterly. We spoke to her and we thought she was an excellent person. It wasn't up to the servants to argue with us." He looked acutely unhappy.

"We have already had this conversation," Alastair said with irritation. "No one could have known."

"Oh yes." Quinlan shot a look at Monk. "You asked us what we thought had happened. I don't recall that anyone ever answered you, did they?"

"Not yet," Monk conceded, his eyes wide. "Perhaps you would begin, Mr. Fyffe?"

"I? Well, let me see." Quinlan sipped his wine, his eyes thoughtful, but if there was distress in him, it was well masked. "The wretched woman would not have killed poor Mother-in-law unless she had already seen the brooch, so that must have happened fairly early on. . . ."

Deirdra winced and Eilish set down her glass, untasted.

"I don't know what you hope to gain with this," Kenneth said angrily. "It is an appalling conversation!"

"Appalling or not, we have to know what happened," Quinlan said viciously. "There's no point pretending it will go away decently just because we don't like it."

"For God's sake, we do know what happened!" Kenneth's voice rose also. "The damned nurse murdered Mother! What else do we have to know—isn't that enough? Do you want every jot and tittle of the details? I certainly don't."

"The law will want it," Alastair said icily. "They won't hang the woman without absolute proof. Nor should they. We must be sure, beyond any doubt at all."

"Who doubts it?" Kenneth demanded. "I don't."

"Do you know something that the rest of us do not?" Monk asked, his voice polite, his eyes glittering.

Kenneth stared at him, frustration, self-justification and resentment flaring in his face.

"Well, do you?" Alastair demanded.

"Of course he doesn't, my dear," Oonagh said soothingly. "He just hates thinking of the details."

"Does he imagine the rest of us enjoy it?" Alastair's voice rose suddenly and for the first time his composure seemed in danger of slipping. "For God's sake, Kenneth, either say something useful or hold your tongue."

Oonagh moved a little closer to him and put her hand lightly on his arm.

"Actually, Quin has made a point," Deirdra said with her face screwed up in concentration. She did not appear to have noticed Alastair's distress. "Miss Latterly must have seen the brooch before she decided to give Mother-in-law a double dose of medicine...." She avoided using the word *poison*. "And since Mother-in-law was not wearing it, then either she saw it in her case, which does not make a lot of sense—"

"Why not?" Alastair said tersely.

There was no anger in Deirdra's face, only deep thought. "How could she? Did she look all through Mother's case at some time when she was supposed to be resting? And then mix the medicine at the same time?"

"I don't know why you say that." Alastair looked at her irritably, but already there was a quickening in his expression belying his words.

All heads turned from Alastair to Deirdra.

"Well, she couldn't mix it in front of her," Deirdra said quickly. "And she couldn't give her two doses. Mother would not have taken them."

Monk smiled with the first real satisfaction he had felt since Rathbone had broken the news.

"You have an excellent point, Mrs. Farraline. Your mother-in-law would not have taken the double dose."

"But she did," Alastair said with a frown. "The police informed us of that, the day before you arrived. That is precisely what happened."

Oonagh looked very pale, a flicker of tension between her brows. She turned from Alastair to Monk without speaking, waiting for him to explain.

Monk chose his words with intense care. Could this be the key to it all? He refused to hope, but still he found his body rigid, muscles aching.

"Was Mrs. Farraline sufficiently forgetful that she might either have accepted two doses of her medicine or have taken one herself and then allowed Miss Latterly to have given her another?" He remembered Crawford's dismissal of such an idea and he knew what the answer would be.

Oonagh opened her mouth, but in the minute's hesitation before she spoke, Eilish interrupted.

"No, certainly not. I don't know what the answer is, but it is not that."

Baird was very pale. He looked at Eilish with something so fierce in his eyes it seemed to be agony, even though it was apparently Monk to whom he was speaking.

"Then the answer must be that Miss Latterly saw the brooch in the house, before it was packed, and decided then on her plan. She must have doubled the dose before she left."

"How?" Deirdra asked.

"I don't know." He was not disconcerted. "She was a nurse, after all. Presumably she knew how to make some medicines as well as give them. Any fool can pass out a vial or present it to someone."

"Make it out of what?" Monk asked with assumed innocence. "The ingredients would hardly be lying about the house."

"Of course not," Deirdra agreed, looking from one to another of them, her face puckered. "It doesn't make sense, does it. I mean, it doesn't sound remotely likely. She was only here for one day . . . less than that. Did she go out, does anyone know? Mr. Monk?"

"I assume you have questioned the local apothecaries?" Quinlan asked.

"Yes, and none has sold digitalis that day to any woman answering Miss Latterly's description," Monk replied. "Or indeed to anyone else not already known to him personally."

"How confusing," Quinlan said without any apparent unhappiness.

Monk felt himself beginning to hope. He had the essence of doubt already.

"I think you are missing the point," Oonagh said very gently. "The brooch will have been packed in Mother's traveling jewel case, which was in the carriage with them. And of course Mother had the key. Miss Latterly saw it when she was preparing the medicine, or perhaps she looked through it out of curiosity when Mother may have alighted at the station to use the convenience. There would be plenty of opportunities during a long evening."

"But the digitalis," Baird argued. "Where did she get that? She didn't find that in a railway station."

"Presumably she carried it with her," Oonagh replied with a tiny smile. "She was a nurse. We have no idea what she had in her case."

"On the chance of having someone to poison?" Monk said incredulously.

Oonagh looked at him with amusement and something like patience.

"Possibly, Mr. Monk. It does seem the most likely explanation. You yourself have pointed out that the other ways and means that we assumed were, after all, not possible. What else is left?"

Monk felt as if the fire had died. The light and the warmth faded all around him. It had been stupid to hope for anything so easy, and yet in spite of all intelligence, he had hoped. He realized it now with anger and self-criticism.

"Of course—" Alastair began, but was interrupted by a large man with fading red-gold hair and blurry eyes walking uncertainly in, leaving the doors gaping behind him. He looked at the walls, his gaze finishing on Monk with a lift of curiosity.

There was a moment's total silence.

Alastair let his breath out in a sigh.

Monk caught a glimpse of Oonagh's face, her expression fierce and unreadable for an instant before she stepped forward and took the man by the arm.

"Uncle Hector—" Her voice caught in her throat, then was smooth again. "This is Mr. Monk, who has come up from London in order to help us in the matter of Mother's death."

Hector swallowed hard, as if there were something tight around his neck and he could not free himself from it. The distress in his face was so naked it would have been embarrassing had he not been oblivious of anyone watching him.

"Help?" he said incredulously. He looked at Monk with disgust.

"What are you, an undertaker?" He scowled at Alastair. "Since when did we have the undertaker to dinner?"

"Oh God!" Alastair said desperately.

Kenneth turned away, his face white.

Deirdra looked helplessly to one, then another.

"He's not the undertaker," Quinlan began.

"Griselda took care of all that, Uncle Hector," Oonagh said gently, passing him her glass of wine. "In London. I did tell you, don't you remember?"

He took the glass and drank it all in one long gulp, then looked at her with slight difficulty in focusing.

"Did you?" He hiccupped loudly and waved his hand in embarrassment. "I don't think I . . ."

"Come on, dear, I'll have your dinner sent up. I don't think you are well enough to enjoy it down here."

Hector turned to Monk again.

"Then what the hell are you?"

Monk had an uncharacteristic moment of tact.

"I have to do with the law, Mr. Farraline. There are details to be dealt with."

"Oh—" He seemed satisfied.

Oonagh half turned and shot Monk a look of gratitude, then gently steered Hector towards the door and out.

By the time she came back they were in the dining room and seated at the table. The meal was served, and while they were eating, Monk had the opportunity to observe them individually, conversation requiring no effort on his part.

He turned over in his mind what the errand boy had said. He looked discreetly at Deirdra Farraline. Her face still pleased him. It was thoroughly feminine, soft curves to the cheek and jaw, neat nose, good brow, and yet it was full of determination; there was nothing weak or apathetic about her. He was stupidly disappointed that she was apparently dedicated to spending her time in society and using extravagant amounts of money to impress others.

Of course she was dressed entirely in black now, as mourning required, and it became her, but looking at it with a critical eye, her gown was hardly high fashion. Indeed, he would have said by London standards it was really very ordinary. The gossip was right; she had no taste. It angered him to concede the point.

He turned to look at Eilish, unwilling to be caught staring at her. Her beauty irritated him enough as it was, without his being observed watching her. The last thing he wished was to pander to her vanity.

He need not have worried. She kept her head bent towards her plate, and only twice did she glance upward, and then it was to Baird.

Her gown was also black, naturally, but more becomingly cut, and certainly more up-to-the-minute in detail. In fact, it could not have been bettered by any London beauty, whatever the cost.

He turned to Oonagh. She was surveying the table, watching everyone to assure herself they had sufficient and were comfortable. He could afford only a moment to look at her, or she would see him. Her gown also was well cut, simple, and more fashionable than Deirdra's. It was not just her fire and her intelligence which made it so. Whatever Deirdra spent her money on, it was not her mourning clothes.

The meal progressed with polite conversation about nothing in particular, and when it was over Kenneth excused himself, to Alastair's annoyance and a sarcastic comment from Quinlan, and the rest of the company retired to the withdrawing room to take up occupations suitable to the Sabbath. Alastair shut himself away in his study to read, although whether it was the Scriptures or not he did not say, and the question from Quinlan went unanswered. Oonagh and Eilish took up embroidery; Deirdra said she had a duty visit to make to a neighbor who was ill, which passed without remark. Apparently she was known to the family, and Deirdra called upon her her regularly. Quinlan picked up a newspaper—to one or two looks of disapproval, which he ignored—and Baird said he was going to write letters.

Monk took the opportunity to find the domestic staff and question them about the day Hester had been in the house.

It was a difficult task. Their memories were clouded and distorted by their knowledge of Mary's death and their conviction that Hester was to blame. Impressions were useless, only facts had any hope of representing truth, and even they were suspect. Hindsight blurred previous certainties and lent conviction to others which had been only thoughts at the time.

No one argued as to when she had arrived or left, or that she had taken breakfast in the kitchen, then Oonagh had taken her to meet

Mary Farraline. The women had had both elevenses and luncheon together. Presumably what Hester had done between was uncertain. One maid recalled seeing her in the library; someone else thought she might have gone upstairs, but she would not swear to it. Undoubtedly she had taken a rest upstairs in the afternoon, and yes of course she could have been in Mary's dressing room and done all manner of things.

Yes, the lady's maid had shown her Mary's clothes, her cases and most particularly the medicine chest. That was her job, wasn't it? She was employed to give Mrs. Farraline her medicine. How could she do it if she were not shown where it was?

No one blamed her for that.

Didn't they indeed? Just look at the expressions on their faces, if that was what you thought. Listen to what they whispered to one another when they thought she wasn't listening.

By five o'clock, as it was getting dusk, Monk gave up. It was extremely dispiriting. There was very little that he could prove, or disprove, and in view of what Oonagh had said about the jewel case being with Mary on the train, it was hardly of any importance anyway.

He was bitterly discouraged. All he had learned in three days was nebulous, nothing was certain except that Hester had had the opportunity, the means were to hand and she had the knowledge to use them more than almost anyone else, and the motive was apparent—the pearl brooch—hardly a motive for any member of the family.

He returned to the withdrawing room angry and fighting despair.

"Did you learn anything?" Eilish asked as he came in.

He had already decided what he would say, and he composed himself with an effort.

"Only what I expected," he replied, forcing a smile that was a matter of lips bared over his teeth.

"I see."

"Well, what did you think?" Quinlan looked up from his newspaper. "You don't imagine one of us did it, do you?"

"Why not?" Baird snapped. "If I were defending Miss Latterly, that is exactly what I would think."

"Indeed?" Quinlan swung around to face him. "And why would you have murdered Mother-in-law, Baird? Did you quarrel with her? Did she know something about you that the rest of us don't? Or was it for Oonagh's inheritance? Or was Mary going to make you keep your eyes off my wife?"

Baird shot out of his chair and lunged towards Quinlan, but Oonagh was there before him, standing between them, her face white.

He stopped abruptly, almost knocking into her.

Quinlan sat perfectly still, the sneer frozen on his face, his eyes wide.

"Stop it!" Oonagh said between her teeth. "This is indecent and quite ridiculous." She took a deep, shaking breath. "Baird, please . . . we are all upset with what has happened. Quin is behaving very badly, but you are only making it worse." She smiled at him, staring into his angry face, and very slowly he relaxed and took a step backwards.

"I'm sorry. . . ." he apologized, not to Quin but to his wife.

Oonagh's smile became a little more certain. "I know you were defending me, as well as yourself, but there is no need. Quin has always been jealous. It happens to men with such beautiful wives. Although, heaven knows, there is no need." She swung around to Quinlan, smiling at him also. "Eilish is yours, my dear, and has been for years. But she is part of the whole family, and everyone with eyes will admire her beauty. You shouldn't resent that. It is a compliment to you also. Eilish, dear . . ."

Eilish looked at her sister, her face scarlet.

"Please assure Quin of your undivided loyalty. I'm sure you do so often . . . but once again? For peace?"

Very slowly Eilish obeyed, turning to her husband, then back towards Baird, and forcing herself to look into her husband's face and curve her lips into a smile.

"Of course," she said softly. "I wish you wouldn't say such things, Quin. I have never done anything to give you cause, I swear."

Quinlan looked at Eilish, then at Oonagh. For a second no one moved, then slowly he relaxed and smiled as well.

"Naturally," he agreed. "Of course you haven't. You are quite right, Oonagh. A man with a wife as beautiful as mine must expect the world to look at her and envy him. Isn't that right, Baird?"

Baird said nothing. His face was unreadable.

Oonagh turned to Monk.

"Is there anything further we could do to assist you, Mr. Monk?" she asked, leaving Baird and coming towards him. "Perhaps you may think of something in a day or two . . . that is, if you will still be in Edinburgh?"

"Thank you," he accepted quickly. "I shall certainly remain a little longer. There are other things to look into, proof I might find that would place it beyond question."

She did not ask him what he had in mind, but walked gracefully towards the door. Accepting the gesture of parting, he followed her, bidding good-night to the others and thanking them for their hospitality.

Outside in the hall Oonagh stopped and faced him, her expression grave. Her voice when she spoke was low.

"Mr. Monk, do you intend to continue investigating this family?"

He was uncertain how to answer. He searched for fear or anger in her face, for resentment, but what he saw was that same curious interest and sense of challenge, not unlike the emotion she stirred in him.

"Because if you do," she continued, "I have something to ask of you."

He seized the chance.

"Of course," he said quickly. "What is it?"

She looked down, masking her thoughts. "If—if in your . . . discoveries, you learn where my sister-in-law manages to spend so much money, I would . . . we would all be much obliged if you would advise us . . . at least advise me." She looked up at him suddenly, and yet there was neither candor nor anxiety in her eyes. "I may be able to speak to her privately and forestall a great deal of unpleasantness. Could you do that? Would it be unethical?"

"Certainly I can do it, Mrs. McIvor," he said without hesitation. It was a gauntlet thrown down, whether she cared for the answer in the slightest, and it was precisely the excuse he needed. He liked Deirdra, but he would sacrifice her in an instant if it would help him find the truth.

She smiled, humor and challenge under the cool tones of her voice and behind the composure of her features. "Thank you. Perhaps in two or three days you will return and dine with us again?"

"I shall look forward to it," he accepted, and as McTeer appeared and handed him his hat and coat, he took his leave.

It was quite by chance as he was hesitating on the footpath, deciding whether to walk the entire distance to the Grassmarket or go east and down to Princes Street to look for a hansom, that he glanced back towards the Farraline house and saw a small, neat figure in wide skirts emerge from near the side entrance and run down to the carriageway. He knew it must be Deirdra; no maid would have such a sweeping crinoline, and it was too small to be either Eilish or Oonagh.

The next moment he saw the other figure, coming across the road. As he passed underneath the gas lamp the light fell on him and Monk saw his rough clothes and dirty face. He was intent on the silhouette of Deirdra, going towards her eagerly.

Then he saw Monk. He froze, turned on the spot, hesitated a moment, then loped off up the way he had come. Monk waited nearly fifteen minutes, but he did not come back again, and at last Deirdra returned alone into the house.

CHAPTER
SIX

On the train northwards Monk had comforted himself with the thought that Hester had endured the Crimea, so a time in Newgate would not be beyond her experience, or even markedly worse than that with which she was already familiar. Indeed, he had thought in many ways it would even be better.

He was mistaken. She found it immeasurably worse. Certainly there were elements that brought back memory so sharply her breath caught in her throat and her eyes prickled. She was intensely cold. Her body shook with it, her extremities lost sensation, and at night she was unable to sleep except for short spells because the cold woke her.

And she was hungry. Food was regular, though it was minimal, and not pleasant. That was like the Crimea, but rather better: she had no fear of being allowed to starve. The chance of disease was present, but it was so slight she gave it no thought. The fear of injury did occur to her once or twice, not from shell or bullets, of course, simply of being beaten or knocked down by wardresses who were quite open in their loathing for her.

If she became ill, she treasured no illusions that anyone would care for her, and that thought was far more frightening than she had foreseen. To be ill alone, or with malicious eyes looking on and enjoying your distress, your weakness and indignity, was a horror that brought out the cold sweat on her skin, and her heart beat faster in near panic.

That was the greatest difference. In the Crimea she had been respected by her colleagues, adored by the soldiers to whom she had dedicated so much. Such love and purpose can be food to the hungry, warmth in the hardest winter, and anesthetic to pain. It can even blind out fear and spur on exhaustion.

Hatred and loneliness cripple everything.

And then there was time. In the Crimea she had worked almost every moment she was awake. Here there was nothing to do but sit on the cot and wait, hour after hour, from morning till night, day after day. She could do nothing herself. Everything rested with Rathbone or Monk. She was endlessly idle.

She had resolved not even to think of the future, not to project her mind forward to the trial, to picture the courtroom as she had seen it so many times before from the gallery when watching Rathbone. This time she would be in the dock, looking down on it all. Would they try her in the Old Bailey? Would it be the same courtroom she had been in before, feeling such compassion and dread for others? She rolled her fear around in her mind, although she had sworn she would not, testing it, trying to guess how different the reality would be from the imagining. It was like touching a wound over and over again, to see if it really hurt as much as you had thought, if it was any better yet, or any worse.

How often had she criticized injured soldiers for doing just that? It was both stupid and destructive. And here she was doing exactly the same. It was as if one had had to look at one's own doom all the time, deluding oneself that it might change, that it might not have been as it had seemed.

And there was the other idea at the back of her mind, that if she absorbed all the pain now, in some way when it really happened she would be prepared.

Her misery was interrupted by the sound of a key in the lock and the door swinging open. There was no privacy here; it was both totally isolated and yet open at any time to intrusion.

The wardress she hated most stood glaring at her, her pale hair drawn back in a knot on her head so tightly it dragged the skin around her eyes. Her face was almost expressionless. Only a tiny flicker at the corner of her mouth betrayed both her contempt and the satisfaction she had in showing it.

"Stand up, Latterly," she ordered. "There's someone 'ere ter see yer." She invested the announcement with both surprise and anger. "Yer lucky. Better make the best of it. Can't be long now till yer goin' ter trial, then there won't be people comin' and goin' all hours."

"I shan't be here to care," Hester said tartly.

The wardress's thin eyebrows rose.

"Think yer goin' 'ome, do yer? That'll be the day! They'll 'ang yer, my fine lady, by yer skinny white neck, until ye're dead. No point nobody comin' te see ye then!"

Hester looked at her slowly, carefully, meeting her eyes.

"I've seen too many people hanged, and found innocent afterwards, to argue with you," she said clearly. "The difference is that that doesn't bother you. You want to see someone hanged, and the truth doesn't interest you."

A dull red color washed up the woman's face and the heavy muscles in her neck tightened. She took half a step forward.

"You watch yer mouth, Latterly, or I'll 'ave yer! You just remember who 'olds the keys 'ere—an' it ain't you. I got power—and yer'll be glad enough to 'ave me on yer side—when the end comes. I seen a lot o' people think 'emsleves brave—till the night before the rope."

"After a month in your charge, the rope may not seem so bad," Hester said bitterly, but inside her stomach was knotted and her breath came unevenly. "Who is my visitor?"

She had hoped it would be Rathbone. He was her lifeline to sanity, and hope. Callandra had been twice, but somehow Hester found herself very emotional when she saw her. Perhaps it was Callandra's very obvious affection and the depth of her concern. Hester had felt uncontrollably lonely after she had gone. It had taken all the willpower she possessed not to give in to a fit of weeping. It was primarily the thought of the wardress's returning, and her contempt and satisfaction, that prevented her.

Now beyond the wardress's powerful shoulder she could see not Rathbone but her brother Charles. He looked pale and profoundly unhappy.

Suddenly memory overwhelmed her. She was almost drowned in the recollection of his face when she had arrived home from the Crimea after her parents' deaths and Charles had met her at the house to tell her the full extent of the tragedy, not only the death by suicide of their father, but the broken heart so shortly afterwards which had taken their mother also, and the financial ruin left behind. He had just the same, familiar look of embarrassment and anxiety now. He looked curiously emotionally naked, and seeing him, Hester felt like a child again.

He came in past the wardress, walking a little around her, his eyes intent on Hester.

Hester was standing, as she had been bidden. Charles's eyes glanced around the cell, taking in the details of the bare walls, the single deep window high above the level of anyone's sight, the gray sky beyond the bars. Then he looked at the cot with its built-in commode. Lastly he looked at Hester, in her plain blue-gray nursing dress. He looked at her face reluctantly, as if he could not bear to see what must be there in it.

"How are you?" he asked, his voice husky.

She had been going to tell him, unburden herself of the loneliness and the fear, but looking at his tiredness, his red-rimmed eyes, and knowing he could do nothing whatever to help, except hurt as well and feel guilty because he was powerless, she found it impossible. She did not even consider it.

"I'm perfectly well," she said in a clear, precise voice. "No one could say it is pleasant, but I have survived a great deal worse without coming to any harm."

His whole body relaxed and some of the tension eased out of his face. He wanted to believe her and he was not going to question what she said.

"Yes—yes, of course you have," he agreed. "You are a remarkable woman."

The wardress had been waiting to give him instructions to recall her, but she felt excluded by the exchange, and she withdrew and slammed the door without speaking again.

Charles jumped at the sound, and swung around to see the blank, iron barrier, handleless on the inside.

"It's all right," Hester said quickly. "She'll be back when your time is up."

He looked at her, forcing himself to smile, but it was a sickly gesture.

"Do they feed you properly? Keep you warm enough? It feels cold here to me."

"It's not bad," she lied. "And really it isn't so important. There must be many people who never have better."

He was struggling for something to say. Polite conversation seemed so ridiculous, and yet he dreaded the realities.

Hester took the decision for him, otherwise the whole visit would have come and gone and they would never have said anything that mattered.

"Monk has gone up to Edinburgh to find out what really happened," she began.

"Monk? Oh, that policeman you were ... acquainted with. Do you " He stopped, changed his mind about what he had been going to say.

"Yes," she finished for him. "I think he has as good a chance as anyone of learning the truth. In fact, better. He won't accept lies, and he knows I did not kill her, so he will keep on asking and watching and thinking until he finds out who did." She felt better for putting it into words. It had been said to convince Charles, but it had lifted her at least as much.

"Are you sure?" he said anxiously. "You couldn't have made a mistake, could you? You were tired, unfamiliar with the patient...." He looked acutely apologetic, his face pink, his eyes desperately earnest.

She wanted to be furious with him, but her anger died in pity and long familiarity. What was the point in hurting him? He was going to suffer enough as it was.

"No," she said quickly. "There was one vial of medicine for each dose. I gave her one vial. She wasn't some vague little old lady who didn't know what she was doing, Charles. She was interesting, funny, wise, and very much aware of everything. She wouldn't have allowed me to make a mistake, even if I had been in a frame of mind to do so."

He frowned. "Then you mean someone else killed her deliberately?"

It was a very ugly thought, but inescapable.

"Yes."

"Could the apothecary have made up a wrong medicine altogether?" He struggled for a more acceptable answer.

"No—I don't think so. That was not the first one to be taken. If the whole lot had been wrong, the first one would have killed her. And who put the brooch in my bag? That certainly wasn't the apothecary."

"The lady's maid?"

"That would be impossible to do by mistake. All her jewelry was together in her own traveling case, which was put in her bag for overnight. This one piece was loose in my bag, which was nothing like hers anyway, and the two were never together until we were on board the train."

His face pinched with unhappiness. "Then I suppose someone meant to kill her . . . and to blame you." He bit his lip, his eyes narrowing and his brows drawing down. "Hester, for God's sake, why couldn't you be content to work at some more respectable occupation? You are always getting involved in crimes and disasters of one sort or another. First the Grey case, then the Moidores, and the Carlyons, and that appalling business at the hospital. What is the matter with you? Is it that man Monk who is involving you in all this?"

The suggestion caught her on the raw, mostly her pride, and the idea that somehow Monk, or her affection for him, ruled her life.

"No it is not," she said tartly. "Nursing is a vocation that is bound to be involved with death, now and again. People do die, Charles, most especially those who are ill to begin with."

He looked confused. "But if Mrs. Farraline was so ill, why did they assume she was murdered? That seems most unreasonable to me."

"She wasn't ill!" Hester said furiously. She was caught in a trap of her own making, and she knew it. "She was just elderly, and had a slight condition of the heart. She could have lived for years."

"You can't have it both ways, Hester. Either her death was normal, and to be expected, or it wasn't! Sometimes women are most illogical." He smiled very slightly. It was not unkind, not even critical, merely patient.

It was like a spark to tinder.

"Rubbish!" she shouted. "Don't you dare stand there and call me 'most women.' Anyway, most women are no more illogical than most men. We are just different, that's all. We take less account of your so-called facts and more of people's feelings. And we are more often right. And we are certainly a great deal more practical. You are all theories, half of which don't work because there was something wrong in them, or something you didn't know which makes nonsense of the rest." She stopped abruptly, out of breath and conscious of the pitch and volume of her voice, and now suddenly aware that she was quarreling with the one person in the entire building, perhaps in the whole city, who was truly on her side, and who was finding nothing but grief from the whole affair. Perhaps she should apologize, pompous and quite mistaken as he was?

He preempted her by making the matter even worse.

"So who did kill Mrs. Farraline?" he asked with devastating practicality. "And why? Was it money? She was obviously far too old for any sort of romantic involvement."

"People don't stop being in love just because they are over thirty," she snapped.

He stared at her. "I have never heard of a woman over sixty being the victim of a crime of passion," he said, his voice rising slightly with disbelief.

"I didn't say it was a crime of passion."

"You are really being very trying, my dear. Why don't you at least sit down, so we can talk a little more comfortably?" He indicated the cot, where they could sit side by side, and suited his own actions to his words. "Is there anything I may bring you to ease your situation at all? If they will allow it, I will certainly do so. I did bring some clean linen from your lodgings, but they took it from me on my way in. No doubt they will give it to you in due course."

"Yes please. You could ask Imogen to find me some toilet soap. This carbolic takes the skin off my face. It's fearful stuff."

"Of course." He winced in sympathy. "I am sure she will be pleased to. I shall bring it as soon as I am able."

"Could Imogen not bring it? I should like to see her." Even as she said it she knew it was foolish, and only inviting hurt.

A shadow crossed his eyes, and there was the faint beginning of a flush to his cheeks, as if he were aware of something wrong, but not certain what, or why.

"I am sorry, Hester, but I could not allow Imogen to come to this place. It would distress her fearfully. She would never be able to forget it, it would come back to her mind again and again. She would have nightmares. It is my duty to protect her from all that I can. I wish it could be more." He looked hurt as he said it, as if the pain were within his own mind and body.

"Yes, it is a nightmare," she said chokingly. "I dream about it too. Only when I wake up I'm not lying in my own bed in a safe home, with someone to look after me and protect me from reality. I'm still here, with the long, cold day in front of me, and another tomorrow, and the day after."

His face closed over, as if he could not bear to grasp the knowledge.

"I know that, Hester. But that is not Imogen's fault, nor mine. You chose your path. I did everything I could to dissuade you. I never ceased to try to convince you to marry, when you had offers, or could have had if you had given a little encouragement. But you would not listen. No, I'm afraid it is too late. Even if this matter is resolved as I pray it will be, and you are exonerated of all fault, you are unlikely to find any man offering you an honorable marriage, unless there is some widower who wishes for a decent woman to—"

"I don't want some widower to keep house for," she said, the tears thick in her voice. "I'd rather be paid as a housekeeper—and have my dignity, and the freedom to leave—than married as one, with the pretense that there was some kind of love in it, when he only wanted a servant he didn't have to pay and I only wanted a roof over my head and food on my plate."

Charles stood up, his face pale and tight.

"A great many marriages are merely convenient and practical to begin with. Often a mutual respect comes later. There is no loss of dignity in that." His smile brightened his eyes and touched his lips. "For a woman, and you say women are so practical, you are the most romantic and totally impractical creature I ever knew."

She stood up as well. Too full of emotion to answer.

"I shall bring you some soap next time I come. Please . . . please do not lose hope." He said the words awkwardly, as if they were a matter of duty rather than anything he could mean. "Mr. Rathbone is the best possible—"

She cut him off. "I know!" She could not bear the rehearsed insincerity of it. "Thank you for coming."

He made a move forward, as if to kiss her cheek, but she backed away from him sharply. He looked surprised for an instant, but accepted the rebuff with something like relief that at last he was excused and could escape, both from the encounter and from the place.

"I'll . . . I'll see you . . . soon," he replied, turning to go to the door and bang on it for the wardress to release him.

It was the following day before she had another visitor, and this time it was Oliver Rathbone. She was too miserable to feel any lift of spirits seeing him, and the perception of her mood was instant in his face. And then after formal greetings had been exchanged, with a leaden heart, she realized it was also a reflection of his own feelings.

"What's wrong?" she demanded shakily. She had not thought she was capable of any further emotion, but she was suddenly sickeningly afraid. "What's happened?"

They were standing face-to-face in the whitewashed room with its table and wooden chairs. He took hold of both her hands. It was not a calculated move, but instinctive, and its gentleness only added to her fear. Her mouth was dry and she took a breath to ask again what was wrong, but her voice would not come.

"They have ordered that you are tried in Scotland," he said very quietly. "In Edinburgh. I have no grounds on which to fight it. It appears to them that the poison was administered on Scottish soil, and since we contend it was actually prepared in the Farraline house, and had nothing to do with you, then it was beyond question a Scottish crime. I'm so sorry."

She did not understand. Why was that so crippling a blow? He looked devastated, and there seemed no reason.

He closed his eyes for a second, then opened them again, dark, dark brown and filled with misery.

"You will be tried under Scottish law," he explained. "I am English. I cannot represent you."

At last she understood. It hit her like a physical blow to the body. In a single move the only help she could hope for had been removed from her. She was absolutely alone. She was too stunned to speak, even to cry.

He was gripping her hand so hard the pressure of his fingers hurt. The slight pain of it was her only link with reality. It was almost a relief.

"We will find the best Scottish lawyer we can," he was saying. His voice seemed far away. "Callandra will remunerate him of course. And don't argue about that. Such things can come later. Naturally I will come up to Edinburgh and advise him in every way I know how. But he will have to speak, even if some of the words are mine."

She wanted to ask him if there was not some way in which he could still conduct the case. She had seen his skill, the power of his brain, his charm and serpentine subtlety to delude, to seem harmless, and then to strike mortally. It had been the one thread of hope she had clung to. But she knew he would not have told her had there been any chance whatever that he could still do it. He would have tried every avenue already, and failed. It was childish, and pointless, to rail against the inevitable. Best to accept it and hoard one's strength for whatever battles were still to be fought.

"I see. . . ."

He could think of nothing to say. Wordlessly he moved a step forward and took her in his arms, holding her tightly, standing perfectly still, not even stroking her hair or touching her cheek, just holding her.

It was three more largely fruitless days before Monk returned to Ainslie Place to dine. He had spent the intervening time learning more about the reputation of the Farralines, which was interesting, but as far as clearing Hester was concerned, quite useless. They were well respected, both in business and in their private lives. No one had any criticism of them apart from the small jibes that fairly obviously sprang from envy. Apparently Hamish had founded the printing company when he retired from the army and returned to Edinburgh a short time after the end of the Napoleonic Wars. Hector had played no part in that, and still did not. He lived, as far as anyone knew, on his army pension, having remained in the service until he was well past middle age. He had visited his father's family frequently and was always made welcome, and now lived there en-

tirely, in a luxury far beyond anything he could have afforded himself. He drank too much, a great deal too much, and so far as anyone
knew, contributed nothing either to the family or the community,
but apart from that he was agreeable enough, and caused no one else
any trouble. If his family were prepared to put up with him, that was
their affair. Every family seemed to have its black sheep, and if there
were any disgrace attached to him, it was not known outside the
four walls of the Farraline house.

Hamish had been an entirely different matter. He had been
hardworking, inventive, daring in business and obviously extremely
successful. The company made a magnificent profit, and had grown
from very small beginnings into one of the finest printers in Edinburgh, if not in Scotland. It did not employ a large number of people, preferring quality to quantity, but its reputation was without
stain.

Hamish himself had been a gentleman, but not in the least
pompous. Maybe he had sown a few wild oats here and there, but
that was usual enough. He had been discreet. He had never embarrassed his family and there was no scandal attached to his name. He
had died eight years ago, after declining health for some time. Towards the end he had left the house very little. Possibly he had suffered a series of strokes; certainly his movement had been impaired.
It was not an uncommon occurrence. Very sad to lose such a fine
man.

Not that his son was not an excellent man also. Less able in
business, and not unwilling to turn over the management of the
company largely to his brother-in-law Baird McIvor. McIvor was a
foreigner, mind: English, but not a bad man for all that. A bit moody
now and then, but very capable, and was honest as you like. Mr.
Alastair was the Procurator Fiscal, and that could hardly leave him
time for affairs of business as well. And a fine Fiscal he was, too, an
ornament to the community. A trifle pompous for some tastes, but
then a Fiscal should be of a serious mind. If the law was not a grave
matter, what was?

Did he sow a few wild oats as well? No one had heard tell of it.
He hardly seemed the type of man to do that. No scandal attached to
his name at all.

Well, there was the Galbraith case, but that scandal was around Mr. Galbraith, not the Fiscal.

Monk asked about the Galbraith case, although he thought he already knew.

He was told largely what he had heard before: Galbraith had been charged with fraud; a very large sum of money was involved. Everyone felt sure there would be a conviction when the matter came to trial, then the Fiscal had declared that there was insufficient evidence to bring the case before the court, so Galbraith had escaped prison—but not disgrace, at least not in the public opinion. Hardly the Fiscal's fault.

And Mary Farraline?

Now there was a lady indeed! Every attribute one could admire, dignity, unfailingly courteous to all, no arrogance about her, civil to everyone, rich and poor. That was the mark of quality, was it not? Always elegant, never ostentatious.

Her personal reputation?

Don't be absurd. One would not even think of such a question in regard to Mrs. Farraline. Charming, but never overfriendly with anyone at all. Devoted to her family. Well yes, she had been a fine-looking woman in her youth, and naturally there would have been admirers. She was not without humor and enjoyment of life, but that was quite a different thing from suggesting improper behavior or the breath of scandal.

Of course. And the present generation?

Well enough, but not of her quality, except perhaps Miss Oonagh. Now there was another lady. Like her mother, she was, quiet, strong, intensely loyal to family . . . and clever too. Some said it was as much her brains that ran the company as her husband's. That could be true. But if it was, it was no one else's affair.

Monk arrived at Ainslie Place armed with a great deal more knowledge of the family's status in society and their good reputation, but nothing that he could see in any way would gain him the least idea of who killed Mary Farraline, let alone proof of it.

He was received civilly by McTeer, who now regarded him with discreet interest, albeit still total disapproval. As on previous occasions he was shown into the withdrawing room, where most of the family was assembled. Only Alastair seemed to be missing.

Oonagh came forward to greet him, a half smile on her lips.

"Good evening, Mr. Monk." She met his eyes with a level look, far too candid and intelligent to be flattering in the usual sense, but he found the fact that she was interested enough not to be merely polite of more value than another woman's flirtation would have been. "How are you?"

"Very well, thank you, and finding Edinburgh a most remarkable city," he replied, meeting her look with an equal mixture of ardor in his eyes and conventions on his lips.

She turned to the others, and he followed her, exchanging polite acknowledgments, words on health and the weather and the other trivialities people use when they have nothing of importance to say.

Hector Farraline was present this evening. He looked appalling. His face was so pale the freckles across his cheeks stood out and his eyes were red-rimmed. Monk guessed he must be taking a bottle of whiskey a day to be looking so ill. At this rate it would only be a short time before he drank himself to death. He was sitting slightly splayed out on the largest sofa. He regarded Monk with puzzled interest, as if he were measuring up his role in events.

Monk saw Deirdra with the same pleasure as before. She really was a most individual woman, but not even her dearest friend could have said her gown was highly fashionable. Monk accepted that she was apparently extravagant with dress, but his own immaculate taste knew a good gown when he saw one, and hers was certainly not. The fabric was excellent and there was carefully stitched jet beadwork on the bodice, but the skirt was poorly proportioned. The lowest tier was too short, which on a small woman was all the more unfortunate. The sleeves seemed to have been lifted at the shoulder, and caused something of a pleat where there should not have been one.

But none of these things were of any importance. They showed individuality and made her seem curiously vulnerable, a quality which always appealed to him.

He accepted the wine offered, and stood a little closer to the fire.

"Have you occupied your time successfully?" Quinlan inquired, looking at him over the top of his own glass. It was impossible to tell if his question was ironic or not.

Monk could think of nothing to reply that would elicit a useful response. He was beginning to feel desperate. Time was running short and so far he had heard nothing at all of use to Hester. How much had he to lose by more dangerous tactics?

"I know a great deal more about your family," he said with a smile of amusement rather than warmth. "Some of it facts, some opinion, much of it of interest one way or another." That was a lie, but he could not afford the truth.

"About us?" Baird said quickly. "I thought you were investigating Miss Latterly?"

"I'm investigating the entire circumstance. But certainly, if you recall, I said that I knew a great deal more, not that I had pursued the knowledge as my primary goal."

"The difference seems academic." Quinlan for once sided with Baird. "And what is interesting about it? Did they tell you I married the beautiful Eilish Farraline almost out of the arms of her previous suitor? A young man of good breeding and no money, of whom her family disapproved."

Baird's face darkened, but he bit his tongue rather than respond.

Eilish looked momentarily unhappy, glanced at Baird, but he was looking away from her, then at Quinlan with dislike.

"How fortunate that they approved of you," Monk said expressionlessly. "Was that personal charm, an influential family, or merely wealth?"

Oonagh drew her breath in sharply, but there was amusement glittering in her eyes, and an appreciation of Monk which he could not fail to see was growing increasingly personal. He felt an acute satisfaction in it; in fact, were he honest he would have acknowledged it as pleasure.

"You would have to have asked Mother-in-law," Deirdra said at last. "I imagine she was the person whose approval mattered. Of course in many ways Alastair . . . but he would be guided in such things. I don't know why he did not care for the other young man. He seemed perfectly agreeable to me."

" 'Perfectly agreeable' is neither here nor there," Kenneth said with a touch of bitterness. "Not even money is everything, unless it is thousands. It is all respectability—isn't it, Oonagh?"

Oonagh looked at him with patience and acute perception.

"Well, it certainly isn't beauty, wit or the ability to enjoy yourself—still less to give enjoyment to others, my dear. Women like that have their place, but it is not at the altar."

"For heaven's sake, please don't tell us where it is," Quinlan said quickly, looking at Kenneth. "The answer is only too obvious."

"Well, I am still none the wiser," Baird said, staring at Quinlan. "You have no fortune, your family has never been mentioned, and personal charm is not even worth considering."

Oonagh looked at him with an unreadable expression. "We Farralines do not need money or family allegiances. We marry where we wish to. Quinlan has his qualities, and as long as they please Eilish, and we gave our approval, that is all that matters." She smiled at Eilish. "Isn't it, dear?"

Eilish hesitated; a curious play of emotions fought in her expression, then finally it softened with something like apology and she smiled back. "Yes, of course it is. I loathed you at the time for agreeing with Mother. In fact, I thought you were largely to blame. But now I can see I would never have been happy with Robert Crawford." She glanced at Baird, and away again. "He was certainly not the right person for me."

A flush of color spread up Baird's cheeks, and he looked away.

"Romantic love," Hector said, more to himself than apparently to anyone else. "What a dream ... what a beautiful dream." There was reminiscence in his tone and his eyes were not focused on anything.

They all studiously ignored him.

"Does anyone know what time we may expect Alastair?" Kenneth asked, looking from Deirdra to Oonagh. "Are we going to have to wait dinner for him ... again?"

"If he is late," Oonagh replied coolly, "it will be for an excellent reason, not because he is inconsiderate or has some social entertainment he prefers."

Like a small boy Kenneth pulled a face, but he said nothing. Monk formed the distinct impression he did not dare to, dearly as he would have liked.

Conversation struggled on for another ten or fifteen minutes. Monk found himself talking with Deirdra, mostly by design, not to obtain Oonagh's information but because he enjoyed her company. She was an intelligent woman, and seemed to be devoid of the sort of artifice he disliked. He watched Eilish out of the corner of his eye, but her luminous beauty did not appeal to him. He preferred character and wit. Sheer beauty lent an aura of invulnerability, and was peculiarly unattractive to him.

"Have you really found out anything about poor Mother-in-law's death, Mr. Monk?" Deirdra asked gravely. "I do hope the affair is not going to drag on and cause more and more distress?" The lift in her voice made it a question and her dark eyes were full of anxiety.

She deserved the truth—although he would not have hesitated to lie even to her, had he thought it would serve its purpose.

"I am afraid I can think of no way in which it will be resolved easily," he replied. "Criminal trials are always unpleasant. No one is going"—he forced himself to say it—"to be hanged without doing everything they know how to avoid it."

Suddenly and ridiculously he was overwhelmed with a blinding hatred for them all, standing in this warm room waiting to be called in to dinner. One of them had murdered Mary Farraline and was going to allow the law to murder Hester in his or her place. "And no doubt a good defense lawyer will try to spread blame and suspicion somewhere else," he added between his clenched teeth. "Of course it will be unpleasant. She is fighting for her life. She is a brave woman who has faced loneliness, privation and physical danger before. She won't surrender. She will have to be beaten."

Deirdra was staring at him, her face drawn, her eyes wide.

"You speak as if you knew her well," she said in little more than a whisper.

Monk checked himself instantly, like a runner tripping and regaining his balance.

"It is my business to, Mrs. Farraline. I can hardly defend the prosecution's interest if I am unfamiliar with the enemy."

"Oh . . . no, I suppose not. I had not thought of that." She frowned. "I had not thought very much about it at all. Alastair would have known better. I expect you have talked with him." It was an assumption rather than a question. She looked a trifle crestfallen. "You should really speak with Oonagh. She is most observant of people. She always seems to know what a person really means, rather than what they say. I have noticed it often. She is most gifted at reading character." She smiled. "It is really rather a comforting quality, to feel someone understands you so well."

"Except in Miss Latterly's case," Monk said with more sarcasm than he had meant to show.

She caught his tone and looked at him with a mixture of perception and defense.

He found himself annoyed, both for having been rude to her and for having betrayed himself.

"You must not blame her for that," she said quickly. "She was so busy caring for poor Mother-in-law. It was she whom Mother confided in. She seemed to be most concerned about Griselda." A slight frown puckered her brows. "I had not thought there was anything really wrong. She always was rather a worrier. But perhaps it was something more serious? A first confinement can be difficult. So can any, for that matter, of course. But I know Griselda wrote several times a week, until eventually even Oonagh agreed that it really was necessary that Mother should travel down to London to reassure her. Now, poor soul, she will never know what Mother would have told her."

"Can Mrs. McIvor not write to her in such a way as to help?" he suggested.

"Oh I am sure she has done," Deirdra said with certainty. "I wish I could help myself, but I have no idea what was the subject of her anxiety. I think it was some family medical history over which Mother-in-law could have set her mind at ease."

"Then I am sure Mrs. McIvor will have done so."

"Of course." She smiled a sudden warmth.

"Oonagh will help if anyone can. I daresay Mother confided in her anyway. She will know precisely what to say to make Griselda feel better."

Further conversation was cut off by the arrival of Alastair, looking tired and a trifle harassed. He spoke first to Oonagh, exchanging only a word or two, but then he acknowledged his wife and apologized to Monk for being late. The moment after, the gong sounded and they went into the dining room.

They were into the second course when the embarrassment began. Hector had been sitting in relative silence, only making the occasional monosyllabic reply, until suddenly he looked across at Alastair, frowning at him and focusing his eyes with difficulty.

"I suppose it's that case again," he said with disgust. "You should leave it alone. You lost. That's the end of it."

"No, Uncle Hector," Alastair said wearily. "I was meeting with the sheriff over something quite new."

Hector grunted and looked unconvinced, but it might have been that he was too drunk to have understood.

"It was a bad case, that. You ought to have won. I'm not surprised you still think about it."

Oonagh filled her glass with wine from the decanter on the table and passed it across to Hector. He took it with a glance at her but he did not drink it straightaway.

"Alastair does not win or lose cases, Uncle Hector," she said gently. "He decides whether there is sufficient evidence to prosecute or not. If there isn't, there would be no point in bringing it to court. It would only waste public money."

"And subject the person, most probably innocent, to a harrowing ordeal and public shame," Monk added rather abruptly.

Oonagh flashed him a look of quick surprise. "Certainly, and that also."

Hector looked at Monk as if he had only just remembered his presence.

"Oh yes . . . you're the detective, aren't you. Come to make sure of the case against that nurse. Pity." He looked at Monk with acute disfavor. "I liked her. Nice girl. Courage. Takes a lot of courage for a woman to go out to a place like the Crimea, you know, and look after the wounded." There was distinct hostility in his face. "You'd better be sure, young man. You'd better be damned sure you've got the right person."

"I shall be," Monk said grimly. "I am more dedicated to that than you can possibly know."

Hector stared at him, then at last almost reluctantly began to drink Oonagh's wine.

"There isn't any doubt, Uncle Hector," Quinlan said irritably. "If you were a little closer to sober you'd know that."

"Would I!" Hector was annoyed. He put down the glass, very nearly spilling it. It was only saved by Eilish, on the other side, reaching forward and pulling a spoon handle out of the way. "Why would

I?" Hector demanded, ignoring Eilish. "Why would I know that, Quinlan?"

"Well, apart from the fact that if it was not her then it was one of us," Quinlan said, baring his teeth in a mockery of a smile, "she was the only one who had any reason. The brooch was found in her case."

"Books," Hector said with satisfaction.

"Books?" Quinlan was derisive. "What are you talking about? What books?"

A flash of temper crossed Hector's face, but he changed his mind about letting go of it. "Company books," he said with a smile. "Ledgers."

There was a moment's silence. Kenneth put down his knife and fork.

"Miss Latterly didn't know anything about our company books, Uncle Hector," Oonagh said quietly. "She only arrived in Edinburgh that morning."

"Of course she didn't," Hector agreed crossly. "But we do."

"Naturally we do," Quinlan agreed. Monk thought he only just avoided adding "you fool."

"And one of us knows whether they are right or wrong," Hector went on doggedly.

Kenneth's face was pink. "I do, Uncle Hector. It is my job to keep them. And they are right . . . to the farthing."

"Of course they are," Oonagh said frankly, looking first at Kenneth, then at Hector. "We all know you are distressed over Mother's death, but you are beginning to speak irresponsibly, Uncle Hector. That does not do any of us justice. It would be a good idea if you were to stop discussing that subject before you say something we shall all regret." Her eyes were very steady on his. "Mother would not have wished us to quarrel with each other, or make hurtful remarks like that."

Hector looked numbed, as if for a moment he had forgotten Mary's death, and then suddenly the whole weight of grief struck him again. The color fled from his face and he seemed about to collapse.

Eilish leaned towards him to give him physical support, which seemed necessary to keep him upright in his chair, and immediately Baird rose and came around to him, half lifting him up.

"Come on, Uncle Hector. Let me take you to your room. I think you had better lie down for a while."

A look of fury crossed over Quinlan's face as Eilish and Baird between them helped Hector to his feet and led him, shambling erratically, out of the room. They could hear their footsteps lurching across the hall, and Eilish's voice in encouragement, and then Baird's deeper tones.

"I'm so sorry," Oonagh apologized, looking at Monk. "I am afraid poor Uncle Hector is not as well as we would wish. This has all struck him very hard." She smiled gently, tacitly seeking Monk's understanding. "I am afraid he sometimes gets confused."

" 'Not as well,' " Quinlan said viciously. "He's blind drunk, the old ass!"

Alastair shot him a look of warning, but refrained from saying anything.

Deirdra rang the bell for the servants to clear away the dishes and bring the next course.

They were finished with dinner and back in the withdrawing room before Oonagh found her opportunity to speak privately with Monk. They were all in the room, but so discreetly that it seemed unnoticed by anyone else, she led him farther and farther from the others until they were standing in front of the large window, now closed against the rapidly chilling night, and out of earshot of anyone. He was suddenly aware of the perfume of her.

"How is your errand progressing, Mr. Monk?" she said softly.

"I have learned little that might not have been expected," he replied guardedly.

"About us?"

There was no point in prevaricating, and she was not a woman to whom he would lie, or wished to over this.

"Naturally."

"Have you discovered where Deirdra spends so much money, Mr. Monk?"

"Not yet."

She pulled a small, rueful face, full of apology, and something else beyond it, deep within her which he could not read.

"She manages to go through enormous amounts, quite unexplained by the running of this house, which has been largely in my mother's hands until her death, and of course mine." She frowned. "Deirdra says she spends it on clothes, but she is exceptionally extravagant, even for a woman of fashion and some social position to maintain." She took a deep breath and looked at Monk very squarely. "It is causing my brother Alastair some concern. If . . . if you should find out, in the course of your investigations, we would be most grateful to learn." The ghost of a smile curved her lips. "We would express that gratitude in whatever manner was appropriate. I do not wish to insult you."

"Thank you," he said frankly. He was obliged to admit, his pride could be quite easily offended. "If I should learn the answer to that, which I may do, I will inform you directly I am certain."

She smiled, in a moment's candid understanding, and a moment later fell back into ordinary, meaningless chatter.

He took his leave shortly before a quarter to eleven, and was in the hall waiting for McTeer to emerge through the green baize door when Hector Farraline came lurching down the stairs and slid the last half dozen steps to land clinging to the newel post, his face wearing an expression of intense concentration.

"Are you going to find out who killed Mary?" he said in a whisper, surprisingly quiet for one so inebriated.

"Yes," Monk replied simply. He did not think rational argument or explanation would serve any purpose, only prolong an encounter which was going to be at least trying.

"She was the best woman I ever knew." Hector blinked and his eyes filled with a terrible sadness. "You should have seen her when she was young. She was never beautiful, like Eilish, but she had the same sort of quality about her, a light inside, a sort of fire." He gazed across the hall past Monk, and for a moment his glance caught the huge portrait of his brother, which until now Monk had noticed only vaguely. The old man's lip curled and his face filled with a vortex of emotions, love, hate, envy, loathing, regret, longing for things past, even pity.

"He was a bastard, you know—at times," he said in little more than a whisper, but his voice shook with intensity. "The handsome Hamish, my elder brother, the colonel. I was only a major, you know? But I was a better soldier than he ever was! Cut a fine figure. Knew how to speak to the ladies. They adored him."

He slid down to sit on the lowest step. "But Mary was always the best. She used to walk with her back so straight, and her head so high. She had wit, Mary. Make you laugh till you wept . . . at the damnedest things." He looked regrettably close to weeping now, and impatient as he was, Monk felt a twinge of pity for him. He was an old man, living on the bounty of a younger generation who had nothing but contempt for him, and a sense of duty. The fact that he probably deserved nothing more would be no comfort at all.

"He was wrong," Hector said suddenly, swiveling around to look straight at the portrait again. "Very wrong. He shouldn't have done that to her, of all people."

Monk was not interested. Hamish Farraline had been dead over eight years. There could be no connection with Mary's death, and that was all that mattered now. Impatience was gnawing inside him. He moved away.

"Watch for McIvor," Hector called after him.

Monk turned back.

"Why?"

"She liked him," Hector said simply, his eyes wide. "You could always tell when Mary liked someone."

"Indeed."

He could not be bothered to wait for McTeer. The old fool was probably asleep in his pantry. He took his own coat off the hall stand and made for the front door just as Alastair came out of the withdrawing room, apologizing for McTeer's absence.

Monk said good-night again, nodded towards Hector on the stairs, and went out of the front door. He had refused the offer of assistance to call a cab, and had set out to walk southwards when he saw an unmistakable figure pass beneath the lamplight so rapidly he almost missed her. But no one else could have quite that ethereal grace, or that flame of hair. Most of her head was covered by the hood of her cape, but as she turned towards the light her brow was pale and the copper red clear above it.

Where on earth was Eilish Fyffe going alone, and on foot, at eleven o'clock at night?

He waited until she was well past him, across the grass of the circle to the far side of Ainslie Place, where she was about to disappear either east into St. Combe Street or south into Glenfinlas Street. Then he ran quickly and soundlessly after her, arriving at the corner just in time to see her pass under the lamp at the beginning of Charlotte Square.

Had she an assignation? It seemed not only the obvious conclusion but the only one. Why else would she be out alone, and obviously wishing not to be seen?

She was moving rapidly past the square. It was only two very short blocks before it ended in a big junction with Princes Street and Lothian Road, Shandwick Place and Queensferry Street. Where on earth was she going? He had never cared much for her, but now his opinion took a rapid and decisive turn for the worse.

She crossed the junction without a glance either way, still less behind her, and continued at a fast walk along Lothian Road. To their left were the Princes Street Gardens, and looming over them, brooding and medieval, the huge mass of the mound with the castle clinging to its top.

Monk kept an even hundred yards behind her, and was almost taken by surprise when she turned left and disappeared into Kings Stables Road. He was familiar with the way. It was his own route home, were he to walk. Not long and it would lead into the Grassmarket, and then Cowgate. Surely she could not be going that way? What would these dark, crowded buildings and narrow alleys possibly hold for a lady like Eilish?

His mind was still turning over the contradictions and impossibilities of it when suddenly he was engulfed in sharp, numbing pain and a black hole opened up in front of him.

He regained his senses, still on the pavement, propped up against the wall, his head aching abominably, his body cold and his temper volcanic. Eilish was nowhere to be seen.

The following day he returned to Ainslie Place in a vicious and desperate frame of mind, and set up vigil as soon as it was dark.

However it was not Eilish he saw, but a scruffy-looking man in soiled and very worn clothes approaching number seventeen nervously, looking from right to left as if he feared observation.

Monk moved farther back into the shadows, then remained absolutely motionless.

The man passed under a streetlamp and for a moment his face was visible. It was the same man Monk had seen several days before, not with Eilish, but with Deirdra. The man fished out a watch from his pocket, glanced at it, and put it back.

Curious. He did not look like a man who would be able to read a watch, far less own one.

Several minutes passed by. The man fidgeted in acute discomfort. Monk stood without moving even the angle of his head. Along the footpath the lamps made little pools of light. Between was a no-man's-land of gathering mist and shadows. It was growing colder. Monk was beginning to feel it in his motionless state. It ate into his bones and crept up through the soles of his feet.

Then suddenly she was there. She must have come around through the areaway gate, into the street from the side—not Eilish, but the small, urgent figure of Deirdra. She did not even glance down the street or to the grass center of the Place, but went straight to the man. They stood close together for several minutes, heads bent, talking in voices so low that from where he stood Monk could not even hear a murmur.

Then suddenly Deirdra shook her head vigorously, the man touched her arm in a gentle reassuring gesture, and she turned and went back inside the house. He departed the way he had come.

Monk waited until long after midnight, growing colder and colder, but no one else came or went in the Farraline house. He could have kicked himself for not having followed the man.

Two more cold and increasingly desperate days followed in which Monk learned nothing useful, indeed nothing that common sense could not have deduced for him. He wrote at some length to Rathbone, detailing everything he had learned so far, and when he returned to his lodgings about noon on the third day there were two letters for him, one from Rathbone outlining the general provisions of Mary Farraline's will. She had left her very considerable property, both real and personal, more or less equally among the children. Alastair had already inherited the house and most of the business on the death of his father. The second letter was from Oonagh, inviting him to attend a large civic dinner that evening and apologizing for the invitation's being so extremely late.

Monk accepted. He had nothing left to lose. Time was treading hard on his heels, and fruitless nights spent watching the Farraline house had yielded nothing. Neither Deirdra or Eilish had appeared again.

He dressed very carefully, but his mind was too absorbed in rehearsing every piece of information he had to be nervous as to his elegance or social acceptability. How could Hester have been idiotic enough to get herself into this appalling situation? The few impressions she had given him were useless. What if Deirdra and Eilish were both conducting clandestine affairs with men from the heart of the slums? What if Mary knew? It made no sense to murder her because of it. If she had not made it public already, then she was not going to. A family quarrel, no matter how fierce, was not cause for murder by anyone but a lunatic.

If Eilish had been the victim, that would be readily explainable. Either Quinlan or Baird McIvor might have excellent cause. Or even Oonagh, if Baird was really in love with her.

But that made little sense either. It could hardly be Baird she was creeping along Kings Stables Road at night to see.

He arrived at the huge hall in which the dinner was to be held with his letter from Oonagh in his hand, ready to show to any doorman who might question his right to be there, but his assurance must have been sufficient and no one accosted him.

It was a dazzling occasion. Chandeliers blazed from every ceiling. He could imagine them being lowered and footmen with tapers spending hours lighting them before winding them back up again. Every niche in the gorgeous ceilings seemed to be ablaze. Fiddlers played a nameless accompaniment while guests milled around nodding and smiling and hoping to be recognized by all the right people. Servants mixed discreetly offering refreshments, and a resplendent liveried doorman announced the arrival of those whom Society considered important.

It was easy to see Eilish. Even in black she seemed to radiate a warmth and a light. Her hair was a more gorgeous ornament than the tiaras of duchesses, and her pale skin against the black of her gown seemed luminous.

From the gallery where Monk was standing he soon observed Alastair's pale head, and the moment after, Oonagh. Even from above, where he could see only an angle of her face, she carried with her an aura of calm and a sense of both power and intelligence.

Had Mary been like that? That was what the drink-sodden Hector had suggested. Why would anyone murder such a woman? Greed for the power she exercised, or the purse strings? Jealousy because she had the innate qualities which would always make her the natural leader? Fear, because she knew something which was intolerable to someone else, that threatened their happiness, even their continued safety?

But what? What could Mary have known? Did Oonagh know it now, albeit without being aware of its danger to her?

Mercifully Hector was absent, and so, as far as Monk could see, was Kenneth. There was nothing to be gained remaining alone. Reluctantly, more tense than he could account for, he straightened up and went down the steps into the throng.

At dinner he was seated next to a large woman in a burgundy and black dress with skirts so huge no one could get within a yard and a half of her. Not that Monk wished to. He would like to have been spared the obligation of conversation also, but that was more than he was granted.

Deirdra was sitting opposite at the farther side of the table, and several times he caught her eye and smiled. He was beginning to think it was a waste of his time, although he knew at least one reason why Oonagh had invited him. She wished to know if he had progressed in discovering where Deirdra spent her money. Did she already know, and was she only looking for him to provide proof so she could confront Deirdra, and perhaps precipitate the quarrel Mary had been killed in order to avoid?

Looking across the table at Deirdra's warm, intelligent, stubborn face, he did not believe it. She might be what some people would refer to as immoral, apparently she was extravagant, but he did not believe she had murdered Mary Farraline, certainly not over something as easily curbed as extravagance.

But he had been wrong before, especially where women were concerned.

No—that was unfair. He had been wrong as to their strength, their loyalty, even their ability to feel passion or conviction—but not their criminality. Why did he doubt himself so deeply?

Because he was failing Hester. Even as he sat there eating a sumptuous meal amid the clatter of cutlery, the chink of glasses, the blaze of lights and murmur of voices, the rustle of silks and creak of stays, Hester was in Newgate Prison awaiting trial, after which, if she were found guilty, they would hang her.

He felt a failure because he was failing.

". . . most becoming gown, Mrs. Farraline," someone was saying to Deirdra. "Most unusual."

"Thank you," Deirdra acknowledged, but without the pleasure Monk would have expected her to show at such a compliment.

"Charming," the large lady next to him added with a downward turn of her ungenerous mouth. "Quite charming. I am very fond of those lines, and jet beading is so elegant, I always think. I had one very like it myself, very like it indeed. Cut a little differently around the shoulder, as I recall, but the design of the stitching was just the same."

One gentleman looked at her with surprise. It was an odd thing to remark, and not altogether polite.

"Last year," the large lady added with finality.

On a wild impulse, a flicker of thought, Monk asked an inexcusable question.

"Do you still have it, ma'am?"

She gave an inexcusable answer.

"No . . . I disposed of it."

"How wise," Monk retorted with sudden viciousness. "That gown"—he glanced at her ample figure—"is more becoming to your . . . station." He had so nearly said "age"; everyone else had, in their minds, said it for him.

The woman turned puce, but said nothing. Deirdra also blushed a light shade of pink, and Monk knew in that moment, although he could not yet prove it, that whatever Deirdra spent her money on, it was not gowns, as she had claimed. She bought hers secondhand, and presumably had a discreet dressmaker alter them to fit her and change them just enough that they were no longer completely identifiable.

She stared at him across the salmon mousse and cucumber and the remains of the sorbet, her eyes pleading.

He smiled and shook his head fractionally, which was ridiculous. He had no reason to keep her secret.

When he encountered Oonagh later, he met her eyes and told her he was investigating the matter but as yet had found no conclusive evidence. The lie troubled him not in the slightest.

In the morning post there was a letter from Callandra. Monk tore it open and read:

My dear William,

I am afraid the news from here is all of the very worst. I have visited Hester as often as I am permitted. She has great courage, but I can see that the strain is telling on her profoundly. I had foolishly imagined that her time in the Scutari hospital would have inured her to at least some of the hardships that Newgate would offer. Of course it is wildly different. The physical portion is relatively negligible. It is the mental suffering, the endless tedium of day after day with nothing to do but let her imagination conjure the worst. Fear is more debilitating than almost anything else.

In Scutari she was endlessly needed, respected, even loved. Here she is idle and the object of hatred and contempt from warders who have no doubt of her guilt.

I hear from Oliver that you have made no significant progress in learning who else may have killed Mary Farraline. I wish I could offer some assistance. I have asked Hester over and over for every memory or impression she might have, but nothing has come to mind which she has not already told you.

I am afraid the worst news of all is something we should have foreseen, but I regret we did not. Not that we could have helped it, even had we known from the outset. Since the crime was committed while the train was in Scotland, whoever is guilty, they have demanded that Hester be tried in Edinburgh. We have no grounds whatever upon which to contest it. She will be returned to stand trial in Edinburgh High Court, and Oliver will not be able to do anything more than offer his personal assistance. Since he is qualified only to practice English Law, he cannot appear for her.

Of course I shall make provision for the best Scottish lawyer I can find, but I confess I feel deeply distressed that Oliver cannot do it. He has the unparalleled advantage that he believes entirely in her innocence.

Still, we must not lose courage. The battle is not yet over, and as long as it is not, we have not lost—nor shall we.

My dear William, spare nothing to learn the truth, neither time nor money are of the least importance. Write to me for anything at all you might need.

Yours faithfully,
Callandra Daviot

He stood in the bitter autumn sunlight with the white paper a blur in front of him; his body was shaking. Rathbone could not defend her. He had never even thought of that—but now that Callandra wrote it, it seemed so obvious. He had not realized until now just how much he had been counting on Rathbone's skill, how the lawyer's past victories had weighed unconsciously on his mind, making him hope the impossible. Now, with one blow, that was ended.

It was minutes before his mind cleared. A dray stopped in the street outside. The cellarman shouted and the driver swore. The sound of the horses stamping on the cobbles and the rattle of wheels came up clearly through the window ajar.

Someone in the Farraline house had tampered with Mary's medicine, with the knowledge it would kill her. Someone had put her pearl brooch in Hester's bag. Greed? Fear? Revenge? Some motive not yet guessed at?

Where did Eilish go down the Kings Stables Road? Who was the rough, uncouth man who waited for Deirdra, and whom she met with such intense and secret conversation before running back into the house? A lover? Surely not, not in such clothes. A blackmailer? More probable. Over what? Her extravagance. Did she gamble, pay off old debts, keep a lover, a relative, an illegitimate child? Or was the extravagance simply to pay off a blackmailer? One thing, it was not to buy fashionable dresses. She had unquestionably lied about that.

It was an ugly resolution, but he decided he must follow her, or the man, and find the truth of it, whatever it was. And he must follow Eilish too. If it was a love affair with her sister's husband, or with anyone else, that also must be known, and beyond doubt.

The first night was totally fruitless. Neither Deirdra nor Eilish appeared. But the second night at a little after midnight the man in the torn coat came again, and after lingering furtively beyond the arc of light from the streetlamp, and again looking at his watch, Deirdra appeared, creeping like a shadow out of the side gate. After a brief, intense exchange, but no overt gesture of affection, they turned away from the house and, side by side, walked rapidly across the grass and down Glenfinlas Street south, exactly the same way Eilish had gone.

This time Monk kept well behind them, which was not difficult because they moved extremely rapidly. For a small woman, Deirdra had a remarkable stride, and did not seem to tire, almost as if something lay ahead of her which filled her with energy and enthusiasm. Monk also stopped and turned around several times to make sure he was not being followed. He still remembered with pain his previous foray along here after Eilish.

He could see no one, apart from two youths going in the opposite direction, a black dog scavenging in the gutter, and a drunk propped against the wall and beginning to slide down.

There was a light wind with a smell of grime and damp on it, and overhead thin clouds darkened the three-quarter moon. Between the pools of the streetlamps the spaces melted into impenetrable shadow. The great mound of the castle towering above them and to the left showed a jagged, now-familiar line against the paler sky.

Deirdra and the man turned left into the Grassmarket. The pavement was narrower here and the five-story buildings made the street seem like the bottom of a deep ravine. There was little sound but that of footsteps, muffled by damp and echo, and the occasional shout, bang of a door or gate, and now and again horses' hooves as some late traveler passed.

The Grassmarket was only a few hundred yards long, then it turned into Cowgate until it crossed South Bridge, running parallel to Canongate, and turned into Holyrood Road. To the right lay the Pleasance and Dumbiedykes, to the left the High Street, the Royal Mile, and eventually Holyrood Palace. In between was an endless maze of alleys and yards, passages between buildings, steps up and steps down, a thousand nooks and doorways.

Monk increased his pace. Where on earth was Deirdra going? Her pace had not slackened at all, nor had she glanced behind her.

Ahead of him Deirdra and the man crossed the road and abruptly disappeared.

Monk swore and ran forward, tripping over a cobble and all but losing his balance. A dog sleeping in a doorway stirred, growled, and then lowered its head again.

Candlemaker Row. He swung around the corner and was just in time to see Deirdra and the man as they passed the beginning of the graveyard to the right, stop, hesitate barely a moment, then go into one of the vast, shadowy buildings to the left.

Monk ran after them, reaching the spot only minutes after they had gone. At first he could see no entrance. The street walls and high wooden gates were a seamless barrier against intrusion.

But they had been here, and now they were not. Something had yielded to their touch. Step by step he moved along, pushing gently, until under his weight one wooden gate swung open just enough to allow him to squeeze inside and to find himself in a cobbled yard facing a building something like a barn. Yellow gaslight streamed from the cracks around an ill-fitting door which would have let through a horse and dray, were it open.

He moved forward gingerly, feeling every step before putting his weight down. He did not want to brush against something and set off an alarm. He had no idea where he was, or what manner of place to expect, or even who else might be inside.

He reached the door in silence and peered in through the wide crack. The sight that met his eyes was so extraordinary, so wildly fanciful and absurd, he stared at it for several minutes before his brain accepted its reality. It was a huge shed, big enough to have built a boat in, except that the structure that crouched in the center of the floor was surely never intended to sail. It had no keel and no possible place for masts. It would have resembled a running chicken, but it had no legs. Its body was large enough for a full-grown man to sit inside, and the wings were outspread as if it fully intended to take off and fly. It seemed to be constructed primarily of wood and canvas. There was some kind of machinery where the heart would have been, were it a real bird.

But more incredible, if anything could be, was Deirdra Farraline, dressed in old clothes, a leather apron over her gown, thick leather gloves over her small, strong hands, her hair scraped back out of her eyes. She was bent forward earnestly laboring over the contraption, tightening screws with delicate, intense efficiency. The man who had come for her was now stripped to his shirtsleeves and was pushing and heaving at another piece of structure which he seemed to be intending to attach to the rear of the bird, by which to extend its tail by some eight or nine feet.

Monk had little enough to lose. He pushed the door open far enough for him to squeeze through and get inside. Neither of the two workers noticed him, so engrossed were they in their labors. Deirdra bent her head, her tongue between her teeth, her brow drawn down in the power of her thought. Monk watched her hands. She was quick and very certain. She knew exactly what she was doing, which tool she wanted and how to use it. The man was patient, and skilled also, but he appeared to be working under her direction.

It was fully five minutes before Deirdra looked up and saw Monk standing in the doorway. She froze.

"Good evening, Mrs. Farraline," he said quietly, moving forward. "Pardon my technical ignorance, but what are you making?" His voice was so normal, so devoid of any criticism or doubt, he might have been discussing the weather at some polite social function.

She stared at him, her dark eyes searching his face for ridicule, anger, contempt, any of the emotions she expected, and finding none of them.

"A flying machine," she said at last.

It was a remark so preposterous no explanation seemed adequate, or even worth attempting. Her companion stood with a spanner in his hand, waiting to see whether she needed support, protection or silence on his part. He was quite clearly embarrassed, but Monk judged it was for her reputation, not his own, and certainly not for their project.

All kinds of questions raced through Monk's head, none of them relevant to Hester's dilemma.

"It must be expensive," he said aloud.

She looked startled. Her eyes widened. She had been ready to counter with defense of the possibility of flying, the necessity to try, the previous ideas and drawings of da Vinci or of Roger Bacon, but the cost was the last thing she had imagined he would mention.

"Yes," she said at last. "Yes, of course it is."

"More expensive than a few fashionable dresses," he went on.

That brought a rush of color to her cheeks as she realized his thoughts.

"It is all my own money," she protested. "I've saved by buying secondhand clothes and having them made over. I never took anything from the family. I know someone has falsified the company books, but I never had a farthing from them. I swear it! And Mary knew what I was doing," she rushed on. "I can't prove it, but she did. She thought it was quite mad, but she enjoyed it. She thought it was a wonderful piece of insanity."

"And your husband?"

"Alastair?" she said incredulously. "Good heavens, no. No." She came towards him, her face puckered with anxiety. "Please, you must not tell him! He would not understand. He is a good man in so many ways, but he has no imagination, and no sense of . . . of . . ."

"Humor?" he suggested.

A flash of temper lit her face, then after a second softened into amusement.

"No, Mr. Monk, not humor either. And you may laugh, but one day it will fly. You don't understand now, but one day you will."

"I understand dedication," he said with a twisted smile. "Even obsession. I understand the desire to do something which is so powerful that all other desires are sacrificed to it."

The man moved forward a step, the spanner held firmly in his hand, but at least for the moment he judged Monk constituted no danger to her, and he remained silent.

"I swear I did not harm Mary, Mr. Monk, nor do I know who did." Deirdra took a deep breath and let it out in a sigh. "What are you going to do about this?"

"Nothing," Monk replied, amazed at his own answer. He had spoken before he had weighed the matter; his reply was instinctive and emotional. "Providing you give me all the help you can to learn who did kill Mrs. Farraline."

She looked at him with dawning perception in her eyes, and as far as he could judge, not so much anger as amazement.

"You are not here for the prosecution, are you?"

"No. I have known Hester Latterly for a long time, and I will never believe she poisoned a patient. She might kill someone in outrage, in self-defense, but never for gain."

The color drained out of her face; her eyes shadowed.

"I see. That means one of us did ... doesn't it?"

"Yes."

"And you want me to help you find out who it is?"

He hesitated, on the edge of reminding her that it was the price of his silence, then decided it would be wiser not to. She already understood as much.

"Don't you want to know?" he asked instead.

She waited only a moment.

"Yes."

He held out his hand, and she took it in her leather-gloved one and clasped it in silent agreement.

CHAPTER
SEVEN

Monk returned to his lodgings cold, tired and faced with a dilemma. He had promised to tell Oonagh if he learned where Deirdra spent her money—or, more accurately, Alastair's money. Now that he knew the answer, every instinct and desire was to tell no one at all, most especially not Oonagh.

Of course her whole enterprise was quite mad, bereft of any connection with reality, but it was an absurd and glorious madness, and harmed no one at all. What if she did spend money on it? The Farralines had plenty of money, and better on a wild and innocuous folly like a flying machine than on gambling, a lover, or to deck herself in silks and jewels in order to look wealthier or more beautiful than her peers. Certainly she should continue.

He found himself striding out with his head high and a lift in his step, and he very nearly went straight past the establishment of Wm. Forster, Innkeeper, in his exhilaration.

In the morning, however, he realized he should have taken the opportunity to strike a better bargain with her. He could have asked her about the company books, and whether there was any basis for Hector's charge. And there was the matter of what he would say to Oonagh. She would never allow him simply to let the subject fade away. And if he were to avoid her, he would have to avoid the Farraline house, which was an impossibility.

Memory of that returned Hester to his thoughts sharply and with a pain that surprised him. At the forefront of his mind he had always considered Hester intelligent, and certainly a useful colleague, but a person about whom his feelings were very mixed. He respected her qualities, at any rate some of them, but he did not really like her. A great many of her mannerisms and attitudes irritated him enormously. Being in her company was like having a small cut on the hands, a paper cut, which was always in danger of being reopened. It was not really an injury, but it was a constant source of discomfort.

And now came the awareness that if he did not succeed in finding proof of who had really killed Mary Farraline, Hester would be gone. He would never see her or speak with her again, never see her square shoulders and proud, rather angular figure come walking towards him, ready to pick a quarrel or enthuse about some cause or other, order him around and express her opinions furiously and with total, blind conviction. If he was facing an impossible case, desperate and defeated, there would be no one who would fight beside him to the end, and beyond, even when reason told them both defeat was already a reality.

He was overwhelmed with a loneliness so deep, staring at the gray cobbles of the Grassmarket and the leaden sky between the heaped and jumbled roofs, the light was worse than the darkness had been, and unreasonably colder. The thought of a world without her was desolating, and the realization that it hurt him so profoundly choked him with anger.

He set out at a brisk walk towards Kings Stables Road, and eventually Ainslie Place. At the front of his mind, his reason for going was to speak to Hector Farraline and press him further to make some sense in the dark and extremely vague accusations he had been making about the company books. If they were indeed being falsified, it might be a motive for murder—if Mary had known, or was about to be told.

His excuse was to report to Oonagh that he was still investigating Deirdra but that so far all he had learned was that she was indeed a poor judge of how to obtain a bargain, and given to extravagance in her attire. If she pressed him for details he would find it difficult to reply, but he was too consumed with emotion for his mind to take heed of such things.

It was a brisk morning after the previous night's frost, but striding up the rise towards Princes Street, it was not at all unpleasant. He was not in any way familiar with Edinburgh, except the immediate vicinity of the Grassmarket now, but he had already developed a liking for the city. The old town was steep and narrow with high buildings, lots of alleys, closes and leg-aching flights of steps, sudden courtyards, and wynds, as they were called; especially eastward towards the Royal Mile, at the far end of which stood Holyrood Palace.

He arrived at Ainslie Place and McTeer let him in with his usual air of gloom and foreboding.

"Good morning to ye, Mr. Monk." He took Monk's hat and coat. "Looks like more rain, I'll be thinking."

Monk was in the mood for an argument.

"More?" he said with wide eyes. "It's quite dry outside. In fact, it's really very agreeable."

McTeer was not put off. "It'll no last," he said with a shake of his head. "Ye'll be to see Mrs. McIvor, no doubt?"

"If I may? I should also like to see Major Farraline, if he is available?"

McTeer sighed. "I couldn't say if he is or no, until I inquire, sir. But I'll be about seein' for ye. If ye'll take a seat in the morning room in the meanwhile."

Monk accepted, and stood in the somber room with its half-drawn blinds and crepe ribbons with surprising apprehension. Now that it actually came to facing Oonagh and lying to her, it was even more difficult than he had expected.

The door opened and he swung around, his mouth dry. She was facing him with calm, measured intelligence. She was not really beautiful, but there was a power of character in her which demanded not only his attention but his admiration as well. Mere form and color bore so quickly, no matter how startling at first. Intelligence, strength of will, the ability to feel great passions and the courage to follow them through, these lasted. And above all he was drawn to the mystery of her, that part he did not understand and she would always hold aloof and apart. It flashed through his mind to wonder about Baird McIvor. What sort of man was he that Mary had liked him? He had won Oonagh's hand in marriage, and yet had fallen in love with Eilish so profoundly he could not mask his feelings even in front of his wife. How could he be so shallow—and so cruel? Surely she had seen? Did she love him so much she forgave his weakness? Or did she love Eilish? The depths to her were immeasurable.

"Good morning, Mr. Monk." She interrupted his thoughts and jerked him into the present. "Have you something to report?" Her words were no more than courteous, but her voice had a vibrancy to it. She was asking a friend, not an employee.

If he hesitated he would betray himself. He was acutely conscious of the sharpness of the perception behind those clear, level eyes.

"Good morning, Mrs. McIvor," he replied. "Not a great deal, I am afraid, except that my investigation so far indicates that your sister-in-law is involved in nothing discreditable. I do not believe she gambles or keeps company with people of poor reputation or habits. I am sure she does not keep a lover, nor is there anyone putting pressure upon her for payment, either of old debts or to keep silent about some unfortunate act of the past." He smiled straight at her, not boldly, but quite casually. Liars could give themselves away by appearing overconfident. "In fact, it would seem she is simply an extravagant woman who has little idea of the value of money and no idea at all how to obtain a bargain, or even a reasonable purchase."

Somewhere beyond the door a maid giggled, and was instantly silent again.

She looked at him steadily, her eyes searching his. It was many years since he had faced anyone with such a penetrating gaze, one which he felt was able to perceive a person's character and read not only judgments but emotions as well, even to sense weaknesses and hungers.

Suddenly she smiled and the light filled her face.

"I'm so relieved, Mr. Monk."

Did she believe him, or was this a polite way of dismissing the subject for the time being?

"I am glad," he acknowledged, surprised how relieved he was that the intensity of the moment had passed.

"Thank you for telling me so rapidly." She walked farther into the room and automatically adjusted an ornament of dried flowers on the central table. It was a desiccated-looking piece and reminded him of funerals.

As if reading his thoughts, or perhaps his face, she pulled the corners of her mouth into a grimace. "It doesn't look well in here, does it? I think I shall have it removed. I would prefer fresh leaves to this, wouldn't you?"

It was unnerving to have one's thoughts so easily observed. It made him wonder if she had seen the lies he had told as well, and simply chose not to remark on them.

"I don't care for artificial flowers," he agreed, forcing himself to keep the smile on his face.

"You must have worked very hard," she went on quite casually.

For a moment he had no idea what she meant, then with a jolt he realized she was referring to his report on Deirdra again. Had he overstated his findings? How could he substantiate such answers if she were to ask him how he knew?

"You are quite sure of what you say?" she pressed. There was a flicker of amusement in her eyes—or was it perception?

There was nothing to do but be brazen. He made the same laughter reflect in his own face. It was not difficult.

"Yes, I am quite certain that I have no evidence that she is anything more than extravagant and unaware of the amount she needs to pay rather than can be persuaded to pay," he answered. "And there is much evidence that she is, in all ways that matter, a thoroughly respectable woman."

She was standing with her back to the window and the light made a halo of her hair.

"Hmm." She sighed a little. "All in so short a time, and yet it has taken you many days to search for evidence that will convict Miss Latterly. . . ."

He should have foreseen that, and he had not. He thought quickly.

"Miss Latterly has taken a great deal of trouble to hide any such evidence, Mrs. McIvor. Mrs. Farraline had nothing to hide. Murder hardly compares with a little extravagance in one's dressmaker, milliner, glover, hosier, bootmaker, haberdasher, furrier, jeweler or perfumier."

"Great heavens!" She laughed, turning to face him. "What an array of people! Yes, perhaps I begin to understand. Anyway, I am obliged to you, and also for having the courtesy to tell me so rapidly. How is your own investigation proceeding?"

"So far I can find nothing with which the defense could trap us," he said truthfully. "I should like very much to learn where she obtained the extra digitalis, but either it was not from an apothecary locally or, if it was, they prefer to remain silent about it."

"I suppose that would not be altogether surprising. The sale would make them, however innocently, party to the murder," she said, watching his face. "People do not like to compromise their reputations, especially if they are in business. It would not improve his trade."

"No." He pursed his lips. "Although I would like to have found him. The defense will point out that she had very little time in which she could have left the house. She was in a city she did not know— she cannot have gone far."

Oonagh drew breath as if to say something, then let it out in a sigh.

"Have you given up, Mr. Monk?" There was only the faintest shadow of challenge in her voice, and disappointment.

He too nearly spoke before thinking. It was on the edge of his tongue to deny it fiercely, then he realized how the emotion would betray him. Carefully he masked his feelings.

"Not yet," he said casually. "But I am close to it. I may soon have done all I can to assure the outcome."

"I hope you will call on us again before you leave Edinburgh?" There was nothing in her face. She needed no artifice and she knew it. Such a thing would be beneath her.

"Thank you, I should like to. You have been most courteous."

He excused himself, and in the empty hall, after she had returned to the nether part of the house, he ran lightly to the stairs and up them to search for Hector Farraline. If he waited for McTeer he would have to explain why he wished to see Hector, and would very likely be politely refused.

He knew the geography of the house from his earlier visits, when he had questioned the servants and been shown Mary's bedroom, the boudoir and the dressing room where the cases and the medicine cabinet had been.

He found Hector's room without difficulty and knocked on the door. It was opened almost immediately with eagerness which was explained when Hector's face fell, and Monk realized he had been expecting someone else, probably McTeer with a little refreshment. Monk had observed that the family did not restrict Hector his liquid sustenance, or seem to make any stringent efforts to keep him sober.

"Oh, the detective, again," Hector said disapprovingly. "Not that ye've found out a damn thing all the time ye've been here! Some poor fool's paying ye money for naught."

Monk went in and closed the door behind him. In other circumstances he might have lost his temper at such language, but he was too intent upon what he might learn from Hector.

"I came looking to find evidence that the defense would put up to clear Miss Latterly," he answered with a candid glance at the older man. He still looked ill, red-eyed and pale-faced, his movement shambling.

"Why did she kill Mary?" Hector said wretchedly, crumpling into the large leather chair near the window. He did not bother to invite Monk to sit down. The room was very masculine; there were scores of books in an oak case against one wall, too far away for Monk to read the titles. A very fine watercolor painting of a Napoleonic hussar hung above the mantelpiece, and another of a soldier of the Royal Scots Greys was on the wall opposite. A little below it was a portrait of an officer in full Highland dress. He was a young man, handsome, with fine features, thick fair hair and wide level eyes. It was several minutes before Monk recognized it as Hector himself, probably thirty years ago. What on earth had happened to the man in that time to change him from what he had been to the pathetic wreck he was now? Surely it must have been more than simply an elder brother with more character, more intelligence and more courage? Were envy and defeat such virulent diseases?

"Why would a woman like that risk everything for a few pearls?" Hector demanded, his voice suddenly sharp with irritation. "It makes no sense, man. She'll be hanged . . . there'll be no mercy for her, ye know?"

"Yes," Monk said very quietly, his throat dry. "I do know. You said something the other day about the company books being falsified. . . ."

"Oh, aye. So they are." Hector said it without the slightest hesitation, and almost without expression.

"By whom?"

Hector blinked. "By whom?" he repeated, as if the question were a curious thing to ask. "I've no idea. Maybe Kenneth. He's the bookkeeper—but he'd be a fool to do it. It'd be so obvious. But then he is a fool."

"Is he?"

Hector looked at him, realizing he was asking a question, not merely responding to a casual remark.

"Not over anything specific," he said slowly. "Just a general opinion."

Monk was certain he was lying, and equally certain he had no intention of telling anyone precisely what Kenneth had done to earn his contempt.

"How do you know?" he asked, sitting down on the smaller, more upright chair opposite him.

"What?" Hector looked composed. "I live in the same house with him, for heaven's sake. Have done for years. What's the matter with you, man?"

Monk was surprised with himself that he was so little irritated.

"I realize how you know he's a fool," he said calmly. "I don't know how you know the books have been meddled with."

"Oh, I see."

"Well, how do you know?"

Hector looked far away. "Something Mary said. Can't remember what, exactly. Annoyed about it though. Very."

Monk leaned forward sharply. "Did she say it was Kenneth? Think, man!"

"No she didn't," Hector replied, puckering his brow. "She was just annoyed."

"But she didn't send for the police?"

"No." He opened his eyes wide and looked at Monk with satisfaction. "That's why I thought it was Kenneth." He shrugged. "But Quinlan is a clever swine. Wouldn't put anything past him either. Upstart. All brains and ambition, greedy for power. Does everything sideways. Never knew why Oonagh was so nice with him. I wouldn't have let him marry Eilish. I'd have sent him on his way, for all that he was charming enough to begin with."

"Even if she loved him?" Monk asked quietly.

Hector said nothing, for several seconds staring out of the window.

"Aye, well, maybe if I thought that . . ."

"Didn't you?"

"Me?" Hector's fair eyebrows rose, wrinkling his brow. "What do I know about it? She doesn't tell me things like that." A look of grief came into his face, so intense and so sudden Monk was embarrassed to have seen it. It was a rare feeling for him, and surprisingly painful. For a moment he was confused, not knowing what to say or do.

But Hector was oblivious of him. The emotion was too consuming and too immediate for him to care what others thought of him.

"But I'd be surprised if he embezzled," he said suddenly. "He's a fly beggar, that one, far too clever to steal."

"What about Mr. McIvor?"

"Baird?" Hector looked up again, his expression changed to one of amusement and pity. "Maybe. Never understood that one. Deep. Mary was fond of him, for all his moods. Used to say there was more good in him than we knew. Which'd no be hard, as far as I'm concerned."

"Has he been married to Oonagh long?"

Hector smiled and it altered his face startlingly. The years of self-abuse dropped away and Monk saw the shadow of the man in the Highland dress thirty years ago. The resemblance to the portrait of Hamish Farraline in the hall was stronger, and yet also in some ways less. The pride and the bearing were more alike, the dignity and self-assurance. But there was a humor in Hector that was absent in his older brother, and oddly, considering the man he was now, a sense of peace.

"Ye'll be thinking they're an odd pair," Hector said, regarding Monk knowingly. "So they are. But I'm told Baird was very dashing when he first came here, very romantic. All dark, brooding looks and hidden passion. Should have been a Highlander, not an Englishman. Oonagh turned down a perfectly good Scots lawyer to take Baird on. Good family, too, the lawyer, very good."

"Mother-in-law?" Monk asked.

Hector's face was incredulous, as if he had seen a sudden flash of light.

"Oh aye! A mother-in-law, right enough. A fair dragon of a woman. Ye know, ye're no half as daft as I thought. That'd make sense, so it would. I can easy imagine Oonagh'd far rather stay here in this house with a man like Baird McIvor than marry an Edinburgh man with a mother of any sort, let alone one like Catherine Stewart. Then she'd no a' bin mistress in her own house, nor kept her hand in the Farraline business as she does now."

"Does she? I thought it was Alastair who was head of the company?"

"Aye, he is, but it's her brains, and Quinlan's, devil take him."

Monk rose to his feet. He did not wish to be caught here by McTeer coming with refreshment for Hector, or Oonagh, as he crossed the hall so long after she had bidden him farewell.

"Thank you, Major Farraline. You have been most interesting. I think I shall take your advice and go and see if I can find out who has meddled with the books of Farralines. Good day to you."

Hector lifted a hand in a half salute, and sat back on his chair again, staring miserably out of the window.

Monk already knew quite a lot about the Farraline printing company, including where to find it, and consequently as soon as he had left Ainslie Place he took a cab along Princes Street into Leith Walk, the long road that led to the Firth of Forth and the dockyards of Leith. The distance from the end of Princes Street was about two miles altogether, and the printing house was halfway. He alighted, paid the driver, and went to look for Baird McIvor.

The building itself was large, ugly and entirely functional. It immediately adjoined other industrial buildings on either side, the largest of which was, according to the legend on the doorway, a rope manufacturer. Inside was a single, vast, open space with the newest part cleared to form a sort of entrance, from which rose a wrought-iron staircase to a landing. There were several doors in sight, presumably offices for the managers of different divisions and for whatever bookkeepers and other clerks were necessary. The rest of the interior was given over to the printing itself, being filled with presses, typesetting equipment, racks of type and inks. Bales of paper were stored in enormous piles at the far end, along with cloth for binding, thread and yet further machinery. There was no bustle, but a steady hum of industry and regulated movement.

Monk asked the clerk who approached him if he might speak with Mr. McIvor. He did not state his business, and the man must have assumed it had something to do with the company, because he did not inquire but led him up to the first fine hardwood door, knocked and opened it.

"A Mr. Monk to see you, Mr. McIvor."

Monk thanked him and went in before Baird could have the opportunity to refuse. He barely glanced at the neat bookshelves, the bright gas lamp hissing on the wall, the odd pieces of blank paper on the desk (presumably there for McIvor to judge their comparative quality), and the piles of books sitting on the floor. His attention was on Baird and the surprise and alarm on his face.

"Monk?" He half rose from his desk. "What do you want here?"

"Just a little of your time," Monk said without a smile. He had already concluded that he would learn nothing from Baird by simply asking him. He would have used subtlety had he the time, or the cool- ness of brain, but he had not. He must resort to force. "I have evi- dence which strongly suggests that the company books have been tampered with and money has been taken."

Baird blanched and anger filled his dark eyes, but before he could protest or deny, Monk went on. This time he smiled, but it was wolf- ish, a baring of the teeth, and offered no comfort at all.

"I understand the defense has employed a brilliant barrister." That was hope ahead of knowledge, but if it was not true now, he would do everything within his power to see that it became true. "We don't want them finding this and making some suggestions to the jury that it was the true motive for Mrs. Farraline's murder, in order to cause reasonable doubt that it was in fact this nurse."

Baird sat back in his chair and stared at him, comprehension fill- ing his face and resentment dying away.

"No . . . no, of course not," he said grudgingly, but his eyes were still wary and Monk noticed that there was a very fine bead of sweat on his brow. It sharpened his attention and he determined to pursue it to the end.

"After all," he added, "if it were so, it might provide an excellent motive for murder. I imagine Mrs. Farraline would not have permitted such a crime to pass unpunished, even if privately rather than pub- licly?"

Baird hesitated, but the expression on his face was as much anger and grief as any overt fear. He was a more complex man than Monk had at first assumed—his rather contemptuous assessment of a man who would prefer Eilish to Oonagh.

"No," Baird conceded. "She would deal with embezzlement one way or another. I imagine, if it were a member of the family, she would do it herself. In fact, even if it were not, she would still choose not to make it public. Such things are not good for a company's reputation."

"Quite. But it would not be pleasant for the culprit."

"I imagine not. But what makes you think there is anything wrong with the books? Has Kenneth said something? Oh . . . is it Kenneth you suspect?"

"I don't suspect anyone in particular." Monk said it in such a way as to leave it open whether he was speaking the truth or deliberately being evasive. Fear was a most effective catalyst from which might come all manner of other revelations.

Baird considered for several minutes before continuing. Monk tried to judge whether it was guilt or the desire not to be unjust to someone else which held him. On balance he thought guilt; there was still that beading of sweat on his face, and his eyes, for all their straight, steady gaze, had an evasiveness about them.

"Well, I know of no way in which I can help you," Baird said at last. "I have little to do with the financial side of the business. I work with the paper and the binding. Quinlan works with the print itself. Kenneth does the accounting. When Alastair is here, he makes the major decisions: which clients to accept, new business, that sort of thing."

"And Mrs. McIvor? I understand she is also concerned in the management. I have heard she is most gifted."

"Yes." His expression was beyond Monk's ability to read; it could have been pride, or resentment, or even humor. A dozen thoughts flashed across Baird's face, and were equally quickly gone. "Yes," he repeated. "She has a remarkable acumen. Alastair very often takes her advice, both in business decisions and technical ones. Or to be more accurate, it is Quinlan who takes her advice on matters of print style, typeface and so on."

"So Mr. Fyffe has nothing to do with the accounting?"

"Quinlan? No, nothing at all." He said it with regret, and then savage self-mockery the instant after.

Monk found himself more deeply confused about him. How could a man of such emotion, self-perception and sense of irony be in love with Eilish, who seemed to have nothing to offer except physical beauty? It was so shallow, so short-lived. Even the loveliest thing on earth grows tedious if there is no art of companionship, no laughter, wit, imagination, power to love in return, even at times to provoke, to criticize, to lift by struggle, quarrel and change.

The thought brought Hester back to his mind with sharpness like a shooting pain.

"Then I had better look into it," he said with a curtness totally unwarranted by the conversation.

Baird looked reluctant.

"That would be better than sending in auditors," Monk went on. It was a threat, and Baird recognized it as such.

"Oh certainly," he said too quickly. "By all means. That would be expensive, and make people anxious that we have cause to think there is something wrong. Yes, you look into it by all means, Mr. Monk."

Monk smiled, or perhaps it was more of a grimace. So Baird was quite happy that Monk could find nothing wrong in the books, or if he did, it was not Baird who had put it there. And yet he was afraid. For what?

"Thank you," he accepted, and turned to go back out into the corridor again as Baird rose from his desk.

He spent all the rest of the day at the Farraline printing company, and found nothing whatever that furthered his cause. If the books had been tampered with, he had not the requisite skill to find the evidence of it. Tired, his head aching and his temper extremely short, he left at half past five and went back to his lodgings in the Grassmarket, to find a letter from Rathbone awaiting him. It was devoid of good news, simply informing him of his own progress, which was woefully little.

Monk spent over three hours of that evening standing in Ainslie Place, growing colder and more wretched, hoping Eilish would make another sortie to wherever it was she visited, somewhere beyond Kings Stables Road. But midnight came and went, and no one stirred from number seventeen.

The following night he took up the same position, by now sunk into an icy gloom. And at a little after midnight he was rewarded by seeing a shadowy figure emerge, cross the open area of the center, pass within ten feet of where he stood motionless, his body trembling with cold and excitement, and once again walk rapidly along Glenfinlas Street, past Charlotte Square towards the crossroads.

He moved after her, keeping thirty yards' distance between them except close to junctions where she might turn and he lose sight of her. And this time he also looked back over his shoulder at regular intervals. He had no intention of being struck from behind again, and ending up senseless on the ground, with Eilish vanished into who knew where?

The night was colder than last time, a rime of frost forming on the stones of the pavement and making the air tingle on his lips and in his lungs. He was glad enough to move quickly, although the speed and ease of her pace surprised him. He had not expected so languid and lazy a woman to have the stamina.

As before, she went past the Princes Street Gardens along Lothian Road and turned left along the Kings Stables Road, passing almost under the shadow of the castle, tonight its massive, rugged outline only a denser black against the cloudy, starless sky.

She crossed Spittal Street, making towards the Grassmarket. Surely she could not have a tryst with anyone who lived in such an area? It was full of tradesmen, innkeepers and transients like himself. And what about Baird McIvor? If the emotion he had thought between them was in fact only one-sided, then he had been more profoundly misled than ever before.

No, that was not true. His ability to be misled by women, beautiful women, was almost boundless. He remembered with chagrin Hermione, and how he had believed her softness of word and deed to be compassion, and it had proved to be merely a profound desire to avoid anything that might cause her pain. She chose the easier path, in anything, because she had no hunger in her soul that would drive her beyond hurt in order to win what she wished for. There was no passion in her at all, no need either to give or to receive. She was afraid of life. How more grossly mistaken could he have been in anyone?

So was Eilish deceiving the gullible Baird every bit as much as her sharper, more critical husband? And Oonagh? Had she any idea what her beloved little sister was doing?

Had Mary known?

There were still people around the Grassmarket. The sparse gas lamps casting pools of yellow light showed them standing around or leaning idly, staring about them. An occasional burst of laughter, jerky

192

ANNE PERRY

and more than a little drunk, gave indication of their state. A woman
in a ragged dress sauntered past and one of the men shouted at her.
She called back in a dialect so broad Monk did not understand her
words, although her meaning was plain enough.

Eilish took no notice, but she did not seem afraid and her pace
was steady as she passed them and continued on.

Monk remembered to look behind him, but if there was anyone
following, he did not know it. Certainly there were others about. One
man, black-coated, was ambling along about thirty feet behind him,
but there was nothing to indicate he was following Monk, and he did
not take any notice when Monk stopped for several seconds before going on again. By now the man was almost up to him.

They were approaching the corner of Candlemaker Row where
Deirdra had turned off, and then the towering, cavernous slums of
Cowgate, and all the steps and wynds between Holyrood Road and
Canongate. Eilish had walked almost a mile and a half, and showed no
signs of slowing down, still less of having reached her destination.
What was even stranger, she seemed to be completely familiar with
the surroundings. Never once did she hesitate or check where she was.

She crossed the George IV Bridge, and behind her Monk glanced
up towards the beautiful Victorian terrace with its classical facade, like
the old town from which they had come. He had thought perhaps she
would turn and go up there. It was the sort of place where a lover
might live, although what manner of lover would expect, or even allow, a woman to come to him, let alone walk it alone, and at night?

At the far end, only a hundred yards away, was the Lawnmarket,
and the home of the infamous Deacon Brodie, that portly, dandy figure who had been a pillar of Edinburgh's society by day, sixty years before, and a violent housebreaker by night. According to tavern gossip,
which Monk had listened to readily in the hope of learning something
about the Farralines, Deacon Brodie's infamy rested in the duplicity of
a man who in daylight inspected and advised on the security of the
very premises he robbed by night. He had lived in the utmost respectability, in the Lawnmarket, and kept not one mistress with an illegitimate family, but two. He had escaped capture when his accomplices
were arrested, fleeing to Holland, only to be caught by a simple trick
and returned to Edinburgh, where he was hanged with a jest on his
lips in 1788.

But Eilish did not turn up towards the Lawnmarket; she continued on and plunged into the filthy cavernous gloom of Cowgate.

Monk followed resolutely after her.

Here the lamps were farther between and the pavement in places only eighteen inches wide. The cobbles of the street were rough and he had to go carefully to avoid turning his ankle. Huge tenements reared above him, four and five stories high, every room filled with a dozen or so people, crowded in without water or sanitation. He knew it from long familiarity with London. The smell was the same, dirt, weariness and all-pervasive human effluent.

Then suddenly the darkness was total and he fell into a violent sensation of pain, both before and behind.

When he woke up he was numb with cold, so stiff he had difficulty in making his arms and legs obey him, and his head ached so badly he hated to open his eyes. There was a small brown dog licking his face in friendly and hopeful curiosity. It was still dark, and Eilish was nowhere to be seen.

He climbed to his feet with difficulty, apologizing to the dog for having nothing he could give it, and set off on the short, bitter walk back to the Grassmarket.

However, he was all the more determined not to be beaten, least of all by a shallow and worthless woman like Eilish Fyffe. Whether her midnight trysts had any relevance to her mother's death or not, he was going to find out exactly where she went and why.

Accordingly the following night he waited for her, this time not in Ainslie Place but at the corner where the Kings Stables Road ran into the Grassmarket. At least he would save himself the walk. During the day he also purchased a stout walking stick and a very well constructed tall hat, which he jammed on his still-throbbing head.

During the day he had taken the precaution of walking the length of Cowgate so he would know every yard of it in the semidarkness of its sporadic gas lamps. In the shortening autumn light it had been a grim sight. The buildings were in ill repair, crumbling stonework, battered, half-obliterated signs, walls stained and weatherworn, gutters shallow and running with water and refuse. The narrow wynds leading off it up towards the High Street were crowded with people, carts, washing and piles of vegetables and rubbish.

Now as he stood in the doorway of an ironmonger's, waiting for Eilish, he could picture every yard of it in his mind, and he was determined not to be caught again.

It was twenty minutes past midnight when he saw her slender figure emerge from the Kings Stables Road and turn into the Grassmarket. She was going a little more slowly this time, perhaps because she was carrying a large parcel of some sort, which, to judge from her less graceful, more awkward gait, was quite heavy.

He waited until she was about fifteen yards past him, then he moved out of the doorway and walked after her, keeping close to the wall and swinging his stick casually, but with an extremely firm grip.

Eilish walked the length of the Grassmarket, crossed the George IV Bridge without looking right or left, and went into Cowgate. She gave no sign whatever of knowing that anyone was following her. Never once did she hesitate or glance backwards.

What on earth was she doing?

He closed the gap between them now that they were in the dim cavern of Cowgate. He must not lose sight of her. She might stop any minute and disappear into one of these high buildings and he would have great difficulty in finding her again. They were all at least four or five stories high, and inside would be like a rabbit warren, passages and stairs, half landings, room after room, all crowded with people.

And of course there were the stairways and alleys and wynds, any one of which she might have taken.

Why did she know no fear, a beautiful woman walking alone after midnight in such a place? The only conceivable answer was that she was perfectly aware of someone following her to protect her. Baird McIvor? It seemed absurd. Why on earth meet here? It made no kind of sense. No stretch of the imagination, short of insanity in both of them, accounted for it as a lovers' tryst. There were any number of easier, safer and more romantic places far nearer home.

They passed South Bridge, and ahead of Eilish he saw a shadowy figure, body bent, a sack across its shoulders, hurry from a side alley and disappear into another, heading towards the Infirmary. With an involuntary shudder he remembered the grotesque crimes of Burke and Hare, as if he had seen a thirty-year ghost heading towards Surgeon's

Hall with a newly murdered corpse on his back to present to the huge, one-eyed anatomist Dr. Knox.

He glanced backwards nervously, but there was no one unwarrantably close.

They were level with Blackfriars' Wynd and Cardinal Beaton's house on one corner with its jutting overhang and crumbling stone. His information earlier that day had told him it had been built in the early fifteen hundreds by the then-archbishop of Glasgow and chancellor of Scotland during the regency and the monarchy of King James V, before England and Scotland were united.

Next was the Old Mint, a dilapidated building with a walled-up doorway with the inscription over it BE MERCIFUL UNTO ME, O GOD. He knew from the daytime that there was also an advertisement for Allison the chimney sweep, and a little picture of two sweeps running, but he could not see it now.

Eilish continued on her way, and Monk gripped his stick more tightly. He disliked carrying it. The feeling of it in his hand brought back sickening memories of violence, confusion and fear, and above all overwhelming guilt. But the prickling in the back of his neck was a primal fear even greater, and against his conscience his hand closed more tightly. He turned every now and again to look behind him, but he saw only indeterminate shadows.

Then suddenly at St. Mary's Wynd she turned sharply left and he almost lost her. He ran forward and only just prevented himself from colliding with her as she stopped in front of a dark doorway, the parcel still in her hands.

She turned and looked at him, for an instant afraid, then as her eyes, used to the darkness, went beyond him she cried out.

"No!"

Monk swung around just in time to raise his stick and fend off the blow.

"No!" Eilish said again, her voice powerful with complete authority. "Robbie, put it down! There is no need. . . ."

Reluctantly the man lowered the cudgel and stood waiting, still gripping it ready.

"You are very determined, Mr. Monk," Eilish said quietly. "You had better come in."

Monk hesitated. Out here in the street he had a fighting chance if he were attacked, inside he had no idea how many men there might be. In an area like Cowgate he could be disposed of without trace or necessity for explanation. Grisly visions of Burke and Hare came back like nightmares yet again.

Eilish's voice was full of laughter, although he could not see her face in the gloom.

"There is no need to be alarmed, Mr. Monk. It is not a den of thieves, it is simply a ragged school. I'm sorry you were struck when you followed me before. Some of my pupils are very jealous for my protection. They did not know who you were. Creeping along the Grassmarket behind me, you cut a very sinister figure."

"A ragged school?" He was stunned.

She mistook his amazement for ignorance.

"There are a lot of people in Edinburgh who can neither read nor write, Mr. Monk. Actually this is not a ragged school in the legal sense. We don't teach children. There are others doing that. We teach adults. Perhaps you didn't realize what a handicap it is to a man not to be able to read his own language? To be able to read is the doorway into the rest of the world. If you can read, you can make the acquaintance of the best minds of the present, no matter where they live, and all the past as well!" Her voice rose with enthusiasm. "You can listen to the philosophy of Plato, or you can go on adventures with Sir Walter Scott, see the past unfold before you, explore India or Egypt, you can—" She stopped abruptly, then continued in a lower tone. "You can read the newspapers and know what the politicians are saying, and form some judgment for yourself whether it is true or not. You can read the signs in the streets and shop windows, and on labels and medicine bottles."

"I understand, Mrs. Fyffe," he said quietly, but with a sincerity that was totally new to him where she was concerned. "And I know what ragged schools are. It is simply an explanation which had not occurred to me."

Then she laughed aloud. "How very candid of you. You thought I had some assignation? In Cowgate? Really, Mr. Monk! With whom, may I ask? Or you thought I was a master thief, perhaps, come to divide the spoils with my accomplices? A sort of female Deacon Brodie?"

"No. . . ." It was a long time since a woman had embarrassed him in this way, but honesty compelled him to admit he deserved it.

"You had better come in, all the same." She turned back to the door. "Unless that is all you wanted to know? Had you better not prove me truthful?" There was mockery in her voice, and underneath the amusement it was charged with emotion.

He agreed, and followed her into the narrow corridors of the tenement. She climbed up rickety stairs, along another corridor, the man Robbie a few steps behind, his cudgel at his side. They mounted more stairs and finally came into a large room overlooking the street. It was clean, especially for such a place, and by now he was used to the general smell of such a region. There was no furniture at all except one frequently repaired wooden table, and on it was a pile of books and papers, several inkwells and a dozen or so quills, a penknife for recutting the nibs, and several sheets of blotting paper. Her students were a collection of some thirteen or fourteen men of all ages and conditions, but everyone dressed in clean clothes, although ragged enough to have earned the school its epithet. Their faces lit with enthusiasm when they saw her, then closed in sudden, dark suspicion as Monk came in behind her.

"It's all right," she assured them quickly. "Mr. Monk is a friend. He has come to help tonight."

Monk opened his mouth to protest that that was not so, then changed his mind and nodded agreement.

Soberly they all sat on the floor, mostly cross-legged, and balancing books on their knees, and papers on top of the books, with others on the floor between them, they slowly and painstakingly wrote their alphabets. Frequently they looked at Eilish for help and approval, and in total solemnity she gave it, offering a correction here, a word of praise there.

After two hours of writing, they moved to reading, their reward for labor. With many stumbles and a lot of encouragement, one by one, they lurched through a chapter of *Ivanhoe*. Their elation at the end of it, at twenty-five to four in the morning, as they thanked her, and Monk, was abundant reward for Monk's own weariness. Then they filed out for an hour's sleep before starting the long day's work.

When the last of them had gone, Eilish turned to Monk wordlessly.

"The books?" he asked, although he knew the answer and did not care in the slightest if it robbed Farraline & Company of its entire profits.

"Yes of course they are from Farralines," she said, looking directly into his eyes. "Baird gets them for me, but if you tell anyone, I shall deny it. I don't think there is any proof. But you wouldn't do that anyway. It has nothing to do with Mother's death, and won't either exonerate or condemn Miss Latterly."

"I didn't know Baird could get to the company accounts." That would explain why he had been so nervous.

"He can't," she agreed with amusement. "I want books, not money. And I wouldn't steal money, even if I did need it. Baird prints extra books, or declares the print runs short. It has nothing to do with accounting."

That made sense.

"Your uncle Hector said someone had been falsifying the accounts."

"Did he?" She sounded only slightly surprised. "Well, maybe they have. It must be Kenneth, but I don't know why. Although Uncle Hector does drink an awful lot, and sometimes talks the most terrible nonsense. He remembers things I don't think ever happened, and confuses one time with another. I wouldn't take a lot of notice."

He was about to say that he had to, in order to guard the prosecution, but he was weary of lies, especially useless ones, and this was not the night for more of them. He had had to reverse all his judgments of Eilish. She was anything but shallow or lazy, and far from stupid. Of course she had to sleep half the morning; she gave up most of the night. And gave it to those who returned her no public or financial reward for it. And yet she was obviously more than pleased with what she received. In this bare lamplit room she glowed with a deep joy. Now he knew why she walked with her head high and her step proud, where the secret smile came from and the thoughts that were removed from the family conversations.

And he knew why Baird McIvor loved her above his own wife.

Actually he knew in that moment also that Hester would have liked her, even admired her.

"I'm not trying to prove that Miss Latterly killed your mother," he said impulsively. "I'm trying to prove that she did not."

She looked at him curiously. "For money? No. Do you love her?"

"No." Then instantly he wished he had not denied it so quickly. "Not in the way you mean," he added, feeling his face burn. "She is a great friend, a very deep friend. We have shared many experiences in the pursuit of justice in other cases. She . . ."

Eilish was smiling. Again there was a faint hint of mockery in her eyes.

"You don't need to explain, Mr. Monk. In fact, please don't. I don't believe you anyway. I know what it is to love when you really don't want to at all." Without warning the laughter vanished totally from her face and deep pain replaced it. Perhaps pain had been closer to the surface all the time. "It changes all your plans and alters everything. One moment you are playing on the shore, the next the tide has you, and struggle as you might, you cannot get back to the land again."

"You are speaking of your own feelings, Mrs. Fyffe. I am a friend of Miss Latterly. I don't feel in the least like that about her." He said all the words clearly and vehemently, and he knew from her face that she did not believe him. He was angry, and there was a curious choking in his throat. He felt absurdly disloyal. "It is perfectly possible to be friendly with someone without a feeling anything like the one you describe," he said again.

"Of course it is," she agreed, moving to the door. "I will walk with you as far as the Grassmarket, to see you are safe."

It was ludicrous. He was a powerful man, armed with a stick, and she was a slender woman, six inches shorter and built like a flower. She made him think of an iris in the sun. He laughed outright.

She led the way down the dim stairs back to the way out, talking to him over her shoulder as he followed.

"How many times have you been struck on the way, Mr. Monk?"

"Twice, but . . ."

"Was it painful?"

"Yes, but . . ."

"I'll see you home, Mr. Monk." There was only the faintest shadow of a smile on her lips.

He took a deep breath. "Thank you, Mrs. Fyffe."

In Newgate, Hester swung from moods of hard-fought-for hope, down to engulfing despair, and up the long incline back to hope again. The boredom and the sense of helplessness were the worst afflictions. Physical labor, however pointless, would have dulled the edges of pain, and she would have slept. As it was she lay awake in almost total darkness, shivering with cold, her imagination torturing her with infinite possibilities—and always returning to the same one, the short walk from the cell to the shed where the rope awaited her. She was not afraid of death itself, it was that she realized with icy pain that the belief she thought she had as to what lay after was simply not strong enough to stand in the face of reality. She was frightened as she had never been before. Even in the battlefield death would have been sudden, without warning or time to think. And after all she had not been alone. She had faced it with others, almost all of them suffering far more than she. Her mind had been filled with what she could do for them; it had left no room for thoughts of herself. Now she realized what a blessing that had been.

The wardresses continued to treat her with a coldness and unique scorn, but she became accustomed to it and the small irritant gave her something to fight against, as one digs nails into the palm of the hand when fighting a greater agony.

One particularly cold day the cell door opened and, after the briefest word from the wardress, her sister-in-law, Imogen, came in. Hester was surprised to see her; she had accepted Charles's word as final and had not expected him to relent. The darker the outlook became, the less likely was he to do so.

Imogen was fashionably dressed, as if going to pay afternoon calls on Society, her skirts broad-sweeping and flounced, her bodice tight and her sleeves elaborately decorated. Her bonnet was trimmed with flowers.

"I'm sorry," she said instantly, seeing Hester's face and glancing only momentarily at the bare cell. "I had to tell Charles I was going to call on the Misses Begbie. Please don't tell him I was here, if you don't mind. I—I would rather not face a quarrel just now." She looked both embarrassed and apologetic. "He—" She stopped.

"He commanded you not to come," Hester finished for her. "Don't worry, of course I shall not tell him." She wanted to thank Imogen for coming—she really was grateful—and yet the words stuck in her mouth. It all sounded artificial, when it should have been most real.

Imogen fished in her reticule and brought out sweet-smelling soap and a little bag of dried lavender so fragrant Hester could smell it even from two yards distance, and the femininity of it brought the tears uncontrollably to her eyes.

Imogen looked up quickly and her polite expression vanished and emotion flooded her face. Impulsively she dropped the soap and lavender and moved forward, taking Hester in her arms and holding her with a strength Hester would not have thought her to possess.

"We'll win!" she said fiercely. "You didn't kill that woman and we'll prove it. Mr. Monk may not be very nice, but he is wildly clever, and quite ruthless. Remember how he solved the Grey case when everyone thought it was impossible. And he is on your side, my dear. Don't ever give up hope."

Hester had managed to keep her composure with every other visitor she had had, even Callandra, difficult as that had been, but now she found it too much. The long denial would not last anymore. Clinging on, she wept in Imogen's arms until she was exhausted and a kind of peace of despair came over her. Imogen's words had been intended to comfort, but perversely they had focused her mind on the truth she had been struggling against all the time since she had first been moved here from the Coldbath Fields. All that Monk, or anyone else, could do might not be enough. Sometimes innocent people were hanged. Even if Monk or Rathbone were to prove the truth afterwards, it would be no comfort to her, and certainly no help.

But now instead of the struggle against it, against the fear and the injustice, there was something inside her close to acceptance. Perhaps it was only tiredness, but it was better than the desperate struggle. There was a sort of release in it.

Now she did not want to listen to talk of hope, because she had passed beyond it, but yet it would be cruel to tell Imogen so, and the new calm was too fragile to be trusted. Perhaps there was still something in her which clung to unreality? She did not want to put it into words.

Imogen stepped back and looked at her. She must have seen or sensed some change, because she said nothing more about it but bent and picked up the dropped soap and the lavender.

"I didn't ask if you could have them," she said matter-of-factly. "Maybe you should hide them?"

Hester sniffed and took out her handkerchief to blow her nose. Imogen waited.

"Thank you," Hester said at last, reaching out to take them and push them down the front of her dress. The soap was a trifle uncomfortable, but even that had its own kind of satisfaction.

Imogen sat down on the cot, her skirts in a huge swirl around her, exactly as if she were visiting a lady of Society; although since Mr. Latterly Senior's disgrace, she did not do that anymore. The Misses Begbie were now the height of her aspirations.

"Do you ever see anyone else?" she asked with interest. "I mean other than that fearful woman who let me in. She is a woman, I suppose?"

Hester smiled in spite of herself. "Oh yes. If you saw the way she looks at Oliver Rathbone, you'd know she was."

"You don't mean it?" Imogen was incredulous, laughter touching her in spite of the place and the occasion. "She makes me think of Mrs. MacDuff, my cousin's governess. We used to rag her terribly. I blush when I think how cruel we were. Children can be devastatingly candid. Sometimes the truth is better not told. It may be in one's own heart one knows it, but one can behave so much better if one is not forced to keep looking at it."

Hester smiled wryly. "I think I am in exactly that situation, but I have very little else to take my attention."

"Have you heard from Mr. Monk?"

"No."

"Oh." Imogen looked surprised, and suddenly Hester felt as if Monk had let her down. Why had he not written? Surely he must know how much it would have meant to have received even a word of encouragement? Why was he so thoughtless? And that was a stupid question, because she knew the answer. There was little tenderness in his nature, and what there was was directed towards women like Imogen, gentle, sweet-natured, dependent women who complemented his own strengths, not women like Hester, whom he regarded at the best of times as a friend, like another man, and at the worst as opinionated, abrasive, dogmatic, and an offense to her own sex.

Loyalty and justice would demand that he search for the truth, but to expect or look for comfort as well was bound to end in hurt and in an inevitable sense of having been let down.

And that was precisely what she did feel.

Imogen was watching her closely. She read her as only another woman could.

"Are you in love with him?" she asked.

Hester was horrified. "No! Certainly not! I would not go so far as to say he is everything I despise in a man, but he is certainly a great deal. Of course he is clever, I would not take that from him for a moment, but he is on occasion both arrogant and cruel and I would not trust him to be gentle, or not to take advantage of weakness, for a minute."

Imogen smiled.

"My dear, I did not ask if you trusted or admired him, or even if you liked him. I asked if you were in love with him, which is quite a different matter."

"Well I am not. And I do like him . . . sometimes. And . . ." She took a deep breath. "And there are matters in which I would trust him absolutely. Matters of honor where justice is concerned, or courage. He would fight against any odds, and without counting the cost, to defend what he believed to be right."

Imogen looked at her with a strange mixture of amusement and pain.

"I think, my dear, you are painting him with your own virtues, but that is no harm. We all tend to do that. . . ."

"I am not!"

"If you say so." Imogen dismissed the matter with disbelief. "What about Mr. Rathbone? I must say I rather like him. He is such a gentleman and yet I formed the opinion he is extremely clever."

"Of course he is." She had never doubted it, and as she spoke, memories of a startling moment of intimacy returned with a sweetness she was not sure now if she imagined or not. She would never in the world have kissed a man in such a way without meaning it intensely. But she did not know men in that way, and perhaps they were very different. All she had observed told her that they were. She was disinclined to attach any importance to it at all. She realized with a hollow ache how little she knew, and that now she would almost certainly die without ever having loved or been loved in return. Self-pity welled up inside her like a tide, and ashamed of it as she was, it still filled her.

"Hester," Imogen said gravely, "you are giving in. It is not like you to be pathetic, and when all this is over you are going to hate yourself for not having matched up to the moment."

"Brave words are all very well when you are talking to somebody else," Hester replied with a twisted smile. "It is a different matter when you are facing the reality of death. Then there isn't any afterwards."

Imogen looked very pale and there was distress plain in her eyes, but she did not flinch. "You mean your death would be somehow different from other peoples'? Different from the soldiers you nursed?"

"No ... no, of course not. That would be arrogant and ridiculous." Being reminded of the soldiers brought back their agonized faces and broken bodies to her mind. She would die quickly, without being mutilated or wasted with fevers or dysentery. She should be ashamed of her cowardice. Many of them had been younger than she was now; they had tasted even less of life.

Imogen forced a smile, and their eyes met for a long, steady moment. There was no need for Hester to speak her thanks. She was still painfully afraid, still uncertain what lay after the hangman's shed and the sudden darkness, but she would face it with the same dignity she had seen in others, and be fit to belong to the vast company who had already taken that path, and done it with head high and eyes unblinking.

Imogen knew when to leave, and she did not mar what was achieved by staying and talking of trivialities. She hugged Hester quickly, then with a swirl of her skirts, went to the door and demanded to be let out. The wardress came, regarded Imogen with contempt in her scrubbed face with its screwed-back hair, and then as Imogen stared back at her without flinching or averting her eyes, the contempt died away and was replaced by something that held envy and a flicker of respect. She held the door open and Imogen sailed through it without a word.

———

The last visitor in Newgate was Oliver Rathbone. He found Hester much calmer than on the previous occasion. She faced him with none of the barely suppressed emotion of earlier times, and far from being comforted, he found himself alarmed.

"Hester! What has happened?" he demanded. The moment the cell door was closed and they were alone, he went straight to her and took her hands in his. "Has someone said or done something to distress you?"

"Why? Because I am not so afraid anymore?" she said with a ghost of a smile.

It was on his tongue to say that she had given up. The very lack of anguish in her face meant that she was no longer struggling between hope and despair. There was no possibility of knowledge that she would be exonerated. At this late date that could not be. She must have accepted defeat. Not for an instant did it occur to him that she had in fact killed Mary Farraline, either intentionally or by accident. He was furious with her for surrendering. How could she, after all the battles they had fought together for other people, and won? She had known physical danger the equal of most soldiers in the field, long hours, hardship, privation, and come through it all with high heart and passionate spirit intact. She had faced her parents' ruin and death and survived it. How dare she crumble now?

And yet he was bitterly aware that she could lose. The courage required was that which goes on fighting when there is no cause to hope, a blind courage without reason, even in the face of reason. How could he expect that of anyone?

Except that to see her vilified and snuffed out, her spirit silenced, never to be able to speak with her again, was a prospect which filled him with a void which was intolerably painful. His own professional failure did not even cross his mind. It was only long afterwards that the realization occurred to him with amazement.

"I have had a great deal of time to think about it," she went on quietly, cutting across his thoughts. "All the fear in the world is not going to change anything, only rob me of what little I have." She laughed a little jerkily. "And perhaps I am just too tired for anything which requires so much energy of mind."

All sorts of words of encouragement hovered on his lips: that there was plenty of time yet in which they could still learn something damning to one of the Farraline family, at least enough to raise doubts in any juror's eyes; that Monk was brilliant and ruthless, and would never give up; that Callandra had hired the services of the finest criminal lawyer in Edinburgh, and Rathbone would be at his elbow throughout; even that prosecutors frequently tripped themselves with overconfidence or that witnesses lied, were afraid, condemned each other out of fear or spite or greed, that they recanted lies when faced with the majesty of the law in session, contradicted themselves and each other. And all of the words died before he spoke them. All the truth had already been thought and known between them. To put words to them yet again, now when it was too late, would only show that after all he had not understood.

"We leave the day after tomorrow," he said instead.

"For Edinburgh?"

"Yes. I cannot travel with you; they will not permit it. But I shall be on the same train, and with you in heart." It flashed across his mind that the words sounded sentimental, but he had said precisely what he meant. All his emotions would be with her, with the mounting shame and embarrassment, the physical discomfort, because he knew she would be in manacles and that the wardress would not leave her for an instant, even for the most intimate necessities. But immeasurably more than that, they both knew it might be the last journey she would make, out of England forever.

"They danced all night on the eve of Waterloo," he said suddenly for no reason, except that the British had won that epochal battle.

"Who did?" she said with a wry smile. "Wellington—or the Emperor of the French?"

He smiled back. "Wellington, of course. Remember you are British!"

"The charge of the Light Brigade?" she countered.

He held her hands very hard. "No, my dear, never under my command. I have been desperate at times, but never foolhardy. If we must have that miserable war, then the Thin Red Line." He knew they were both familiar with those incredible hours when the Highland infantry had withstood charge after charge of the Russian cavalry. At times they had been only one man deep, and as each man had fallen another had replaced him. All through the dreadful slaughter the line had not broken, and in the end it was the enemy who had retreated. Hester would have nursed men injured in that stand, perhaps she had even seen it from the heights.

"All right," she said with a catch in her voice. "The Heavy Brigade—win or lose."

CHAPTER
EIGHT

———

Rathbone had written to Monk telling him which train he would take, without mentioning that it would be the same one on which Hester would be brought. Therefore when they pulled into Edinburgh's Waverley Station on a gray morning he was fully expecting to see Monk on the platform. A small part of him even hoped he would have some news, however slight, something which would provide a new thread to follow. Time was desperately short, and all he had so far were a few possible motives for other people, which a competent prosecutor would thrust aside as malicious and born of despair. They might or might not be malicious, but the despair was certainly there. He alighted onto the platform carrying his case and made his way towards the gates, oblivious of the people bumping against him.

He was not looking forward to meeting the Scottish lawyer, James Argyll. His reputation was formidable. Even in London his name was mentioned with admiration. Heaven knew what Callandra was paying him. He was not in the least likely to take any advice from Rathbone, and Rathbone had no idea whether he believed Hester innocent or was merely willing to take on what would undoubtedly be a celebrated case, for the sake of the victim, if not the accused. He was an Edinburgh man. He might have known the Farralines, certainly by repute if not in person. How hard would he try? How undivided would his loyalty be, or his dedication to victory?

"Rathbone? Rathbone, where the devil are you going?"

Rathbone swung around and came face-to-face with Monk, dressed immaculately and looking grim and angry. He knew without asking that there was no good news.

"To meet Mr. James Argyll," Rathbone said tartly. "He seems to be our only hope." He raised his eyebrows, opening his eyes wide. "Unless you have uncovered something you have not yet told me?" He was being sarcastic, and they both knew it. Without words Monk had understood as well as he that neither of them had any practical ideas to follow, and the same desperation choked in each of them, the same sense of panic rose and made them breathless. They each felt towards the other the desire to hurt, to find fault. It was one of the many masks of fear. Behind them on the platform there was a commotion as people were pushing each other and craning to look, not forwards as might be expected, but back towards the rear of the platform where the guard's van stood.

"Oh God!" Rathbone said wretchedly.

"What?" Monk demanded, his face white.

"Hester . . ."

"What? Where?"

"In the guard's van. They've brought her up."

Monk looked as if he were about to strike him.

"It's the way they always do it," Rathbone said between his teeth. "You must know that. Come on. There's no point in standing here gaping with the rest of the crowd. We can't help her."

Monk hesitated, loath simply to leave. The shouting and the catcalls were getting worse.

Rathbone looked up the platform towards the exit, then back down its length where a crowd was gathering. He was in an agony of indecision.

"Train murderess on trial!" a newsboy called out. "Read all about it here! Here, sir, ye want one? Penny, sir. . . ."

There was a constable wending his way alone towards them, shouldering people aside.

"Now then, now then! On about your business. There's nothing to see. Just some poor woman come to stand trial. It'll all come out then. On your way, please! Come on, move along there."

Rathbone made up his mind, turning and starting off again towards the way out.

"When does the trial start?" Monk asked, matching him stride for stride, and at last the other passengers also scrambling with loss of dignity, and corresponding loss of temper.

"Impudent beggar!" an elderly man said furiously, but neither

Monk nor Rathbone heard him. "Watch where you're going, sir! I really don't know . . . as if the police weren't enough. One can hardly travel decently anymore. . . ."

"What are you basing the defense on?" Monk demanded as he and Rathbone strode through the gate and out towards the street. "That way." He indicated the steps up to Princes Street.

"I'm not," Rathbone said bitterly. "It's all up to Argyll."

Monk knew what the letter had said, and all the reasons, but it did nothing to ease his fear.

"For God's sake, doesn't Hester have anything to say about it?" he demanded as they burst out into Princes Street, nearly knocking over a pretty woman with a child in tow.

"I beg your pardon," Rathbone said abruptly to her. "Not a great deal, I imagine. I haven't met the man yet, I have only corresponded with him, and that was kept to the formalities. I have no idea whether he even believes she is innocent."

"You bloody incompetent!" Monk exploded, swinging around to face him. "You mean you have hired a lawyer to defend her without even knowing if he believes in her?" He grasped Rathbone by the lapels, his face twisted with fury.

Rathbone slapped him away with surprising violence. "I did not hire him, you ignoramus! Lady Callandra Daviot hired him. And belief in her innocence is a very pleasant thing to have, but in our parlous state it is a luxury we may not be able to afford. For a start, such a thing may not exist—in Edinburgh."

Monk opened his mouth to retaliate, then realized the truth of the remark and let it go.

Rathbone smoothed down his lapels.

"Well, what are you standing there for?" Monk said acidly. "Let us go and see this man Argyll, and find out if he is any good."

"There is no point in being a crack shot if you have no ammunition," Rathbone said bitterly, turning to face the way they had been going and resuming his journey. He knew Argyll's address was in Princes Street itself, and had been advised it was easy walking distance from the station. "If you have no idea who did kill Mary Farraline, at least tell me who could have, and why. I presume you have something since you last wrote. It is three days."

Monk's face was tight and very pale as he fell in step with

Rathbone again. For several moments they walked in silence, then finally he spoke, his voice rasping.

"I've been over the apothecaries again. I can't find the source of the digitalis, for Hester or anyone else. . . ."

"So you wrote."

"Apparently there was a digitalis poisoning a few months ago here in Edinburgh. It received some attention. It may have given our killer the idea."

Rathbone's eyes widened. "That's interesting. Not much, but you are right, it may have prompted the idea. What else?"

"Our best chance still seems the bookkeeper. Kenneth Farraline has a mistress. . . ."

"Not unusual," Rathbone said dryly. "And hardly a crime. What of it?"

Monk kept his temper with momentary difficulty. "She's expensive, and he is the company bookkeeper. Old Hector Farraline says the books were tampered with. . . ."

Rathbone stopped and swung around.

"Why in God's name didn't you tell me that before?"

"Because it happened some time ago, and Mary already knew about it."

Rathbone swore.

"Very helpful," Monk said acidly.

Rathbone glared at him.

Monk continued walking. "The weakest point in this case seems to be the questions of timing. Hester could not have purchased the digitalis here in Edinburgh—at least it is almost impossible. And she could not have seen the pearl brooch until she was already in the train on the way back. She could only have done it if she had brought the digitalis with her from London, which is absurd."

"Of course it's absurd," Rathbone said between his teeth. "But I've seen people hanged on evidence as poor—when public hatred is deep enough. Haven't you sense, man?"

Monk swung around to face him. "Then you'll have to change the public mood, won't you." It was not a question but a demand. "That's what you're paid for. Make them see Hester as a heroine, a woman who gave up her own family and happiness to minister to the sick and injured. Make them see her in Scutari, passing all night along the rows of wounded with a lamp in her hand, mopping brows, comforting the dying, praying—anything you like. Let them see her braving shot and shell to reach the wounded without thought for herself . . . then returning home to fight the medical establishment for better conditions here . . . and losing her post for her impertinence, so she has to nurse privately, moving from post to post."

"Is that how you see Hester?" Rathbone asked, standing still in the middle of the footpath opposite him, his eyes wide, his lips almost in a smile.

"No, of course not!" Monk said. "She's an opinionated, self-willed woman doing precisely what she wants to do. But that is not the point." There was a faint color in his face as he said it, and it occurred to Rathbone that there was more truth in what Monk had said than he was prepared to admit. And Rathbone also realized with a shiver of surprise that he would not have found it difficult to put forward that picture of Hester himself.

"I can't," he said bitterly. "You seem to have forgotten that this is Scotland."

Monk swore viciously, and with several words Rathbone had not heard before.

"Oh very helpful," Rathbone said, mimicking his earlier tone exactly. "But I shall do all I can to see that Argyll uses that to the best advantage. I have achieved one thing." He tried to sound casual, and not too smug.

"Oh good—do tell me," Monk said sarcastically. "If there is something, I should like to know it!"

"Then hold your tongue long enough and I will!" They were walking again and Rathbone quickened his pace. "Florence Nightingale herself will come and testify as a character witness."

"That's marvelous!" Monk shouted with such exuberance two passersby pulled faces and shook their heads, supposing him intoxicated. "That's brilliant of you . . . it's . . . ."

"Thank you. We have established that physically any member of the household could have killed Mary Farraline. What about motive?"

The elation vanished from Monk's face. "I thought I had two. . . ."

"You didn't tell me!"

"They disappeared on examination."

"Are you sure?"

"Perfectly. Alastair's wife is extravagant, and goes out at night to meet a scruffy-looking individual dressed in working clothes and carrying a pocket watch."

Rathbone stopped in disbelief. "And that's not a motive?"

Monk snorted. "She's building a flying machine."

"I beg your pardon?"

"She is building a large machine, big enough to carry a passenger, which she hopes will fly," Monk elaborated. "In an old warehouse in the slum quarter. All right, she's eccentric. . . ."

"Eccentric? Is that what you call it? I would have said insane."

"Most inventors are a trifle strange."

"A trifle? A flying machine?" Rathbone pulled a face. "Come on, man, she'll be locked up if anyone finds out."

"Probably that is why she does it in secret, and at midnight," Monk agreed, beginning to walk again. "But from what I've heard of Mary Farraline, she'd have been entertained by it. She certainly wouldn't have had her committed."

Rathbone said nothing.

"The other one is the middle daughter, Eilish," Monk resumed. "She also goes out at night, secretly, but alone. I followed her." He omitted mentioning that twice he had been knocked senseless for his pains. "And I found where she goes: down in Cowgate, which is a slum tenement area."

"Not another fantastical machine?" Rathbone said wryly.

"No, something far more elementary," Monk replied with a tone of surprise in his voice. "She is conducting her own ragged school for adults."

Rathbone frowned. "Why in the middle of the night? That seems a highly honorable thing to do!"

"Because presumably her pupils are at their labors during the day," Monk said waspishly. "Added to which, she has coerced her brother-in-law, who is in love with her, into giving her books from the family company for her pupils' use."

"You mean pilfering?" Rathbone chose to ignore the sarcasm.

"If you like. But again, I'm damned sure Mary would have approved heartily had she known. And she might have."

Rathbone raised his eyebrows. "You didn't think to ask?"

"Ask whom?" Monk inquired. "Eilish would have said yes, if it mattered and she hadn't. . . . The only other person to ask would have been Mary."

"And is that all?"

"The only other thing is the company books."

"We've no evidence to raise it," Rathbone pointed out. "You said Hector Farraline is as tight as a newt most of the time. His drunken ramblings, even if he's right, won't be enough to demand an audit. Is he fit to put in the witness-box?"

"God knows."

They had stopped, having reached the building where James Argyll had his offices.

"I'm coming in," Monk stated.

"I really don't think . . ." Rathbone began, but Monk had marched ahead of him through the doors and up the stairs and there was nothing for him to do but follow.

The office was quite small, and not nearly as imposing as Rathbone had expected, being lined with shabby books on three sides, the fourth having a small fireplace with a hotly burning fire and paneled in wood of some African origin.

But the man himself was an entirely different matter. He was tall with powerful shoulders and muscular body, but it was his face which commanded attention. In his youth he must have been very dark, what was referred to as a black Celt, with fine eyes and olive complexion. Now what was left of his hair was grizzled gray, and his deeply lined face was full of humor and intelligence. When he smiled he had marvelous teeth.

"You must be Mr. Oliver Rathbone," he said, looking past Monk. His voice was deep and his accent was savored with relish, as if he were proud of being a Scot. He held out his hand. "James Argyll at your service, sir. I feel we have a great challenge in front of us. I have your letter stating that Miss Florence Nightingale is prepared to travel to Edinburgh to appear as a character witness for the defense. Excellent, excellent." He waved to one of the leather chairs and Monk sat in it. Without being asked, Rathbone took the other, and Argyll resumed his own seat.

"Did you have an agreeable journey?" he asked, looking at Rathbone.

"We have no time for chatter," Monk cut across him. "All we

have to fight with are Miss Latterly's reputation and what we can make of Miss Nightingale. I presume you are well acquainted with her role in the war and how she is greatly regarded? If you were not before, you should be now."

"I am, Mr. Monk," Argyll said with unconcealed amusement. "And I am also aware that so far, it is all we have with which to fight. I presume you have still uncovered nothing factually relevant within the Farraline household? We will naturally consider the possible value of innuendo and suggestion, but as you will be aware by now, if you were not before, the family is well thought of in Edinburgh. Mrs. Mary Farraline was a woman of remarkable character, and Mr. Alastair is the Procurator Fiscal, a position close to that of your own Crown Prosecutor."

Monk took the irony and knew it was well deserved.

"You are saying that to make an unsubstantiated attack would count against us?"

"Yes, without question."

"Can we get the company books audited?" Monk leaned forward.

"I doubt it, unless you have evidence of embezzlement, and that it is likely to be connected with Mrs. Farraline's murder. Have you?"

"No ... one can hardly count old Hector's ramblings."

Argyll's expression sharpened. "Tell me more about old Hector, Mr. Monk."

In precise detail and without interruption, Monk recounted what Hector had said to him.

Argyll listened intently.

"Will you put him in the box?" Monk finished.

"Aye ... I think I may," Argyll said thoughtfully. "If I can manage to do it without warning."

"Then he may be too drunk to be any use," Rathbone protested, sitting upright.

"And if I warn the family, they may make sure he is too drunk to stand up at all," Argyll pointed out. "No, surprise is our only weapon. Not good, I grant you, but all we have."

"What will you do?" Rathbone asked. "Elicit something which will necessitate your calling him as if by chance?"

Argyll's mobile mouth curved upward in appreciation. "Precisely. And I gather you have also obtained another Crimean colleague to appear for Miss Latterly?"

"Yes. A doctor who will speak very highly of her."

Monk stood up impatiently and swung away from the chair to pace the floor.

"None of that is any use if we cannot suggest who else killed Mrs. Farraline. She didn't die by accident, nor did she kill herself. Someone gave her a lethal dose, and someone put that pearl brooch in Hester's baggage, certainly to implicate her. You can't create doubt it was Hester unless you can point to someone else."

"I am aware of that, Mr. Monk," Argyll said quietly. "That is where we still look to you. I think we may safely assume it was one of the family. You have effectively ruled out the servants, so Mr. Rathbone has told me."

"Yes, they can all account for their time in each other's company," Monk agreed. "And more importantly, there seems no earthly reason for any of them to have harmed her." He drove his hands into his pockets savagely. "It was one of the family, but I have no more idea now of which one than I had when I stepped off the train, except I don't believe it was Eilish. I think our best chance is Kenneth. He has a mistress the family doesn't approve of, and he is the company bookkeeper. He is also one of the weaker ones. You ought to be able to rattle him in the witness-box, if you are any good at your job."

Rathbone winced at Monk's abruptness, but he shared his emotion. He would tie Kenneth into a knot he'd never undo, if only he had the chance. Damn the differences between English and Scots law. Frustration churned inside him so violently he found it hard to keep still. He did not blame Monk for his restlessness or his manner.

Argyll leaned back in his chair, resting his fingertips together and staring at Monk without anger. "I'll be better at it, Mr. Monk, if you can find me cause to have those company books examined. I think young Mr. Kenneth may very well have embezzled a bawbee here and there to keep his mistress . . . but we'll need more than a suggestion if we are to say that to the High Court of Justiciary in Edinburgh."

"I'll get it for you," Monk said grimly.

Argyll raised his black eyebrows. "Legally, if you please. It will be no use to us otherwise."

"I know that," Monk said between his teeth. "There won't be a mark on him, nor will he have cause for a complaint of any sort. Just do your part."

Rathbone winced again.

Monk shot another glance at Argyll, then without speaking again opened the door and went out.

Hester had passed the journey from London to Edinburgh in the guard's van, in a state which was certainly not sleep, or anything like the rest that sleep should bring, and yet it had all the qualities of a dream. There was no sense of direction, she could as easily have been traveling south as north, and this time there was no footwarmer. She was manacled to the wardress, who sat rigid with anxiety, her face set like iron. Every time Hester closed her eyes she expected to see Mary Farraline when she opened them again, and hear her soft, cultured Highland voice with the Edinburgh intonation recounting some memory from the past, filled with humor and enjoyment.

She was the last to disembark from the train, and by the time she and the wardress stepped out onto the platform, most of the other passengers were moving towards the gates up into the street.

The police escort was there, four large constables holding truncheons and looking nervously from left to right.

"Come on, Latterly," the wardress said sharply, yanking at Hester's manacled hands. "No dithering around, now!"

"I'm not going to escape!" Hester said with wry contempt.

The wardress gave her a filthy look, and it was several seconds before Hester realized why. Then as the constables closed in around her, and there was an angry shout from a few yards away, suddenly she understood. They were here not to prevent her escape but to protect her.

A woman screamed.

"Murderess!" someone yelled hoarsely.

"Hang 'er!" another shouted out, and a surge of bodies buffeted the constables and they lurched forward, unwittingly almost knocking Hester off her feet.

A dozen yards away a newsboy was calling out about the trial.

"Burn her!" a voice shouted quite clearly and chillingly, a woman's voice, shrill with hatred. "Burn the witch! Put her to the fires!"

Hester felt herself chilled as if by ice. It was terrifying to feel such a passion thick in the air, it was a kind of madness. There was no reasoning with it, no logic, no pity. She had not even been tried yet.

A missile flew past her cheek and clattered against the carriage door.

"Now then, now then!" another constable's voice said with rising panic barely suppressed. "Move along. You got no business here. Move along or I'll have to take you in charge for disturbing the peace. You let the courts do their job. Time enough then for hanging. Move along. . . ."

"Don't stare there, stupid!" The wardress tugged at Hester again, bruising her wrists where the manacles dug into her.

"Come on, miss, we can't stand about here," the largest constable said, more gently. "We got to keep you safe."

Hurriedly and awkwardly, still pushed and heaved by the crowd, now sullen, they made their way off the platform and up to the street.

They were driven in a closed van straight to the prison, where more wardresses awaited her, their faces hard, eyes angry.

She said nothing, asked no questions, and passed into the cell in silence, her head high, her thoughts islanded from them. She remained there until the middle of the afternoon, when she was escorted to another small room, bare but for a wooden table and two hard wooden chairs.

There was a man already there, tall and broad-shouldered, and to judge from his gray hair and beard and from the lines around his mouth, he was nearer sixty than fifty, but there was a quality of intense vitality in him which dominated the room, even though he remained motionless.

"Good afternoon, Miss Latterly," he said with courtesy, the irony of which reflected in his dark eyes. "I am James Argyll. Lady Callandra has retained me to represent you, since Mr. Rathbone cannot appear before the bar in Scotland."

"How do you do," she replied.

"Please sit down, Miss Latterly." He indicated the wooden chairs, and as soon as she had taken one, he took the other. He was watching her with curiosity and some surprise. She wondered with self-mockery what he had expected of her—perhaps a big, rawboned woman with the physical strength to carry wounded men off the battlefield, like Rebecca Box, the soldier's wife who had dared the shot and walked alone onto the field between the lines to bring back the fallen across her shoulders. Or maybe he had envisioned a drunkard, or a slut, or an ignorant woman who could find no better employment than emptying slops and winding bandages.

Her heart sank, and she found it difficult to control her sense of despair so it did not show in her face or spill in tears down her cheeks.

"I have already spoken with Mr. Rathbone," Argyll was saying to her.

With a tremendous effort she mastered herself and looked back at him calmly.

"He has told me that Miss Nightingale is prepared to testify for you."

"Oh?" Her heart leapt and without warning hope came back with a ridiculous pain. All sorts of things that she held dear seemed possible again, things for which she had already endured the parting, at least in her mind: people, sights, sounds, even the habits of thinking of tomorrow, having time for which to plan. She found her body shaking; her hands on the table trembled and she had to grip them so hard the nails dug into the flesh to keep them still enough that he would not see. "That must be good. . . ."

"Oh it is excellent," he agreed. "But showing the qualities of your character will not be sufficient if we cannot also show that someone else had both the opportunity and the motive to murder Mrs. Farraline. However, in discussing the matter with Mr. Monk . . ."

It was absurd how mention of his name made her stomach turn over and her breath catch in her throat.

He continued as if he had noticed nothing.

". . . it seems as if Mr. Kenneth Farraline may have tampered with the company books in order to finance his affair with someone whom the family obviously consider unsuitable. How unsuitable and why, and how deeply he is entangled with her, whether there is a child or not, just what hold she has over him, we have yet to learn. I have dispatched Mr. Monk posthaste to uncover that. If he is as excellent as Mr. Rathbone assures me, it should not take him above two days. Though I confess I wonder why he has not made it his business to learn it before now."

Her heart was tight in her throat. "Because unless you can prove that he has embezzled from the company, the fact that he has a mistress is irrelevant," she said gravely. "A great many men do, especially young, well-bred men who have no other involvements. In fact, I would hazard a guess it is more common than not."

His eyes widened in momentary surprise, then in undisguised admiration for her candor and her courage. He was a man whose admiration was not easily stirred.

"Of course you are right, Miss Latterly. And that is my task. It will require some legal endeavor to obtain audit for the company books, and I propose to put Mr. Hector Farraline in the witness-box in order to obtain it. Now if you please, we shall go through the order of the witnesses Mr. Gilfeather will call for the prosecution and what we may expect them to say."

"Of course."

He frowned. "Have you attended a criminal trial, Miss Latterly? You speak almost as if you are familiar with the procedure. Your composure is admirable, but this is not the time to mislead me, even in the name of dignity."

A flicker of amusement crossed her face. "Yes, Mr. Argyll, I have attended several, in the cause of my occasional assistance to Mr. Monk."

"Assistance to Mr. Monk?" he questioned. "Is there something of importance I have not been told?"

"I don't think it is of importance." She pulled a slight face. "I cannot imagine that the jurors, or the public, would find it respectable, and certainly not mitigating."

"Tell me," he demanded grimly.

"I first met Mr. Monk when he was investigating the murder of a Crimean officer named Joscelin Grey. Because of Mr. Grey's involvement with my late father, I was able to give Mr. Monk some assistance," she explained obediently, although she found her voice shaking. Funny how memory made that time now seem so dear. The quarrels dimmed into episodes which now seemed almost amusing. She could no longer feel the anger or the contempt she had for him then.

"Continue," Argyll pressed. "You speak as though it were not a single instance."

"It wasn't. I used my nursing experience to obtain a position with

Sir Basil Moidore when Mr. Monk was investigating the death of Sir Basil's daughter."

Argyll's black eyebrows rose. "In order to assist Mr. Monk?" he said with unconcealed amazement. "I had not realized your devotion was so deep."

She felt a tide of color burn up her face.

"It was not a devotion to Mr. Monk," she said tartly. "It was the desire to see some sort of justice done. And it was my devotion to Lady Callandra which made me obtain a position in the Royal Free Hospital in order to learn more of the death of Nurse Barrymore. And the fact that I had known her in the Crimea, and formed a considerable regard for her. I became involved with General Carlyon's death because I was asked to by his sister, who is a friend of mine." She looked him very directly in the face, defying him to doubt her.

An almost imperceptible touch of color stained his cheeks, but there was still amusement in his eyes.

"I see. So you are indeed very familiar with the rules of evidence and the procedure of trial?"

"I . . . I think so."

"Very well, forgive me for having seemed to patronize you, Miss Latterly."

"Of course," she said graciously. "Please continue."

The following day Monk spent from dawn until slightly before midnight investigating Kenneth Farraline and writing his findings to give to James Argyll, a pursuit which he believed to be largely pointless.

Rathbone had a wretched day. There was almost nothing he could accomplish. He had never cared so much about the outcome of a case, or been so helpless to influence one. A dozen times he almost set out to see Argyll again, and each time he resisted with difficulty, telling himself it would serve no purpose at all. But it was only the sting to his pride of running around after another barrister, particularly when it was the one taking his place, and the certainty that Argyll would read his nervousness like a billboard, that finally stayed him.

He knew that Callandra Daviot would be in Edinburgh for the trial, which began on the next morning, so she would have to come up on that day's train, unless she had already traveled and was here before him. By midafternoon he was at his wit's end and had paced the floor uselessly ever since picking without appetite over what should have been an excellent luncheon.

Late in the evening he was tired, but unable to relax sufficiently to retire. There was a knock on the door of the room he had taken. He whirled around.

"Come in!" he shouted, striding towards the doorway and almost being struck as the door opened and Callandra appeared in the entrance, followed immediately by Henry Rathbone, Rathbone's father. Of course he had told his father of the whole affair before he could read of it in the newspapers. The elder Rathbone had met Hester on several occasions and had formed a fondness for her. The sight of his tall, slightly stooped figure now, with his ascetic face and benign expression, was ridiculously comforting. And at the same time it awoke in the younger man emotions of both dependence and fierce protection he would rather not have been burdened with in the circumstances.

"Please excuse me, Oliver," Callandra said briskly. "I realize it is late, and I am possibly interrupting you, but I could not contain myself until morning." She came in as he stepped back, smiling in spite of himself. Henry Rathbone followed immediately after, searching Oliver's face.

"Come in," Rathbone invited, closing the door behind him. He very nearly said that they were not interrupting anything at all, then pride prevented him from such an admission. "Father! I had not expected you. It is good of you to have come."

"Don't be absurd." Henry Rathbone dismissed it with a shake of his head. "Of course I came. How is she?"

"I have not seen her since the night before she left London," Rathbone replied. "I am not her barrister here in Edinburgh. They will only allow Argyll in now."

"So what are you doing?" Callandra demanded, too restless to sit in either of the large armchairs available.

"Waiting," Rathbone answered bitterly. "Worrying. Racking my brain to think of anything we have left undone, any possibilities we could still pursue."

Callandra drew in her breath, then said nothing.

Henry Rathbone sat down and crossed his legs. "Well, pacing the floor is not going to help. We had better approach the matter logically. I presume there is no possibility this poison was administered accidentally, or intentionally by Mrs. Farraline herself? All right, there is no need to lose your temper, Oliver. It is necessary to establish the facts."

Rathbone glanced at him, smothering his impatience with difficulty. He knew perfectly well that his father did not lack emotion or care, indeed he felt painfully; but his ability to suppress his feelings and concentrate his brain irritated him, because he was so far from that kind of control himself.

Callandra sat down on the other chair, staring at Henry hopefully.

"And the servants?" Henry continued.

"Ruled out by Monk," Rathbone replied. "It was one of the family."

"Remind me again who they are," Henry directed.

"Alastair, the eldest son, the Procurator Fiscal; his wife, Deirdra, who is building a flying machine . . ."

Henry looked up, awaiting an explanation, his blue eyes mild and puzzled.

"Eccentric," Rathbone agreed. "But Monk is convinced she is otherwise harmless."

Henry pulled a face.

"Eldest daughter Oonagh McIvor; her husband, Baird, who is apparently in love with his sister-in-law, Eilish, and is taking books from the company for her to use in her midnight occupation of teaching a ragged school. Eilish's husband, Quinlan Fyffe, married into the family and into the business. Clever and unappealing, but Monk knows of no reason why he should have wished to kill his mother-in-law. And the youngest brother, Kenneth, who seems our best hope at the moment."

"What about the daughter in London?" Henry asked.

"She cannot have been guilty," Rathbone reasoned with a sharp edge to his voice. "She has nowhere near Edinburgh or Mary, or the medicine. We can discount her and her husband."

"Why was Mary going to visit her?" Henry asked, ignoring Rathbone's tone.

"I don't know. Something to do with her health. She is expecting her first child and is very nervous. It's natural enough she should wish her mother to be there."

"Is that all you know?"

"Do you think it would matter?" Callandra asked urgently.

"No, of course not." Rathbone dismissed it with a sharp flick of his hand. He stood leaning a little against the table, still unwilling to sit down.

Henry ignored his reply. "Have you given any thought as to why Mrs. Farraline was killed at that precise time, rather than any other?" he asked.

"Opportunity," Rathbone replied. "A perfect chance to lay the blame on someone else. I would have thought that was obvious."

"Perhaps," Henry agreed dubiously, resting his elbows on the arms of the chair and pressing his fingertips together in a steeple. "But it seems to me also very possible that something provoked it at this precise time. You do not kill someone simply because a good opportunity presents itself."

Rathbone straightened up, at last a tiny spot of instinct caught inside him.

"Have you something in mind?"

"Surely it is worth giving close examination to anything that happened within three or four days immediately before Mrs. Farraline set out for London?" Henry asked. "The murder may have been an opportunist act after years of desire, but it may also have been precipitated by something that happened very shortly before."

"Indeed it may," Rathbone agreed, moving away from the table. "Thank you, Father. At last we have another avenue to explore. That is, if Monk has not already done it and found it empty. But he said nothing."

"Are you sure you cannot see Hester?" Callandra asked quickly.

"Yes I am sure, but I shall be in court, of course, and I may be permitted a few moments then."

"Please . . ." Callandra was very pale. Suddenly all the emotion they had been trying so hard to smother beneath practical action, intelligence and self-control poured into the silence in the warm, unfamiliar room, with its anonymous furnishings and smell of polish.

Rathbone stared at Callandra, then at his father. The understanding between them was complete; all the fear, the affection, the knowledge of loss hanging over them, the helplessness were too clear to need words.

"Of course I'll tell her," Rathbone said quietly. "But she knows already."

"Thank you," Callandra said.

Henry nodded his head.

The morning of the trial was cold, sharp and threatening rain. Oliver Rathbone walked briskly from the rooms he had taken just off Princes Street, up the steps of the mound towards the castle, then up Bank Street and sharp left onto the High Street. Almost immediately he was faced with the great Cathedral of St. Giles, half hiding Parliament Square, on the farther side of which was Parliament House, unused now since the Act of Union, and the High Court of Justiciary.

He crossed the square. No one knew or recognized him. He passed newspaper sellers not only pressing their news of today but promising all sorts of scandal and revelation for the next issue. The murderess of Mary Farraline was on trial. Read all about it. Learn the secrets known only to a few. Incredible stories for the price of a penny.

He walked past them impatiently. He had heard all these things before, but they had not hurt when it was only a client. It was to be expected and brushed aside. When it was Hester it had a power to wound in quite a new way.

He went up the steps, and even there, amid the black-gowned barristers, he was unknown. It was surprisingly disorienting. He was accustomed to recognition, even considerable respect, to younger men moving aside for him in deference, muttering to each other of his past successes, hoping to emulate them one day.

Here he was merely another spectator, albeit one who might sit near the front and occasionally pass a note to the counsel for the defense.

He had already made arrangements and obtained permission to see Hester for a few moments before court was in session. The stated time had been precise. He preceded it by two minutes exactly.

"Good morning, Mr. Rathbone," the clerk said stiffly. "If you will come this way, sir, I'll see if you can speak with the accused for a moment." And without waiting to see if Rathbone agreed, he turned and led the way down the narrow, steep steps to the cells where prisoners

were held before trial—or after, awaiting transport to a more permanent place of incarceration.

He found Hester standing white-faced inside the small cell. She
was dressed in her usual plain blue-gray which she used for working
and she looked severe. The ordeal had told on her health. She had
never been softly rounded, but now she was considerably thinner and
her shoulders looked stiff and fragile and there were hollows in her
cheeks and around her eyes. He imagined this was how she must have
looked during the worst days of the war, hungry, cold, worked to exhaustion and racked with fear and pity.

For a second, less than a second, a spark of hope lit in her eyes,
then sight of his face made sense prevail. There would be no reprieve
now. She was embarrassed that he should have seen such foolishness
in her face.

"G-good morning, Oliver," she said almost steadily.

How many more times would he be able to speak to her alone?
Then they might part forever. There were all manner of things he
wanted to say, emotional things, about caring for her, how intolerably
he would miss her, the place in his life no one else would ever enter,
let alone fill. He was uncertain exactly what that was, in a romantic
sense, but he had no doubt at all about the love of friends, even its
nature or its ineffable value.

"Good morning," he replied. "I have met Mr. Argyll, and I am
very impressed with him. I think he will not fall short of his reputation. We may have every confidence in him." How dismally formal,
and so little of what was in his mind.

"Do you think so?" she asked, watching his face.

"I do. I imagine he has given you all the appropriate advice about
your conduct and your replies to him or Mr. Gilfeather?" Perhaps it
was best to speak of nothing but business. It would burden her unbear-
ably to be emotional now.

She smiled with an effort. "Yes. But I already knew it, from having
heard you speak. I shall answer only as I am asked, speak clearly and
respectfully, not stare too directly at anyone. . . ."

"Did he say that?"

"No . . . but you would have, would you not?"

His smile was uncertain, even painful.

"I would—to you. Men do not like a woman who is too confident."

"I know."

"Yes . . ." He swallowed. "Of course you do."

"Don't worry. I shall behave myself meekly," she assured him. "And he also warned me what to expect the other witnesses to say, and that the crowd will be hostile." She gave a shaky sigh. "I should have expected that, but it is a very unpleasant thought that they have already judged me guilty."

"We will change their minds," he said fiercely. "They have not heard your evidence yet; they have only heard the prosecutor's view of things."

"I—"

But she got no further. There was a brisk knock on the door and it swung open to allow the warder in.

"Sorry, sir, but you'll have to be on your way. Got to take the prisoner up."

There was no time for anything further. Rathbone glanced at Hester once, forced a smile to his lips, then obeyed the orders and withdrew.

The High Court of Justiciary in Edinburgh was not like the Old Bailey, and Monk was reminded again with an ugly jolt that they were in a different land. Although united by many common bonds and governed by one queen and one parliament, the law of the land was different, the history and the heritage were different, and until very recently in a long national memory, they had been as often enemies as friends. The borders were drenched with the blood of both sides, and the Auld Alliance was not with England but with France, England's foe down the centuries.

The titles were different, the clothes marginally so, and there were not twelve men to the jury, but fifteen. Only the majestic implacability of the law was unchanged. The jury had been empaneled, the prisoner charged and the proceedings commenced.

The prosecution was conducted by a huge, rambling man with a soft voice and flyaway gray hair. His face was benign and the lights shone on the bald crown of his head. Monk knew from deep instinct that his affability and gentle air of disorganization were a total sham. Behind the smile was a brain whetted to scalpel sharpness.

On the other bench, equally courteous but utterly different in attitude, was James Argyll. He looked grizzled and dangerous, like an old bear, his black eyes and sharp brows accentuating his air of intense concentration and the fact that he feared nothing and was deceived by no one.

How much was it a personal battle, with Hester's life to win or lose as the prize? These two must have met many times before. They must know each other as one can know only an adversary tested and tried to the limit. One can never know a friend in quite that way.

Monk looked at Hester in the dock. She was very white, her eyes focused far away, as if she were in a daze. Perhaps she was. This was reality so intense it was like no other, and therefore would seem unreal. Each sense would at times be so keen she would remember every grain of wood in the dock railing and yet not hear what was said. Or hear even an intake of breath from the clerk before her, or the wardress behind, or the crackle of the fires in the two grates at each side of the room, and yet not see the people in the gallery even if they moved or jostled each other the better to see.

The judge was seated above them, an elderly man with a narrow, clever face and crooked teeth, a long nose and fine hair. He must have been handsome in his youth. Now his character was too deeply marked and his erratic temper stamped his features.

The first witness for the prosecution was Alastair Farraline. There was a hush in the court and then a slow letting out of breath as his name was called. Everyone knew he was the Procurator Fiscal, a title to elicit both fear and respect in the law. A woman in the gallery gave a little scream of sheer pent-up emotion as he climbed to the witness-box, and the judge glared at her.

"Control yourself, madam, or I shall have you removed," he warned grimly.

She clapped both hands over her mouth.

"Proceed," the judge commanded.

Gilfeather thanked him and turned to Alastair with a smile.

"First of all, Mr. Farraline, may I extend to you the court's sympathy on the loss of your mother. A lady we all held in the highest esteem."

Alastair, pale and very upright, the light shining on his hair, tried to smile back, and failed.

"Thank you," he said simply.

Monk glanced at Hester, but she was immobile and staring at Alastair.

Immediately behind Argyll, Oliver Rathbone was so rigid that even from across the room Monk could see the fabric of his coat stretched across his shoulders.

"Now, Mr. Farraline," Gilfeather continued. "When your mother planned this journey south into England, did you always intend to send someone with her to care for her?"

"Yes."

"Why, sir? Why not one of her own servants? You have a sufficiency of servants, do you not?"

"Of course." Alastair looked puzzled and unhappy. "Mother's lady's maid had never traveled, and did not wish to. We were afraid her own nervousness would make her unsuitable as a companion, and possibly inefficient, especially at dealing with any difficulty or inconvenience which might arise."

"Naturally," Gilfeather agreed, nodding sagely. "You wished someone competent to take care in any contingency, therefore a woman who had traveled before."

"And a nurse," Alastair added. "Just in case the . . . ." He swallowed. He looked wretched. "In case the tension of the journey should make Mother unwell."

The judge's mouth tightened. There was a rustle in the gallery.

Oliver Rathbone winced. Argyll sat expressionless.

"So you advertised for someone suitable?" Gilfeather prompted.

"Yes. We had two or three replies, but Miss Latterly seemed to us to be the best qualified and most suitable."

"She gave you references, of course?"

"Of course. She seemed excellent."

"Did you at any time have cause to doubt the wisdom of your choice prior to your seeing her off in Edinburgh station for the journey to London?"

"No. She seemed a perfectly acceptable young woman," Alastair answered. Never once did he glance at Hester, but kept his eyes studiously away from her.

Gilfeather asked him a few more questions, all fairly trivial. Monk's attention wandered. He looked for Oonagh's fair head and did not find her, but Eilish was easy to see, and Deirdra. He was surprised to see Deirdra looking straight back at him with pity, and something like conspiracy, in her eyes.

Or perhaps it was only the lamplight reflecting.

Gilfeather sat down amid a stir of excitement from the gallery. James Argyll stood up.

"Mr. Farraline . . ."

Alastair looked at him with a fixed, polite expression of dislike.

"Mr. Farraline." Argyll did not smile at him. "Why did you choose someone from London rather than Edinburgh? Have we no acceptable nurses in Scotland?"

Alastair's face tightened noticeably.

"I imagine so, sir. None of them answered our advertisement. We wished for the best we could find. A woman who had served with Florence Nightingale seemed to us above reproach."

There was a murmur around the crowd and mixed emotions, patriotic approval of Florence Nightingale and all she stood for in their minds, anger that her reputation should be besmirched, even vicariously, surprise, doubt and anticipation.

"You really considered such qualification necessary for so simple a task as administering a prepared dose to an intelligent and far from incapacitated lady?" Argyll said curiously. "Members of the jury may wonder why a local woman of sound reputation would not have served at least as well, and far less expensively in railway fares than sending for a stranger from London."

This time the rustle was agreement.

Monk shifted impatiently. It was a point so minor as to be worthless, too subtle for the jury even to understand, much less recall when the time came.

"We wanted someone accustomed to travel," Alastair repeated doggedly, his face pink, although it was impossible to tell what emotion lay behind the flushed cheeks and unhappy eyes. It could have been no more than grief, and certain embarrassment at being required to stand so publicly for everyone to stare at with such morbid interest. He was used only to honor, respect, even awe. Now his private affairs, his family and its emotions, were displayed and he was helpless to defend himself.

"Thank you," Argyll said politely, conveying neither belief nor disbelief. "Did Miss Latterly seem an entirely satisfactory person to you while she was in your house?"

Even if Alastair had wished to deny it, he was now in a position where he could not, or he would seem to have connived at whatever ill he had implied.

"Yes, of course," he said sharply. "I should never have permitted my mother to travel if I had suspected anything at all."

Argyll nodded and smiled. "In fact, would it be true to say that your mother seemed to get along particularly well with Miss Latterly?"

Alastair's face hardened. "Yes . . . I feel it would. A remarkably—" He stopped.

Argyll waited. The judged looked inquiringly at Alastair. The jurors all sat staring.

Alastair bit his lip. Apparently he had thought better of what he was going to say.

There was a murmur of sympathy around the room. Alastair's face tightened, loathing the public pity.

Argyll knew when he had stopped winning, even if he did not know why.

"Thank you, sir. That is all I have to ask you."

Gilfeather nodded benignly, and the judge excused Alastair with a further expression of sympathy and respect which Alastair accepted tight-lipped.

The next witness to be called was Oonagh McIvor. She caused even more of a stir than Alastair. She had no title, no public position, but even if no one had known who she was, her air of dignity and suppressed passion would have commanded both respect and attention. Of course she was dressed entirely in black, but she was anything but drab. Her fair skin was delicate and warm and the gleam of her hair was plain beneath her black bonnet.

She climbed the steps deliberately and took the oath with an unwavering voice, then stood waiting for Gilfeather to begin. Not one of the fifteen jurors took his eyes from her.

Gilfeather hesitated, as if wondering how much to play on the jury's sympathy, then decided against it. He was a subtle man and saw no need to gild the lily.

"Mrs. McIvor, did you concur in your brother's decision to employ a nurse from London for your mother?"

"Yes I did," she said slowly and calmly. "I confess I thought it an excellent idea. I thought as well as her professional abilities, and her experience in travel, she would be an interesting companion for my mother." She looked apologetic. "Mother had traveled considerably in her youth, and I think at times she missed the excitement of it. I thought such a woman would be able to talk with her about foreign parts and experiences that would be bound to entertain her."

"Most understandable." Gilfeather nodded. "I think in your circumstances I should have felt the same. And presumably that part of your arrangement lived up to your hopes."

Oonagh smiled bleakly, but did not answer.

"Were you present when Miss Latterly arrived, Mrs. McIvor?" Gilfeather continued.

The questions were all as Monk had foreseen. Gilfeather asked them and Oonagh answered them, and the court listened with rapt attention, all except Monk, who stared around at first one face, then another. Gilfeather himself looked satisfied, even smug. Watching him, the jury could only believe he was completely in command of the whole procedure and held no doubt as to its outcome.

Monk resented it bitterly, while admiring the man's professionalism. He could not recall the trial of his mentor all those years ago. He did not even know in which court it had been held, but his helplessness now brought back waves of old emotion and grief. Then he had known the truth and had watched impotently while someone he had both loved and admired had been convicted of a crime he had not committed. Then Monk had been young and looking with incredulity at the injustice, not believing until the last possible moment that it could really happen. Afterwards he had been stunned. This time it was all too familiar, an old wound with scar tissue ripped away to reveal the unhealed depths, and probed anew.

At the defense table James Argyll sat with his black brows drawn down in thought. His was a dangerous face, full of strength and subtlety, but he was a man without weapons. Monk had failed him. Deliberately he used the word over and over to himself. Failure. Someone had killed Mary Farraline, and he had not found any trace of who it was or why it had happened. He had had weeks in which to seek, and all he had produced was that Kenneth had a pretty mistress with long yellow hair, white skin and a determination never to be cold and hungry again, or to sleep in some strange bed at some man's favor, because she had not one of her own.

Actually Monk sympathized with her more than he did with Kenneth, who had been forced to part with more expensive gifts than he had wished, in order to keep her favors.

But unless someone could raise adequate suspicion of embezzlement to have the company books audited, and embezzlement was in fact proved true, then it was possibly scandalous, although not probably, and it was certainly no cause for murder.

Monk looked at Rathbone and in spite of himself felt a stab of sympathy. To a stranger he appeared merely to be listening, his head a trifle to one side, his long face thoughtful, his dark eyes heavy-lidded as if his attention were entirely involved. But Monk had known him long enough and seen him under pressure before. He could see the angle of his shoulders hunched under his beautiful jacket, the stiffness of his neck and the slow clenching and unclenching of his hand on the table, and he felt the frustration boiling inside him. Whatever he thought or whatever emotions churned inside him, there was nothing he could do now. Whatever he would have done differently, whether it was a whole strategy or as little as an intonation or an expression of the face, he could only sit silently and watch.

Oonagh was answering Gilfeather's questions about the preparation for Mary's journey.

"And who packed your mother's case, Mrs. McIvor?"

"Her lady's maid."

"Upon whose instructions?"

"Mine." Oonagh hesitated only a fraction of a moment, her face pale, her head high. No one in the court moved. "I prepared a list of what should go in, so Mother would have everything she needed and . . . and not too many dinner gowns rather than plain day dresses, and skirts. It . . . it was not a social visit . . . not really."

There was a murmur of sympathy like a breath of wind around the room. The personal details brought the reality of death more sharply.

Gilfeather waited a second or two, allowing the emotions time.

"I see. And naturally you included the appropriate jewelry on this list?"

"Yes, of course."

"And you packed this list in the case?"

"Yes." The ghost of a smile crossed her face. "So the maid who packed for her return would have something by which to know what should be there, and nothing would accidentally be left behind. It can be very tiresome . . ." She did not need to finish.

Again the sense of the dead woman filled the room. Someone in the gallery was weeping.

"Which brings me to another point, Mrs. McIvor," Gilfeather said after several moments. "Precisely why was your mother making this long journey to London? Would it not have been more sensible for your sister to have returned to Edinburgh, and then been able to visit the whole family?"

"Normally speaking, of course," Oonagh agreed, resuming her calm, intelligent tone. "But my sister is recently married and expecting her first child. She could not travel, and she was very anxious to see Mother."

"Indeed? And do you know why that was?"

There was a complete silence in the court. One woman coughed discreetly and the sound was like gunfire.

"Yes . . . she was concerned . . . afraid that her child might not be quite normal, might be afflicted with some hereditary illness. . . ." The words dropped one by one, carefully enunciated, into a pool of expectancy. There were gasps around the room. The jurors sat motionless. The judge turned sharply towards her.

Rathbone's head came up, his expression tense.

Argyll's eyes searched Oonagh's face.

"Indeed," Gilfeather said very softly. "And what did your mother propose to do about these fears, Mrs. McIvor?" He did not ask what the illness was, and Monk heard the whisper and rustle around the crowd as a hundred people let out their breath in release of tension and disappointment.

Oonagh paled a little. Her chin lifted. She knew their thoughts.

"She was going to assure her that the disease of which my father died was contracted long after she was born and was in no way hereditary." Her voice was very level, very clear. "It was a fever he developed while serving in the army abroad, and it damaged his internal organs, eventually killing him. Griselda was too young to have remembered it accurately, and I suppose at the time of Father's death she was not told. No one thought it would matter to her." She hesitated. "I am sorry to say so, but Griselda worries about her health far more than is necessary or natural."

"You are saying her anxiety was without cause?" Gilfeather concluded.

"Yes. Quite without cause. She would not believe that easily, and Mother was going to see her in person to convince her."

"I see. Very natural. I am sure any mother might well have done the same."

Oonagh nodded but did not reply.

There was a faint air of disappointment around the room. Some people's attention wandered.

Oonagh cleared her throat.

"Yes?" Gilfeather said immediately.

"It is not only my mother's gray pearl brooch which was missing," she said carefully. "Although of course we have that back now."

Now the attention was returned in full. No one fidgeted anymore.

"Indeed?" Gilfeather looked interested.

"There was also a diamond brooch of a great deal more value," Oonagh said gravely. "It was commissioned from our family jeweler, but it was not among my mother's effects."

In the dock Hester straightened up sharply and leaned forward, amazement in her face.

"I see." Gilfeather stared at Oonagh. "And the estimated worth of the two pieces, Mrs. McIvor?"

"Oh, a hundred pounds or so for the pearls, and perhaps a little more for the diamonds."

There was a gasp of breath around the room. The judge frowned and leaned forward a little.

"A very considerable sum indeed," Gilfeather agreed. "Enough to buy a great many luxuries for a woman living from one chance job to another."

Rathbone winced, so slightly perhaps only Monk saw it, but he knew exactly why.

"And was this diamond brooch on the list to be packed for London?"

"No. If Mother took it, it was a last-minute decision of her own."

"I see. But you have not found it among her effects?"

"No."

"Thank you, Mrs. McIvor."

Gilfeather stepped back, indicating graciously that Argyll might proceed.

Argyll thanked him and rose to his feet.

"This second piece of jewelry, Mrs. McIvor; you did not mention it earlier. In fact, this is the first time we have heard it referred to. Why is that?"

"Because we did not previously realize that it was missing," Oonagh answered reasonably.

"How odd! Such a valuable piece must surely have been kept in a safe place, a locked jewel casket or something of the like."

"I presume so."

"You don't know."

She looked uncertain. "No. It was my mother's, not mine."

"How many times have you seen her wear it?"

"I—" She watched him carefully with that same clear, direct look Monk remembered facing himself. "I don't recall seeing her wear it."

"How do you know she had it at all?"

"Because it was commissioned from our family jeweler, paid for and taken."

"By whom?"

"I see your point, Mr. Argyll," she granted. "But it is not mine, nor my sister's, nor does it belong to my sister-in-law. It can only have been my mother's. I daresay she wore it on some occasion when I was not present and so I have never noticed it."

"Is it not possible, Mrs. McIvor, that it was a gift for someone else, and not for a member of your family at all?" he suggested. "That would account for why no one has seen it and it is not there now, would it not?"

"If it were the truth, yes," Oonagh said dismissively. "But it was very expensive indeed to give someone who is not a member of the family. We are generous, I hope, but not extravagant."

Heads nodded. One woman stifled a giggle, and the man next to her glared at her.

"So you are saying, Mrs. McIvor, that the brooch was commissioned and yet no one has seen it, although it was paid for, is that right? You are not saying that you have any evidence to suggest that Miss Latterly has it, or ever has had?"

"She had the pearl brooch," Oonagh pointed out. "Even she does not deny that."

"No, indeed not," Argyll agreed. "She made every effort to return it to you as soon as she discovered it. But she has not seen the diamond brooch, any more than you have."

Oonagh flushed, opened her mouth, and then changed her mind and remained silent.

Argyll smiled. "Thank you, Mrs. McIvor. I have nothing further to ask you."

It was another tiny point gained, but the momentary elation vanished almost as soon as it came. Gilfeather was amused. He could afford to be.

He called the conductor from the train on which Mary Farraline and Hester had traveled. He said exactly what was expected. No one else, as far as he knew, had gone into the carriage. The two women had been alone the entire journey. Yes, Mrs. Farraline had left the compartment at least once, to attend the requirements of nature. Yes, Miss Latterly had called him in a state of some distress to report the death of the elder lady. He had gone along to see, and indeed, he deeply regretted to say so, but she had been dead. He had done his duty as soon as he had arrived in London. It was all very sad.

Argyll knew well enough not to alienate the jury by questioning what was too well established to state, and he would only harass an ordinary little man following his calling. He waved away his opportunity to cross-examine with a flick of his hand and an inclination of his head.

The stationmaster also said only what was entirely predictable, if in places self-important, nervous and melodramatic.

Again Monk's attention wandered to the faces around the room. He was able to watch Hester for several moments because she was staring at the witness-box. He regarded her curiously. She was not beautiful, but tense, frightened as she was now, there was a quality of refinement in her which was like a kind of beauty. It was stripped of all artifice or pretense, even the mask of usual good manners, and its very honesty caught the emotions. He was surprised how familiar she seemed, as if he had known every line of her entire being, every flicker of expression that would cross her features. He thought he knew what she was feeling, but he was powerless to give her anything.

The sense of helplessness was so intense it was like a pain in his chest. But even if he could have spoken to her, he knew there was nothing to say which she did not already know. Perhaps it would have helped if he could have lied. He would never know that, because he could not. He would not do it well, and to do it badly would only place a barrier between them which would make it all worse.

Oonagh had remained in the courtroom. He could see her fair hair across her brow beneath the brim of the dark bonnet. She looked calm and brave, as if she had spent hours alone in deep thought and self-mastery before she had left Ainslie Place to come here, and now nothing would break through her composure.

Did she know who had killed her mother? Did she guess, knowing her siblings as well as she did? He studied her features, the smooth brow, the level eyes, the long straight nose, the full mouth, almost perfectly shaped. Each feature was good, and yet the whole had too much power in it for ordinary beauty. Had she taken over the mantle of leadership on Mary's death? Was she protecting the family honor, or one individual member's weakness or evil?

Even if he found out who it was, he might never know that.

If?

Coldness enveloped him. He had unwittingly voiced the fear he had denied so scrupulously ever since he had come to Edinburgh. He dismissed it violently.

It was one of the Farralines. It had to be.

He turned from Oonagh to Alastair, sitting beside her, his eyes fixed unwaveringly on the stationmaster giving his evidence. He looked haunted, as though the burden of the public trial of his family's tragedy were more than he could bear. As Monk had seen once or twice before, it seemed to be his sister upon whom he leaned for support rather than his wife. Deirdra was there, certainly, and sitting next to him, but his body was inclined to the left, closer to Oonagh, and his right shoulder was half turned, excluding Deirdra.

Deirdra stared straight ahead of her, not ignoring Alastair so much as simply more interested in the proceedings. There was barely any concern or anxiety in her face with its calm brow, tip-tilted nose, and sturdy chin. If she suspected any impending tragedy, she was a consummate actress.

Kenneth was not in the room, nor had Monk expected him to be. He would be called to testify, and therefore was not permitted in yet, in case he overheard something that in some way altered what he would say. It was the law. Eilish was here, like a silent flame. Baird, on the far side of Oonagh, was also turned a little away, not obviously, simply a withdrawing of himself. He did not look at Eilish, but even from the far side of the room, Monk felt the iron control he was exerting on himself not to.

Quinlan Fyffe was absent, presumably because he too would be called.

The stationmaster finished his evidence and Argyll declined to question him. He was excused and replaced by the doctor who had been sent for and had certified that Mary Farraline was indeed dead. Gilfeather was very kind to him, seeking not to embarrass him for having diagnosed the death as due to ordinary heart failure and in no way worthy of further investigation. Even so, the man was uncomfortable and answered in monosyllables.

Argyll rose and smiled at him, then sat down without saying anything at all.

It was late in the afternoon. Court was adjourned for the day.

Monk left immediately, hurrying to find Rathbone and learn his judgment of how the day had gone. He saw him on the steps and caught up with him just as he and James Argyll climbed into a hansom cab.

Monk stopped at the curb and swore vehemently. His better sense knew perfectly well that Rathbone could tell him nothing he did not know for himself, and yet he was infuriated not to have been able to speak to him. He stood still for several minutes, too angry to think what to do next.

"Were you looking for Oliver, or just for the cab, Mr. Monk?"

He turned around sharply to find Henry Rathbone standing a few feet away. There was something in the anxiety in his gentle face, and vulnerability in it, which robbed him of his rage and left only his fear, and the need to share it.

"Rathbone," he replied. "Although I don't suppose he could have told me anything I haven't seen for myself. Were you in the court? I didn't see you."

"I was behind you," Henry Rathbone replied with a faint smile. "Standing. I was too late for a seat." They started to walk and Monk fell in step beside him. "I hadn't realized there would be so much public interest. It is the least attractive side of people, I think. I prefer people individually; in a crowd I find they so often take on each other's least admirable qualities. A pack instinct, I suppose. The scent of fear, of something wounded—" He stopped abruptly. "I'm sorry."

"You're right," Monk said grimly. "And Gilfeather is good." He did not add the rest of the thought. It was unnecessary.

They walked in a strangely companionable silence for several yards. Monk was surprised. The man was Rathbone's father, and yet he felt a liking for him as if he had known him for years and the relationship had always been comfortable. Instead of resenting Hester's liking for him, he was pleased. There was something in Henry Rathbone's face, his rather awkward gait, his long legs, not quite straight, which brought back faint, indistinct memories of being a young man, admiring his mentor intensely, almost without question. He had been very naive then. It seemed like another man whose innocence he looked at as he would a stranger's, only the feeling was within him, unaccountably sharp for just those few moments.

There was a legless beggar sitting on the footpath, an old soldier from some war gone from the public mind. He was selling small pieces of white heather bound into nosegays for luck.

Suddenly Henry Rathbone's eyes filled with agonized tears of pity. Wordlessly he smiled at the man and offered him sixpence for two bunches. He took them and walked in silence for several more paces before passing one to Monk.

"Don't lose hope," he said abruptly as they stepped off the curb and across the street. "Argyll is clever too. One of the family is responsible. Think what that person must be feeling! Think of the guilt, no matter what passion drove him or her to do it, whether it was fear or greed, or hatred for some wrong, real or imagined. There is still a terror, in all but the totally mad, for having taken such an irretrievable step."

Monk said nothing, but kept in step with him, thoughts turning over in his mind. What Henry Rathbone said was true. Someone was laboring under a driving passion which must include both fear and guilt.

"And perhaps a kind of elation," Henry went on. "The culprit seems to have won, to be on the brink of victory."

Monk grunted. "What kind of victory? Achievement of something or escape from some danger? Is it elation or relief?"

Henry shook his head, his face troubled. The darkness of it touched him, both for Mary Farraline and for whichever of her children, or children by marriage, had killed her.

"Pressure," he said, continuing to shake his head. "The process of the law may reach them, you know. That is what Oliver would do. Question. Probe. Play on their doubts of each other. I hope Argyll will do the same."

Neither of them said anything about Hester, but Monk knew Henry Rathbone was thinking of her too. There was no need to talk of winning or losing. It was always just below the surface of their words anyway, too painful to touch.

They walked on together in silence up the Lawnmarket.

CHAPTER
NINE

Hester felt uniquely alien as she stood in the cage in the cells waiting to be drawn up through the extraordinary trapdoor affair which would bring her into the courtroom without the necessity of passing through the crowd. The day was bitterly cold and here below the courtroom there was no heat at all. She shivered uncontrollably, and told herself with a flash of mockery that it had nothing to do with fear.

But when the time came and she was winched up into the packed court, even the warmth of the two coal fires and the expectant crowd of people crammed together to fill every space did not reach inside her and stop the shaking or ease the locked muscles.

She did not search their faces to see Monk, or Callandra, or Henry Rathbone. It was too painful. It reminded her of all she valued and might so very soon have to leave. And that was looking more and more likely with every witness who spoke. She had seen Argyll's tiny victories—and was not deceived. They were not enough to light hope in anyone but a fool. They kept the battle alive, futile as it was so far. They prevented surrender—but not defeat.

The first witness of the day was Connal Murdoch. The last time she had seen him had been in the railway station in London. He had been stunned with the news of Mary's death, confused by it, and anxious for his wife and her state both of health and of mind. Now he looked quite different. The frantic, slightly disheveled air was totally gone. He was neatly dressed in plain black, well cut but unimaginative. It was expensive without being elegant, probably because the man himself had no conception of grace, only of what was fitting.

But she could not deny the intelligence in his face with its hooded eyes, nervous mouth and slightly receding hair.

"Mr. Murdoch," Gilfeather began with an amiable air. "Allow me to take you through the events of that tragic day, as you are aware of them. You and your wife were expecting to meet Mrs. Farraline on the overnight train from Edinburgh?"

Murdoch looked grim and nodded slightly as he replied.

"Was it Mrs. Farraline herself who wrote to you of her visit?"

"Yes." Murdoch looked a trifle surprised, although presumably Gilfeather had taken him through the questions before the session began.

"Was there any indication in her letters that she was anxious or concerned for her safety?"

"Of course not."

"No mention of a family difficulty, a quarrel of any sort, any kind of ill feeling whatsoever?"

"None at all!" Murdoch's voice was growing sharper. The idea was repellent to him and the fact that Gilfeather had raised it clearly displeased him.

"So you had no sense of foreboding as you traveled to the station to meet her, no thought whatever that there could be anything wrong?"

"No sir, I have said not."

"What was the first intimation you received that all was not well?"

There was a stir in the room. Interest was awoken at last.

In spite of herself Hester looked at Oonagh and saw her pale face with its lovely hair. She was sitting next to Alastair again, their shoulders almost touching. For a moment Hester felt sorry for her. Absurdly she remembered quite clearly opening the letter from Charles which told her of her own mother's death. She had been standing in the sharp sunlight on the quayside at Scutari. The mail boat had come in while she had a few hours off duty, and she and another nurse had walked down to the shore. Many of the men were already embarking on the homeward journey. The war was all but over. The heat had gone out of the battle. It was the time when the cost could so clearly be seen, the wounded and the dead counted, the victory shabby and the whole fiasco pointless. One day the heroism would be remembered, but then it had all seemed only a matter of pain.

England had been a dream of such strangely mixed values: all the calm of old culture, a land at peace, quiet lanes and rich fields with trees bending low, people going quietly about their undoubting business. And at the same time old buildings of ineffable grace housing men whose bland, entrenched stupidity had sent untold young men to their deaths with a complacency that was still without the guilt she felt it should have had.

She had torn the letter open eagerly, and then stood with the black words dazzling on the white paper, reading them over and over as if each time there were some hope they might change and say something different. She had grown cold in the wind without realizing it.

Was that how Oonagh McIvor had felt when the letter had come telling her that Mary was dead?

From her face now it was impossible to tell. All her concentration seemed to be on supporting Alastair, who looked ashen pale. They were the two eldest. Had they been peculiarly close to Mary? She remembered Mary saying how they had comforted each other in childhood.

Connal Murdoch was relating how the news had been broken to him first, and how he had then told his wife. He was a good witness, full of quiet dignity and understated emotion. His voice quivered only occasionally, and no one could have told whether it was grief or anger, or any other powerful emotion.

Hester looked for Kenneth Farraline but could not see him. Had he embezzled from the company? And when his mother found out, murdered her? Weak men had done such things before, especially if they were besottedly in love, and then, afraid of the consequences of a rash action, done something even more panic-stricken in trying to conceal it.

Would Oonagh conceal it for him?

Hester stared at her strange powerful face and could not even guess.

Connal Murdoch was talking about meeting Hester in the stationmaster's office. It was an extraordinary thing to stand and hear it recounted through someone else's eyes and be unable to speak to correct lies and mistakes.

"Oh certainly," he was saying. "She appeared very pale, but quite composed. Of course we had no idea then that she herself was responsible for Mother-in-law's death."

Argyll rose to his feet.

"Yes, yes, Mr. Argyll," the judge said impatiently. He turned to the witness stand. "Mr. Murdoch, whatever your own convictions, we in the court presume a person is innocent until the jury has returned a verdict of guilty. You will please remember that in your replies."

Murdoch looked taken aback.

Argyll was obviously aching to put the criticism in his own words, far more decisively than the judge, and he was not to be permitted. Behind him Oliver Rathbone was sitting rigidly, motionless except for the fingers of his left hand, drumming on a sheaf of notes.

Hester looked at the rest of the Farralines. One of them had killed Mary. It was absurd that she should stand here fighting for her life, and be able to stare at their faces one after another, and not know which one it was, even now.

Did they know, all of them—or only the one who had done it?

Old Hector was not there. Did that mean he was drunk as usual, or that Argyll intended to call him? He had not told her.

Sometimes it was better to have someone else plan the defense and conduct the battle. And there were other times she felt so agonizingly helpless she would have given anything at all to be able to stand up and tell them herself, question people, force the truth out of them. And even while the thought raced through her mind, she knew it would be totally futile.

Gilfeather concluded his questions and sat down with a smile. He looked comfortable, well satisfied with his position, and so he should. The jury was sitting in solemn and disapproving silence, their faces closed, their minds already set. Not one of them looked towards the dock.

Argyll rose to his feet, but there was little he could say and nothing at all to contest.

Behind him Oliver Rathbone was fuming with impatience. The longer this evidence took, the more firmly entrenched in the jurors' mind was Hester's guilt. Men were reluctant to change a decision once made. Gilfeather knew that as well as he did. Clever swine.

The judge's face also was narrow and hard. His words might be full of legally correct indecision, but one had only to see him to know what his own verdict was.

Argyll sat down again almost immediately, and Rathbone breathed a sigh of relief.

The next person to be called was Griselda Murdoch. It was a piece of emotional manipulation. She had recently given birth and she looked pale and very tired, as if she had traveled only with difficulty for so tragic an event. The sympathy from the crowd was palpable in the air. The hatred for Hester increased with a bound till it hung thick like a bad smell in a closed space.

For Rathbone it was a nightmare. He did not know whether he would have attempted to tear her apart rather than allow the sympathy to build, or whether it would only make matters immeasurably worse. He was almost glad it was not his decision to make.

And yet to sit there helplessly was almost beyond bearing. He looked at Argyll, and could not read his face. He was staring through furrowed brows at Griselda Murdoch, but he could have been merely listening to her with concentration, or he could have been planning how to trap her, discredit her, attack her character, her veracity, or any other aspect of the effect she would have upon the jury.

"Mrs. Murdoch," Gilfeather said softly, as if he were addressing an invalid or a child. "We are deeply sensible of your courage in coming to testify in this tragic matter, and of the cost it must have been for you to travel this distance in your present state of health."

There was a murmur of sympathy around the room and someone spoke his approval aloud.

The judge ignored this.

"I will not trouble you to relive your emotions at the railway station, Mrs. Murdoch," Gilfeather continued. "It would distress you for no purpose, and that is the furthest thing from my intention. If you would be so kind as to tell us what transpired after you returned to your home, with your husband, knowing that your mother had died. Do not hurry, and choose your words exactly as you please."

"Thank you, you are most kind," she said shakily.

Monk, staring at her, thought how unlike her sisters she was. She had not the courage of either of them, nor the passion of character. She might well be far easier for a man to live with, less demanding, less testing of patience or forbearance, but dear heaven she would also be infinitely less interesting. She was uncertain, timid, and there was a streak of self-pity in her that Oonagh would have found intolerable.

Or was it all an act, an outer garment designed to appeal to the court? Did she know who had killed her mother? Was it even conceivable, in a wild moment of insanity, that they had all conspired together to murder Mary Farraline?

No, that was absurd. His wits were wandering.

She was telling Gilfeather how she had unpacked Mary's cases and found her clothes and the list of items, and in so doing had failed to find the gray pearl pin.

"I see." Gilfeather nodded sagely. "And you expected to find it?"

"Certainly. The note said that it should be there."

"And what did you do, Mrs. Murdoch?"

"I spoke to my husband. I told him it was missing and asked his advice," she replied.

"And what did he advise you should do?"

"Well, of course the first thing we did was to search thoroughly again, through everything. But it was quite definitely not there."

"Quite. We now know that Miss Latterly had it with her. This is not in dispute. What then?"

"Well—Connal, Mr. Murdoch, was most concerned that it had been stolen, and he . . ." She gulped and took several seconds to regain her composure. The court waited in respectful silence.

Behind Argyll, Rathbone swore under his breath.

"Yes?" Gilfeather encouraged.

"He said we should be wise to call in our own doctor to give another opinion as to how my mother had died."

"I see. And so you did exactly that?"

"Yes."

"And whom did you call, Mrs. Murdoch?"

"Dr. Ormorod, of Slingsby Street."

"I see. Thank you." He turned with a disarming smile to Argyll. "Your witness, sir."

"Thank you, thank you indeed." Argyll uncurled himself from his chair and stood up.

"Mrs. Murdoch . . ."

She regarded him warily, assuming that he was essentially inimical.

"Yes sir?"

"These clothes and effects of your mother's that you unpacked . . .

I take it that you did it yourself, rather than having your maid do it? You do have a maid, I imagine?"

"Of course I do!"

"But on this occasion, possibly because of the uniquely tragic circumstances, you chose to unpack them yourself?"

"Yes."

"Why?"

There was a rustle of disapproval around the room. One of the jurors coughed sharply. The judge frowned, seeming on the edge of speech, then at the last moment restrained himself.

"Wh-why?" Griselda looked nonplussed. "I don't understand."

"Yes, Mrs. Murdoch," Argyll repeated, standing grim and motionless, every eye fixed on him. "Why did you unpack your mother's belongings?"

"I—I did not wish the maid to," Griselda said chokingly. "She —she was . . ." She stopped, knowing that the sympathy of the court would finish it for her.

"No, madam, you have misunderstood me," Argyll said carefully. "I do not mean why did you not have the maid do it. The answer to that, I am sure, we all understand perfectly, and would probably have felt the same in your position. I mean, why did you unpack them at all? Why did you not simply leave them packed, ready to return them to Edinburgh? It was tragically obvious she would no longer need them in London."

"Oh." She let out her breath in a sigh, her face very pale except for the faint splash of pink burning in her cheeks.

"One wonders why you unpacked them with such care when it was now quite irrelevant. I would not have done so in your position. I would have left them packed, ready to return." Argyll's voice dropped to a low rumble, and yet every word was hideously clear. "Unless, of course, I was looking for something myself?"

Griselda said nothing, but her discomfort was now only too apparent.

Argyll relaxed a little, leaning forward.

"Was the diamond brooch on this list of contents, Mrs. Murdoch?"

"Diamond brooch? No. No, there was no diamond brooch."

"You are sure?"

"Yes, of . . . of course I am sure. Just the gray pearl and the topaz and the amethyst necklace. Only the gray pearl one was missing."

"Do you still have that list, Mrs. Murdoch?"

"No . . . no. No I don't. I . . . I don't know what happened to it." She swallowed. "What does it matter? You know Miss Latterly had the brooch. The police found it in her belongings."

"No, Mrs. Murdoch," Argyll corrected. "That is not true. The police found it in the home of Lady Callandra Daviot, where Miss Latterly had discovered it and had already taken it to her hostess in order to have it returned to Edinburgh. She had reported the matter to her solicitor and obtained his advice."

Griselda looked confused—and considerably shaken.

"I don't know about that. I only know it was missing from my mother's effects and Miss Latterly had it. I don't know what else you want me to say."

"I don't want you to say anything, madam. You have answered my questions admirably and with great frankness." There was only a thread of sarcasm in his voice, but the doubt had been raised. It was enough. Now everyone wondered exactly why Griselda Murdoch had gone through her mother's possessions, and many thought they knew the answer. It was not a flattering one. It was the first rift in family solidarity, the first suggestion that there could be greed or distrust.

Argyll sat down with an air of satisfaction.

Behind him, Rathbone felt as if the first salvo of return shot had at last been fired. It had hit the mark, but the wound was trivial, and Gilfeather knew that as well as they did. Only the crowd had seen blood and the air was tingling sharp again with the sudden scent of battle.

The final witness of the day was Mary Farraline's lady's maid, a quiet, sad woman dressed in unrelieved black, devoid of even the simplest piece of mourning jewelry.

Gilfeather was very polite with her.

"Miss McDermot, did you pack the clothes of your late mistress for her trip to London?"

"Yes sir, I did."

"Did you have a list of all that you put in the cases, for the maid at the other end, whom Mrs. Murdoch would supply?"

"Yes sir. Mrs. McIvor wrote it out for me to work from."

"Yes, I understand. Was there a diamond brooch included?"

"No sir, there was not."

"You are quite sure?"

"Yes sir, I'd swear to it."

"Quite so. But there was a gray pearl brooch of unusual design?"

"Yes sir, there was."

Gilfeather hesitated.

Rathbone stiffened. Was he about to ask if everything she had packed had been returned with Mary's luggage? It would clear Griselda of the slur.

But he declined. Perhaps he too was uncertain if she might have taken something. It would only have to be the slightest memento, and its loss would seem theft to this straining crowd, eager for drama and guilt of any sort.

Rathbone leaned back in his chair and, for the first time, smiled. Gilfeather had made a mistake. He was vulnerable after all.

"Miss McDermot," Gilfeather resumed. "Did you meet Miss Latterly that day when she came to the house in Ainslie Place in order to escort Mrs. Farraline to London?"

"Certainly, sir. I showed her Mrs. Farraline's medicine chest so she would know what to do."

There was a sharp snap of attention in the court again. Three jurors who had relaxed suddenly sat upright. Someone in the gallery gave a little squeak and was instantly criticized.

"You showed her the medicine chest, Miss McDermot?"

"Aye, I did. I couldn't know she was going to poison the poor soul!" There was anguish in her voice and her face looked on the brink of tears.

"Of course not, Miss McDermot," Gilfeather said soothingly. "No one blames you for your quite innocent part in this. It was your duty to show her. You presumed her a good nurse who quite obviously had need to know her patient's requirements and how to meet them. But the court has to be sure of precisely what happened. You did show her the medicine chest, and the vials in it, and you told her what they contained, and how and when to administer the dose?"

"Aye—I did."

"Thank you. That is all, Miss McDermot."

She made as if to leave, turning in the box to fumble her way down again.

Argyll rose to his feet.

"No . . . Miss McDermot. A few minutes of your time, if you please!"

She gasped, blushed scarlet, and turned back to face him, chin high, eyes terrified.

He smiled at her, and it only made it worse. She looked about to faint away.

"Miss McDermot," he began softly, his voice like the growl of a sleeping bear. "Did you show Miss Latterly your mistress's jewels?"

"Of course not! I'm not . . ." She stared at him wildly.

"Not a foolish woman," he finished for her. "No, I had not thought you were. I imagine you would not dream of showing your mistress's jewels to a relative stranger, or indeed to anyone. On the contrary, you would be most discreet about them, would you not?"

Gilfeather half rose. "My lord . . ."

"Yes, Mr. Gilfeather," the judge said sharply. "I know what you are going to say. Mr. Argyll, you are leading the witness. Ask questions if you please, do not assume answers."

"I apologize, my lord," Argyll said with outward humility. "Now, Miss McDermot, please enlighten the court as to the duties of a good lady's maid. What would your mistress have said had you shown her jewels, or any other of her valuable possessions, to anyone outside the family? Did she give you instructions on this matter?"

"No sir. It wouldn't be necessary. No servant would do such a thing and expect to keep her position."

"So you are quite certain you did not show the pearl brooch, or any other piece, to Miss Latterly?"

"Aye, I'm absolutely positive I did not. The mistress kept her jewelry in a case in her bedroom, not in the dressing room, sir. And I didn't have a key to it."

"Quite so. Thank you. I had not doubted you, Miss McDermot. I imagine the Farralines can afford to have the best servants in Edinburgh, and would not keep anyone who disregarded so basic a rule."

"Thank you, sir."

"Now, this medicine cabinet. Please think very carefully, Miss McDermot. How many vials does this cabinet hold?"

"Twelve sir," she said, staring at him warily.

"And each one is a separate and complete dose."

"Aye sir, it is."

"How are they laid out, Miss McDermot?"

"In two rows of six."

"Side by side, one above the other, in two trays? Please describe it for us," he instructed.

"One above the other, in the same tray ... like ... like two halves of a book ... not like drawers," she replied. Something of her anxiety seemed to lessen.

"I see. A very precise description. Do you have new vials each time the medicine is prescribed?"

"Oh no. That would be most wasteful. They are glass, with a stopper in. It is quite airtight."

"I commend your thrift. So the apothecary refills the vials when the medicine is obtained?"

"Yes sir."

"Especially for traveling?"

"Yes."

"What about when Mrs. Farraline is at home?"

"It still comes from the apothecary separately, sir. It has to be very exact, or it could be"—she swallowed hard—"fatal, sir. But we have to add the liquid to make it palatable—at least ..."

"I see, yes, that is quite clear. And this was a new supply, a full dozen vials for Mrs. Farraline to travel with?"

"Aye sir. If she were gone more than six days then it would be simple enough to get an apothecary in London to provide more."

"A very practical arrangement. She took the prescription with her, of course?"

"Aye, sir."

"So there was no anxiety if she ran out?"

"N-no ..."

Gilfeather stirred restlessly in his seat. He was impatient, and had his adversary been a lesser man, he would have dismissed the line of questioning as time-wasting.

"Mr. Argyll," the judge said irritably, "have you some purpose in mind? If you have, it is more than time you arrived at it."

"Yes, my lord," Argyll said smoothly. He turned back to the witness stand. "Miss McDermot, would it have mattered had you been a little hasty in your care for Mrs. Farraline and, instead of sending her off with a full complement of vials, used one to give her her morning dose on the day she traveled, rather than make one up. I simply ask if it would have mattered, not if you did so."

She stared at him as if she had suddenly seen a snake.

"Miss McDermot?"

"You must answer," the judge informed her.

She swallowed. "N-no. No sir, it would not really have mattered."

"It would not have placed her in any danger?"

"No sir. None at all."

"I see." He smiled at her as if he were totally satisfied with the answer. "Thank you, Miss McDermot. That is all."

Gilfeather rose rapidly. There was a stir of excitement around the room like a ripple of wind through a cornfield. Gilfeather opened his mouth.

Miss McDermot stared at him.

Gilfeather looked at Argyll.

Argyll's smile did not change in the slightest.

Rathbone sat with his hands clenched so hard his nails scarred his palms. Would Gilfeather dare to ask if she had used the first vial? If she admitted it, his case was damaged, severely damaged. Rathbone held his breath.

Gilfeather did not dare. She might have used it. She might not have the nerve to deny it on oath. He sat down again.

There was a sigh of breath around the room, a rustle of fabric as everyone relaxed, disappointed. One juror swore under his breath, mouthing the words.

Miss McDermot had to be assisted at the bottom of the steps when she stumbled in sheer unbearable relief.

Argyll's lips still curved in the same smile.

Rathbone offered up a prayer of thanks.

Gilfeather's next witness was the doctor whom Connal Murdoch had called, a rotund man with black hair and a fine black mustache.

"Dr. Ormorod," he began smoothly, as soon as the doctor's credentials had been thoroughly established, "you were called by Mr. Connal Murdoch to attend the deceased, Mrs. Mary Farraline, is that correct?"

"Yes sir, it is. At half past ten in the morning of October the seventh, of this year of our Lord," the doctor replied.

"Did you respond immediately?"

"No sir. I was in attendance upon a child who was seriously ill with whooping cough. I had been informed that Mrs. Farraline was deceased. I saw no urgency."

There was a nervous giggle in the gallery. One of the jurors, a large man with a mane of white hair, scowled at the offender.

"Was any reason given why you should be sent for, Dr. Ormorod?" Gilfeather asked. "It was a somewhat unusual request, was it not?"

"Not really, sir. I imagined at the time that my main duty would be to attend Mrs. Murdoch. The shock of bereavement can in itself be a cause for medical concern."

"Yes . . . I see. And what did you find when you reached Mrs. Murdoch's residence?"

"Mrs. Murdoch, poor soul, in a state of considerable distress, which was most natural, but the cause of it was not entirely what I had expected." The doctor became increasingly sensible that he was the focus of all attention. He straightened up even farther and raised his chin, measuring his words like an actor delivering a great monologue. "She was, of course, deeply grieved by her mother's passing, but she was also most troubled by the possible manner of it. She feared, sir, that in view of the missing jewels, it may not have been entirely of natural causes."

"That is what she said to you?" Gilfeather demanded.

"Indeed sir, it is."

"And what did you do, Dr. Ormorod?"

"Well, at first, I confess, I did not entirely believe her." He pulled a face and glanced at the jury. One or two of them obviously sympathized with him. There were nodding heads. At least two thirds were middle-aged to elderly gentlemen of high repute, and were used to the vagaries of women, especially young women in a delicate condition.

"But what did you do, sir?" Gilfeather insisted.

Ormorod returned his attention to the matter. "I conducted an examination, sir, in some considerable detail." Again he waited, for dramatic effect.

Gilfeather kept his composure.

Rathbone swore under his breath.

Argyll sighed silently, but his expression was easily readable.

Ormorod's face tightened. This was not the reaction he had intended.

"It took me a long time," he said tightly. "And I was obliged to conduct a full postmortem examination, most particularly the contents of the stomach of the deceased. But I concluded that there was no doubt whatsoever that Mrs. Farraline had met her death as a result of having been given a massive overdose of her usual medicine, a distillation of digitalis."

"How massive a dose, sir? Can you say?"

"At least twice what any responsible practitioner would prescribe for her," Ormorod answered.

"And you have no doubt of that?" Gilfeather persisted.

"None whatsoever. But you do not need to rest on my opinion alone, sir. The police surgeon will have told you the same."

"Yes sir. We have the result of that to be read into evidence," Gilfeather assured him. "And it confirms precisely what you say."

Ormorod smiled and nodded.

"Did you form any opinion as to how it had been administered?"

"By mouth, sir."

"Was any force used?"

"There was nothing to suggest it, no sir. I would think it was taken quite voluntarily. I imagine the deceased lady had no idea whatever that it would do her harm."

"But you have no doubt that it was indeed the cause of her death?"

"No doubt whatsoever."

"Thank you, Dr. Ormorod. I have no further questions for you."

Argyll thanked Gilfeather and faced Dr. Ormorod.

"Sir, your evidence has been admirably clear and to the point. I have only one question to ask you. It is this. I assume you examined the medicine chest from which the deceased's dose had been taken? Yes. Naturally you did. How many vials were there in it, sir . . . both full and empty?"

Ormorod thought for a moment, furrowing his brow.

"There were ten full vials, sir, and two empty."

"Are you quite sure?"

"Yes . . . yes, I am positive."

"Would you describe their appearance, sir?"

"Appearance?" Ormorod clearly did not see any purpose to the question.

"Yes, Doctor; what did they look like?"

Ormorod held up his hand, finger and thumb apart. "About two, two and a half inches long, three quarters of an inch in diameter, sir. Very unremarkable, very ordinary medical vials."

"Of glass?"

"I have said so."

"Clear glass?"

"No sir, dark blue colored glass, as is customary when a substance is poisonous, or can be if taken ill-advisedly."

"Easy to see if a vial is full or empty?"

At last Ormorod understood. "No sir. Half full, perhaps; but completely full or quite empty would appear exactly the same, no line of liquid to observe."

"Thank you, Doctor. We may presume one of them was used by Miss Latterly on the previous evening, the other we may never know ... unless Miss McDermot should choose to tell us."

"Mr. Argyll!" the judge said angrily. "You may presume what you please, but you will not do it aloud in my court. Here we will have evidence only. And Miss McDermot has said nothing about the subject."

"Yes, my lord," Argyll said unrepentantly. The damage was done, and they all knew it.

Ormorod said nothing.

Argyll thanked him and excused him. He left somewhat reluctantly. He had enjoyed his moment in the limelight.

On the third day Gilfeather called Mary Farraline's own doctor to describe her illness, its nature and duration, and to swear that there was no reason why she should not have lived several more years of happy and fulfilled life. There were all the appropriate murmurs of sympathy. He described the medicine he had prescribed for her, and the dosage.

Argyll said nothing.

The apothecary who had prepared the medicine was called, and described his professional services in detail.

Again Argyll said nothing, except to ascertain that the medicine could have been distilled to become more concentrated, and thus twice as powerful, while still in the same volume of liquid, and that it did not need a nurse's medical knowledge or skills to do so. It was all totally predictable.

Hester sat in the dock watching and listening. Half of her wished that it could be over. It was like a ritual dance, only in words, everyone taking a carefully rehearsed and foreordained part. It had a nightmarish quality, because she could only observe. She could take no part in it, although it was her life they were deciding. She was the only one who could not go home at the end of it, and would certainly not do it all again next week, or next month, but over a different matter, and with different players walking on and off.

She wanted the suspense to stop, the judgment to be made.

But when it was, then perhaps it would be all over. There would be condemnation. No more hope, however slight, however little she set her heart on it. She thought now that she had resigned herself. But had she really? When it came to the moment that it was no longer a matter of imagination that the judge put on the black cap and pronounced the sentence of death, would she still really keep her back straight, her knees locked and supporting her weight?

Or would the room spin around her and her stomach churn and rise in sickness? Perhaps after all she needed a little longer to prepare herself.

The next witness was Callandra Daviot. Somehow word had been whispered around until almost everyone in the gallery knew that she was Hester's friend, and they were therefore hostile to her. A battle of wits was expected. It was almost as if there were a scent of blood in the air. People craned forward to see her stiff, broad-hipped figure walk across the floor of the courtroom and climb the steps to the witness stand.

Watching her, Monk had an almost sickening lurch of familiarity. It was as if she were not only a woman he had known in the last year and a half, and who had helped him financially, a woman whose courage and intellect he admired, but as if she were a part of his own emotional life. She was not beautiful; even in her youth she had been charming at best. Her nose was too long, her mouth too individual, her hair was too curly and tended to frizz and fly away at odd and uncomplimentary angles. No pins had yet been devised which would make it sit fashionably. Her figure was broad at the hip and a trifle too rounded at the shoulders.

And yet the whole had a dignity and honesty about it that superceded the elegance of other Society women, a reality where artifice ruled. He ached to be able to help her, impossible as that was, and was disgusted with his own sentimentality.

He sat in his seat with his body rigid, all his muscles locked, telling himself he was a fool, that he did not care overmuch, that his whole life would continue much the same in all that mattered, regardless of what happened there. And he did not feel one iota better for any of it.

"Lady Callandra." Gilfeather was polite but cool. He was not naive enough to imagine he could charm her, or that the jury would think he could. He had occasionally overestimated the subtlety of a jury; never had he erred in the other direction. "How long have you known Miss Hester Latterly?"

"Since the summer of 1856," Callandra replied.

"And the relationship has been friendly, even warm?"

"Yes." Callandra had no alternative but to admit it. To deny it might have strengthened her embracement of Hester's honesty, but it would have required explanation of its own as to why it was cool. She and Gilfeather both knew it and the jury watched her with growing understanding of all the nuances of both what she would say and leave unsaid.

"Were you aware that she intended to take the position with the Farraline family?"

"Yes."

"She informed you of it?"

"Yes."

"What did she tell you about it? Please be precise, Lady Callandra. I am sure you are aware that you are on oath."

"Of course I am," she said tartly. "Added to which, I have no need and no desire to be anything less."

Gilfeather nodded but said nothing.

"Proceed," the judge directed.

"That she would enjoy the journey and that she had not been to Scotland before, so it would be a pleasure in that respect also."

"Are you familiar with Miss Latterly's financial position?"

Gilfeather asked, his eyebrows raised, his flyaway hair wild where he had pushed his fingers through it.

"No I am not."

"Are you quite certain?" Gilfeather sounded surprised. "Surely as a friend, a friend with considerable means of your own, you have ascertained from time to time whether she was in need of your assistance or not?"

"No." Callandra stared back at him, defying him to disbelieve her. "She is a woman of self-respect, and considerable ability to earn her own way. I trust that if she were in difficulty she would feel close enough to me to ask, and I should have noticed for myself. That situation has never arisen. She is not someone to whom money is important, provided she can meet her commitments. She does have a family, you know—who would be perfectly happy to offer her a permanent home, did she wish it. If you are trying to paint a picture of her as desperate to keep body and soul together, you are totally mistaken."

"I was not," Gilfeather assured her. "I was thinking of something far less pitiable, and understandable, Lady Callandra, simply greed. A woman without pretty things, who sees a brooch she likes, and in a moment of weakness takes it, then is obliged to conceal her crime by an infinitely worse one."

"Balderdash!" Callandra said furiously, her face burning with anger and disgust. "Complete tommyrot. You know little of human nature, sir, if you judge her that way, and cannot see that most crimes of murder are committed either by practiced villains or else are within the family. This, I fear, is one of the latter. I am quite aware that it is your professional duty to obtain a conviction, rather than to seek the truth . . . which is a pity, in my view. But—"

"Madam!" The judge banged his gavel on the bench with a clap like gunfire. "The court will not endure your opinion of the Scottish legal system and what you believe to be its shortcomings. You will answer counsel's questions simply and add nothing of your own. Mr. Gilfeather, I suggest you endeavor to keep your witness in control, hostile or not!"

"Yes, my lord," Gilfeather said obediently, but he was not as entirely angry as perhaps he should have been. "Now, your ladyship, if we may address the matter in hand? Would you be good enough to tell the court exactly what happened when Miss Latterly called upon you on her return from Edinburgh, after Mrs. Farraline's death. Begin with her arrival at your home, if you please."

"She looked extremely distressed," Callandra answered. "It was about a quarter to eleven in the morning, as I recall."

"But surely the train arrives in London long before that?" he interrupted.

"Long before," she agreed. "She had been detained by Mrs. Farraline's death, and advising the conductor, and then the station-master, and finally by speaking to Mr. and Mrs. Murdoch. She came straight from the station to my house, tired and deeply grieved. She had liked Mrs. Farraline, even in the short time she had known her. She was, according to Hester, a remarkably charming woman, full of humor and intelligence."

"Indeed, so I believe," Gilfeather said dryly, glancing at the jury and then back at Callandra. "She is already deeply missed. What did Miss Latterly tell you had happened?"

Callandra replied as accurately as she could remember, and no one else stirred or made a sound while she was speaking. She went on, at Gilfeather's prompting, to tell how Hester had gone upstairs to wash and had returned with the gray pearl pin, and what had transpired after that. Gilfeather tried his best to keep her answers brief, to cut her off, to best rephrase his questions so that a confirmation or denial would be sufficient, but she was not to be led.

Rathbone sat still behind Argyll listening to every word, but his eyes as often as not were upon the faces of the jury. He could see their respect for Callandra, and indeed that they liked her, but they also knew that she was biased towards the prisoner.

How much would they discount for that reason?

It was impossible to tell.

He turned to watch the Farralines instead. Oonagh was still composed, her face totally calm, watching Callandra with interest and not without respect. Beside her, Alastair looked unhappy, his aquiline face drawn, as if he had slept poorly, which was hardly surprising. Did he know about the company books? Had he begun his own inquiries since his mother's death? Had he suspected his weaker younger brother?

What quarrels were there in that family when the door was closed and the outside, public world could neither see nor hear?

It was not surprising that none of them looked at Hester. Did they know, or at least believe, that she was innocent?

He leaned forward and tapped Argyll on the shoulder.

Very slowly Argyll leaned backward so he could hear if Rathbone bent and whispered.

"Are you going to play on the family's guilt?" he said under his breath. "It is very probable at least one of them knows who it is—and why."

"Which one?"

"Alastair, I should guess. He is head of the family, and he looks wretched."

"He won't break as long as his sister is there to support him," Argyll said in reply so softly Rathbone had to strain to hear him. "If I could drive a wedge between those two, I would, but I don't know how yet, and to try it and fail would only strengthen them. I'll only get one chance. She is a formidable woman, Oonagh McIvor."

"Is she protecting her husband?"

"She would, I think, but why? Why would Baird McIvor have killed his mother-in-law?"

"I don't know," Rathbone confessed.

The judged glared at him and for several moments he was obliged to keep silent, until Callandra again earned the judge's disapproval and his attention returned to her.

"Fear," he whispered to Argyll again.

"Of whom?" Argyll asked, his face expressionless.

"Play on fear," Rathbone replied. "Find the weakest one and put him on the box, and make the others fear he or she would give them away, either out of panic and clumsiness or to save his own skin."

Argyll was silent for so long Rathbone thought he had not heard.

He leaned forward again and was about to repeat it when Argyll replied.

"Who is the weak one? One of the women? Eilish, with her ragged school, or Deirdra, with her flying machine?"

"No, not the women," Rathbone said with a certainty that surprised him.

"Good," Argyll agreed dryly, the shadow of a smile curving his lips. "Because I wouldn't have done it."

"How gallant." Rathbone was bitingly sarcastic. "And damned useless."

"Not gallant at all," Argyll said between his teeth. "Practical. The jury will love Eilish; she is both beautiful and good. What else can you ask? And they'll deplore Deirdra's deceit of her husband, but they'll secretly like her. She's small and pretty and full of courage. The fact that she's as mad as a hatter won't make any difference."

Rathbone was relieved that Argyll was not as stupid as he had feared. It mattered too much for him to be angry at his own discomfort.

"Go after Kenneth," he replied to the earlier question. "He is the weak link—and possibly the murderer. Monk has the information about his mistress. Get old Hector, if he's sober enough, and that will be sufficient to raise the question of the books."

"Thank you, Mr. Rathbone," Argyll said tightly. "I had thought of that."

"Yes, of course," Rathbone conceded. "I apologize," he added as an afterthought.

"Accepted," Argyll murmured. "I am aware of your personal involvement with the accused, or I would not."

Rathbone felt his face burning. He had not thought of his relationship with Hester as an "involvement."

"Your witness, Mr. Argyll," the judge said sharply. "If you would be good enough to give us your attention, sir."

Argyll stood up, his temper flushing in his face. He did not reply to the judge. Perhaps he did not trust himself to.

"Lady Callandra," he said courteously. "Just to make sure we have understood you correctly, Miss Latterly brought the pin to you while you were downstairs? You did not find it in her luggage, nor did any of your servants?"

"No. She found it when she went to wash before luncheon. None of my servants would have occasion to look in her luggage, nor would she, had she not decided to stay with me during the meal."

"Quite so. And her immediate reaction was to bring it to you."

"Yes. She knew it was not hers, and feared something was seriously wrong."

"In which she was tragically correct. And your advice was to seek a solicitor's counsel in the matter, so it might be returned to Mrs. Farraline's estate?"

"Yes. She took it to Mr. Oliver Rathbone."

"The matter, Lady Callandra, or the pin itself?"

"The matter. She left the pin in my house. I wish now that she had thought to take it with her."

"I doubt it would have forestalled this sorry situation, madam. The plan had been very carefully laid. She did all a sensible person could, and it availed her nothing."

"Mr. Argyll," the judge snapped. "I will not warn you again."

Argyll inclined his head graciously. "Thank you, Lady Callandra. I have no more questions."

The last witness for the prosecution was Sergeant Daly, who recounted his having been called in by Dr. Ormorod, the whole of his procedure from that time until he had arrested Hester and finally charged her with murder. He spoke levelly and carefully and with great sadness, every now and again shaking his head, his mild, clear face regarding the whole courtroom with benign interest.

Gilfeather thanked him.

Argyll declined to question him. There was nothing to say, nothing to argue with.

Gilfeather smiled. The prosecution rested its case.

The jury nodded to one another silently, already certain of their verdict.

CHAPTER
TEN

The defense began the following morning. The crowd which filled the gallery was in an unusual mood, shifting and whispering in a strange mixture of apathy and then sudden interest, its tenor changing every few moments. Some believed it was all over, and the defense was merely a legal nicety in order that there could be no appeal against unfair process of law. Others were half expecting a battle of wits, however futile. The former were admirers of Gilfeather, the latter of James Argyll. Almost everyone was partisan; those who had no interest in either combatant were sure of the outcome and had not bothered to attend at all.

Rathbone was so on edge he had kept clearing his throat and it now ached. He had not slept until it was nearly time to get up, then he had been deeply in nightmare and waking had been difficult. The previous evening he had gone first to spend time with his father, then, realizing how short his temper, he had not wished to inflict it on anyone else, particularly Henry. He had spent from half past eight until nearly midnight alone, going over and over the case in his mind, rehearsing every scrap of evidence they knew, and when that proved fruitless, repeating as well as he could remember all the testimony Gilfeather had presented. It was not conclusive, of course it was not. Hester was not guilty! But she could have killed Mary Farraline, and in the absence of anything to suggest someone else had, suggest it powerfully, believably, any jury would convict her.

Argyll might be the best lawyer in Scotland, but it would take more than skill now, and as he sat in the crowded, tingling courtroom he dared not look up at the dock at Hester. She might see the despair in his face, and he could at least spare her that.

Nor did he look for Monk's smooth, dark head in the gallery. He half hoped he would not be there. Possibly he had thought of something to pursue, some further idea. Had he asked the apothecaries if anyone else had purchased digitalis? Yes, he must have. It was elementary. Monk was not a man to rest on pure defense. He would attack; it was his nature. Dear heaven, it was the essence of the man.

Neither did Rathbone look for his father; he avoided the gallery altogether. It was not only emotional cowardice—or, to give it a kinder name, self-preservation—it was tactical sense. At this point feelings were redundant, a clear mind was needed, a sharp brain and logical thought.

The judge looked cold and complacent. It was not a difficult case from his view. He had no doubt of conviction. Sentencing a woman to hang would be unpleasant, but he had done it before, and would no doubt do it again. Then he would go home to his family and a good dinner. Tomorrow there would be a new case.

And the public would applaud him. Emotion was running high. There were people whom Society had set high in its estimation, had given a certain honor, attributed to them emotions nobler than the ordinary man. They included the religious and medical worlds. They had been set above others in esteem, and more was required of them in return. When they fell, they fell farther. Condemnation was accompanied by disillusion and all its discomfort to the beliefs. It was bitter, born of pain, anger and self-pity, because something precious had been attacked. The offense was not only against Mary Farraline. If one could not trust a nurse, the whole world was not what one had taken for granted. All safety was threatened. For that, the punishment was terrible.

He saw it in the faces of the jurors also. Judgment was touched with fear. And few men forgave one who frightened them.

The court came to order. James Argyll rose to his feet. There was total silence. Not a soul whispered or moved.

"May it please my lord, gentlemen of the jury," he began. "So far you have heard much factual evidence as to how Mary Farraline met her death, and much indication as to how it may well have happened. You have heard a little of what manner of woman she was. The defense would be the last to wish to quibble with what has been said of her. Indeed, we would have added more. She was charming, intelligent, courteous, honorable; possessed of those rare qualities, both generosity and humor. While we do not contend that she was perfect—which of us mortals is—we know of no ill in her and have nothing to say of her but praise. Her family is not alone in mourning her."

The judge sighed audibly, but no one in the gallery moved their eyes from Argyll. One or two of the jury frowned, uncertain what he was leading to.

Argyll regarded them seriously.

"However, we have heard very little of the character of the accused, Miss Hester Latterly. We have heard from the Farraline family that she met all the requirements for the brief task she was to undertake for them, but that is all. They saw her as an employee, for less than a day. Hardly time to get to know a person."

The judge leaned forward as if to speak, then changed his mind. He looked to Gilfeather, but Gilfeather was quite serene, his flyaway hair on end, his smile amiable and totally unconcerned.

"I propose to call two witnesses to that end," Argyll continued. "Just in case you feel one to be inadequate, possibly biased. To begin with I shall call Dr. Alan Moncrieff."

There was a stirring of interest as the usher repeated the name, then a distinct rustle as heads craned to look when the door opened and a tall, lean man with an unusually handsome aquiline face walked across the open space between the gallery and the witness-box and climbed up the steps. He was sworn in and faced Argyll expectantly.

"Dr. Moncrieff, is the prisoner, Miss Hester Latterly, known to you?"

"Yes sir, I know her quite well." In spite of his Scottish name, his voice was beautifully modulated, and very English.

Rathbone swore under his breath. Could Argyll not have found a man who sounded more like a native, less alien? Moncrieff might have been born and bred in Edinburgh, but he did not sound like it. He should have checked it himself. He should have said something. Now it was too late.

"Would you tell the court in what circumstances you knew her, sir?" Argyll requested.

"I served in the Army Medical Corps during the late war in the Crimea," Moncrieff replied.

"With what regiment, sir?" Argyll asked innocently, his eyes wide.

"The Scots Greys, sir," Moncrieff said with an almost imperceptible lift of his chin and straightening of his shoulders.

There was a second's silence, and then an indrawing of breath by the half dozen or so who knew their military history. The Scots Greys, the Inniskilling Dragoons and the Dragoon Guards, a mere eight hundred men in all, had marshaled on the field of disaster at Balaclava and held a Russian charge of three thousand cavalry, and in eight blood-soaked minutes the Russians had broken and fled back the way they had come.

One man in the jury blew his nose fiercely and another was not ashamed to wipe his eyes.

Someone in the gallery called out "God save the Queen!" and then fell silent.

Argyll kept a perfect gravity, as if he had heard nothing. "An odd choice for an Englishman?" he observed.

Gilfeather sat like stone.

"I am sure you have no intention of being offensive, sir," Moncrieff said quietly. "But I was born in Stirling and studied medicine in Aberdeen and Edinburgh. I have spent some time in England, as well as abroad. You may blame my accent upon my mother."

"I beg your pardon, sir," Argyll said grimly. "It was a hasty conclusion, upon appearances—or rather, upon sound." He did not add anything about the foolishness of such prejudgments. It would have been clumsy. The jury had taken the point as it was.

There was a murmur of approval around the gallery.

The judge scowled.

Rathbone smiled, in spite of himself.

"Please proceed, Mr. Argyll," the judge said with exaggerated weariness. "Wherever the good doctor was born, or studied, is neither here nor there. I assume you are not going to say that he knew Miss Latterly in either place? No, I thought not. Do get on with it!"

Argyll was not in the slightest disturbed. He smiled at the judge and turned back to Moncrieff.

"And you encountered Miss Latterly while you were in the Crimea, Doctor?"

"Yes sir, on many occasions."

"In the pursuit of your mutual profession?"

The judge leaned forward, a sharp frown between his brows making his face look even longer and narrower.

"Sir, this court requires that you be precise. You are misleading the jury. Dr. Moncrieff and Miss Latterly do not have a mutual profession, as you well know; and if you do not, then let me inform you. Dr. Moncrieff is a physician, a practitioner of the art of medicine. Miss Latterly is a nurse, a servant to such doctors in their care of the sick, to roll bandages, make beds, fetch and carry. She does not diagnose disease, she does not prescribe medicines, she does not perform operations of even the slightest nature. She does as she is told, no more. Do I make myself clear?" He turned to the jury. "Gentlemen?"

At least half the jurors nodded sagely.

"Doctor," Argyll said smoothly, addressing Moncrieff. "I do not wish you to presume upon jurisprudence. Please confine yourself to medicine as your skill, and Miss Latterly as your observation."

There was a titter around the room, hastily suppressed. One man in the gallery guffawed, and someone squeaked with alarm.

The judge was scarlet-faced, but events had overtaken him. He searched for words, and found none.

"Of course not, sir," Moncrieff said quickly. "I know nothing about it, beyond what is open to every layman."

"Did you work with Miss Latterly, sir?"

"Frequently."

"What was your opinion of her professional ability?"

Gilfeather rose to his feet. "We are not doubting her professional ability, my lord. The prosecution is not charging she made any error in judgment as to procedure. We are quite sure all her acts were precisely what she intended them to be, and with full understanding of the consequences . . . at least medically speaking."

There was another nervous giggle somewhere, instantly stifled.

"Proceed to what is relevant, Mr. Argyll," the judge directed. "The court is waiting to hear Dr. Moncrieff's testimony as to the character of the prisoner. Relevant or not, it is her right to have it heard."

"My lord, I believe that competence to perform one's duties, and to place the care of others before one's own safety, while in great personal danger, is a profound part of a person's character," Argyll said with a smile.

There was a long, tense silence. No one in the gallery moved.

In spite of himself Rathbone's eyes flickered up to Hester. She was staring at Argyll, her face white, the shadow of hope struggling in her eyes.

He felt an overwhelming sense of despair, so total for a moment he could hardly catch his breath. It was as if someone had knocked the air out of his lungs.

Perhaps it was as well Argyll was conducting the case. He cared too much to be in command of himself.

The jury was waiting, all fifteen faces turned towards the judge. This time their emotion was with Argyll, and it was plain to see.

The judge was tight-lipped with anger, but he knew the law.

"Proceed," he said curtly.

"Thank you, my lord." Argyll inclined his head and turned back to Moncrieff. "Dr. Moncrieff, I ask you again, what is your opinion of Miss Latterly's professional ability, in all circumstances with which you are acquainted and competent to form a judgment?"

"Excellent, sir," Moncrieff answered without hesitation. "She showed remarkable courage on the battlefield when there were enemy skirmishers about, working with the wounded when her own life was in danger. She worked very long hours indeed, often all day and half the night, ignoring her own exhaustion or hunger and cold." A shadow of amusement crossed Moncrieff's handsome face. "And she had exceptional initiative. I have on occasions thought it is unfortunate it is impossible to train women to practice medicine. More than one nurse, in cases when there was no surgeon, has performed successful operations to remove musket balls or pieces of shell, and even amputated limbs badly shattered on the field. Miss Latterly was one such."

Argyll's face registered the appropriate surprise.

"Are you saying, sir, that she was a surgeon . . . in the Crimea?"

"In extremis, yes sir. Surgery requires a steady hand, a good eye, a knowledge of anatomy, and a cool nerve. All of these qualities may be possessed by a woman as much as by a man."

"Stuff and nonsense!" someone shouted from the gallery.

"Good God, sir!" one of the jurors exploded, then blushed scarlet.

"That is an extraordinary opinion, sir," Argyll said very distinctly.

"War is an extraordinary occupation, thank God," Moncrieff replied. "Were it commonplace, I fear the human race would very soon wipe itself out. But appalling as it is, it does on occasion show us qualities we would not otherwise know we possessed. Both men and women rise to heights of gallantry, and of skill, that the calm, more ordered days of peace would never inspire.

"You called me to testify as to what I know of Miss Latterly's character, sir. I can in honesty say no other than I found her brave, honest, dedicated to her calling, and compassionate without sentimentality.

"On the negative side, so you will not believe me biased, she was opinionated, at times hasty to judge others whom she believed to be incompetent. . . ." He smiled ruefully. "In which I regret she had much cause. And at times her sense of humor was less than discreet. She could be dictatorial and arbitrary, and when she was tired, short-tempered.

"But no one I ever knew saw a single act of personal greed or vindictiveness in her, whatever the circumstances. Nor had she personal vanity. Good heavens, man, look at her!" He waved one arm towards the dock, leaning over the railing of the witness-box. Every head in the courtroom turned at his word. "Does she look to you like a woman who would commit murder to gain a piece of personal adornment?"

Even Rathbone turned, staring at Hester, gaunt, ashen-faced, her hair screwed back, dressed in blue-gray as plain as a uniform.

Argyll smiled. "No sir, she does not. I confess, it seems you are right; a little personal vanity might be more becoming. It is a falling short, I think."

There was a ripple around the room. In the gallery one woman put her hand on her husband's arm. Henry Rathbone smiled wanly. Monk gritted his teeth.

"Thank you, Dr. Moncrieff," Argyll said quickly. "That is all I mean to ask you."

Gilfeather rose slowly, almost ponderously, to his feet.

Moncrieff faced him steadily. He was not naive enough to think the next few minutes would be easy. He was aware that he had altered, if not the tide of the battle, at least the pitch and the heat of it. In Argyll he had been facing a friend; Gilfeather was the enemy.

"Dr. Moncrieff," he began softly. "I expect few of us here can imagine the horror and privation you and other workers in the medical field must have faced during the war. It must have been truly terrible. You spoke of hunger, cold, exhaustion and fear. Is that true, no dark exaggeration?"

"None," Moncrieff said guardedly. "You are correct, sir. It is an experience that cannot be adequately imagined."

"It must place the most extraordinary strain upon those called upon to endure it?"

"Yes sir."

"I accept that you could not share it with me, for example, other than in the most superficial and unsatisfactory way."

"Is that a question, sir?"

"No, unless you disagree with me?"

"No, I agree. One can communicate only those experiences for which there is some common language or understanding. One cannot describe sunset to a man who has not sight."

"Precisely. That must leave you with a certain loneliness, Dr. Moncrieff."

Moncrieff said nothing.

"And a closeness to those with whom you have shared such fearful and profound times."

Moncrieff could not deny it, even though to judge from his face he could perceive where Gilfeather was leading him.

The jurors leaned forward, listening intently.

"Of course," he conceded.

"And very naturally a certain impatience with the blandness and uncomprehension, perhaps even uselessness, of certain of the women who have no idea whatever of anything more dangerous or demanding than household management?"

"These are your words, sir, not mine."

"But accurate, sir? Come, you are on oath. Do you not ache to share the past you speak of with such passion now?"

Moncrieff's expression did not flicker.

"I have no need to, sir. It is beyond sharing by me, or anyone else, except in words that are spoken by the shabby and believed by the ignorant." He leaned forward, his hands gripping the rail. "But neither do I insult the women who remained at home caring for homes and children. We all have our own challenges, and our virtues. It is too easy to compare, and I think a profitless exercise. As women who manage the domestic economy do not understand the women who went to the Crimea, so, perhaps, those who went away do not know, or pretend to know, the hardships of those who stayed at home."

"Very well, sir. Your courtesy does you credit," Gilfeather said between his teeth, the smile vanished from his face. "But nevertheless a closeness must exist, a relief to share what must still cause you deep emotion?"

"Of course."

"Tell me, sir, did Miss Latterly always appear as dowdy as she does here today? She is a young woman, and not of displeasing form or feature. This must have been an extraordinary ordeal for her. She has been confined first in Newgate Prison in London, and now here in Edinburgh. She is on trial for her life. We cannot judge fairly her charms from the way in which we see her now."

"That is true," Moncrieff agreed carefully.

"Did you like her, Doctor?"

"There is little time for friendship, Mr. Gilfeather. Your question admirably illustrates your assumption that those who were not there cannot comprehend what it was like. I admired her and found her excellent to work with, as I have already said."

"Come, sir!" Gilfeather said grimly, his voice suddenly raised and harsh. "Do not be disingenuous with me! Do you expect us to believe that in two years you were so dedicated to your duty day and night that the natural man never emerged in you?" He spread his hands wide, his face smiling. "You never once, during lulls in battle, times when the summer sunshine shone in the fields, when there was time for picnics . . . oh yes, we are not totally ignorant of what happened out there! There were war correspondents, you know . . . even photographs! Do you expect us to believe, sir, that all that time you never saw Miss Latterly as a young and not unpleasing woman?"

Moncrieff smiled.

"No sir, I do not ask you to. I had not even thought of the matter, but since you raise it, she is not at all unlike my wife, who has many of the same qualities of courage and honesty."

"But who was not a nurse in the Crimea, and thus able to share your emotions, sir!"

Moncrieff smiled.

"You are mistaken, sir. She was most certainly in the Crimea, and most able to understand as much of my feelings as another person could."

Gilfeather was defeated, and he knew it.

"Thank you, Doctor. That is all I have to ask you. Unless my learned friend has anything to add, you may go."

"No, thank you," Argyll declined generously. "Thank you, Dr. Moncrieff."

The court adjourned early for lunch, newspaper correspondents racing out to send messengers flying with the latest word, jostling each other, even knocking people over in their excitement. The judge had retired in considerable ill humor.

A hundred things were on the edge of Rathbone's tongue to say to Argyll. In the end he said none of them; each seemed too obvious when it came to the point, unnecessary, merely betraying his own fears.

He had not thought himself hungry, and yet in the dining room of the inn he ate luncheon without even being aware of it. He looked down and found his plate empty.

At last he could contain himself no longer.

"Miss Nightingale this afternoon," he said aloud.

Argyll looked up, his fork still in his hand.

"Aye," he agreed. "A formidable woman from what I have seen of her—which is little enough, just a few brief words this morning. I confess, I am not sure how much to lead her and how much I should simply point her in the right direction and let her destroy Gilfeather, if he is rash enough to attack her."

"You must have her say something he will have to attack," Rathbone said urgently, laying down his knife and fork. "He is too experienced to say anything to her unless you force him to. He will not

274

leave her on the stand a moment longer than she has to be, unless you have her say something he cannot leave uncontested."

"Yes . . ." Argyll said thoughtfully, abandoning what little was left of his meal. "I think you are right. But what? She is not a material witness to anything here in Edinburgh. She has presumably never heard of the Farralines. She knows nothing of what happened. All she can testify is that Hester Latterly was a skilled and dilligent nurse. Her sole value to us is her own reputation—the esteem in which she is held. Gilfeather will certainly not challenge that."

Rathbone thought wildly, his brain in a whirl. Florence Nightingale was not a woman to be manipulated into anything, not by Argyll, and not by Gilfeather. What possible thing was there she could say that was pertinent to the case and which Gilfeather would have to challenge? Hester's courage was not in doubt, nor her capability as a nurse.

Then the beginning of an idea formed in his mind, just a shadow. Slowly, feeling for its shape, he explained it to Argyll, fumbling for words, then, as he saw Argyll's eyes brighten, gathering confidence.

By the time the court commenced its afternoon session, he was sitting behind Argyll, in precisely the same position as before, but feeling a spark of excitement, something which might even be mistaken for hope. But still he did not look at the gallery, and only once, for a moment, at Hester.

"Call Florence Nightingale," the usher's voice boomed out, and there were gasps of indrawn breath around the room. A woman in the gallery screamed and stifled the sound with her hand clasped over her face.

The judge banged his gavel. "I will have order in the court! Another outburst like that and I shall have the place cleared. Is that understood? This is a court of law, not a place of entertainment. Mr. Argyll, I hope this witness is relevant to the case, and not merely a piece of exhibitionism and an attempt to win some kind of public sympathy. If it is, I assure you it will fail. Miss Latterly is on trial here, and Miss Nightingale's reputation is irrelevent!"

Argyll bowed gravely and said nothing.

Every eye was turned towards the doorway, necks were craned and bodies twisted to see as a slender, upright figure came in, crossed the floor without looking to right or left, and climbed the steps to the witness-box. She was not imposing. She was really quite ordinary looking, with brownish hair, straight and severely swept from her face, very level brows and regular features. The whole cast of her countenance was too determined to be pretty, and without the inner light and serenity which fires beauty. It was not an easy face; it was even a little frightening.

She swore as to her name and place of residence in a firm and clear voice, and stood waiting for Argyll to begin.

"Thank you for traveling this considerable distance and leaving your own most important work to testify in this case, Miss Nightingale," he said gravely.

"Justice is also important, sir," she replied, staring very directly at him. "And in this instance, also a matter of life"—she hesitated—"and death."

"Quite so."

Rathbone had warned him passionately about the danger of patronizing her, or seeming in the slightest way to condescend to her, or state the obvious. Please heaven he remembered!

"We are all aware that you have no knowledge of the facts of this case, ma'am," Argyll proceeded. "But the prisoner, Hester Latterly, has been well known to you in the past, has she not? And you feel able to speak of her character?"

"I have known Hester Latterly since the summer of 1854," Florence replied. "And I am willing to answer any questions as to her character that you care to put to me."

"Thank you." Argyll adopted a relaxed posture, his head a little to one side. "Miss Nightingale, there has been some speculation as to why a young lady of gentle birth and good education should choose an occupation such as nursing, which previously has been carried out largely by women of low degree and, frankly, of pretty rough habits."

Behind Argyll, Rathbone sat forward on the edge of his seat, his body aching with tension. The courtroom was silent. Every juror was watching Florence as if she had been the only living person there.

"Indeed, prior to your noble and pioneering work," Argyll continued, "it was the sort of task to occupy those women who were not able to find a respectable domestic position. For example, if I may ask you, why did you yourself undertake such an arduous and dangerous task? Were your family agreeable to your doing such a work?"

"Mr. Argyll!" the judge said angrily, jerking forward in sudden movement.

"No sir, they were not," Florence replied, ignoring the judge. "They put up considerable argument against it, and it took me many years, and a great deal of pleading, before they succumbed. As to the reason why I persisted against their will, there is a higher duty even than that to family, and a higher obedience." Her face was lit with a simple, blinding conviction, and even the judge's protest died unspoken. Every man and woman in the room, juror or spectator, was listening to her. Had the judge spoken he would have been ignored, and that he would not invite. It would have been intolerable.

Argyll waited expectantly, black eyes wide.

"I believe that is what God has called me to do, sir," she answered him. "And I shall devote my life to that end." She gave a little shiver of impatience. "Indeed, I wrong myself and am cowardly to express it so. I know He has called me. I believe that others have the same desire to serve their fellow men, and the conviction that nursing the sick is the finest way in which they can do it. There can be no higher calling, and none more urgently needed at such times than the relief of suffering, and where possible the preservation of life and restoration to health of men who have fought for their country. Can you doubt it, sir?"

"No, madam, I cannot, and I do not," Argyll said candidly.

Gilfeather stirred in his seat as if to make some interruption, but knew his time was not yet, and restrained himself with some difficulty.

With a supreme effort of self-control, Rathbone also remained motionless.

"And Hester Latterly served in the hospital at Scutari?" Argyll asked, his face expressionless except for a mild interest. Whatever emotions of triumph or expectancy boiled inside him, there was nothing in his features to betray them.

"Yes, she was one of the best nurses there."

"In what way, ma'am?"

"Dedication—and skill. There were too few surgeons and too

many patients." Her voice was calm and controlled, but there was an intensity and feeling in it which commanded the attention of everyone in the room. "Often a nurse had to act as she thought he would have done, or a man's life would be lost which she could have saved."

There was a gasp somewhere in the gallery, a hissing of anger at such suggested arrogance.

The judge's face registered his acknowledgment of it.

Florence took no more notice than if it had been a fly on the windowpane.

"Hester had both the courage and the knowledge to do so," she went on. "There are many men alive in England now who would be buried in the Crimea were she a lesser woman."

Argyll waited several seconds to allow the full impact of what she had said to sink into the minds of the jury. Their faces were filled with battling emotions: awe of Florence, which was almost a religious reverence; and memories of their own of war and the losses of war, brothers and sons buried in the carnage, or perhaps saved by the efforts of such women. Mixed with those feelings were outrage at the challenge to centuries of masculine leadership, previously unquestioned rights. The confusion was painful, the doubts and the fears profound.

"Thank you," Argyll acknowledged at last. "And did you also find her personally honest, both truthful and careful of the rights and possessions of others?"

"Absolutely and without exception," Florence replied.

Argyll hesitated.

The tension was unbearable. Rathbone sat hardly daring to draw breath. The decision Argyll made now might be the difference between winning and losing, between life and the hangman's noose. Only he and Argyll knew the weight of what hung in that moment. If he succeeded in maneuvering Gilfeather into attacking Florence she would retaliate with a passion and emotional force that would sweep away all the quibbles and arguments he could raise. On the other hand, if he had the wisdom to retreat, and dismiss her, her value to Hester would be lost.

Was it enough? Had he goaded Gilfeather sufficiently, masked the hook by the bait?

Very slowly Argyll smiled at Florence Nightingale, thanking her again for having come, and resumed his seat.

Rathbone sat with his heart pounding. The room seemed to sway around him. Seconds stretched into eternity.

With a scrape of chair legs, Gilfeather stood up.

"You are one of the most deeply loved and highly respected women in the nation, madam, and I do not wish to seem to detract from that in any way," he said carefully. "However, the cause of justice is higher than any individual, and there are questions I must ask you."

"Of course," she agreed, facing him squarely.

"Miss Nightingale, you say that Miss Latterly is an excellent nurse—indeed, that she has displayed skills equal to those of many field surgeons when faced with cases of emergency?"

"That is true."

"And that she is diligent, honest and brave?"

"She is." There was no hesitation in her voice, no shred of uncertainty.

He smiled. "Then, madam, how is it that she is obliged to earn her living, not in some senior position in a hospital, using these remarkable qualities, but traveling on an overnight train from Edinburgh to London, administering a simple dose of medicine to an elderly lady whose health is no worse than that of most persons of her age? Surely that could have been done quite adequately by a perfectly ordinary lady's maid?" There was challenge and triumph even in the angle of his body where he stood, the lift of his shoulders.

Rathbone clenched his hands, digging his nails into his palms with unbearable tension. Would she retaliate as he had hoped, as he had counted?

In front of him Argyll sat rigid, only a tiny muscle flicking at the side of his temple.

Florence's face hardened as she looked at Gilfeather with dislike.

Please—please— Rathbone prayed in his head.

"Because she is an outspoken woman, with more courage than tact, thank God," Florence said sharply. "She does not care for hospital life, having to obey the orders of those who are on occasion less knowledgeable than herself but are too arrogant to be told by someone they consider inferior. Perhaps it is a fault, but it is an honest one."

The jury smiled.

Somewhere in the gallery a man cheered, and then instantly fell silent.

"And an impetuous one," Gilfeather added, taking a step forward. "Even, perhaps, a self-indulgent one, would you not say, Miss Nightingale?"

"I would not."

"Oh I would! Sometimes self-indulgent, and unquestionably arrogant. It is the weakness, the fault, of a woman who considers herself above others, believes her own opinions count more than those of men trained and qualified in their profession, a profession perhaps she aspires to, but for which she has no training but practice, in extraordinary circumstances—"

"Mr. Gilfeather," she cut across him imperiously, her eyes blazing, her body quivering with the fierceness of her emotion. "You are either intending to provoke me to anger, sir, or you are more naive than a man in your position has a right to be! Have you the faintest idea of the 'extraordinary circumstances' to which you refer so glibly? You are well dressed, sir. You look in the best of health. How often do you go without your dinner? Do you even know what it is like to be so hungry you would be glad to boil the bones of a rat?"

There were gasps around the room. A woman in the gallery slid forward in her seat. The judge winced.

"Madam—" Gilfeather protested, but she barely heard him.

"You have your sight, sir, and your limbs. Have you seen a man with his legs shot away? Do you know how quickly one must act to stop him hemorrhaging to death? Could you find the arteries in all that blood and save him? Would your nerve hold you, and your stomach?"

"Madam—" Gilfeather tried again.

"I am sure you are master of your profession," she swept on, not leaning forward over the railing as another might have, but standing stiff and straight, head high. "But how often do you work all day and all night for days on end? Or do you return home to a nice soft bed— one that is warm enough, and in which you may lie safely until the morning? Have you lain on a canvas sheet on the earth, too cold to sleep, listening to the groans of those in agony, and hearing in your memory the rattle of the dying, and knowing tomorrow and tomorrow and tomorrow there will always be more, and all you can do will only ease it a little, a very little!"

There was utter silence in the court.

The judge waved his hands at Gilfeather.

Gilfeather shrugged.

"And when you are ill, sir, vomiting and with a flux you cannot control, is there someone to hold a bowl for you, wash you clean, bring you a little fresh water, change your sheets? I hope you are suitably grateful, sir—because, dear God, there are so many for whom there is not, because there are too few of us willing to do it, or with the heart and the stomach for it! Yes, Hester Latterly is an extraordinary woman, molded by circumstances beyond most people to imagine. Yes, she is headstrong, at times arrogant, capable of making decisions that would quail many a heart less brave, less passionate, less moved by intolerable pity." She barely took a breath. "And before you ask me, I can believe she would kill to save her own life, or that of a patient in her charge. I would prefer not to think she would kill out of revenge, no matter how gross or intolerable the wrong, but I would not swear to it on oath." Now at last she did lean forward, facing Gilfeather with a burning eye. "But I would take my oath before God, she would not poison a patient for gain of a paltry piece of jewelry and then give it back unasked. If you believe that, sir, you are a lesser judge of mankind than you have a right to be and hold the calling you do."

Gilfeather opened his mouth, then closed it again. He was well beaten and he knew it. He had provoked a force of nature, and the storm had broken over him.

"I have no more questions," he said grimly. "Thank you, Miss Nightingale."

Rathbone had been staring at her.

"Go and help her," he hissed at Argyll.

"What?"

"Assist her!" Rathbone said fiercely. "Look at her, man!"

"But, she's . . ." Argyll began.

"Strong! No she's not! Get on with it!"

The sheer fury of Rathbone's voice impelled him to his feet. He plunged forward just as Florence reached the bottom of the steps and all but collapsed.

In the gallery people craned forward anxiously. One man rose as if to leave his place.

"Allow me, madam," Argyll said, grasping Florence's arm and holding her up. "I feel you have exhausted yourself on our behalf."

"It is nothing," she said, but she clung to him all the same, allowing him to take a remarkable amount of her weight. "Merely a little breathlessness. Perhaps I am not as well as I had imagined."

Quite slowly he escorted her, without asking the court's permission, as far as the doors out, every man and woman in the room watching him with bated breath, and then amid a sigh of approval and respect, he returned to his place.

"Thank you, my lord," he said solemnly to the judge. "The defense next calls the prisoner, Miss Hester Latterly."

"It is growing late," the judge said sharply, his face creased with ill-suppressed rage. "The court will adjourn for today. You may call your witness tomorrow, Mr. Argyll." And he slammed down the gavel as if he would break the shaft of it in his hand.

Hester climbed the steps of the witness-box and turned to face the court. She had slept little, and the few moments she had had were fraught with nightmares, and now that the moment had come, it seemed unreal. She could feel the railing beneath her hands, the wood of it smoothed by a thousand other clenched fingers and white knuckles; the judge with his narrow face and deep-set eyes seemed the figment of yet another nightmare. Her senses were filled with an incomprehensible roaring sound, without form or meaning. Was it people in the gallery talking to each other, or only the blood thundering through her veins, cutting her off from the sights and sounds plain to everyone else?

In spite of all the promises to herself, her eyes searched the gallery for Monk's hard, smooth face, and she found instead Henry Rathbone. He was looking at her, and although from that distance she could not see him clearly, in her mind's eye his clear blue eyes had never been plainer, and the gentleness and the hurt for her brought a rush of emotion beyond her control. She knew him ridiculously little. She had

had just a few moments with Oliver in his house on Primrose Hill, a quiet evening supper (overcooked because they were late), the summer evening in the garden, the starlit sky above the apple trees, the scent of honeysuckle on the lawn. It was all so familiar, so sweet, the pain of it almost intolerable. She wished she had not seen him, and yet she could not tear her eyes away.

"Miss Latterly!"

Argyll's voice jerked her back to the present and to the proceedings that had at last begun.

"Yes . . . sir?" This was her chance to speak for herself, the only chance she would be given between now and the verdict. She must be right. She could not afford a mistake of any sort, not a word, a look, a gesture that could be interpreted wrongly. She might live, or die, upon such tiny things.

"Miss Latterly, why did you respond to Mr. Farraline's advertisement for someone to accompany his mother from Edinburgh to London? It was a post of short duration, and far beneath your skill. Did it pay extraordinarily well? Or were you so greatly in need of funds that anything at all was welcome?"

"No sir, I accepted it because I thought it would be interesting, and agreeable. I had never been to Scotland before, and all I had heard of it was in its praise." She forced a wan smile at memory. "I had nursed many men from Scottish regiments, and formed a unique respect for them."

She felt the ripple of emotion through the room, but she was not sure if she understood it or not. There was no time to think about it now. She must concentrate on Argyll.

"I see," he said smoothly. "And the remuneration, was it good?"

"It was generous, considering the lightness of the task," she said honestly. "But it was perhaps balanced by the fact that in order to accept it, one would have to forgo other, possibly longer, engagements. It was not undue."

"Indeed. But you were not in grave need, were you?"

"No. I had just completed a very satisfactory case with a patient who was well enough no longer to require nursing, and I had another post to go to a short time afterwards. It was ideal to take up the time between."

"We have only your word for that, Miss Latterly."

"It would be simple enough to check on it, sir. My patient—"

He held up his hands and she stopped.

"Yes, I have done so." He turned to the judge. "There is a disposition for Miss Latterly's past patient, my lord, and another from the lady who was expecting her, and who of course has now had to employ someone else. I suggest that they be read into the evidence."

"Yes, yes, of course," the judge conceded. "Proceed, if you please."

"Had you ever heard of the Farraline family, before the post?"

"No sir."

"Did they receive you courteously?"

"Yes sir."

Gradually, in precise detail, he led her through her day at the Farraline house, not mentioning any other members of the family except as they affected her movements. He asked about the dressing room when the lady's maid was packing, had her describe everything she could recall, including the medicine chest, the vials she had been shown, and the exact instructions. The effort to remember kept her mind too occupied for fear to creep into her voice. It stayed submerged like a great wave, forever rolling, its great power never breaking and overwhelming her.

Then he moved on to the journey on the train. Stumblingly, filled with sadness, her eyes focused on him, ignoring the rest of the room, she told him how she and Mary had talked, how she had recalled some of the journeys of her youth, the people, the laughter, the scenes, the things she had loved. She told him how she had been reluctant to end the evening, how only Oonagh's warning about Mary's lateness had made her at last insist. In a low quiet voice, only just above tears, she recited opening the chest, finding one vial gone, and giving the second vial to Mary before closing the chest again and making her comfortable, and then going to sleep herself.

In the same voice, with only the barest hesitation, she told him of waking in the morning, and finding Mary dead.

At that point he stopped her.

"Are you quite sure you made no error in giving Mrs. Farraline her medicine, Miss Latterly?"

"Quite sure. I gave her the contents of one vial. She was a very intelligent woman, Mr. Argyll, and not shortsighted or absentminded.

If I had done anything amiss she would certainly have known, and refused to take it."

"This glass you used, Miss Latterly, was it provided for you?"

"Yes sir. It was part of the fitments of the medicine chest, along with the vials."

"I see. Designed to hold the contents of one vial, or more?"

"One vial, sir; that was its purpose."

"Quite so. You would have had to fill it twice to administer more?"

"Yes sir."

There was no need to add anything further. He could see from the jurors' faces that they had taken the point.

"And the gray pearl brooch," he continued. "Did you see it at any time prior to your finding it in your baggage when you had arrived at the home of Lady Callandra Daviot?"

"No sir." She nearly added that Mary had mentioned it, and then just in time refrained. The thought of how close she had come to such an error sent the blood rushing burningly up her face. Dear heaven, she must look as if she were lying! "No sir. Mrs. Farraline's baggage was in the goods van, along with my own. I had no occasion to see any of her things once I had left the dressing room at Ainslie Place. And even then, I only saw the topmost gowns as they were laid out."

"Thank you, Miss Latterly. Please remain where you are. My learned friend will no doubt wish to question you also."

"Indeed I will." Gilfeather rose to his feet with alacrity. But before he could begin, the judge adjourned the court for luncheon, and it was afternoon before he could launch his attack. And attack it was. He advanced towards the witness stand with flying hair an aureole around his head. He was a large man, shambling like a newly awoken bear, but his eyes were bright and gleaming with the light of battle.

Hester faced him with her heart beating so violently her body shook and her breath caught in her throat so she feared she might choke when she was forced to speak.

"Miss Latterly," he began smoothly. "The defense has painted a picture of you as a virtuous, heroic and self-sacrificing woman. Because of the circumstances which bring you here, you must give me leave to doubt the total accuracy of that." He pulled a small face. "People of the sort depicted by my learned friend do not suddenly stoop to murder, especially the murder of an old lady in their trust, and for the gain of a few pearls set in a pin. Would you agree?

"In fact," he went on, looking at her with concentration, "I presume the burden of his argument to be that it is inconceivable that a person should change her nature so utterly, therefore you could not be guilty. Is that not so?"

"I did not prepare the defense, sir, so I cannot speak for Mr. Argyll," she said levelly. "But I imagine you are correct."

"Do you agree with the hypothesis, Miss Latterly?" His voice was sharp, demanding an answer.

"Yes sir, I do, although at times we may misjudge people, or fail to read them aright. If it were not so, we should never be taken by surprise."

There was a ripple of amusement around the room. One or two men nodded in appreciation.

Rathbone held his breath in an agony of apprehension.

"A very sophisticated argument, Miss Latterly," Gilfeather conceded.

She had seen Rathbone's face, and knew why he had stared at her with such pleading. She must make amends.

"No sir," she said humbly. "It is merely common sense. I think any woman would have told you the same."

"That is as may be, ma'am," Gilfeather said. "However, you will appreciate why I shall endeavor to disprove their high estimation of you."

She waited in silence for him to do so.

He nodded, pulling a very slight face. "Why did you go to the Crimea, Miss Latterly? Was it like Miss Nightingale, in answer to a call to serve God?" He invested no sarcasm or condescension in the question, his voice and his expression were innocent, but there was a waiting in the room, a readiness for disbelief.

"No sir." She kept her voice low and her tone as gentle as lay within her power. "I intended to serve my fellow men in a way best suited to such skills as I possessed, and I believed it would be a fine and daring thing to do. I have but one life, and I had rather do something purposeful with it than at the end look back and regret all the chances I had missed, and what I might have made of myself."

"So you are a woman to take risks?" Gilfeather said with a smile he could not hide.

"Physical ones, sir, not moral ones. I think to stay at home, safe and idle, would have been a moral risk, and one I was not prepared for."

"You draw a fine argument, madam."

"I am fighting for my life, sir. Would you expect anyone to do less?"

"No madam. Since you ask, I expect you to use every art and argument, every subtlety and persuasion that your mind can devise or your desperation conceive."

She looked at him with loathing. All Rathbone's warnings rang in her head as clearly as if he were saying them now, and her emotion overrode them all. She was going to lose anyway. She would not do it without honesty and what dignity was possible.

"You make it sound, sir, as if we were two animals battling for mastery of each other, not rational human beings seeking to find the truth and serve our best understanding of justice. Do you wish to know who killed Mrs. Farraline, Mr. Gilfeather, or do you merely wish to hang someone, and I will do?"

For a moment Gilfeather was startled. He had been fought with before, but not in these terms.

There was a gasp and a sigh of suspended breath. A journalist broke his pencil. One of the jurors choked.

"Oh God!" Rathbone said inaudibly.

The judge reached for his gavel, and mistook the distance. His fingers closed on nothing.

In the gallery Monk smiled, and his stomach knotted inside him with grief.

"Only the right person will do, Miss Latterly," Gilfeather said angrily, his hair standing on end. "But all the evidence says that that is you. If it is not, pray tell me who is it?"

"I do not know, sir, or I should already have told you," Hester answered him.

Argyll rose to his feet at last.

"My lord, if my learned friend has questions for Miss Latterly, he should put them to her. If not—although she seems well able to defend herself—this baiting is unseemly, and not the purpose of this court."

The judge looked at him sourly, then turned to Gilfeather.

"Mr. Gilfeather, please come to the point, sir. What is it you wish to ask?"

Gilfeather glared first at Argyll, then at the judge. Finally he turned to Hester.

"Miss Nightingale has painted you as a ministering angel, tending the sick regardless of your own sufferings." This time he could not entirely keep the sarcasm from his tone. "She would have us envision you passing gently between the hospital beds wiping a fevered brow, bandaging a wound; or else braving the battlefield to perform operations yourself by the light of a flickering torch." His voice grew louder. "But in truth, madam, was it not a rough life, most of it spent with soldiers and camp followers, women of low degree and even lower morals?"

Vivid memories surged back into her mind.

"Many camp followers are soldiers' wives, sir, and their humble birth equals that of their husbands," she said angrily. "They work and wash for them, and care for them when they are sick. Someone must do these things. And if the men are good enough to die for us in our bloody battles, then they are worthy of our support when we are safe in our own houses at home. And if you are suggesting that Miss Nightingale, or any of her nurses, were army whores, then—"

There was a roar of anger from the gallery. One man rose to his feet and shook his fist at Gilfeather.

The judge banged his gavel furiously and was totally ignored.

Rathbone sank his head in his hands and slid farther down in his chair.

Argyll swiveled around and said something to him, his expression incredulous and accusing.

Henry Rathbone closed his eyes and offered up a silent prayer.

Gilfeather abandoned that line of attack altogether and tried another.

"How many men have you seen die, Miss Latterly?" he shouted above the general clamor.

"Silence!" the judge said furiously. "I will have order in court! Silence! Or I shall have the gallery cleared!"

ANNE PERRY

The noise subsided almost immediately. No one wished to be removed.

"How many men, Miss Latterly?" Gilfeather repeated when the uproar had finally abated.

"You must answer," the judge warned even before she had had time to speak.

"I don't know. I never thought to count. Each one was a person, not a number."

"But a great many?" Gilfeather persisted.

"Yes, I am afraid so."

"So you are accustomed to death; it does not frighten you, or appall you, as it might most people?"

"All people who care for the sick become accustomed to death, sir. But one never ceases to grieve."

"You are argumentative, madam! You lack the gentleness of manner and the delicacy, the humility, which is the chief ornament of your sex."

"Perhaps," she responded. "But you are trying to make people believe that I hold life cheaply, that I have somehow become inured to the death of others, and it is not true. I did not kill Mrs. Farraline, or anybody else. I am far more grieved by her loss than you are."

"I do not believe you, madam. You have shown the court your mettle. You have no fear, no sense of decorum, no humility whatsoever. They are well able to judge you for a woman who will take from life what she wishes and defy anyone to prevent her. Poor Mary Farraline never had a chance once you had determined upon your course."

Hester stared at him.

"That is all!" Gilfeather said impatiently, flicking his hand to dismiss her. "There is little edifying to the jury in listening to me ask question after question, and you standing there denying it. We may assume it as read. Do you wish to reexamine your witness, Mr Argyll?"

Argyll thanked him with more than a touch of sarcasm, and turned to Hester.

"Was Mrs. Farraline a pathetic little old lady, easily browbeaten, timid?"

"Not in the least," Hester said with some relief. "She was quite the opposite: intelligent, articulate and very much in command. She

289

had had a most interesting life, traveled a great deal and known some quite remarkable people and events." She summoned the ghost of a smile. "She told me about dancing the night away at the great ball the night before the Battle of Waterloo. I found her brave, and wise, and funny . . . and . . . and I admired her."

"Thank you, Miss Latterly. Yes, that is the opinion of her which I had formed myself. I imagine she also found you to be most worthy of her admiration. That is all I have to ask you. You may return to the dock for the time being."

The judge adjourned the court. Newspaper reporters knocked each other over in their efforts to be first out of the door. The gallery erupted in noise, and the wardresses on both sides of Hester closed in on her and demanded that the cage be let down into the bowels of the building so that she might safely be locked up again before riot broke loose.

Monk walked the streets. Rathbone and Argyll sat up till long after midnight. Callandra sat with Henry Rathbone, and they talked of everything else they could imagine. And all of their thoughts were of nothing but Hester and what the morrow would bring.

Argyll rose to his feet.

"I call Hector Farraline to the stand."

There was amazement in the gallery. Alastair rose to protest and was pulled back into his seat. It was useless, and Oonagh at least understood that. Alastair looked on in an agony of embarrassment.

Hector appeared and walked very slowly, his feet uncertain, his eyes wandering. He crossed the floor to the foot of the stairs up to the box.

"Do you need assistance, Mr. Farraline?" the judge inquired.

"Assistance?" Hector said with a frown. "What for?"

"To mount the steps, sir. Are you well?"

"Quite well, sir. And you?"

"Then take your place, sir, to be sworn in." The judge looked at Argyll with acute disfavor. "I presume this is necessary, sir?"

"It is," Argyll assured him.

"Very well, get on with it!"

Hector climbed the steps, was sworn in, and waited for Argyll to begin.

Gilfeather was watching intently.

"Major Farraline," Argyll said courteously. "Were you in the house when Miss Latterly first arrived?"

"What? Oh . . . yes. Of course I was. I live there."

"Did you see her arrive?"

Gilfeather rose. "My lord, Miss Latterly's arrival is not in dispute Surely this is irrelevant, and wasting the court's time."

The judge looked at Argyll, his eyebrows raised.

"I am coming to the point, my lord, if my learned friend will permit me," Argyll replied.

"Then be a little more rapid, if you please," the judge ordered.

"My lord, Major Farraline, did you see Miss Latterly moving about the house on that day?"

Hector looked confused. "Moving about? What do you mean . . . going up and down stairs, that sort of thing?"

Gilfeather rose again. "My lord, this witness is obviously not . . . not well! He is not competent to tell us anything of value. Of course Miss Latterly moved about the house. She could hardly have remained and not been seen the entire day. My learned friend is wasting time."

"It is you who are wasting time," Argyll countered. "I could get to my point a great deal faster if I were not constantly interrupted."

"Get to it now, sir," the judge commanded. "Before I also lose my patience. I am inclined to agree that Major Farraline is not in sufficient command of himself to offer anything of use."

Argyll gritted his teeth.

Rathbone was leaning forward again, his hands clenched.

"Major Farraline," Argyll resumed. "Did you meet with Miss Latterly alone, in the hallway, on that day, and have some conversation with her about the Farraline family business and its wealth?"

"What?"

"Oh really!" Gilfeather exploded.

"Yes," Hector said with a moment of clarity. "Yes. On the stairs, as I recall. Spoke to her for several moments. Nice girl. Liked her. Pity."

"Did you tell her that there had been money embezzled from the company books?"

Hector stared at him as if he had been bitten.

"No—no, of course not." Then his eyes wandered away from Argyll and across to the gallery. He found Oonagh, and looked at her imploringly. She was pale-faced, her eyes wide.

"Major Farraline," Argyll said firmly.

"My lord, this is inexcusable," Gilfeather protested.

Argyll ignored him.

"Major Farraline, you are an officer of one of Her Majesty's most renowned and battle-honored regiments. Remember yourself, sir! You are under oath! Did you not tell Miss Latterly that someone had been embezzling from the Farraline printing company?"

"This is monstrous," Gilfeather cried, waving his arms furiously. "And completely irrelevant. Miss Latterly is on trial for the murder of Mary Farraline. This can have nothing to do with the case at issue."

Alastair made as if to rise to his feet, then subsided again, his expression anguished.

"No I didn't," Hector said with another sudden rush of clarity. "I can remember it now. That was Mr. Monk I told. He went off to find McIvor about it, but he didn't learn anything. Poor fool. I could have told him that. That's all covered up now."

There was a moment's utter silence.

Rathbone sank onto the table in devastated relief.

Argyll's dark face split into a grin.

The judge looked furious.

Monk punched his clenched fist into his open palm again and again till the flesh was bruised.

"Thank you, Major Farraline," Argyll said quietly. "I am sure that you are right. It must have been Mr. Monk, and not Miss Latterly. That is my error, and I apologize."

"Is that all?" Hector said curiously.

"Yes, thank you."

Gilfeather swung around in a complete circle, staring at the gallery, the jurors, then at Hector.

Hector gave a discreet hiccup.

"Major Farraline, how many glasses of whiskey have you drunk this morning?" Gilfeather asked.

"I have no idea," Hector said politely. "I don't think I used a glass. Have one of those flasks, you know. Why?"

"No matter, sir. That is all, thank you."

Hector began to fumble his way down the steps.

"Oh . . . " Gilfeather said quickly.

Hector stopped three steps from the bottom, clinging on to the rail.

"Do you keep the company books, Major Farraline?"

"Me? No, of course not. Young Kenneth does."

"Have you seen them lately, Major? Say, within the last two weeks?"

"No. Don't think so."

"Can you read company accounts, sir?"

"Never tried. Not interested."

"Quite so. Do you need assistance down the steps, sir?"

"No I don't, sir. Make my own way." And with that he missed his footing and slid the last three steps, landing inelegantly at the bottom. He straightened himself and walked unaided and quite steadily back to the gallery and was given a seat.

"My lord"—Argyll turned to the judge—"in view of Major Farraline's evidence, I would like to call Kenneth Farraline."

Gilfeather was on his feet. He hesitated, a protest on his lips.

The judge sighed. "Do you object, Mr. Gilfeather? It seems there is some question of embezzlement, real or imagined."

Argyll smiled. If Gilfeather gained the impression he was perfectly happy to be denied Kenneth, and leave doubt in the jury's minds, or a question of appeal, so much the better.

"No objection, my lord," Gilfeather conceded. "It would be advisable to clear up all doubts." He shot a tight smile at Argyll.

Argyll inclined his head in thanks.

Kenneth Farraline was called and took the stand looking acutely unhappy. He could feel the brooding, almost violent tension in the court, and he saw Argyll advance on him like a bear closing in for the kill.

"Mr. Farraline, your uncle, Major Hector Farraline, has told us that you keep the company books. Is that correct?"

"Irrelevant, my lord," Gilfeather objected.

The judge hesitated.

"My lord, if there is embezzlement from the company books, and the head of that family has been murdered, it can hardly be irrelevant," Argyll reasoned. "It provides an excellent motive, unconnected with Miss Latterly."

The judge conceded the point, but with displeasure.

"You have not proved it yet, sir. So far it is merely a suggestion, indeed the ramblings of a man the worse for drink. If you cannot show something more substantial, I shall disallow it next time Mr. Gilfeather objects."

"Thank you, my lord." Argyll turned back to Kenneth. "Mr. Farraline, was your mother aware of Major Farraline's beliefs that the books had been tampered with?"

"I ... I ..." Kenneth looked wretched. He stared at Argyll with eyes unfocused, as if he longed to be looking elsewhere.

"Sir?" Argyll prompted.

"I've no idea," Kenneth said abruptly. "It's ..." He swallowed. "Nonsense. Complete nonsense." He faced Argyll with something like a challenge. "There is no money missing whatsoever."

"And you are the bookkeeper, so you would know?"

"Precisely."

"And you would also be in the best position to conceal it, if there were?"

"That ..." Kenneth swallowed. "That is slanderous, sir, and quite unjust."

Argyll affected innocence.

"You would not be in the best position?"

"Yes ... yes, of course I would. But there is nothing missing, nothing whatever."

"And your mother was quite satisfied on that point?"

"I have said so!"

There was a murmur of disbelief around the room.

Gilfeather rose to his feet.

Argyll smiled. Kenneth was a very poor witness. He looked as if he were lying even if he were not.

"Very well, to another subject. Are you married, Mr. Farraline?"

"Irrelevant, my lord!" Gilfeather protested.

"Mr. Argyll," the judge said wearily. "I will not tolerate any more of this meandering around. I have given you a great deal of latitude, but you have abused it."

"It is relevant, my lord, I assure you."

"I fail to see how."

"Are you married, Mr. Farraline?" Argyll repeated.

"No."

"Are you courting, sir?"

Kenneth hesitated, his face a dull red, sweat glistening on his lip. His eyes searched the gallery till they found Oonagh. He looked back at Argyll.

"No . . . no . . ."

"Have you then a mistress? One of which your family would not approve?"

Gilfeather started to rise, then realized the futility of it. Everyone in the room was waiting upon the answer. A woman moved and her stays creaked in the silence. A coal settled in one of the fires.

Kenneth gulped.

"No."

"If I were to call Miss Adeline Barker to the stand, would she agree with you, Mr. Farraline?"

Kenneth's face was scarlet.

"Yes . . . I mean, no. I . . . God damn it, it is none of your business. I did not kill my mother! She—" He stopped again just as suddenly.

"Yes? She knew about it?" Argyll prompted. "She did not know about it?"

"I have nothing else to say. I did not kill my mother, and the rest is none of your affair."

"A lady of expensive tastes," Argyll went on. "Not easy to keep her satisfied—and generous, and loyal—on a bookkeeper's salary, even when he works for the Farraline company."

"There is no money missing," Kenneth said sullenly. "Count it for yourself." There was confidence in his voice now, a ringing quality as if he knew he could not be proved wrong.

Argyll heard it too.

"I daresay there is none missing now, but was that always the case?"

The confidence was gone. Now it was defense.

"Certainly. I told you, I have taken nothing, and I was not responsible for my mother's death. For all I knew it was Miss Latterly, for the wretched pearls."

"So you say, sir, so you say." Argyll smiled politely. "Thank you, Mr. Farraline, I have nothing further to ask you."

Gilfeather shrugged. "I have nothing to ask this witness, my lord. As far as I can see he has nothing whatever to do with the case."

Rathbone leaned forward again, grasping Argyll's shoulder. "Call Quinlan Fyffe," he whispered fiercely.

Argyll did not turn.

"I have nothing to ask him," he whispered back. "I'll only weaken my case by looking desperate."

"Think of something," Rathbone insisted. "Get him up there. . . ."

"There's no point! Even if he knows who killed her, he isn't going to say so. He's a clever and very self-possessed man. He isn't going to flounder. He's no Kenneth. Anyway, I've nothing to rattle him with."

"Yes you have." Rathbone leaned even farther forward, aware of the judge glaring at him, and the jury waiting. "Use his emotions. He's a proud man, vain. He's got a beautiful wife, and a brother-in-law who's in love with her. He hates McIvor. Use his jealousy."

"What with?"

Rathbone's mind raced. "The company accounts. Eilish has been systematically taking books, with McIvor's help, to teach her ragged school. I'll wager Fyffe doesn't know about that. For God's sake, man, you're supposed to be the best advocate in Scotland. Twist him. Use his emotions against him."

"What about betraying Eilish?" Argyll asked. "Monk will be furious."

"To hell with Eilish," Rathbone said. "And Monk too! This is Hester's life!"

"Mr. Argyll," the judge said loudly. "Are you concluding your case, or not?"

"No, my lord. The defense calls Quinlan Fyffe, may it please the court."

The judge frowned. "For what purpose, Mr. Argyll? Mr. Gilfeather, are you aware of this?"

Gilfeather looked surprised, but interested, and not displeased.

The judge glanced at him.

Gilfeather lifted his shoulders slightly in the shadow of a shrug. "No, my lord, but if the court is prepared to wait for Mr. Fyffe to be sent for, I do not object. I think he will prove as useless to the defense's case as Mr. Farraline."

"Call Quinlan Fyffe!" the usher cried out. The words were echoed by the clerk at the door, and a messenger was duly dispatched.

In the interim the court was adjourned for luncheon.

When they returned over an hour later, Quinlan took the stand and was sworn in. He faced Argyll with outward politeness but a coldness of glance that bordered on insolence.

"Mr. Fyffe," Argyll began carefully, measuring his words. "You are one of the principal officers in the management of the Farraline printing company, are you not?"

"Yes sir."

"In what capacity?"

Gilfeather made as if to rise, and then changed his mind.

"Is this relevant, Mr. Argyll?" the judge said with a sigh. "If you are about to raise the matter of the company accounts, I must warn you that unless you provide real evidence that there has indeed been embezzlement, I shall not allow you to proceed."

Argyll hesitated.

"The missing books Eilish took," Rathbone whispered furiously behind him.

"No, my lord," Argyll said blandly, looking at the judge with an innocent smile. "That is not the area I wish to pursue at the moment."

The judge sighed again. "Then I don't know what you do want. I thought that was what you called this witness for."

"Yes my lord, but after I have laid suitable groundwork."

"Then proceed, Mr. Argyll, proceed," the judge said irritably.

"Thank you, my lord. Mr. Fyffe, in what capacity do you serve the Farraline company?"

"I am in control of the printing, and make all printing decisions," Quinlan replied.

"I see. Are you aware, sir, that several of your books have been stolen over the last year or more?"

There was a sharp stir of interest in the court. Quinlan looked incredulous.

"No sir, I was not aware of it. And to tell you the truth, I am disinclined to believe it now. Such a loss would have been apparent."

"To whom, sir?" Argyll asked. "To you?"

"No, not to me, but certainly . . ." He hesitated only a second or so, but a look of brilliance came into his eyes, a flash of thought. "To Baird McIvor. He manages that area of the company."

"Precisely so," Argyll agreed. "And he did not report such a loss to you?"

"No sir, he did not!"

Again Gilfeather half rose, but the judge waved him back.

"Would you be interested to know," Argyll said carefully, "that it was your wife who took them, sir, with Mr. McIvor's assistance?"

There was a gasp from the gallery. Several jurors turned towards Eilish, then towards Baird.

Quinlan stood motionless, the blood rushing scarlet up his face, then receding again, leaving him ashen. He started to say something, but his voice died away.

"You did not know this," Argyll said unnecessarily. "It would seem at a glance to make no sense, but she had a most excellent reason. . . ."

There was a sigh of breath around the entire room, then utter silence.

Quinlan stared at Argyll.

Argyll smiled, just a slow lift of the corners of his mouth, his eyes brilliant.

"She teaches people to read," he said distinctly. "Grown men who labor by day and come to learn from her by night how to read and write their names, to read street signs, warnings, instructions, who knows, perhaps in time even literature and the Holy Bible."

There was a sharp rustle of movement in the gallery. Eilish sat white-faced, her eyes wide.

The judge leaned forward, frowning.

"I assume you must have some proof of this extraordinary allegation, Mr. Argyll?"

"I quibble with your word *allegation*, my lord." Argyll stared up at the bench. "I do not see it as any kind of charge. I think it is a most praiseworthy thing to do."

Quinlan leaned forward over the edge of the witness-box, his fingers gripping the rail.

"It might be, if that were all it was," he said fiercely. "But McIvor is inexcusable. I always knew he lusted after her." His voice was rising and growing louder. "He tried to seduce her from any kind of morality or honor. But that he should use this excuse for it—and to corrupt her honesty as well—is beyond pardon."

There was a whisper around the room. The judge banged his gavel sharply.

Argyll cut in before there could be any direction from the bench or Gilfeather could protest.

"Are you not leaping to conclusions, Mr. Fyffe?" he asked with a lift of surprise displayed for the judge's sake. "I did not say that Mr. McIvor had done more than procure the books for her."

Quinlan's face was still white, his eyes narrowed to gleaming slits. He regarded Argyll with contempt.

"I know you did not. Do you take me for a fool, sir? I've watched him for years, staring at her, making excuses to be with her, the whispers, and laughter, the sudden falling into silence, the moods of temper and depression when she ignored him, the sudden elation when she did not." Again his voice was becoming shrill. "I know when a man is in love with a woman and when his desire has consumed him beyond his control. He has at last devised a way to gain her trust—and God knows what else!"

"Mr. Fyffe . . ." Argyll began, but he did not seriously attempt to stop him.

"But I recognize what I should have guessed before now," Quinlan went on, staring at Argyll and ignoring the rest of the court. "It is amazing how blind one can be until one's attention is forced to that which is painful."

At last Gilfeather rose to his feet.

"My lord, this is all most regrettable, and I am sure the court feels for Mr. Fyffe's shock and dismay, but it is entirely irrelevant as to who murdered Mary Farraline. My learned friend is only wasting time and attempting to divert the jury's attention from the issue."

"I agree," the judge said, and closed his mouth in a thin hard line.

But before he could add any further ruling, Quinlan turned to him, his eyes blazing.

"It is not irrelevant, my lord. Baird McIvor's behavior is very relevant indeed."

Gilfeather made as if to protest again.

Argyll gestured with his hands, intentionally ineffectual.

Rathbone said a prayer under his breath, his hands clenched, his body aching with the strain. He dared not look at Hester. He had forgotten Monk as if he had never existed.

In the box Quinlan stood upright, his face white, two sharp furrows at the bridge of his nose.

"The family solicitor asked me to go through certain of Mrs. Farraline's papers, relating to her estate—"

"Yes, sir?" the judge interrupted.

"I frequently handled her financial affairs," Quinlan replied. "My brother-in-law Alastair is too busy with his own commitments."

"I see. Proceed."

"I have discovered something which has shocked and appalled me," Quinlan said. "And also explained many circumstances previously beyond my understanding." He swallowed hard. He had the attention of every person in the room, and he knew it.

Gilfeather frowned, but made no attempt to interrupt.

"And this discovery, Mr. Fyffe?" Argyll asked.

"My mother-in-law owned a property, a family inheritance, in the far north, a croft—a smallholding, to be precise—in Rossshire. It is not of great worth, only twenty-five acres or so and a house, but quite sufficient to provide one or two people with an adequate living."

"I do not find that shocking or appalling, Mr. Fyffe," the judge said critically. "Pray explain yourself, sir."

Quinlan glanced at him, then once again faced the court.

"The property has been leased out for at least six years, through the agency of Baird McIvor, but no money from it, whatsoever, has ever reached Mrs. Farraline's accounts."

There was a gasp from the court. Someone cried out. One of the jurors jerked forward. Another searched for Baird McIvor in the gallery. One bit his lip and looked up at Hester.

"Are you sure of this, Mr. Fyffe?" Argyll asked, struggling to keep the rising excitement out of his voice. "I assume you have documented proof, or you would not make such a charge?"

"Of course I have," Quinlan answered him. "The papers are all there for anyone to see. Baird handled the matter for her, and even he would not deny it. He could not. Whatever rents there were is a mystery. The property is worth several pounds a year. Nothing whatever reached her account. For her, it was as if it never existed."

"Did you tax him with it, Mr. Fyffe?"

"Of course I did! He said it was a private agreement between himself and Mother-in-law, and not my concern."

"And that explanation does not satisfy you?"

Quinlan looked incredulous. "Would it you, sir?"

"No," Argyll agreed. "No, it would not. It sounds highly irregular, to put the kindest possible interpretation upon it."

Quinlan pulled a face of contempt.

"And the circumstances it explained?" Argyll went on. "You spoke of a circumstance that you had previously not understood."

"His relationship with Mrs. Farraline," Quinlan replied, his eyes hard and brilliant. "Shortly before the time he obtained the right to act for her in the matter of the croft, he appeared very depressed. He was sunk in gloom and short temper, spending many hours alone, and in a frame of mind approaching despair."

Not a person in the court moved or let out a whisper.

"Then quite suddenly his mood changed," Quinlan continued. "After many talks with Mrs. Farraline. It is plain now that he convinced her to give him this charge on her behalf, and he used it to clear himself of whatever trouble it was that plagued him."

Gilfeather rose to his feet.

The judge nodded to him, and turned to Quinlan.

"Mr. Fyffe, that is a conclusion which may or may not be accurate. However, you may not draw it, only present to the jury what actual evidence you possess."

"Documents, my lord," he replied. "The ownership deeds of the croft, Mrs. Farraline's written permission that Mr. McIvor may act for her to receive rents, and the fact that he never paid any money to her, for that or any other reason. Is that not proof?"

"It would be adequate for most people," the judge conceded. "But it is not my privilege, but the jury's, to make of it what they will."

"That is not all," Quinlan continued, his face set like a man staring at death. "I believed, like everyone else, that it was the nurse, Miss Latterly, who murdered Mother-in-law in order to conceal the fact that she had stolen a gray pearl pin. But now I find it increasingly harder to maintain that conviction. She seems to be a woman of re-

markable courage and virtue, which of course I did not know earlier."
He took a mighty breath. "And I did not connect the sight of my
brother-in-law, Baird McIvor, in the laundry room, on the lady's
maid's day off, fiddling with jars and vials of liquid, pouring one from
another."

There was a violent moment in the court. Baird shot to his feet,
his face ashen. Oonagh tried to restrain him, clinging on to his arm.
Alastair let out a cry of amazement.

Eilish sat white-knuckled, frozen.

"I had no idea what he was doing at the time, and no interest,"
Quinlan went on in a clear, relentless voice. "Now I fear I may have
witnessed something very terrible, and my failure to grasp its meaning
has cost Miss Latterly the most dreadful experience imaginable, to be
charged with the murder of her patient and tried for her life."

Argyll looked flushed, almost stunned.

"I see," he said with a choking voice. "Thank you, Mr. Fyffe. That
must have been very difficult for you to reveal, prejudicing your own
family as it does. The court appreciates your honesty." If there was sarcasm in his mind, it barely touched his lips.

Quinlan said nothing.

Gilfeather rose immediately to cross-examine. He attacked
Quinlan, his accuracy, his motives, his honesty, but he failed in all.
Quinlan was quiet, firm and unshakable; if anything, his confidence
grew. Gilfeather quickly realized his position was only damaged by pursuing it, and with only one bitter, angry movement, he resumed his
seat.

Rathbone could barely contain himself. He wished to tell Argyll
a hundred things about his summing up, what to say, above all what
to avoid. It was simple. To play on emotion, the love of courage and
honor, not to overplay the reference to Miss Nightingale, but he had
no opportunity, and on reflection, perhaps that was best. Argyll knew
it all.

It was masterful; all the emotion was there, but concealed, latent
rather than overt. He led them by their own passions, not his. When
he sat down there was no sound in the room except the squeak as the
judge sat forward and ordered the jury to retire and consider its verdict.

Then began the longest and the briefest time conceivable, between the moment when the die is cast and that when it falls.

It was one desperate, unbearable hour.

They filed back, their faces pale. They looked at no one, not at Argyll or Gilfeather, and what brought Rathbone's heart to his mouth, not at Hester.

"Have you reached your verdict, gentlemen?" the judge asked the foreman.

"We have, my lord," he replied.

"Is it the verdict of you all?"

"It is, my lord."

"How do you find the prisoner, guilty or not guilty?"

"My lord, we find the case not proven."

There was a thunderous silence, an emptiness ringing in the ears.

"Not proven?" the judge said with a lift of incredulity.

"Yes, my lord, not proven."

Slowly the judge turned to Hester, his expression bitter.

"You have heard the verdict, Miss Latterly. You are not exonerated, but you are free to go."

CHAPTER
ELEVEN

"What does it mean?" Hester asked intently, staring at Rathbone. They were in the sitting room of the lodgings Callandra had taken while in Edinburgh for the trial. Hester was to stay with her at least for this night, and the reconsideration could be made in the morning. Rathbone was sitting in a hard-backed chair, too charged with emotion to relax in one of the spacious softer ones. Monk stood by the mantelshelf, half leaning on it, his face dark, his brows drawn down in concentration. Callandra herself seemed more at ease. She and Henry Rathbone sat opposite in the sofa silently.

"It means that you are neither innocent nor guilty," Rathbone replied, pulling a face. "It is not a verdict we have in England. Argyll explained it to me."

"They think I am guilty, but they are not really quite sure enough to hang me," Hester said with a catch in her voice. "Can they try me again?"

"It means they think you're guilty, but they can't damned well prove it," Monk put in bitterly. He turned to Rathbone, his lip curled. "Can they try her again?"

"No. In that respect it is the same as a verdict of not guilty."

"But people will always wonder," Hester said grimly, her face very pale. She was perfectly aware of what it meant. She had seen the expressions of the people in the gallery, even those who were truly uncertain of her guilt. Who would hire as a nurse a woman who might be a murderess? The fact that she also might not was hardly a recommendation.

No one answered immediately. She looked at Monk, not that she expected comfort from him, but possibly because she did not. His face would reflect the worst she would find, the plain and bitter truth.

He stared back at her with such a blazing anger that for a moment she was frightened. Even during the trial of Percival in the Moidore case, she had never seen such a barely controllable rage in him.

"I wish I could say otherwise," Rathbone said very softly. "But it is a very unsatisfactory conclusion."

Callandra and Monk both spoke at once, but her voice was lost in his, which was harsh, furious, and immeasurably more penetrating. Whatever she said was never heard.

"It is not a conclusion. For the love of God, what is the matter with you?" He glared at them all, but principally at Rathbone and Hester. "We don't know who killed Mary Farraline! We must find out!"

"Monk . . ." Rathbone began, but again Monk overrode him with a snarl of contempt.

"It is one of the family."

"Baird McIvor?" Callandra asked.

"I have doubts," Henry Rathbone began. "It seems . . ."

"Unsatisfactory?" Monk asked with sarcasm, mimicking Oliver's earlier comment. "Very. No doubt they'll find him 'not proven' also, if it ever gets to trial. At least I hope so. I think it was that sniveling little beggar Kenneth. He embezzled from the company books, and his mother caught him."

"If he has covered his tracks, and from his confidence I have no doubt he has," Oliver argued, "then we'll never prove it."

"Well, you won't if you run off back to London and leave McIvor to face trial . . . and maybe hang for it," Monk snapped back at him. "Is that what you intend?".

Rathbone looked temporarily nonplussed. He stared at Monk with acute dislike.

"Do we gather from your remark that you intend to remain, Mr. Monk?" Henry Rathbone asked, his mild face pinched with concern. "Is that because you believe you can accomplish something you have not done so far?"

A faint flush of anger and self-consciousness colored Monk's lean cheeks.

"We have a great deal more to pursue than we did even a day ago.

I'm going to remain here until I have seen the end of it." He looked at Hester with a strange, mixed expression in his face. "You don't need to be so frightened. Whether they can prove it or not, they'll charge someone else." His voice still sounded angry.

She felt absurdly, unreasonably hurt. It was unfair. He seemed to be blaming her because the matter was unresolved, and she was frightened, and only with the greatest difficulty prevented herself from bursting into tears. Now that the worst fear was over, the sense of anticlimax, the confusion and relief, and the continued anxiety were almost more than she could bear. She wanted to be alone, where she could allow herself to stop the pretense and not care in the slightest what anyone else thought. And at the same time she wanted company, she wanted someone to put his arms around her and hold her closely, tightly, and not to let her go. She wanted to feel the warmth of someone, the breathing heartbeat, the tenderness. She certainly did not want to quarrel, least of all with Monk.

And yet because she was so vulnerable, she was furious with him. The only defense was attack.

"I don't know what you are so upset about," she said. "No one accused you of anything, except perhaps incompetence! But they don't hang you for that!" She turned to Callandra. "I am going to remain as well. For my own sake, as well as anyone else's, I am going to find out who killed Mary Farraline. I really—"

"Don't be absurd!" Monk cut across her. "There's nothing you can accomplish here, and you may well be a hindrance."

"To whom?" she demanded. Anger was so much easier than the fear and need she really felt. "You? I would have thought, on your showing so far, you would be grateful for any help you could obtain. You don't know whether it was Baird McIvor or Kenneth. You just said as much. At least I knew Mary, you didn't."

Monk's eyebrows rose. "And what help is that? If she said something useful, don't tell me you have waited until now to reveal it."

"Don't be stupid! Of course—"

"This conversation is not furthering our cause," Henry Rathbone interrupted them. "I think, if you will forgive me saying so, it is well time we exercised a little more logical thought and rather less emotion. It is only natural that after such a fearful experience we may all be excused a little self-indulgence, but it really will serve us ill in learning who is responsible for Mrs. Farraline's death. Perhaps we should retire to our beds and resume our discussion in the morning?"

"An excellent idea." Callandra rose to her feet. "We are all too tired to think usefully."

"There is no decision to make," Monk said irritably. "I shall go back to the Farraline house and continue my investigations."

"How will you explain yourself?" Rathbone asked with pursed lips. "They may not find personal curiosity an acceptable excuse."

Monk regarded him with loathing. "They are acutely vulnerable at the moment," he replied slowly and with sarcastic patience. "It is now apparent to everyone that one of the family is guilty. They will each be pointing the finger at the other. It should not be beyond my ability to convince at least one of them that they require my services."

Oliver's eyebrows rose very high. "At least one? Do you plan to work for several of them? That should provoke an interesting situation, to say the least of it!"

"All right . . . one of them," Monk conceded waspishly. "I'm sure Eilish is not guilty, and she will be very keen to prove that McIvor is not either, since she is in love with him. I think it is not impossible she will prefer him to her brother, if she is driven to choose."

"Which presumably you will do?"

"How perceptive of you!"

"Not particularly. You were rather obvious."

Monk opened his mouth to retort.

"William!" Callandra commanded. "I will be obliged if you will take your leave. Whether you return to your room in the Grassmarket or not is up to you, but it seems more than apparent to me that you need a good night's sleep." She regarded Henry Rathbone with affection. "I am sure you must be ready to retire, and I am. Good night, Mr. Rathbone. You have been of great support to me in this most trying time, and my gratitude to you is immense. I hope we shall remain friends once you have returned to London."

"I am always at your service, ma'am," he said with a smile which warmed his whole face. "Good night. Come, Oliver. We have all but outstayed our welcome."

"Good night, Lady Callandra," Oliver said courteously. He turned to Hester, ignoring Monk. His face was suddenly gentle. The anger fled and a pronounced tenderness took its place. "Good night, my dear. Tonight you are free, and we shall find the solution somehow. You shall not be jeopardized again."

"Thank you," she said with a sudden rush of emotion making her voice hoarse. "I know how much you have done for me already, and I am profoundly grateful. Nothing I can say—"

"Don't," he interrupted. "Just sleep well. Tomorrow is time enough to think of the next step."

She took a deep breath. "Good night."

He smiled and led the way to the door. Henry Rathbone followed immediately after him, smiling at Hester, and leaving without further speech.

Monk hesitated, frowning, then seemed to think better of what he had been going to say.

"Good night, Hester, Lady Callandra."

He was gone and the door closed before she realized it was the first time she could recall his having used her given name. It was odd to hear it on his tongue, and she was torn between relief that he had left and a desire for him to stay. That was ridiculous. She was much too tired and overwrought to make any sense even to herself.

"I think I will go to bed if you don't mind," she said to Callandra. "I think I am really . . ."

"Exhausted," Callandra finished very gently. "Of course you are, my dear. I shall have the innkeeper send us both up hot milk and a spot of brandy. I think I need it about as much as you do. I can confess to you now, I was deathly afraid I was going to lose one of the dearest friends I have. The relief is rather more than I can comfortably cope with. I am very ready to sleep." She held out her hand, and without an instant's hesitation, Hester took it, and walked into her arms to cling to her as fiercely as she was able, and did not move till the innkeeper knocked on the door.

Early the following morning everyone was a trifle self-conscious over the previous night's high emotion. No one referred to it. Henry Rathbone took his leave back to London, stopping for a moment to speak with Hester and then failing to find words for what he meant. It did not matter in the slightest. She had no need of them.

Callandra also went, apparently satisfied that she could add nothing further to the situation.

Oliver Rathbone said that he was going to council with Argyll once more, and that no doubt he would see Monk and Hester again before he also returned to London. Not unnaturally he had other cases awaiting him. He said nothing to Monk about whatever he had intended to do at Ainslie Place, and took only a moment to speak, rather formally, to Hester. She thanked him yet again for his work on her behalf, and he looked embarrassed, so she pursued it no further.

By nine o'clock she and Monk were alone, everyone else having departed for the morning train south. It was a windy day but not unpleasant, and fitful shafts of sunlight gave it a brightness out of keeping with both their moods. They stood side by side on Princes Street, staring up its handsome length towards the rise of the new town, and Ainslie Place.

"I don't know where you think you are going to stay," Monk said with a frown. "The Grassmarket is most unsuitable, and you cannot afford the hotel where Callandra was."

"What is wrong with the Grassmarket?" she demanded.

"It's not suitable for a woman alone," he replied irritably. "For heaven's sake, I thought your own common sense would have told you that! The neighborhood is rough, and a great deal of it none too clean."

She looked at him witheringly. "Worse than Newgate?" she inquired.

"Acquired a taste for it, have you?" he said, tight-lipped.

"Then leave me to attend to my own accommodation," she said rashly. "And let us proceed to Ainslie Place."

"What do you mean 'us'? I'm not taking you!"

"I do not require you to. I am perfectly capable of taking myself. I believe I shall walk there. It is not an unpleasant day and I should welcome a little exercise. I have not had much of late."

Monk shrugged and set out at a smart pace, so smart she was obliged almost to run to keep up with him. She had no breath to continue the conversation.

They arrived after ten, Hester with sore feet and feeling too heated for comfort, and by now in a very different temper. Damn Monk!

He, on the contrary, was looking rather pleased with himself.

The door of number seventeen was opened by McTeer. His dismal expression fell even farther when he saw Monk, and approached disastrous proportions when he saw Hester behind him.

"And who will ye be wanting?" he said slowly, rolling the words on his tongue as if he were making a prognostication of doom. "Have ye come for Mr. McIvor?"

"No, of course not," Monk said. "We have no power to come for anybody."

McTeer snorted. "I thought maybe ye were the po-liss. . . ."

It still jarred Monk that he was no longer a policeman and had no power whatever. His new status gave him freedom, and at the same time robbed him of half the ability to use it to its uttermost.

"Then ye'll be wanting Mrs. McIvor, no doubt," McTeer finished for himself. "Mr. Alastair is no here at this time o' day."

"Of course not," Monk agreed. "I should be obliged to see whoever I may."

"Aye, aye, I daresay. Well, you'd better come in." And reluctantly McTeer pulled the door wide enough open to allow them to pass into the hall, with its giant picture of Hamish Farraline dominating the room.

Hester stared at it with curiosity as McTeer withdrew. Monk waited impatiently.

"What are you going to say?" Hester asked him.

"I don't know," he replied tersely. "It can't be prescribed and followed like a dose of medicine."

"Medicine is not prescribed and followed regardless," she contradicted. "You watch the progress of the patient and do whatever you think best according to his response."

"Don't be pedantic."

"Well, if you don't know now, you had better make up your mind very rapidly," she replied. "Oonagh will be here in a moment, unless she sends a message that she will not receive you."

He turned his back, but remained standing close to her. She was right, and it irritated him almost beyond bearing. There had been too much emotion in the last few weeks, and he was profoundly disturbed by it. He hated his feelings to be beyond his control. The anger brought back memories which frightened him, recent memories of confusion and fear. The possibility of failure was another all too recent memory he preferred not to reawaken. The emotion caused by the knowledge that she might very easily die was a profound and deeply confused turmoil he chose to ignore. If he did so for long enough, he could sink into all the other memories he had lost.

She did not interrupt his thoughts again until McTeer returned to say that they would be received in the library. He did not say by whom.

When he opened the library door and announced them, all three of the women were there: Eilish, pale as a ghost, her eyes dark with fear; Deirdra, tense and unhappy, glancing all the time at Eilish; and Oonagh, composed and grave, and somewhat apologetic. It was she who came forward to greet first Hester, then Monk. As always, she was not lost for words.

"Miss Latterly, no expression of regret can suffice for what you have endured, but please believe that we are truly sorry, and as far as we have any part in it, we apologize profoundly."

It was a noble speech, most especially considering that it was her own husband who now stood so openly accused.

Eilish looked wretched, and Monk felt an unaccustomed wave of pity for her. Quinlan's behavior could only be acutely embarrassing to her.

Hester was generous about it, whatever her underlying feelings.

"You have no call to apologize, Mrs. McIvor. You were newly bereaved in most fearful circumstances. I think you acted with dignity and restraint. I would be pleased to have done as well."

A slight smile touched Oonagh's lips.

"You are very gracious, Miss Latterly, more generous than I think I should be"—the smile broadened for a moment—"were we to change places."

Eilish made a strangled sound in her throat.

Deirdra turned to her, but Oonagh ignored the interruption, and looked at Monk.

"Good morning, Mr. Monk. McTeer gave no indication as to why you have come. Was it simply to accompany Miss Latterly, that we might apologize to her?"

"I did not come for apologies," Hester cut across him before he could speak. "I came to say how highly I regarded your mother, and in spite of all that has happened since we last met, I regard her loss as the worst of it."

"That is generous of you," Oonagh accepted. "Yes, she was a remarkable person. She will be greatly missed, outside the family as well as within it."

They seemed to be on the point of being shown out again, and Monk had asked nothing at all.

"I have already expressed my regrets, long ago," he said somewhat abruptly. "I came to ask if you wished my assistance in the matter. It is far from resolved, and the police will not allow it to rest. They cannot."

"As an agent of inquiry?" Oonagh's fair eyebrows rose curiously. "To help us obtain another verdict of 'not proven'?"

"Do you think Mr. McIvor is guilty?"

It was an appalling thing to ask. There was a shocked, breathless silence. Even Hester gasped and bit her lip. A coal settled in the grate and outside beyond the windows a dog barked.

"No!" Eilish said at last, her voice a sob in her throat. "No, of course not!"

Monk was ruthless. "Then you will need to prove that it was someone else, or he will take Miss Latterly's place at the rope's end."

"Monk!" Hester exploded. "For heaven's sake!"

"You find the truth ugly?" he said. "I would have thought you, of all people, would not now balk at the reality."

She said nothing. He could feel her disgust as if it were a palpable thing radiating from her. It did not disturb him in the slightest.

A bar of pale sunlight came through the clouds and shone on one of the bookcases.

"I fear you are right, Mr. Monk," Oonagh said with distaste, "no matter how bluntly you phrase it. The authorities cannot afford to allow the matter to remain unresolved. They have not yet been here, but no doubt it is merely a matter of time. If not today, then tomorrow. I know of no one else we could call to our assistance in the matter of learning the truth. Of course we do have lawyers, should that be necessary. What would you propose to do?" She did not mention money; it was vulgar, and she had more than sufficient means to meet anything he might charge, probably out of petty housekeeping.

It was an impossible question to answer. He was seeking the truth only to prove once and for all that it was not Hester. The only imaginable alternatives were members of the Farraline family. Looking at Oonagh's face, he saw the depths of her eyes, the black laughter in there, and knew that she understood it as perfectly as he did.

Eilish moved uncomfortably. Deirdra glanced at her.

"Discover which of you it was, Mrs. McIvor," Monk said quietly. "At least let us hang the right man—or woman. Or would you prefer simply to hang the most convenient?"

Hester let out a suppressed groan of anguish.

Oonagh remained entirely composed.

"No one could accuse you of mincing your words, Mr. Monk. But you are correct. I should prefer it to be the right person, whether it is my husband or one of my brothers. How do you propose to proceed? You must know a great deal already, and it has not led you to any conclusion, or doubtless you would have said so in Miss Latterly's interests."

Monk felt himself tighten as if he had been slapped. Once again his respect for Oonagh mounted. She was unlike any woman he had known before, and he could think of few men, if any, who could match her cold courage or her monumental composure.

"I now know a great deal more than I did then, Mrs. McIvor. I think we all do," he replied dryly.

"And you believe it!" Eilish could control herself no longer. "You believe everything Quinlan said, just because it was—"

"Eilish!" Oonagh's voice cut across her firmly, reducing her to agonized silence, staring at Monk with her brilliant eyes. Oonagh turned back to Monk. "I presume you do not believe the matter is ended, or you would not have bothered to come. I imagine, whatever tactics or courtesy require you to say, it is to clear Miss Latterly's name that you have really come. No, you do not need to answer that. Please don't protest, it is unworthy of either of us."

"I was not going to protest," he said tersely. "As I see it, there are at least two avenues to explore on the grounds of evidence, either old or new."

"Mother's property in Ross-shire," Oonagh said. "What else?"

"The diamond brooch which apparently you never found."

She looked a little surprised. "You think it matters?"

"I have no idea, but I shall find out. Who is your jeweler?"

"Arnott and Dunbar, of Frederick Street."

"Thank you." He hesitated only an instant. "Will it be possible to know a little more about the property in . . ."

"Ross-shire," she finished for him, her eyes wide. "If you wish to. Quinlan has naturally given the papers to the police. They took them yesterday evening. But the fact is irrefutable. Mother inherited a small croft in Easter Ross. She gave the leasing of it into Baird's hands, and there are, it would seem, no receipts of money whatever. . . ."

"There will be some explanation for it!" Eilish said desperately. "Baird would never simply steal it!"

"Whatever it is, I doubt it is simple," Oonagh said dryly. "But of course, dear, we all wish to think it is not as it seems, no one more than I!"

Eilish blushed, and then went white.

"Where is Easter Ross?" Monk could not recall the county, if he had ever known anything of it. Presumably it was in the east, but to the east of where?

"Oh, beyond Inverness, I think," Oonagh replied absently. "It is really very far north indeed. Saint Colmac, Port of Saint Colmac, or something like that. Really, it is all rather absurd; the amount cannot be more than a few pounds a year. Hardly worth anyone's life!"

"People have been killed over a hand of cards," Monk said bitterly, then as Hester glanced towards him, suddenly wondered how he knew that. He was not conscious of knowing, and yet he had spoken with certainty. It was another of those little jolts of knowledge that returned every so often, utterly without warning and with no surrounding recollection.

"I suppose so." Oonagh's voice was little more than a whisper. She looked towards the window. "I shall find the precise address for you, if that is what you wish. Perhaps you would dine with us this evening, and I shall have it for you then?"

"Thank you," Monk replied, then suddenly was uncertain whether Hester had been included or not.

"Thank you," Hester accepted, before the question could be answered by anyone else. "That would be most generous of you, especially in the circumstances."

Oonagh drew in her breath, then decided against arguing, and smiled instead.

It was dismissal, and Monk and Hester were in the hall, waiting for the sepulchral McTeer to let them out, when Eilish came hurrying after them, grasping Monk by the arm, hardly seeming to see Hester.

"Mr. Monk! It wasn't Baird. He would never have hurt Mother, whatever anyone thinks. He doesn't even care all that much about money. There has to be another explanation for all this."

Monk felt acutely sorry for her. He knew only too well the bitterness of disillusion, the moment when one realizes that the man or the woman that one has loved intensely is after all not merely imperfect but flawed, and in a way that is ugly, shallow and alien. It is not that he or she has slipped, and needs forgiving, but never was the person one thought. The whole relationship was a mirage, a lie, unwitting perhaps, but still a lie.

"Have you asked him?" he said gently.

She looked very white. "Yes. He simply says that he did not steal anything but it is a subject he cannot speak of. I . . . I believe him, of course, but I don't know what to make of it. Why would he not speak of it, when Quinlan accuses him of something so terrible? What is worth pursuing now, when his"—she gulped—"his life may be at stake?"

The only answer that came to Monk's mind was that it could be some secret even uglier than the accusation, or one that substantiated it. He did not say so to her.

"I don't know, but I promise you I shall do all I can to find out. And if Baird is innocent then he will be proved so."

"Kenneth?" she whispered. "I can't bear to believe that either."

Hester said nothing, although Monk knew she was aching to speak. Perhaps for once she also could think of no words that would not make it worse.

McTeer appeared, his face set in lines of imminent disaster, and immediately Eilish stepped back and began a formal good-bye.

Monk responded appropriately, and turned to leave, only to find Hester speaking to Eilish with total disregard for McTeer. He could not hear what she was saying, her voice was so low, but Eilish gave her a look of intense gratitude, and then a moment later they were out in the street.

"What did you say to her?" he demanded. "There is no point giving her any hope. It may very well have been McIvor."

"Why?" she said crisply, her chin coming up. "What on earth would he do such a thing for? He liked Mary, and the rent of one croft is hardly worth killing anyone for."

He gave up in exasperation and began walking briskly back towards Princes Street and the route to the jeweler's. She was too naive to understand, and too willful to be told.

That night at dinner, Monk arrived in his usual immaculate dress, and Hester came looking, in his opinion, a complete fright, having nothing with her other than the gray-blue dress in which she had stood trial. They were armed with information which altered everything with respect to Baird McIvor and Kenneth. The jeweler had informed them that it was not Mary Farraline who had commissioned the diamond pin at all, in spite of the fact that it was on her account. It was Kenneth. He had at the time assumed it was an errand, and had not questioned it, much to his chagrin when he had learned later, from Mary herself, that she had not requested it, and had indeed never seen it. Of course the matter was settled now, as far as he was concerned. What had passed between Kenneth Farraline and his mother he had no idea.

As usual McTeer met them at the door and ushered them into the withdrawing room, where this time the entire family was assembled, almost as if they might have known a revelation awaited them—although perhaps, in the circumstances, that was not surprising. Hester had been released, if not cleared of the charge, and Quinlan had openly accused Baird McIvor. It was inconceivable that the case could rest as it was. Even if the police pressed it no further, it was beyond imagination that the Farralines themselves could leave matters as they stood.

As always it was Oonagh who acknowledged them first, but Alastair, looking pale and grim-faced, was only a moment behind.

"Good evening, Miss Latterly," he said with studied politeness. "It is good of you to come with such generosity. A lesser woman might have borne a grudge."

It crossed Monk's mind that that remark might have been a question as much as a statement. Alastair had a haunted look in the depths of his eyes, as well he might, knowing either his brother or his dearest sister's husband was guilty of murder, and the murder of his mother at that. Monk did not envy him. As he stood in the gracious withdrawing room with its tall windows and sweeping curtains, the fire blazing in the hearth and the generations of family mementos and embroideries, he felt a sharp touch of pity for Alastair. What if it were Baird McIvor? Alastair and Oonagh had grown up together, sharing their dreams and their fears in a way the other siblings had not. If it were Oonagh's husband, Alastair would feel it almost as deeply as she. And he would be the one person from whom she might not hide her grief, her disillusionment, her intolerable sense of shame. No wonder he stood close to her now, as if he would touch her, were it not so obvious, and so intrusive of a wound not yet delivered.

Hester had already deflected the remark generously, turning it into a mere exchange. They were invited in, offered wine. Eilish caught Monk's eye. She looked painfully embarrassed, knowing that at least some people would associate her with her husband's accusations. And galling as it was, Hester probably owed him her freedom, even though it was brought about by Argyll's questions.

Quinlan was standing at the farther end of the room, his lean face, with its long nose and chiseled lips, deep in thought. He was watching Hester, amusement in his eyes. Perhaps he was wondering how she would approach him, what she would find to say. Monk felt a rush of loathing towards the man, not for Hester's sake—she was well able to take care of herself, or if she were not it was her own fault for being here—but for Eilish, who could not escape.

Baird stood by the fireplace, as far as possible from Quinlan. He looked pale, as if he had not eaten or slept, and there was a haunted air about him, as though he were preparing to fight but had no hope of winning.

Kenneth sat on the arm of one of the easy chairs, regarding Hester with undisguised interest.

They had been indulging in polite conversation about nothing that mattered, but the room seemed to crackle with the underlying silence, the waiting for someone to broach the only subject that mattered. Finally it was Alastair who did it.

"Oonagh says you went to find out about the other brooch which no one has seen. I can't imagine why." A curious look came into his eyes, doubt, incredulity, hope. "Surely you don't think one of the servants took it . . . do you? Isn't it merely lost? Mother does seem to have been somewhat careless . . ." He left the remark hanging in unfinished silence. No one had yet explained the gray pearl brooch, and somehow it seemed crass to mention the subject at all now, in front of Hester.

"No I don't," Monk said grimly. "I am sorry, Mr. Farraline, but the explanation for that is quite simple. Your mother never had it. It was commissioned in the first place by your brother, Kenneth, I assume in order to give to his lady friend, who is so determined never to be poor again. A very understandable resolve, not perhaps to you, but certainly to anyone who has lain awake all night because he or she was too hungry or too cold to sleep."

Alastair pulled a face of distaste, then turned slowly to look at Kenneth.

Kenneth flushed a dull red, and his face tightened defiantly.

Monk glanced at Eilish. Her expression was a painful mixture of anguish and hope, as though she had not expected to be hurt by Kenneth's guilt, and now that it was on the brink of reality, it caught her unaware, both wounded and abashed. She looked across at Baird, but he was sunk in gloom of his own.

Oonagh turned a questioning gaze at her younger brother.

"Well?" Alastair demanded. "Don't just stand there glowering, Kenneth. This requires very considerable explanation. Do you admit buying this piece of jewelry and charging it to Mother? Not that there seems any point in denying it; the proof is there."

"I admit it," Kenneth said in a strangled voice, although there seemed as much anger in it as fear. "If you paid us decently I wouldn't have to—"

"You are paid what you are worth!" Alastair said, the color mounting in his cheeks. "But if you were paid nothing at all beyond your keep, that would not excuse you from buying presents for your mistress on Mother's account. Dear God, what else have you done? Is Uncle Hector right? Have you embezzled from the company accounts?"

The blood fled from Kenneth's cheeks, but he seemed defiant as much as frightened, and there was still no remorse in him that the eye could see.

Oddly, it was Quinlan who stepped forward to speak, not Kenneth himself.

"Yes he did, months ago, over a year now, and Mother-in-law knew about it at the time. She paid it all back."

Alastair exploded with disbelief. "Oh really, Quin! Don't expect me to believe all that. I know how you feel about Baird, but this is absurd. Why on earth would Mother cover up Kenneth's embezzlement and simply repay it all? I presume we are not speaking about a few pennies. That would hardly fund the life he enjoys and keep his poverty-stricken mistress in the diamonds she apparently likes so much."

"Of course not," Quinlan agreed with a twist of his mouth. "If you look at Mother-in-law's will, you will find that Kenneth gets nothing at all. She took his share in settlement of his debt—both for the embezzlement and, I imagine, the brooch. She knew about that too." His eyes stared levelly at Alastair, so absolutely without wavering, Monk wondered if this last was a lie.

Alastair said nothing.

Quinlan smiled. "Come on, Alastair. That is what Mother-in-law would have done, and you know it. She would never have precipitated a scandal by prosecuting her own son. We all knew her better than that—even Kenneth. Not when the remedy lay so easily to hand." He shrugged very slightly. "Certainly she punished him, and redeemed the debt at the same time. If he'd done it again she'd have taken it out of his skin—she would have had him work all day and all night till it was earned again. I daresay she'd received one or two nice presents in her day. . . ."

"How dare you—" Alastair began furiously, but Oonagh cut him off.

"I presume the solicitors will know this much?" she said quietly.

"Of course," Quinlan agreed. "There is no reason given in the will, except that Kenneth himself will understand why he has no inheritance, and have no complaints."

"How do you know this, when the rest of the family doesn't?" Monk asked him.

Quinlan's eyebrows rose. "Me? Because as I said before, I conducted a great deal of her affairs for her. I am extremely good at business, especially investments, and Mother-in-law knew it. Besides, Alastair is too busy, Baird has no head for it, and obviously she would be a complete fool to trust Kenneth."

"If you know so much about the business," Eilish challenged him in a choking voice, "how is it you knew nothing about the land in Easter Ross and that she was getting no rent from it?"

Kenneth seemed to be forgotten, at least temporarily. All eyes turned to Eilish, and then to Baird. No one took the slightest notice of Monk or Hester.

Baird looked up at them, his face wretched.

"Mary knew everything that I did, and it was done with her permission," he said quietly. "That is all I will tell you."

"Well, it is not enough." Alastair swung around at him desperately. "Good God, man! Mother is dead—poisoned by someone. The police aren't going to accept an answer like that. If Miss Latterly didn't do it, then one of us did!"

"I didn't." Baird's voice was barely a whisper between his lips. "I loved Mary, more than anyone else . . . except . . ." He stopped. Few in the room doubted he was going to say "Eilish," not "Oonagh."

Oonagh was very pale, but perfectly composed. Whatever emotions tore her at such a reality, they were too well concealed by time, familiarity, or sheer courage to show now.

"Of course," Alastair said bitterly. "We would hardly expect you to say anything less. But words are immaterial now; it is only facts that matter."

"Nobody knows the facts," Quinlan pointed out. "We only know what Mary's papers say, what the bankers say, and Baird's excuses. I don't know what other facts you think there are."

"I imagine the police may think that sufficient," Monk responded. "At least for trial. What else they find, or need, is their affair."

"Is that what you are going to do?" Eilish was desperate; it stared out of her anguished face and rang in the rising pitch of her voice. "Just accuse, and leave it to the police? Baird is one of the family. We've lived with him in this house, known him every day for years, shared our dreams and our hopes with him. You can't just— just say he's guilty—and abandon him." She looked wildly from one to another of them, all except Quinlan, ending with Oonagh, perhaps to whom she had always turned in times of need.

"We are not abandoning him, my dear," Oonagh said quietly. "But we have no alternative to facing the truth, however terrible it is for us. One of us killed Mother."

ANNE PERRY

Unintentionally Eilish looked again at Hester, then blushed scarlet.

"That won't work, my sweet," Quinlan said sourly. "Of course it is still possible. 'Not proven' is a vicious verdict, but they cannot try her again, whatever they think. And let us face facts, her reason hardly matches Baird's. He could have slipped the brooch into her bag . . . she could hardly have embezzled Mother-in-law's rents."

"For God's sake, Baird, why don't you say something?" Deirdra burst out after her long silence. She went to Eilish and put her arm around her. "Can't you see what this is doing to all of us?"

"Deirdra, please control your language," Alastair reproved almost automatically.

Monk was amused. If Alastair had the faintest idea of his wife's midnight activities, he would be grateful it was so relatively mild. Monk would swear she knew a great deal that was more colorful than that from her mechanic friend.

"There seems only one way." Hester spoke for the first time since the charge had been made against Baird. Everyone looked at her with some surprise.

"I don't know what it can be." Alastair frowned. "Do you know something that we don't?"

"Don't be absurd," Quinlan said. "Mother-in-law would hardly confide her business to Miss Latterly on one day's acquaintance, and not tell at least Oonagh, if not all of us."

"Miss Latterly?" Alastair turned to her.

"One of us must go to the croft in Ross-shire and learn what has happened to the rents," she replied. "I have no idea how far it is, but it hardly matters. It must be done."

"And which of us will you trust?" Deirdra asked dryly. "I can think of no one."

"Monk, of course," Hester replied. "He has no interest whatever in the answer one way or the other."

"As long as it is not you," Quinlan added. "I think his interest in the case is now quite obvious to all. He came here originally talking what, at the kindest, was much less than the truth, what less kindly but more accurately was a complete lie."

"Would you have helped him for the truth?" she asked.

Quinlan smiled. "Of course not. I am not accusing, merely point-

321

ing out that Mr. Monk is not the paragon of honesty you seem to imagine."

"I don't imagine it," she said crossly. "I simply said he has no interest in which of you is lying or what happened to the rents."

"What a charming turn of phrase you have."

Hester blushed hotly.

"Please!" Deirdra interrupted them, turning to Monk. "All this is beside the point now. Mr. Monk, would you learn the particulars from Quinlan and travel north to Easter Ross, find the person who leases the croft and what they have done with the rents, to whom they were paid. I imagine it will be necessary to bring with you some burden of proof, documents, or whatever it may be. Probably a sworn testimony . . ."

"An affidavit," Alastair supplied. "I presume there will be notaries public, or justices of the peace, even up there."

"Yes," Monk said immediately, although he was irritated he had not suggested it himself, before Hester had. Then as quickly he wondered how he was going to find the fare. He lived precariously as it was. Callandra provided for him in lean times, when his clients were few, or poor, in return for his sharing the interesting cases with her. It was her form of both friendship and philanthropy, and her occasional excitement and touch of danger. But she had gone home, and he could not ask her for a contribution towards this. She had already paid him for his part in Hester's defense, sufficient to take him to Scotland and to secure his lodgings, both here and in London during his absence. She had not known such a prolonged trip would be necessary.

"How far is it?" he said aloud. It galled him intensely to have to ask.

Alastair's eyes widened. "I have no idea. Two hundred miles? Three hundred?"

"It isn't so far," Deirdra contradicted him. "Two hundred at most. But we will provide your fare, Mr. Monk. After all, it is our business which takes you there, not your own." She disregarded Alastair's frown and Oonagh's look of faint surprise and a flicker of black humor. She at least understood that it was to remove the final question from Hester's innocence, not because Monk wished to assist Baird McIvor or any of the Farralines. "I expect there is a train as far as Inverness," Deirdra continued. "After that you may have to ride, I don't know."

"Then as soon as I have the information, and a note of authority from you," Monk said, for the first time looking at Quinlan, not Oonagh, for agreement, "I shall collect my belongings and take the first train north."

"Will you travel also?" Eilish said, addressing Hester.

"No," Monk said instantly.

Hester had opened her mouth to speak, but no one knew what she was going to say. She took one look at Monk's face, then at the faces of the assembled company, and changed her mind. "I shall remain in Edinburgh," she said obediently. Had Monk been less consumed by his own forthcoming task, he might have been suspicious of the sudden collapse of her argument, but his thoughts were occupied elsewhere.

They remained for dinner: a good meal, punctiliously served. But there was a gloom over the whole house, not only of recent death, but now of newborn fear, and conversation was stilted and meaningless. Hester and Monk took their leave early, without the necessity or artificiality of excuses.

The journey north was long and extremely tedious for Monk, because he was chafing to be there. No one in Edinburgh had been able to tell him how to proceed into Easter Ross after he should reach Inverness. As far as the ticket clerk was concerned, it was an unknown land, cold, dangerous, uncivilized, and no sensible person would wish to go there. Stirling, Deeside and Balmoral were all excellent places for a holiday. Aberdeen, the granite city of the north, had its qualities, but beyond Inverness was no-man's-land, and you went there at your own risk.

The long journey took nearly all the daylight hours, as it was now deepest autumn. Monk sat morosely and turned over and over in his mind all he knew of the death of Mary Farraline and the passions and characters of her family. He came to no conclusion whatever, only that it was one of them who had killed her; almost certainly Baird McIvor, because he had embezzled the rents from the croft. But it seemed such a futile reason, so incredibly petty for a man who seemed moved by so much stronger emotions. And if he loved Eilish, as he seemed to so apparently, how would he have brought himself to kill her mother, whatever the temptation?

When he disembarked at Inverness it was already too late to think of proceeding farther north that night. Resentfully he found lodgings, and immediately inquired of the landlord about travel to the Port of Saint Colmac on the next day.

"Oh," the landlord said thoughtfully. He was a small man by the name of MacKay. "Oh aye, Portmahomack, ye mean? That'll be the ferry ye'll be wanting."

"The ferry?" Monk said dubiously.

"Aye, ye'll be wanting to go over to the Black Isle, and then across the Cromarty Firth over by Alness and up towards Tain. It's a long way, mind. Can ye no do your business in Dingwall, maybe?"

"No," Monk replied reluctantly. He could not even remember if he could ride a horse, and this was a harsh way to find out. His imagination punished him already.

"Oh well, needs must when the devil drives," MacKay said with a smile. "That'll be out Tarbet Ness way. Fine lighthouse that is. See it for miles on a dark night, so ye can."

"Can I take a horse on the ferry?" Then the instant he had asked, MacKay's face told him it was a foolish question. "Well, can I hire one on the other side?" he said before MacKay could answer.

"Aye, that ye can. And ye can walk to the ferry here that will take you to the Black Isle. Just yonder by the shore there. Ye'll be a southerner, no doubt?"

"Yes." Monk did not debate it. Instinct told him that a Borderer, like himself, from Northumberland, whose men had fought the Scots in raid and battle and foray for close on a thousand years, might be unwelcome, even as far north as this.

MacKay nodded. "Ye'll be hungry," he said sagely. "It's a tidy journey from Edinburgh, so they say." He pulled a face. It was a foreign land to him, and he was well content to leave it so.

"Thank you," Monk accepted.

He was served a meal of fresh herrings rolled in oatmeal and fried, with bread still warm from the oven, butter, and oatmeal-covered cheese named Caboc, which was delicious. He went to bed and slept deeply, with barely the stirring of dreams.

The morning was windy and bright. He rose immediately and instead of eating breakfast at MacKay's hostelry, he took bread and cheese with him and set out to find the ferry across to the Black Isle,

ANNE PERRY

which he had been informed was not literally an island but a large isthmus.

The passage was not broad—it might at some stage conceivably be bridged—but the tide was swift from the Moray Firth into the smaller Beauly Firth and the wide bay within swept around to the left far out of sight.

The ferryman looked at him dubiously when he asked to be taken across.

"There's a fair wind, the day." He squinted eastwards, frowning.

"I'll help," Monk offered instantly, then could have bitten his tongue. He had no idea whether he could row or not. He had absolutely no memory of water or boats. Even when he had gone back home to Northumberland, as soon as he was out of hospital after the accident, and woken in the night to find his brother-in-law with the lifeboat, it stirred no recollection of boats in him.

"Aye, well that'll maybe be needed," the ferryman agreed, still not moving from the spot.

Monk could not afford to anger the man. He had to cross the straits today; riding around the long coastline by Beauly, Muir-of-Ord, Conon Bridge and Dingwall would take him an entire day longer.

"Then shall we begin?" Monk said urgently. "I need to reach Tarbet Ness tonight."

"Ye'll be having a long ride." The ferryman shook his head, looking at the sky, then back at Monk. "But ye might make it. Looks like a fair day, in spite of the wind. Might drop when the tide turns. Sometimes does."

Monk took that as an acceptance and made to step into the boat.

"Ye'll no be wanting to see if there's anyone else, then?" the ferryman asked. "It'll be half the fare if ye're willing to lend a hand yourself?"

Monk might have argued, closer to home, that the fare should have been less if he were prepared to row, whether there was anyone else or not, but he did not wish to provoke ill feeling.

"Aye, well, come on then." The ferryman extended his hand to help Monk. "We'd best be going. There'll maybe be someone on the Black Isle who wants to come to Inverness."

Monk took his hand and stepped into the small boat. As soon as his feet touched the boards and the whole thing rocked with his added weight, he felt a wave of memory so sharp he hesitated in mid-motion, his balance spread between the boat and the quay. It was not visual, but emotional; a fear and a sense of helplessness and embarrassment. It was so powerful he almost withdrew.

"What's the matter wi' ye?" The ferryman looked at him warily. "Ye're no seasick, are ye? We've no even set out yet!"

"No, I'm not," Monk said sharply. He forbore from giving any explanation.

"Aye, well if ye are"—the ferryman was dubious—"ye'll please throw up over the side."

"I'm not," Monk repeated, hoping it was true, and let himself down into the boat, sitting down in the stern rather hard.

"Well, if ye're going to help, ye'll no do it there." The ferryman frowned at him. "Have ye never been in a wee boat before?" He looked as if he doubted it severely.

Monk stared at him. "It was remembering last time that made me hesitate. The people I knew then," he added, in case the man thought he was afraid.

"Oh, aye?" The ferryman made room in the seat beside him and Monk moved over, taking the other oar. "I may be daft doing this." The ferryman shook his head. "I'm hoping I'll no regret it when we're out in the current. But I don't want you trying to move over then, or we'll likely both end up in the water. An' I canna swim!"

"Well, if I have to save you, I'll expect my fare back," Monk said dryly.

"No if ye're the one that upsets us." The ferryman looked him squarely in the eye. "Now hold your hush, man, and bend your back to the oar."

Monk obeyed, principally because it took all his attention to keep in rhythm with the ferryman, and he was intent not to make more of a fool of himself than he had already.

For more than ten minutes he rowed steadily, and was beginning to be satisfied with himself. The small boat skimmed over the water with increasing ease. He began to enjoy it. It was pleasant to use his body for a change from the pent-up anguish of mind over the previous weeks, and the necessity of sitting in the crowded courtroom, completely uselessly. This was not so difficult. The day was bright and the sunlight off the water almost dazzling, giving the sky and water a unity

of blue brilliance which was curiously liberating, as if its very endless-
ness were a comfort, not a fear. The wind in his face was cold, but it
was sharp and clean, and the salt smell of it satisfied him.

Then without any warning they were out of the lee of the head-
land and into the current and the tide sweeping in from the Moray
Firth and into the Beauly, and he almost lost the oar. Involuntarily he
caught sight of the ferryman's face, and the wry humor in the man's
eyes.

Monk grunted and clasped the oar more firmly, bending his back
and heaving as powerfully as he could. He was disconcerted to find
that instead of shooting forward and outrowing the ferryman, turning
the boat on a slew, he merely kept up and the boat plowed through
the water across the current towards the far distant shore of the Black
Isle.

He tried to compose his mind and consider what he might find
when he arrived at Mary Farraline's croft. There did not seem many
possibilities. Either there was no resident tenant, and therefore
there would be no rents, and Baird McIvor had merely been either
lazy or incompetent, or there was a tenant, and Baird had never col-
lected the rents—or he had, and for some reason not given them to
Mary.

Presumably he had kept them, or used them to pay some dishonorable debt, which he could not pay openly out of the money he was
known to have. Another woman was the answer which leaped to
mind. But surely he could not love anyone beside Eilish? Was it a past
indiscretion he was paying to keep silent, both from Oonagh and
Eilish? That had a ring of truth to it that was curiously unwelcome.
Why, for heaven's sake? Someone had killed Mary. Proof that it was
Baird McIvor would clear Hester beyond shadow.

They were halfway across and the current was more powerful. He
had to pull with all his strength, throwing his weight into each stroke,
driving his feet against the boards across the bottom of the boat. The
ferryman was still rowing easily in a long, slow rhythm which made it
look like a natural, almost effortless movement, while Monk's shoulders were already aching. And he still wore the same very slight smile.
Their eyes met for a moment, then Monk looked away.

He began to develop a rhythm within himself, to block out the
pain across his back with each stroke. He must be getting soft for this

to cause him such discomfort. Was that recent? Before the accident, had he been different: ridden horseback perhaps, rowed on the Thames, played some sport or other? There had been nothing in his rooms to indicate so. Yet there was no surplus fat on him, and he was strong. It was just that this was an unaccustomed exercise.

Unwittingly he found himself thinking of Hester. It was quite unreasonable, and yet even while he knew it, he was angry. The loss of her would have hurt him far more than he wished. It made him vulnerable, and he resented it. He could think of courage with power and clarity; it was the one virtue he admired above all others. It was the cornerstone on which all rested. Without it everything else was insecure, endangered by any wind of fortune. How long would justice survive without the courage to fight for it? It was a sham, a hypocrisy, a deceit better unspoken. What was humility unless one possessed the courage to admit error, ignorance and futility, the strength to go back and begin again? What was anything worth—generosity, honor, hope, even pity—without courage to carry it through? Fear could devour the very soul.

And yet the loneliness and the pain were so real. And time was a dimension too easy to overlook. What was bearable for a day, two days, became monstrous when faced without end. Damn Hester!

Suddenly there was water in his face.

"Caught a crab," the ferryman commented with amusement. "Getting tired?"

"No," Monk said tersely, although he was nearly exhausted. His back was aching, his hands were blistered, and his shoulders felt like cracking.

"Oh, aye?" the ferryman said dubiously, but did not slacken his pace.

Monk caught another "crab," skimming the oar over the top of the water instead of digging in, and sending the spray up into their faces, tasting it cold and salty on his lips and in his eyes.

Suddenly memory returned like a blinding moment of vision, except that the actual sight portion of it—the gray, glimmering sea and light on the waves—was gone almost before it registered in his mind. It was the cold, the sense of danger and overwhelming urgency that remained. He was frightened, his shoulders had hurt just as they did now, but he had been younger, far younger, perhaps only a boy. The boat had been bucketing all over the place, tossed on heavy waves, their crests curling white with spume. Why on earth would anyone be out in such weather? Why was he frightened? It was not the waves, it was something else.

But he could not find the memory. There was nothing more, just the cold, the violence of the water, and the terrible overwhelming sense of urgency.

Suddenly the boat shot forward. They were in the lee of the Black Isle and the ferryman was smiling.

"Ye're a stubborn man," he said as they slid into the shore. "Ye'll no be doing this tomorrow, I'll be thinking. Ye'll be hurting sore."

"Possibly," Monk conceded. "Maybe the tide'll be on the turn, and the wind not so hard against us."

"Ye can always hope." The ferryman held out his hand and Monk paid him his fare. "But the train to the south will no wait for ye."

Monk thanked him and went to hire a horse to take him the several miles up over the high hills of the Black Isle, almost due north towards the next ferry across the Cromarty Firth.

He obtained the animal, and rode steadily. It was a comfortable feeling, familiar. He found he knew how to guide the animal with a minimum of effort. He was at home in the saddle, although he had no idea how long it was since he had last ridden.

The land was beautiful, rolling away to the north in soft slopes, some heavily wooded in deciduous trees, some in pines, much of it in meadows dotted with sheep and occasional cattle. He could see at least fifteen or twenty miles, at a guess.

What was the memory that had troubled him in the boat? Was it one he even wanted to find? There was something else at the back of the other matter, something uglier and more painful. Perhaps he would rather leave it lost. There could be mercy in forgetfulness.

It was hard traveling up the rise of the hill. He had used his back to exhaustion rowing across the Firth, but walking would not be unpleasant. He dismounted and gave the horse a break in its labor. Side by side they reached the crest and saw the mass of Ben Wyvis ahead of them, the first snows of winter crowning its broad peak. With the sunlight on it it seemed to hang in the sky. He walked gently, still on foot, while the hill to the left fell away, and he could see mountains beyond mountains, almost to the heart of Scotland: blue, purple, shimmering white at the peaks against the cobalt sky. He stopped, breathless, not with exhaustion but with the sheer wonder of it. It was vast. He felt as if he could see almost limitlessly. Ahead of him and below was the Cromarty Firth, shining like polished steel; to the east it stretched out of sight towards the sea. To the west were range after range of mountains lost in the distance. The sun was strong on his face, and unconsciously he lifted it towards the wind and the silence.

He was glad he was alone. Human companionship would have intruded. Words would have been a blasphemy in this place.

Except he would have liked to share it, have someone else grasp this perfection and keep it in the soul, to bring back again and again in time of need. Hester would understand. She would know just to watch, and feel, and say nothing. It was not communicable, simply to be shared by a meeting of the eyes, a touch, and a knowledge of it.

The horse snorted, and he was returned to the present and the passage of time. He had a long way to go yet. The beast was rested. He must proceed downwards to the shore and the Foulis Ferry.

It took him all day, with many inquiries, to reach Portmahomack, as Saint Colmac was now called, and it was long after dusk had deepened into true night when he finally reached the blacksmith's forge on Castle Street and inquired where he could stable his horse and find lodgings for the night. The smithy was happy to keep the animal, knowing the beast from previous travelers who had hired it at the same place, but he could only suggest Monk go to the nearest inn a few yards down the hill by the shore.

In the morning Monk walked the mile or so along the pale beach and up the hill to find Mary Farraline's croft, which was apparently rented by a man named Arkwright. He was well known in the village—but not, from the intonation of voice, with much love. That could be because, to judge from his name, he was not a Highlander, and probably not even a Scot—although Monk had personally met with only the greatest courtesy, in spite of his very English voice.

He had arrived in the dark, but the morning was brilliant again, as clear as the day before. It was not a long walk, barely a mile at the outside, and at the crown of the ridge was an avenue of sycamore and

ANNE PERRY

ash trees lining the road. To the left was a large stone barn or byre of some sort, and to the right a smaller house which he presumed was Mary Farraline's croft. He could see over the rooftops the chimneys of a larger building, a manor house possibly, but that could not be what he was seeking.

He must compose his thoughts to what he would say. He stopped under the trees and turned back the way he had come . . . and caught his breath. The sea stretched out below him in a silver-blue satin sheet; in the distance lay the mountains of Sutherland, the farthest peaks mounded with snow. To the west a sandbar gleamed pale in the sunlight, and beyond it was blue water stretching inland towards blue hills fading into purple on the horizon, a hundred miles or more. The sky was almost without a blemish and a skein of wild geese threaded its way slowly overhead, calling their way south.

He turned slowly, watching their passage and pondering the miracle of it, as they disappeared. He saw the sea to the south as well, silver-white in the mounting sun, and the outline of a lone castle dark against it.

In another mood he might have been angry at the ugliness which brought him here. Today he could only feel a weight of sadness.

He finished the last few yards of his journey and knocked on the door.

"Aye?" The man who came to answer him was short and stocky, with a smooth face which in no way masked his resentment of strangers.

"Mr. Arkwright?" Monk inquired.

"Aye, that's me. Who are you, and what do you want here?" His voice was English, but it took Monk a moment to discern the intonation. It was mixed, softened by the Highland.

"I've come from Edinburgh—" Monk began.

"You're no Scot," Arkwright said darkly, backing away a step.

"Neither are you," Monk countered. "I said I came from Edinburgh, not that I was born there."

"What of it. I don't care where you're from."

Yorkshire! That was the cadence in his voice, the nature of the vowels. And Baird McIvor had come originally from Yorkshire. Coincidence?

The lie sprang instantly to Monk's lips.

331

"I am Mrs. Mary Farraline's solicitor. I have come to see to her affairs. I don't know if you were informed of her recent death?"

"Never heard of her," Arkwright said intently, but there was a shadow in his eyes. He was lying too.

"Which is odd," Monk said with a smile, not of friendliness but of satisfaction. "Because you are living in her house."

Arkwright paled, but his face set hard. There were the shadows of a hundred other bitter struggles in him. He knew how to fight and Monk guessed he was not particular as to his weapons. There was something dangerous in the man. He found himself measuring his response. What was this alien man doing in this huge, wild, clean place?

Arkwright was staring at Monk.

"I don't know whose name is on the deeds, but I rent it from a man called McIvor, and that is none of your affair, Mr. Crow."

Monk had not introduced himself, but he knew the cant name for a solicitor.

Monk raised his eyebrows skeptically. "You pay rent to Mr. McIvor?"

"Yeah. That's right." There was belligerence in Arkwright, and still a thread of uncertainty.

"How?" Monk pressed, still standing well back.

"What you mean, how? Money, o' course. What you think, potatoes?"

"What do you do, ride over to Inverness and put a purse on the night train to Edinburgh? Weekly? Monthly? It must take you a couple of days."

Arkwright was caught out, and the realization of it blazed in his eyes. For a second he seemed about to swing a fist at Monk, then he looked at Monk's balance, and the leanness of his body, and decided against it.

"None of your business," he growled. "I answer to Mr. McIvor, not you. Anyway, you got no proof who you are, or that Mary Whatsisname is dead." A momentary gleam of triumph lit his eyes. "You could be anybody."

"I could," Monk agreed. "I could be the police."

"Rozzers?" But his face paled. "What for? I keep a farm. Isn't nothing illegal in that. You ain't a rozzer, you're just a nosy bastard who don't know what's good for him!"

"Would it interest you, or surprise you, to know that McIvor never passed on all this money that you sent to him on the train?" Monk asked sarcastically.

Arkwright tried to leer, but there was no laughter behind it, only a strange gleam of anxiety.

"Well, that's his problem, isn't it?"

In that moment Monk knew that Baird McIvor could not betray Arkwright, and Arkwright was totally sure of it. But equally, if Baird lost his power of authority for the croft, Arkwright would lose it too. Blackmail. That was the only conceivable answer. Why? Over what? How would this man ever come to know an apparent gentleman like Baird McIvor? Arkwright was at best bordering on criminal, at worst a fully fledged professional.

Monk shrugged with deliberate casualness and made as if to turn away.

"McIvor'll tell me all about it," he said smugly. "He'll grass you."

"No 'e won't!" Arkwright said victoriously. " 'E daren't, or e'll shop 'imself."

"Rubbish! Who'd believe you against him? He'll grass you all right. To account for the money."

"Anyone as can read'll believe me," Arkwright sneered. "It's all writ. An' 'e's still got the marks o' a cockchafer on 'is backside."

Prison. So that was the answer. Baird McIvor had served a term in jail somewhere. Possibly Arkwright knew about it because he had been there too. Perhaps they had trodden side by side on the "cockchafer," that dreaded machine more properly called a treadmill, where inmates were imprisoned for a quarter of an hour at a time, treading down a wheel of twenty-four steps attached to a long axle and an ingenious arrangement of weather vanes so they always turned at exactly the right speed to cause the most breathlessness, suffocation and exhaustion. The cant name arose because of the agony caused by the leather harness constantly rubbing on the tender flesh.

But had Mary Farraline known all this? Had he killed her to keep that dreadful secret, as he had paid Arkwright with a rent-free croft to keep his? It seemed so obvious it was hard to deny.

Why should it pain Monk? Because he wanted it to be Kenneth? That was absurd.

And yet somehow the shining bay did not seem so warm when he turned to leave, and walked down the gentle slope between the hedges towards the smithy and his horse, to ride long and hard back to Inverness.

He had crossed Cromarty and the Black Isle and was on the ferry across the Beauly, his back aching, pain shooting through his shoulders as he pulled furiously on the oars. He was determined to vent his anger on something, despite the ferryman's smile and his offer to do it all himself. Suddenly, without any warning at all, he remembered the time in his childhood that the first memory had brought back with such pain. He knew what the other emotion was, the one that hovered on the edges, dark and unrecognized. It was guilt. Guilt because they were returning from a lifeboat rescue, and he had been afraid. He had been so bitterly afraid of the yawning gulf of water that had opened up between the lifeboat and the doomed ship that he had frozen in terror, missing the thrown rope and too late seeing it coil and slither back off the deck, into the water. They had thrown it again, of course, but the few precious seconds had been lost, and with it the chance of a man's life.

The sweat broke out on his skin here in the present as he bent his back and dug the oar savagely into the bright water of the Beauly Firth. All he could see in his mind's eye was the gaping chasm of water between the boat sides all those years ago. He could taste the shame as if it were minutes past and feel the tears of humiliation prickle in his eyes.

Why did he remember that? There must have been dozens of happy memories, times he had shared with his family; there must have been successes, achievements. What was it in him that chose this to bring back so vividly? Was there more to it, something else, uglier, that he still did not recall?

Or was it that his pride could not accept failure of any sort, and he clung to the old wound because it still rankled, souring everything else? Was he really so self-obsessed?

"A wee bit dour today," the ferryman observed. "Did ye no fir.d what you wanted up at the port?"

"Yes . . . yes, I found it," Monk replied, heaving on the oars. "It was what I expected."

"Then it's no to your taste, to judge from the dreich look on your face."

"No . . . it's not."

The ferryman nodded and kept his silence.

They reached the far side. Monk climbed out stiffly, paid him, and took his leave. His whole body ached abominably. Served him right for his pride. He should have let the ferryman row.

He arrived back in Edinburgh tired and without any feeling of satisfaction in his discovery. He chose to walk, in spite of the gusty wind blowing in his face and the touch of sleet now and again out of a gray sky. He strode across the Waverley Bridge, right down Market Street, up Bank Street and over the George IV Bridge and right into the Grassmarket. He ended outside Hester's lodgings without having given a thought to why he chose there instead of Ainslie Place. Perhaps in some way he decided she deserved to learn the truth before the Farralines, or to be present when they were told it. He did not even consider the cruelty of it. She had liked Baird, or at least he had formed that impression.

He was already at her door before he realized he simply wanted to share his own disillusion, not with anyone, although there was no one else, but specifically with her. The knowledge froze his hand in the air.

But she had heard his footsteps on the uncarpeted passage and opened the door, her face filled with expectancy, and an element of fear. She saw his own disillusion in his eyes before he spoke.

"It was Baird. . . ." It was almost a question, not quite. She held the door for him to go in.

He accepted without the impropriety of it crossing his mind. The thought never occurred to him.

"Yes. He was in prison. Arkwright, the man on the croft, knew it; in fact, I imagine the bastard served with him." He sat down on the bed, leaving the one chair for her. "I expect McIvor let him use the croft to keep him silent, and when Mary found out, he killed her for the same reason. He could hardly have the Farralines, and all Edinburgh, know he was an old lag."

She looked at him gravely, almost expressionlessly, for several seconds. He wanted to see some reaction in her, a reflection of his own hurt, and he was about to speak, but he did not know what to say. For once he did not want to quarrel with her. He wanted closeness, an end to unhappy surprises.

"Poor Baird," she said with a little shiver.

He was about to ridicule her sentiment, then he remembered with a jolt that she had tasted prison herself, bitterly and very recently. His remark died unspoken.

"Eilish is going to be destroyed," she said quietly, but still there seemed a lack of real horror in her.

"Yes," he agreed vehemently. "Yes she is."

Hester frowned. "Are you really sure it was Baird? Just because he was in prison doesn't necessarily mean he killed Mary. Don't you think it is possible, if this Arkwright creature was blackmailing him, that he might have told Mary, and she helped him by letting him use the croft that way?"

"Come on, Hester," he said wearily. "You're clutching at straws. Why should she? He'd misled them all, lied to them about his past. Why should she do what was virtually paying blackmail for him? She may have been a good woman, but that calls for a saint."

"No it doesn't," she contradicted him. "I knew Mary, you didn't."

"You met her on one train journey!"

"I knew her! She liked Baird. She told me that herself."

"She didn't know he was an old lag."

"We don't know what he did." She leaned forward, demanding he listen. "He may have told her, and she still liked him. We knew about a time when he was very upset and went off by himself. Maybe this was when Arkwright turned up. Then he told Mary about it, and she helped him, and he was all right. It's quite possible."

"Then who killed Mary?"

Her face closed over. "I don't know. Kenneth?"

"And Baird playing with the chemicals?" he added.

A look of scorn filled her face. "Don't be so naive. No one else saw that but Quinlan, and he's green with jealousy. He'd lie about Baird as quick as look at you."

"And hang him for a crime he didn't commit?"

"Of course. Why not?"

He looked at her and saw certainty in her eyes. He wondered if she ever doubted herself, as he did. But then she knew her past, knew not only what she thought and felt now, but what she had always thought, and done. There was no secret room in her life, no dark passages and locked doors in the mind.

"It's monstrous," he said quietly.

She searched his face. "It is to you and me." Her voice was soft. "But to him, Baird has stolen what should be his. Not his wife—but his wife's love, her respect, her admiration. He can't accuse him of that, he can't punish him for it. Perhaps he feels that is monstrous too."

"That . . ." he began, and then stopped.

She was smiling, not with anything like laughter, but a wry, hurting perception.

"We had better go and tell them what you found out."

Reluctantly he rose to his feet. There was no alternative.

They stood in the withdrawing room in Ainslie Place. Everyone was present. Even Alastair had contrived not to be in court or his offices. And presumably the printing was running itself, at least for the day.

"We assumed you would return this morning," Oonagh said, regarding Monk carefully. She looked tired—the fair skin under her eyes was paper thin—but as always her composure was complete.

Alastair looked from Monk to Oonagh and back again. Eilish was in an agony of suspense. She stood beside Quinlan as if frozen. Baird was in the farther side of the room, eyes downcast, face ashen.

Kenneth stood by the mantelshelf with a slight smirk on his face, but it was hard to tell if it was not predominantly relief. Once he smiled at Quinlan, and Eilish shot him such a look of loathing he blushed and turned away.

Deirdra sat in an armchair looking unhappy, and beside her, Hector Farraline was also sunk in gloom. For once he seemed totally sober.

Alastair cleared his throat. "I think you had better tell us what you discovered, Mr. Monk. It is pointless standing here doubting and fearing, and thinking ill of each other. Did you find this croft of Mother's? I confess I knew nothing of it, not even of its existence."

"No reason why you should," Hector said darkly. "Nothing to do with you."

Alastair frowned, then decided to ignore him.

They were all looking at Monk, even Baird, his dark eyes so full of pain, and the knowledge of pain, that Monk could have no doubt he knew exactly what Arkwright would have said, and that it was the truth. He hated doing this. But it was not the first time he had liked someone who was guilty of a crime he deplored.

"I found the man who is living in the croft," he said aloud, looking at no one in particular. Hester was standing beside him silently. He was glad of her presence. In some way she shared his sense of loss. "He claimed that he sent money to Mr. McIvor."

Quinlan gave a little grunt of satisfaction.

Eilish started, as if to speak, but said nothing. Her face looked as if she had been struck.

"But I did not believe him," Monk continued.

"Why not?" Alastair was amazed. "That won't do."

Oonagh touched his sleeve, and as if understanding some unspoken communication, he fell silent again.

Monk answered the question anyway.

"Because he could offer no explanation as to how he contrived the payments. I asked him if he rode to Inverness, a day's ride on a good horse, across two ferries, and put a purse on a train to Edinburgh. . . ."

"That's absurd," Deirdra said contemptuously.

"Of course," Monk agreed.

"So what are you saying, Mr. Monk?" Oonagh asked very steadily. "If he did not pay Baird, then why is he still there? Why has he not been thrown out?"

Monk took a deep breath. "Because he is blackmailing Mr. McIvor over a past association, and is living there freely as the price of his silence."

"What association?" Quinlan demanded. "Did Mother-in-law find out about it? Is that why Baird killed her?"

"Hold your tongue!" Deirdra snapped at him, moving closer to Eilish and glaring at Baird, as if praying for him to deny it, but one look at his face was enough to know that would not happen. "What association, Mr. Monk? I presume you have proof of all you are saying?"

"Don't be fatuous, Deirdra," Oonagh said bitterly. "The proof is in his face. What is Mr. Monk talking about, Baird? I think you had better tell us all, rather than have some stranger do it for you."

Baird looked up and his eyes met Monk's for a long, breathless moment, then he acquiesced. He had no alternative. He began in a low, tight voice, harsh with past hurt and present pain.

"When I was twenty-two I killed a man. He abused an old man

I respected. Made mock of him, humiliated him. We fought. I did not intend to, at least I don't think I did . . . but I killed him. He struck his head against the curb. I served three years in prison for it. That was when I met Arkwright. When I was set free I left Yorkshire and came north to Scotland. I made my way quite successfully, and put the past behind me. I had all but forgotten it, until one day Arkwright turned up and threatened to tell everyone unless I paid him. I couldn't—I had barely enough means for myself, and I would have had to explain to Oonagh. . . ." He said her name as if she were a stranger, some figure that represented authority. "Of course I couldn't. I hesitated for days, close to despair."

"I remember . . ." Eilish whispered, staring at him with anguish, as though even now she yearned to be able to comfort him and heal the past.

Quinlan made a noise of impatience and turned away.

"Mary knew," Baird continued, his voice rasping with hurt. "She knew something was troubling me more than I could bear, and in the end I told her. . . ."

He did not even notice Eilish stiffen and a sudden surprise and pain in her face. He did not seem to realize it was different, no longer an agony for the past, or for him, but a hurt for herself.

Quinlan smiled. "Told her you'd served time in prison," he said with blatant disbelief.

"Yes."

"You expect us to believe that?" Alastair looked grim, doubt written plain in his expression. "Really, Baird, that's asking too much. Could you prove it?"

"No—except that she gave me permission to lease the croft to Arkwright, for his silence." Baird looked up and met Alastair's eyes for the first time.

It was an absurd story. Why would a woman like Mary Farraline accept a man with such a past—and even help him? And yet Monk found himself at least half believing it.

Quinlan gave a sharp bark of laughter.

"Come on, Baird, that isn't even clever," Kenneth said with a smile, letting his foot slide off the fender and sitting down in the nearest chair. "I could think of a better excuse than that."

"No doubt you have—frequently," Oonagh said dryly, regarding her younger brother with contempt. It was the first time Monk had seen an expression of contention or open criticism on her face, and it surprised him. The peacemaker was rattled at last. He looked at her puckered mouth, the anxiety marked deep between her brows, but still could only guess what emotions burned inside her. He could make no hazard as to whether she had known or even suspected her husband had such a shadowed past.

Or was that what she had sought to do all the time? Was that the blindingly obvious thing he had always missed, that Oonagh loved her husband, in spite of his obsession with her younger sister, and that she sought to protect him from both his reckless past and his tortured present.

Quite suddenly he saw her in a different light, and his admiration for her leaped beyond the mere courage and composure she had shown to something of classical magnitude; she was a woman who bore herself with silence and generosity almost immeasurable.

Instinctively he turned to Eilish, to see if she had the remotest conception of what she had done, however unwittingly. But all he could see was disillusion and the scalding pain of rejection. In his desperation Baird had turned not to her, but to her mother. She was excluded. He had not even trusted her with it afterwards. He would not have. She had learned it publicly, from a stranger.

And little as he admired it, in that instant he knew exactly what she felt, all the loneliness, the confusion, the feelings of unworthiness, the longing to strike back and hurt just as much. Because he knew now what else had happened in the lifeboat so long ago. He had tried so hard, and yet someone else had been the hero. Someone else had retrieved his mistake and saved the man on the doomed ship. In his mind's eye he could see the boy, a year or two older, standing balanced on the slippery deck, hurling the rope at risk of being pitched overboard, drenched to the skin, lashing it fast, heaving the man out of that awful chasm.

No one had said anything to him, no one had blamed him, and yet his ears rang with the other boy's praises, not just his skill, but his courage. That was what hurt, his quickness of thought, his self-denial and his courage, the qualities Monk had wanted above all.

It was the same with Eilish. Above all she had wanted to be loved and trusted.

They were each of them regarding Monk now; the judgment awaited.

Quinlan had decided, but then he had from the beginning. "If you believe all that, you're a fool," he said bitterly. "We'd do better to call the police before Monk does. Or do you plan to pay him off as well? It's too late to avoid scandal, if that has occurred to anyone?" He looked around with wide eyes. "One of us did it. No one can escape that."

"Scandal," Deirdra said thoughtfully, her face intent. "Is it not possible that Baird is telling the truth, and Mother-in-law paid off this Arkwright to avoid scandal?"

There was a long silence. Oonagh turned to Baird.

"Why didn't you say that?" she asked him.

"Because I don't believe it is true," he said, answering her very directly, his dark eyes staring into hers. "Mary was not the sort of person to do that."

"Of course she was," Alastair said, then glanced at Oonagh with abject apology, having just realized what he had said.

"I think we had best leave this for the present," Oonagh said decisively. "We do not know the truth. . . ."

Hester spoke for the first time.

"Mrs. Farraline mentioned Mr. McIvor to me several times on the train, always with affection," she said very quietly. "I cannot imagine she was paying blackmail simply to keep the family name out of scandal. If she were doing that, she would have loathed him, perhaps even required that he go away. . . ."

"Thank you for your comments, Miss Latterly," Alastair said dryly. "But I really do not think you are sufficiently informed to—"

Deirdra interrupted him. "Yes she is." But before she could say anything further Alastair commanded she be silent, and he turned to Monk.

"Thank you for your work, Mr. Monk. Do you have documented proof of what you have told us?"

"No."

"Then I think, in that event, you will keep silent about it until we have made a decision as to what is wisest to do. Tomorrow is Sunday. After kirk you will take luncheon with us, and we shall then discuss this matter to its conclusion. Good day to you, Mr. Monk, Miss Latterly."

There was nothing to do but accept their dismissal. Monk and Hester walked together into the hall, past the great picture of Hamish, and out into the steadily falling rain.

CHAPTER
TWELVE

———

Monk and Hester were easily agreed that they also would go to church on Sunday morning. Monk had no intention of worshiping. It was not a subject to which he had given any thought, but it was another opportunity to observe the Farralines. He did not ask Hester her reasons. Presumably they were similar.

They had walked up from the Grassmarket, allowing plenty of time, having previously ascertained the time of the service, and arrived as the congregation was assembling.

They filed in behind a stout matron, leaning on the arm of a grim-faced man carrying his hat in his hand. This couple nodded to acquaintances, and received several acknowledgments in return. Everyone looked extremely sober.

Hester glanced around. It was difficult to recognize the Farraline women because they all wore hats, naturally. To go to church without a hat and gloves would be tantamount to arriving naked. It was easier to distinguish the men; hair color and bearing differed markedly. It did not take her long to find Alastair's fair head with its faintly thinning patch towards the crown.

As if sensing her eyes on him, he turned half towards them, but apparently it was to nod to the couple just ahead of them.

"Good morning, Fiscal," the woman said grimly. "A fine day, is it not?" It was a ritual remark. It was beginning to rain and getting rapidly colder.

"Indeed, Mrs. Bain," he replied. "Very agreeable. Good morning, Mr. Bain."

"Good morning, Fiscal." The man inclined his head respectfully and moved on.

"Poor creature," the woman said as soon as they were past. "What a business for him."

"Hold your peace, Martha," the man said crisply. "I'll not have you gossiping in here of all places. And on the Sabbath too. You should not be talking in kirk at all."

She blushed angrily, but refused to defend herself.

Hester bit her lip with vicarious frustration.

Monk took her arm and led her, with some difficulty and several apologies for injured dignity and trodden toes, into the pew two rows behind the Farralines. Hester bent her head to pray, and he followed her example, at least outwardly.

More and more people arrived, several glancing at Monk and Hester with surprise and irritation. It was some time before either of them realized that apparently they had taken a place which by custom and tacit rule belonged to someone else. They did not move.

Monk watched, noticing how many people nodded or otherwise paid deference to Alastair. Those who spoke addressed him in a whisper, and by his office rather than his name.

"Such a clever man," one woman murmured to her neighbor immediately in front of Monk. "I'm glad he didn't prosecute Mr. Galbraith. I always thought he was innocent anyway. I don't believe a gentleman like that would ever do such a thing."

"And Mrs. Forbes's son as well," her neighbor replied. "I'm sure that was more of a tragedy than a crime."

"Quite. Girl was no better than she should be, if you ask me. I know that sort."

"Don't we all, my dear. Had a maid like that once myself. Had to get rid of her, of course."

"His father was a fine man too." Her eyes returned to Alastair. "Such a pity."

The organ was playing meditatively. Over to the left someone dropped a hymnbook with a crash. No one looked.

"I didn't know you knew them." There was a lift of interest in the woman's voice in front of Hester, as she half turned her head to hear the better, should her neighbor choose to elaborate.

"Oh yes, quite well." The neighbor nodded, the feathers in her hat waving. "So handsome, you know. Not like his miserable brother, who drinks like a fish, they say. Never had the talent either. The colonel was such an artist, you know."

An old gentleman to the right glared at them and was ignored.

"An artist? I never knew that. I thought he owned a printing company."

"Oh he did! But he was a fine artist too. Drew beautifully, and a great hand with his pen. Caricatures, you know? The poor major is a wretched creature beside him. No talent for anything, except sponging from the family, since the colonel died."

Hester leaned forward and tapped her on the shoulder.

She turned around, startled, expecting to be told yet again not to speak in the kirk.

"Would you like a stone?" Hester offered.

"I beg your pardon!"

"A stone," Hester repeated clearly.

"Whatever for?"

"To throw," Hester replied. And then, in case she had missed the point, "At Hector Farraline."

The woman blushed scarlet. "Well really!"

"Hold your tongue, you fool!" Monk whispered, poking Hester with his elbow. "For God's sake, woman, do you want to be recognized?"

She looked puzzled.

" 'Not proven'!" he said sharply, but so quietly she barely heard him. "Not innocent!"

The color burned up her face, and she turned away.

The service began. It was extremely sober and pious, with a long sermon on the sins of undue levity and light-mindedness.

Sabbath luncheon at Ainslie Place was not the rich fare it would have been in a family of such means in London. The servants had also attended the kirk, and although the food was plentiful, it was also cold. No comment was made. The day itself was considered sufficient explanation. Alastair, as head of the family, said a brief prayer before anyone presumed to eat, and then the vegetables were served to complement cold meats. For some time everyone avoided the subject of Mary's croft, the rents, Arkwright, or any question of Baird's culpability in that or any other matter.

Baird himself seemed to have closed his mind and his emotions, like a man who has already accepted his own death.

Eilish looked desolate. She was still beautiful. No grief could take that from her, but the fire that had lit her countenance before had vanished as if it had never been.

Deirdra had dark rings of sleeplessness under her eyes, and she constantly looked from one to another of her family as if seeking anything she might do to ease their pain, and found nothing at all.

Oonagh sat white-faced. Alastair was profoundly unhappy. Hector reached for the wine as often as usual, but seemed to remain stubbornly sober. Only Quinlan appeared to find even a glimmer of satisfaction in anything.

"You cannot put it off forever," he said at last. "Some decision has to be made." He glanced at Monk. "I assume you are going to return to London? If not tomorrow, then some time soon. You don't intend to remain in Edinburgh, do you? We have no more crofts, to pay for your silence."

"Quinlan!" Alastair said furiously, banging his clenched fist on the table. "For heaven's sake, man, have a little decency!"

Quinlan's eyebrows rose. "Is this matter decent? Your ideas differ from mine, Fiscal. I think it's thoroughly indecent. What are you proposing? That we conspire together to keep silence over it and let the shadow hang forever over Miss Latterly?" He swiveled in his chair. "Will you allow that, Miss Latterly? It will make it uncommonly difficult for you to obtain another nursing post. Unless of course it is with someone who wishes the patient's decease?"

"Of course I should like it resolved," Hester answered him, while the rest of the company looked on in horrified silence. "But I do not wish anyone to stand in the dock in my place simply to accomplish that, if they are no more guilty than I am. There is a certain case against Mr. McIvor, but I do not find it compelling." She turned to Alastair. "Is it compelling, Procurator Fiscal? Would you prosecute with the evidence you have so far?"

Alastair blushed, and then paled. He swallowed hard. "They would not expect me to handle the case, Miss Latterly. I am too close to it."

"That was not what she meant," Quinlan said contemptuously. "But Alastair is famous for not prosecuting. Aren't you, Fiscal?"

Alastair ignored him, turning instead to Baird.

"I presume you will be going in to the printing shop as usual tomorrow?"

"It's closed tomorrow," Baird replied, blinking at him as if he had barely understood what he had said.

Hector reached for more wine. "Why?" he asked, frowning. "What's wrong with it? Tomorrow is Monday, isn't it? Why aren't you working on a Monday?" He hiccupped gently.

"There are building alterations being done outside. There will be no gas. We cannot work in the dark."

"Should have built more windows," Hector said irritably. "It's that damn secret room of Hamish's. Always said it was a stupid idea."

Deirdra looked confused. "What are you talking about, Uncle Hector? You can't have windows, except at the front. The other three sides are the back with the doors and the yard, and where it joins to the other warehouses at both sides."

"I don't know what he wanted a secret room for." Hector was not listening to her. "Quite unnecessary. Told Mary that."

"Secret room?" Deirdra smiled wryly.

Oonagh offered Hector the decanter, and when he had fumbled for it ineffectually, filled his glass for him.

"There is no secret room in the printworks, Uncle Hector. You must be remembering something from the old house, when you were boys."

"Don't . . ." he started angrily, then looked into her steady blue eyes, clear and level as his own must have been thirty years earlier, and his words died away.

Oonagh smiled at him, then turned to Monk.

"I apologize, Mr. Monk. We have placed you in an invidious position, and probably embarrassed you as well, with our family quarrels. Of course we cannot expect you to keep silent over your discoveries regarding the very objectionable Mr. Arkwright and his occupancy of Mother's croft. He claims that he has paid rent for it, and my husband claims that he has not, but that my mother allowed him to live there freely in return for his silence. Whether these arrangements were made with my mother's knowledge and consent we shall never know beyond question. Quinlan, for his own reasons, believes they were not. I choose to believe they were. You must do whatever you feel to be right."

She turned to Hester. "And you also, Miss Latterly. I can only apologize to you for involving you in our family's tragedy. I hope that word of it has not reached London in the detail it has been reported here, and it will not affect your life or your livelihood, as Quinlan supposes. If I could undo it for you, I would, but it is beyond my power. I am sorry."

"We all regret it," Hester said quietly. "You should feel no need to apologize, but I thank you for your graciousness. I knew Mrs. Farraline for only a very brief time, but from her conversation that evening on the train, I choose to believe as you do, and do not find it in the least difficult."

Oonagh smiled, but there was no answer in her eyes, no relief from the tension there.

As soon as the meal was over Monk seemed in some haste to depart.

"I shall leave the matter in your hands," he said to Alastair. "You are aware of your mother's property, and of the disposition of it, and of Arkwright's tenancy. You must inform the police of whatever you think appropriate. As Procurator Fiscal, you are far better placed than I to judge what is evidence and what is not."

"Thank you," Alastair accepted gravely, but also apparently without relief. "Good-bye, Mr. Monk, Miss Latterly. I hope your journey back to London is agreeable."

As soon as they were out of the door and on the pavement, Monk pulling his collar higher and Hester wrapping her blue coat tighter around her against the wind, Monk spoke.

"I'm damned if I'm finished yet! One of them killed her. If it wasn't McIvor, it was one of the others."

"I would dearly like it to be Quinlan," Hester said with feeling as they crossed the road and stepped onto the grass. "What a perfectly odious man. Why on earth did Eilish marry him? Any fool can see she loathes him now—and little wonder. Do you think Hector was drunk?"

"Of course he was drunk. He's always drunk, poor old devil."

"I wonder why," she said thoughtfully, increasing her speed to keep up with him. "What happened to him? From what Mary said, he used to be every bit as dashing as Hamish, and a better soldier."

"Envy, I suppose," he replied without interest. "Younger brother, lesser commission, Hamish got the inheritance, and appears to have had the brains as well, and the talent."

They reached the far side of the Place and turned down Glenfinlas Street.

"I meant do you think he was so drunk he was talking nonsense?" she resumed.

"About what?"

"A secret room, of course," she replied impatiently, having to run again to keep at his side, and brushing past a woman with a basket. "Why would Hamish build a secret room in a printing works?"

"I don't know. To hide illegal books?"

"What sort of books would be illegal?" she asked breathlessly. "You mean stolen ones? But that doesn't make any sense."

"No, of course not stolen ones. Seditious—blasphemous—most probably pornographic."

"Oh—oh I see."

"No you don't. But possibly you understand."

She did not quibble. "Is that worth killing over?"

"If it was graphic enough, and there was enough of it," he replied. "It could be worth a lot of money."

Two gentlemen crossed the street ahead of them, one swinging a cane.

"You mean they could *sell* it for a lot." She could be equally pedantic. "It's worth nothing."

He pulled a face. "Didn't think you'd know what it was."

"I've been an army nurse," she said tartly.

"Oh." For a moment he was confused, off balance. He did not wish to think of her as being aware of such things, must less to have seen them. It offended him. Women, especially decent women, should never have to see the obscenities of the darkest human imagination. Unconsciously he increased his speed, almost knocking into a man and woman. The man glared at him and muttered something.

Hester was obliged to break into a trot to keep up.

"Are we going to look for it?" she asked, gasping. "Please slow a little. I cannot speak or listen at this rate."

He obeyed abruptly and she shot a couple of paces past him.

"I am," he answered. "You're not."

"Yes I am." It was a single, contradictory, pigheaded statement. There was no question or pleading in it.

"No you are not. It may be dangerous. . . ."

"Why should it? They said there would be no one there tomorrow, and there certainly won't be today. They'd never break the Sabbath."

"I'm going tonight, while it's dark."

"Of course we are. It would be absurd to go in the daylight; anyone might see us."

"You're not coming!"

Now they were stopped and causing an obstruction on the footpath.

"Yes I am. You'll need help. If it really is a secret room, it won't be all that easy to find. We may have to knock for hollow places, or move—"

"All right!" he said. "But you must do as you're told."

"Naturally."

He snorted, and once again set off at a rapid pace.

It was a little before eleven, and pitch-dark except for the lantern which Hester held, when she and Monk finally stood in the huge print room and began their task. To avoid unnecessary noise they had had to break in. It had taken some time, but Monk possessed skills in that field which startled Hester, though he offered no account of how he had come by them. Possibly he did not recall himself.

For over an hour they searched, slowly and methodically, but the building was very solidly and plainly built. It was simply a barnlike structure, similar to the warehouses on either side of it, for the purpose of printing books. There was no ornament or carving, no alcoves, mantels, sets of shelves or anything else which could mask an opening.

"He was drunk," Monk said in disgust. "He just loathed Hamish so much he was trying to make trouble, anything he could think of, no matter how absurd."

"We haven't been searching very long yet," she argued.

He gave her a withering look, which was exaggerated by the yellow glare of the lantern and the black cavern above them.

"Well, do you have a better idea?" she demanded. "Do you just want to go back to London and never know who killed Mary?"

Wordlessly he turned back to reexamine the wall.

"It's straight along the line of the abutting wall onto the next warehouse," he said half an hour later. "There isn't any space for a secret compartment, let alone an entire room."

"What if it's in the roof?" she said desperately. "Or the cellar?"

"Then there'll be stairs to it—and there aren't."

"Then it must be here. We just haven't found it."

"Your logic is typical," he said tartly. "We haven't found it, so it must be here."

"That's not what I said. You have it backwards."

He raised his eyebrows. "It must be here because we haven't found it! That is a deductive improvement?"

She took the lantern and left him standing in the dark. There was nothing to lose by searching a little longer. This was the last chance. Tomorrow they would leave, and either Baird McIvor would face trial, and maybe be hanged, or else live with another "not proven" verdict over his head. Either way, she would never be sure who had killed Mary. She needed to know, not just for herself but because Mary's wry, intelligent face was still as sharp in her mind as when she had gone to sleep that night on the train to London, thinking how very much she liked her.

She did not find it by accident, but by methodical, furious banging and thumping. A heavy panel of the wall slid away and opened up a narrow door. The room itself must originally have been part of the next-door warehouse and not the Farraline building at all. Its very existence was concealed because a floor plan would have shown no discrepancy. One would have had to have the plans of both buildings and compare them.

"I've got it!" she cried out exultantly.

"Don't shout," he whispered from just behind her, making her start and nearly drop the lamp.

"Don't do that!" she said as she led the way into the hole ahead.

With the lantern high and as far in front as she could hold it, the entire room was visible as soon as they were inside. It was windowless, about twelve feet by ten feet large, low-ceilinged, and there was a single air vent in the far corner leading to the outside. It was at least half filled with printing presses, ink, stacks of paper, and guillotine cutters. More space as taken by a table like an easel and a rack of fine etching and engraving tools and acid. Over the table was a bracket for a large, unshaded gas lamp. When lit it must have shed a brilliant light.

"What is it?" Hester said in bewilderment. "There aren't any books here."

"I think we have just found the source of the Farraline wealth," he said in awe, almost under his breath.

"But there aren't any books. Unless they shipped them all out?"

"Not books, my love—money! This is where they print money!"

Hester felt a shiver run through her, not only for the meaning of what he had said but also for the way in which he had addressed her.

"You mean f-forged money?" she stammered.

"Oh yes, forged . . . very forged. But they must do it damnably well, to have got away with it for so long." He moved forward and bent over the presses to examine them more closely, taking the light from her. "Lots of it," he went on. "Here are several pound notes, five pounds, ten pounds, twenty. Look, all the different banks in Scotland—the Royal, the Clydesdale, the Linen Bank. And here's the Bank of England. And these look like German, and here's French. Very eclectic tastes, but by heaven they're good!"

She peered over his shoulder, staring at the metal plates.

"How do you know they've been doing it for a long time? It could have been just recently, couldn't it?"

"The family wealth goes back a long way," he answered. "Well into Hamish's time—I'll wager he was the original engraver. Remember what that woman said in church? And Deirdra said something about his being a good copyist." He picked up a note and examined it carefully. "This one is current. Look at the signature on it."

"But if they've got new notes as well, who's the artist now? It's not the sort of thing you can go out and hire."

"Of course it isn't. I'll lay any odds you like that it's Quinlan. No wonder he's so damned arrogant. He knows they can't do without him, and they know it too. He has them over a barrel. Poor little Eilish. I expect she was his price."

"That's unspeakable!" she said in horror. "Nobody would . . ." Then she stopped. What she had been going to say was absurd, and she knew it. Women had been given in marriage to suit the ambitions

ANNE PERRY

or the convenience of their families since time immemorial, and for
worse reasons than this. At least she was still at home, and partici-
pated in the wealth. And Quinlan was roughly her own age, and not
uncomely, or drunken, diseased or otherwise repellent. And it was
even possible he had cared for her originally, before she betrayed him
by falling in love, however unwillingly, with Baird. Or was that
Oonagh's attempt at self-protection, to marry her exquisite younger
sister to a man who would possess her and brook no disloyalty?

Poor Oonagh—she had failed. Their acts might be without blemish, but no one could govern their dreams.

Monk laid the notes back gently, exactly as he had found them.

"Do you suppose Mary knew?" Hester asked in a whisper. "I . . . I
hope not. I hate to think of her being party to this. I know it is not
as evil as really hurting people . . . it's only greedy, but . . ."

He looked at her, his face bleak, the lean planes of his cheeks and
brow harsh in the lamp's glow, his nose exaggerated.

"It's a filthy crime," he said between his teeth. "You sound as if
there is no victim, because you aren't thinking. What would you do if
half your money was worth nothing and you didn't know which half?
How would you live? Who could you trust?"

"But . . ." There were no words, and she stopped.

"People would be afraid to sell," he went on savagely. "You might
trade, but who with? Who wants what you have to offer and can give
you what you need? Ever since man acquired goods and leisure, spe-
cialized his skills and learned to cooperate one with another for everyone's benefit, we have used a common means of exchange—money. In
fact, ever since we began anything one could call civilization and
learned that we are more than a collection of individuals, each for
himself, and formed the concept of community, money has been piv-
otal. Pollute that, and you strike at the root of all society."

She stared at him, comprehension of the magnitude of it dawning
inside her, of the totality of the damage.

"And words," he went on, his face burning with the fierceness of
his emotion. "Words are our means of communication, that which
raises man above the beasts. We can think, we have concepts, we can
write and pass our beliefs from one land to another, one generation to
the next. Pollute our relationships with flattery and manipulation, our
language with lies, propaganda, self-serving use of images, the prostitu-

tion of words and meaning, and we can no longer reach each other. We become isolated. Nothing is real. We drown in a morass of the sham, the expedient. Deceit, corruption and betrayal . . . they are the sins of the wolf." He stopped abruptly, staring at her as if he had only just that moment really seen her.

"The wolf?" she urged. "What do you mean? What wolf?"

"The lowest circle of hell," he answered slowly, rolling the words as though one by one. "The last pit of all. Dante. The three great circles of hell. The leopard, the lion and the wolf."

"Do you remember where you read that, who taught it you?" she asked, almost in a whisper.

He waited so long she thought he had not heard her.

"No . . ." He winced. "No, I don't. I'm trying . . . but it's just out of reach. I didn't even know I knew it at all until I started to think about forgery. I . . ." He shrugged very slightly and turned away. "We've learned all we need to here. This could be the reason Mary was killed. If she learned about it somehow, they'd have to keep her silent."

"Who? Which one?"

"God knows. Perhaps Quinlan. Maybe she knew about it anyway. That's for the police to discover. Come on. We can't find out anything more here." He picked up the lantern and went back towards the way they had come in. It took him a moment or two to find the door because it had swung closed again. "Damn," he said irritably. "I could have sworn I left it open."

"You did," Hester said from close behind him. "If it swung shut on its own, it must be weighted. That means we can open it from here somehow."

"Of course we can open it from here," he said. "But how? Hold the lantern up." He ran his fingers over the wall experimentally, covering every inch. It took him something less than three minutes to find the catch. It was not concealed, simply in an awkward place. "Ah . . ." he said with satisfaction, pulling it hard. But it did not move. He pulled again.

"Is it stuck?" she asked with a frown.

He tried it three times before he accepted the truth. "No. I think it is locked."

"It can't be! If it locks just by closing, how did Quinlan get out?

He can't have worked in here without being able to get out if he wished to!"

He turned around slowly, looking at her with the kind of candor they had so often shared. "I don't think it did lock itself. I think we have been locked in deliberately. Someone realized we took Hector at his word, and waited here to see if we would come. This is too precious and secret to allow us to blunder into and repeat."

"But the workers don't come back until Tuesday. Quinlan said it was closed because of the gas lines," she said with mounting realization of what it meant. The room was small, windowless, effectively sealed but for the air vent. Tuesday was at least thirty hours away. She went over to the vent and stretched up her hand to it. There was no breath of air, no chill. It had been blocked—of course. There was no need to add the rest.

"I know," he said quietly. "It looks as if the Farralines win in the end. I'm sorry."

She looked around with sudden fury. "Well, can't we at least destroy this machine that prints the money? Can't we smash the plates or something?"

He smiled, then he started to laugh, quietly and with genuine amusement.

"Bravo! Yes, by all means, let's ruin them. That'll be something accomplished."

"It'll make them very angry," she said thoughtfully. "They might be enraged and kill us."

"My dear girl, if we are not already suffocated to death, they'll kill us anyway. We know enough to hang them . . . we just don't know which ones."

She took a deep breath to steady herself. Although she had already realized it, it was different to hear him say so.

"Yes—yes, of course they will. Well, let us at least ruin their plates. They could still be evidence, in the event the police find them. Anyway, as you say, forgery is very evil; it is a pollution, a corruption of our means of exchange with one another. We ought to end this much of it." And without waiting for him to follow, she went over and lifted up one of the plates, then froze.

"What is it?" he said immediately.

"Don't let's break them," she said with a tingle of quite genuine

pleasure. "Let's just mar them, so little they don't realize it, but enough that when they have printed all the money, unless they look at
it very carefully, they will still pass it. But the first person who does
look at it will know it is wrong. That would be more effective,
wouldn't it? And a better revenge . . ."

"Excellent! Let's find the engraving tools and the acid. Be careful
you don't get any of it on your skin. And not on your dress, in case
they notice it."

They set about it with determination, working side by side, erasing
here and there, making little blotching marks, but always discreetly,
until they had in some way marred every single plate. It took them until after two in the morning, and the lamp was burning low. And now
that there was nothing more to do, they were also growing increasingly aware of the cold. Without thinking, they automatically sat close
together on some boxes of paper, huddled in the corner, and above the
colder floor level. There were no drafts; the room was effectively
sealed. And after their concentration on the plates had gone, they
were also aware that the air was getting stale. A great deal of the space
was already taken up with boxes and machinery.

"I can't believe Mary knew about this," Hester said again, her
mind still hurt by the thought, teased by memories of the woman she
had known, or thought she had known, on the London train. "I really
don't think she would have lived off forgery all those years."

"Perhaps she viewed it as you did," Monk replied, staring into the
little pool of light the lantern made. "A victimless crime, just a little
greed."

She did not reply for several minutes. He had not met Mary, and
she did not know how to convey the sense of honesty she had felt in
her.

"Do you suppose they all did?" she said at length.

"No," he said immediately, then apparently realized the logical position in which he had placed himself. "All right, perhaps she didn't.
If she did, then all this"—he inclined his head towards the presses—
"was no reason to kill her. If she didn't, how do you suppose she found
out? She wouldn't have come down here looking for this room. If she
knew, why did she not call the police? Why go off to London? It was
urgent, but hardly an emergency. There was certainly time to attend
to this first." He shook his head. "But would Mary have exposed her

own family to scandal, ruin and imprisonment? Wouldn't she just have demanded they stop? That would be reason to kill her?"

"If I were a forger," she replied. "I'd have said, 'Yes, Mother,' and moved it somewhere else. It would be infinitely safer than killing her."

He did not reply, but lapsed into thought.

It was getting even colder. They moved closer yet, the warmth of each other comforting, even the steady rhythm of breathing a kind of safety in the threat of enclosing darkness and the knowledge that time was short and every second that passed meant one fewer left.

"What did she say—on the train?" Monk asked presently.

"She talked about the past, for the most part." She thought back yet again to that evening. "She traveled then. She danced at the ball in Brussels on the eve of Waterloo, you know?" She stared into the darkness, speaking softly. It seemed appropriate to the mood and it saved energy. They were sitting so close together whispering would serve. "She described it to me, the colors and the music, the soldiers in their uniforms, all the scarlets and the blues and golds, the cavalrymen, the artillery, the hussars and dragoons, the Scots Greys." She smiled as she pictured Mary's face and the light in it as she relived that night. "She spoke of Hamish, how elegant he was, how dashing, how all the ladies loved him."

"Was Hector sober then?" he asked.

"Oh yes. She spoke of Hector too, he was always quieter, tenderer—that isn't the word she used, but that is what she meant. And she said he was actually a better soldier." She smiled. "She described the band and the gaiety, the laughter at any joke at all, the hectic dancing, whirling 'round and 'round, the lights and color, the brilliance of jewels and the candle flames and the flash of reds." She drew in a deep breath. "And the knowledge in everyone that tomorrow perhaps one in ten of them would die, and two or three be injured, maybe marred for life, limbs lost, blinded, God knows what. Whatever they thought or felt, no one spoke of it, and the musicians never missed a beat. Wellington himself was there. It was the high tide of history. All Europe hung in the balance."

She swallowed and tried to keep her voice from shaking. She must have Mary's courage. She had faced death before, and worse death. She would be with Monk, and in spite of all the enmity they had shared, the quarrels and the anger and the contempt, she would not have had anyone else there, except for his sake. "She said how terrified she was for Hector, but she never allowed him to know," she finished.

"You mean Hamish," he corrected.

"Do I? Yes, of course I do. The air is getting thin, isn't it?"

"Yes."

"She spoke about her children as well, mostly Oonagh and Alastair, how close they had always been, even when they were young." She recounted what she could remember of Mary's story of the night of the storm, and finding the two together, comforting each other.

"A very remarkable woman, Oonagh," he said softly. "A little frightening, so much strength."

"Alastair must have strength too, or he would not be Procurator Fiscal. It must have taken courage to refuse to prosecute Galbraith. Apparently it was a very big case, very political, and everyone expected him to face trial and be found guilty. I think Mary did too."

"From what the woman in front of us in the church said, he has refused to prosecute quite a few. Are you cold?"

"Yes, but it doesn't matter."

"Do you want my coat?"

"No—then you'll be cold."

He took it off. "Don't argue," he said grimly, and began to put it around her.

"Put it 'round both of us." She moved so that was possible.

"It isn't big enough," he complained.

"It'll do."

"Mary expected Galbraith to be prosecuted? How do you know that?"

"She said something about seeing an Archie Frazer in the house, very late one night, rather furtively. I think it worried her."

"Why? Who is he?"

"A witness in the Galbraith case."

He stiffened. "A witness?" He turned around a little to look at her in the lamplight. "What would a witness be doing coming to Alastair's house at night? And Mary was worried?"

"Yes, it seemed to disturb her."

"Because she knew he had no business there. Alastair had no business seeing a witness privately. And then the case was thrown out, never prosecuted?"

She stared at him. Even in the failing light, the yellow glare and shadow, she could see from his eyes that the same thought had come to him as now filled her mind.

"Bribery?" she whispered. "The Fiscal took money, or something else, not to prosecute Mr. Galbraith—and Mary feared it!"

"Once?" Monk said slowly. "Or often? The woman in the church said there had been a few cases dropped unexpectedly. Is our Fiscal a just man brave enough to defy expectations and throw out a poor case, regardless of public opinion; or is he a corrupt man taking some reward, monetary or otherwise, in order not to prosecute those who can and will pay his price?"

"And even if we can answer that," she went on, almost under her breath, "there arises the other question—did Mary know it or fear it? And was he aware of that?"

He sat silently for several minutes, half turned in their cramped corner, his body sideways, legs out in front of him, covered by her skirts, which were keeping them both warm. The lamp was growing lower, the corners of the room completely lost in darkness. The air was getting very thin and stale.

"Maybe not Kenneth or Baird at all," she whispered at last. "Or even Quinlan for the forgery. I'd rather think she didn't know."

"Damn," he said between his teeth. "Damn Alastair Farraline!"

The same anger and frustration stirred within her, but far overriding it was a desire to share the intensity of feeling with all its subtleties and shades of disappointment, fear, memories, understanding and half-glimpsed thoughts, hunger for truth, and sense of self-blame.

He reached his hand over to take hold of hers where it lay on her skirt. For a moment she did not move, then without thinking, she leaned forward, her brow against his cheek, sliding her head down until it rested in the hollow of his neck, her face half turned on his shoulder. The whole gesture seemed oddly familiar and right. A sense of peace filled her and the anger drained away. It was all still true, still unjust and unresolved, but it no longer had the same importance.

The air was painfully thin. She had not the remotest idea what time it was. Daylight would make no difference here.

Gently he pushed her away until there was a space between them.

She looked at him in the last of the lamplight, at the strong planes of his face, the wide gray eyes. In that moment there was no pretense between them, no lingering vestige of reserve or attempt to escape, no denial. It was final and complete.

Very slowly he leaned forward, infinitely slowly, and kissed her mouth with exquisite tenderness, almost a reverence, as if this one gesture with the last of his strength were almost a holy thing, a surrender of the final bastion.

She never thought not to answer him, not to give her inner self with as much generosity as he, in an embrace she had so long ached for, and to admit it in the passionate tenderness of her lips and her arms.

It was not long after when the lamp had finally guttered and gone out and they lay together, cold and almost senseless in the last of the air, when without warning there was a sound, a thump and a scraping. A shaft of light fell across the room, yellow and dim. And most blessedly of all, there was a draft, clean and sweet, smelling of paper.

"Are you there? Mr. Monk?" It was a tentative voice, a little blurred, and with the lift and music of the north.

Monk sat up slowly, his head hurting, eyes difficult to focus. Hester was still beside him; he could barely feel her breathing.

"Mr. Monk?" came the voice again.

"Hector!" Monk said with dry lips. "Hector ... is that ... are you ..." He ended in a spasm of coughing.

Hester sat up awkwardly, holding on to him. "Major Farraline?" she whispered.

Stumbling over a ream of paper left in his path, knocking himself on the corner of the press and letting out a gasp of pain, Hector made his way over to them, setting his lamp on the floor. He looked dreadful in its yellow light, his thinning hair standing out in spikes, his eyes bloodshot and dark-rimmed. His concentration was intense, and obviously costing him effort, but the relief in his face redeemed it all.

"Mr. Monk! Are you all right?" Then he saw Hester. "Good God! Miss Latterly! I—I'm sorry—I didn't even think of you being here, ma'am!" He extended his arm to assist her up. "Are you able to stand, ma'am? Would you like ... I mean ..." He hesitated, uncertain if he was physically capable of lifting her, any more than in his present state Monk would be.

"Yes, I am sure I am all right, thank you." She attempted to smile. "Or at least I will be, when I have a little air."

"Of course, of course!" He stood up again, then realized he still had not given her any aid. However, Monk was there before him, climbing to his feet awkwardly and bending down to pull Hester up.

"Please hasten," Hector urged, retrieving the lamp. "I don't know who locked you in, but it is not inconceivable they may have missed me and will come looking. I really think it would be much better not to be found here."

Monk gave a sharp laugh, more like a bark, and without further comment they left the secret room, closing the door behind them. They followed Hector carefully through the printing works, now barely lit by daylight pouring through the windows at the front and even in the farthest reaches giving a strained light.

"What made you come after us?" Hester asked when they were outside and she had begun to get some strength back from breathing the fresh air.

Hector looked embarrassed. "I—I think I was a little tipsy last night. I don't remember a great deal of what passed at the dinner table. I should have stopped about three glasses before I did. But I woke in the night, I've no idea what time. My head was as thick as a Chinaman's coat, but I knew something was wrong. I could remember that—very wrong." He blinked apologetically and looked profoundly ashamed. "But I could not for the life of me think what it was."

"Never mind," Monk said generously. "You came in time." He pulled a face. "Not a lot to spare, mind you!" He took the older man by the elbow and they started to walk, three abreast, along the unevenly cobbled street.

"But that doesn't explain why you are here," Hester protested.

"Oh . . ." Hector looked unhappy. "Well, when I woke up this morning I remembered. I knew I said something about the secret room. . . ."

"You said you knew there was one," Monk put in. "In the printing works. But you didn't seem very certain. I gathered it was by deduction rather than observation—at least as to what was in there."

"Deduction?" Hector still sounded confused. "I don't know. What is in there?"

"Well, why did you come?" Monk said, repeating Hester's question. "What made you think we would be in there, or that anyone would lock us in?"

Hector's face cleared. "Ah—that's obvious. You fastened onto the idea, that was plain in your expression. I knew you'd go and look for it. After all, you can't let Miss Latterly live the rest of her life under the shadow, can you?" He shook his head. "Though I never thought she'd be there too." He frowned at Hester, walking a little sideways and having to be steered back into a straight course by Monk's pushing his arm. "You are a very original young woman." A flood of sadness filled him, altering his features starkly. "I know why Mary liked you. She liked anyone with the courage to be themselves, to drink life to the lees and drain the cup without fear. She used to say that." He searched her eyes earnestly. And again Monk had to keep him from veering off into the gutter, even though they were walking comparatively slowly.

"And once I realized you'd go looking for it," Hector went on, "I knew, of course, that if it was in use for anything, whoever was using it would go after you and most likely shut you in." He blinked. "To tell you the truth, I was very afraid they would already have killed you. I'm so glad they haven't."

"We are obliged to you," Monk said sincerely.

"Very much," Hester added, holding Hector's arm a little more tightly.

"You're welcome, my dear," he replied. Then a look of puzzlement crossed his face again. "What is in there, anyway?"

"You don't know?" Monk said it almost casually, but there was an edge to his voice.

"No I don't. Is it something of Hamish's?"

"I think so. Hamish's in the past. Quinlan's now."

"That's odd. Hamish never knew Quinlan all that well. He was ill by the time Eilish met him. In fact, he was going blind, and definitely had times of mental confusion and paralysis of his limbs. Why would he leave anything to Quinlan, rather than Alastair, or even Kenneth?"

"Because Quinlan is an artist," Monk answered, guiding Hester across the uneven road and onto the farther pavement.

ANNE PERRY

"Is he?" Hector looked surprised. "I didn't know that. Never seen anything he's done. Knew Hamish was, of course. Didn't like his work much, too much draftsmanship and not enough imagination. Still, matter of taste, I suppose."

"Don't want imagination in bank notes," Monk said dryly.

"Bank notes?" Hector stopped in the middle of the path.

"Forgery," Monk explained. "That's what is in there. Plates and presses for printing money."

Hector let out a long, slow sigh, as if the thought and the fear had been inside him, pent up for years.

"Is it indeed," was all he said.

"Did Mary know?" Hester asked, searching his face.

He looked at her slowly, frowning, his fair brows drawn down, the early sunlight catching the freckles across his cheeks.

"Mary? Of course not. She'd never have stood for it. Mary was a good woman ... she had her ... her ...." He colored painfully. "Her weaknesses—she told lies, she had to...." There was a moment of fierce defensive anger in him. Then as quickly as it had flared up, it died again. "But she was not dishonest. Not in that way. She would never have allowed that! It's—it's not stealing from one person, it's stealing from everyone. It's ... corrupt."

"I didn't think she would," Hester said with satisfaction, although she was puzzled by what else he had said, profoundly puzzled. She turned to Monk. "Where are we going? If you are looking for a carriage of some sort, we have just passed the main road."

"You're going to the offices, aren't you." Hector made it a statement rather than a question. "You're going to face them with it. Are you sure you are ...." He frowned again, looking doubtfully across at Hester, then to Monk. "We three are not the best soldiers you could have.... You have been locked up all night without air, I am an old man too worn with drink and unhappiness to stand upright, and Miss Latterly, begging your pardon, ma'am, is merely a woman."

"I am quite refreshed," Monk said bleakly. "You are a soldier, sir, and will not fail in the hour of need, and Miss Latterly is no ordinary woman. We shall be sufficient."

They continued in silence, each in solitary thoughts. It was actually only another two or three hundred yards; the offices were naturally enough no farther from the printing works than was necessary.

363

Once it was on the edge of Hester's mind to ask how Hector had known of the room at all and why he had never bothered to look for it before. Presumably in his muddled mind the whole thing was a confusion of memory, childhood envies and secrets, and since Hamish was long dead none of it had mattered much at all until he had dimly, through a haze of alcohol, perceived that something was urgently wrong.

They reached the offices and book warehouse still without having spoken any further. Now they stopped, hesitated only a moment, then Monk knocked sharply on the door and, as soon as a clerk opened it, strode in, closely followed by the two others.

The clerk backed away, sputtering expostulations, and was ignored. Monk led the way through the outer area into the large open space, off which led the iron stairway up to Baird's office and the other one which Alastair used on the rare occasions when he came. As always the cavern below was filled with presses, bales of paper, bolts of cloth, reels of twine and, stretching to the distance, rack after rack of books ready to be shipped. There seemed to be no one else about. Even the clerk had disappeared again. If there was anyone else, they were at the far end of the building, packing or loading books.

Hector looked puzzled, his emotions veering between disappointment and relief. He wanted the last battle, but he was too tired to relish it and too unsure of its outcome.

Monk had no such misgivings. His face was set like a steel mask, through which his eyes glittered hard and bright, and he strode up the iron steps.

"Come on," he ordered, without waiting to see if they obeyed. At the top he took the passage in three strides and flung open the door to Baird's office.

Three people were present—Alastair, Oonagh, and Quinlan Fyffe. Alastair looked surprised and angry at the intrusion, Quinlan merely startled, and Oonagh's usual calm was intensified into an icy chill. She stared at Monk, not even seeing Hester behind him, or Hector not yet in the doorway.

"What in God's name do you want now?" Alastair demanded. He looked harassed and weary, but not noticeably alarmed, and certainly not guilty to see Monk still alive.

ANNE PERRY

Monk looked at Quinlan, who looked back with a half smile of ironical humor, and Oonagh, as so often, was unreadable.

"I've come to make my last report," Monk replied with something approaching irony himself.

"You already did, Mr. Monk," Oonagh said coldly. "And we have thanked you for your efforts. We shall tell the police what we choose in the affair of Mother's croft. It is no longer your concern. If the matter troubles your conscience, you will have to act as you think best. There is nothing we can do about it."

"Not, for example, lock me in the secret room in your warehouse and leave me to suffocate to death?" he said with raised eyebrows, glancing quickly at Quinlan and seeing the blood drain from his cheeks, his eyes turned to Oonagh.

So she at least knew!

"I have no idea what you're talking about," Oonagh said levelly. She still had not even noticed Hester and Hector. "But if you were locked in the warehouse, you have only yourself to blame, Mr. Monk. You were trespassing to be there, and I cannot think of any honest purpose you could have had in the middle of a Sunday night. Still, you obviously managed to effect an exit, and you seem none the worse for it."

"I did not effect an exit. I was released by Major Farraline."

"Bloody Hector!" Quinlan said between his teeth. "Trust the drunken old sot to interfere!"

"Hold your tongue," Oonagh said without looking at him. She spoke to Monk. "What were you doing in our warehouse, Mr. Monk? How do you explain yourself?"

"I went to look for the secret room that Major Farraline mentioned at dinner," he replied, watching her as closely as she watched him. For each of them, there might have been no one else present. "I found it."

Her fair brows rose. "Did you? I was not aware of such a place."

He knew she was lying; he had seen it in Quinlan's face.

"It was full of equipment with which to forge bank notes," he replied. "All denominations, and for several banks."

There was still nothing in her face to betray her.

"Good heavens! Are you sure?"

"Quite."

365

"I wonder how long it has been there. Since my father's time, I imagine, if Uncle Hector says it was his secret room."

Alastair shifted his weight with an almost imperceptible sound.

Monk glanced at him for an instant, and then back at Oonagh.

"Almost certainly," he agreed. "But it is also in present use. Some of the plates are as recent as last year."

"How can you tell?" A flash of amusement lit Oonagh's eyes. "Was the ink still wet?"

"Bank notes change, Mrs. McIvor. There are new designs brought in."

"I see. You are saying someone is still using the room to forge money?"

"Yes. You should be pleased." There was a black laughter underlying his voice now. "It will remove some of the burden from your husband. It makes another excellent motive for murder."

"Does it, Mr. Monk? I fail to see how."

"If your mother discovered it—"

This time it was she who laughed.

"Don't be absurd, Mr. Monk! Do you imagine Mother didn't know?"

Hector made a strangled noise, but he did not move.

"You affected not to," Monk pointed out.

"Certainly, but only before I realized that you are aware it is still in use." Her face was cold and implacable now. She no longer concealed her enmity.

Alastair stood rooted to the spot. Quinlan's hand had closed around a bright paper knife on the desk and he was balanced so as to move with violence.

"Not, of course, that this is the only motive for murder," Monk went on, his voice cutting harsh with anger and stinging, bottomless contempt. "There is also the Galbraith case, and God knows how many others."

"The Galbraith case? What in hell are you talking about?" Quinlan demanded.

But Monk was watching Alastair, and had he ever doubted the charge, he could no longer. The blood fled from Alastair's face, leaving him ashen, his eyes terrified, his mouth slack. Instinctively, almost blindly, he looked at Oonagh.

"She knew," Monk said with a depth of emotion that startled him. "Your mother knew, and you murdered her to keep it silent. You were trusted by your fellow men, honored, held above the ordinary citizens, and you sold justice. Your mother could not forgive that, so you killed her and tried to get her nurse hanged for it in your place."

"No!"

It was not Alastair who spoke, he was beyond speech. The voice came from behind him. Monk half turned to see Hector push his way forward, staring at Alastair. "No," he said again. "It wasn't Alastair who made the list of Mary's clothes for Griselda. It was you! You put that brooch in Hester's bag. Alastair wouldn't have known even where to find it. Alastair, God help him, killed her, but it was you who would have hanged Hester in his place."

"Rubbish," Oonagh said sharply. "Hold your tongue, you old fool!"

A spasm of pain crossed Hector's features so sharp it was beyond all proportion to the insult, which he must have heard a hundred times before, even if only in his mind.

Surprisingly it was Hester who spoke, from just behind Monk's elbow.

"It couldn't have been Alastair who put the pin in my case," she said slowly. "Because Mary wore it with only one dress, and he knew she hadn't packed that dress to take with her. He was the one who damaged it so it had to be cleaned."

"Couldn't it have been mended before she took it?" Monk asked.

"Don't be absurd. It takes days to unpick and clean a silk gown and then stitch it back together again."

As one they turned to Oonagh.

She lowered her eyes. "I didn't know she'd marked the dress. I wanted to protect him," she said very quietly.

Alastair looked at her with a ghastly smile filled with despair.

"But she didn't know," Monk said very softly, almost under his breath. The words fell in the room like stones. "She was afraid, because she saw Archie Frazer in the house, but you could have explained that. You killed her for nothing."

Very slowly, as if in a nightmare, Alastair turned to Oonagh, his face like a dead man's, aged and yet with the helplessness of a lost child. "You said she knew. You told me she knew. I didn't have to kill her! Oonagh—what have you done to me?"

"Nothing, Alastair! Nothing!" she said quickly, putting out both her hands and gripping his arms. "She would have ruined us, believe me." Her voice was desperate, urgent that he should understand.

"But she didn't know!" His voice was rising, shrill with betrayal and despair.

"All right! She didn't know that, or the forgery." The gentleness vanished and her features were suddenly ugly. "But she knew about Uncle Hector and Father, and she'd have told Griselda. That is what she was on the way south to do. Griselda and her stupid obsession with health and her child. She'd have told Connal, and then it would have been all over the place."

"Told him what? What are you talking about?" He was utterly lost. He seemed to have forgotten everyone in the room except Oonagh. "Father's been dead for years. What did it have to do with her child? It doesn't make any sense. . . ."

Oonagh's face was as white as his, but with fury and contempt. There was still no fear in it, and no weakness.

"Father died of syphilis, you fool! He was riddled with it! What did you think his blindness was, and his paralysis? We kept him in the house and said it was a stroke . . . what else were we to do?"

"B-but . . . syphilis takes years to get to . . ." He stopped. There was a funny little choking sound in his throat, as if he could not breathe. He was horrified beyond movement, except for his dry lips. It almost seemed as if she were holding him up. "That means . . . that means we are all . . . Griselda . . . her child, all our children . . . Oh sweet Jesus!"

"No it doesn't," she said between clenched jaws. "Mother knew it from the beginning. That is what she was going to tell Griselda. What she had just told me. . . . Hamish was not our father . . . not any of us."

He looked at her as if she had spoken to him in an incomprehensible language.

She swallowed. Now the words seemed to choke her as much as him. Her face was white with pain.

"Hector is our father . . . every one of us . . . right from you to Griselda. You are a bastard, Alastair. We are all bastards . . . our mother was an adulteress, and that drunken sot is our father! Do you want the world to know that? Can you live with it . . . Procurator Fiscal!"

But Alastair was beyond speech. He was stricken as if dead.

The only sound in the whole place was Quinlan's laugh, a wild, hysterical, bitter sound.

"I loved her," Hector said, staring at Oonagh. "I loved her all my life. She loved Hamish to begin with, but after we met, it was me ... it was always me. She knew what Hamish was ... and she never let him touch her."

Oonagh looked back at him with utter, indescribable loathing.

Tears were running down Hector's face. "I always loved her," he said again. "And you killed her, more surely than if you'd done it yourself." His voice was rising, getting stronger. "You sold my beautiful Eilish to that creature ... to get his services for forgery." He did not even look at Quinlan. "You sold her like a horse or a dog. You used flattery and deceit on all of us ... using our weaknesses against us ... even me. I wanted to stay here, to be part of you. You are all the family I have, and you knew that, and I let you use it." He gulped. "Dear God, but what you've done to Alastair ..."

It was Quinlan who reacted at last. He picked up the heavy paper knife and lunged—not at Hector, but at Monk.

Monk reacted only just in time. The blade grazed his arm and he went backwards, knocking Hester off balance and lurching against the iron railing of the spiral stairs. He only just avoided going over them as they caught him in the small of his back and his foot slipped and went from under him, leaving him sprawled at Hester's feet.

Alastair still stood mesmerized.

Oonagh waited only an instant, then realized he was going to be useless. For a terrible moment she stared at Hector, then she ran at him, bending to catch him in the solar plexus and knock him over the railing to fall the twenty feet to the floor below.

He understood from her eyes, but he moved too slowly. She caught him in the chest, to the left, not quite under the heart. He fell sideways against the railing and backed into Hester, sending her flying. She caught Quinlan just as he reached Monk to strike again. There was a shriek, a flailing of limbs, a moment's blind panic, and then a sickening thud from the floor below.

Then total silence closed in, except for Alastair's weeping.

Hester peered over the edge.

Quinlan lay on the floor below them, his blond hair like a silver halo. There was no blood, but his right arm, in which he had held the knife, was bent underneath him, and no one needed to be told he would not move again.

At last Alastair seemed to regain some semblance of control. He looked around for another weapon, his eyes glistening with almost manic hatred.

Oonagh could see there was no more room for words, no excuses anymore. She plunged past the choking Hector and still-sprawling Monk, ignoring Hester, and clattered down the iron stairs, making towards the back of the vast building until she disappeared between the bales of paper.

Alastair stared wildly around him, then after only a split second's hesitation, followed after her.

Monk scrambled to his feet and bent over Hector.

"Are you all right? Did she injure you?"

"No . . ." Hector coughed and gasped to regain his breath. "No . . ." He looked at Monk with wild eyes. "She didn't. How did I beget that? And Mary . . . Mary was . . ."

But Monk had no time for such speculation. He checked to see that Hester was unhurt, that it was no more than a few bruises and a possible abrasion. Then he set off down the stairs after Oonagh and Alastair.

Hester followed after him, tucking her skirts up in an undignified but very effective manner, and Hector lumbered close behind at a surprisingly good speed.

Out in the street Oonagh and Alastair were at least fifty yards ahead and increasing the distance between them. Monk was sprinting with an excellent turn of speed.

They reached the thoroughfare, and Alastair, waving his arms and shouting, leaped directly in the path of an oncoming carriage. The horse shied and the driver, foolishly standing to ward off what he imagined was an attack, overbalanced and crashed to the ground, still grasping the reins. Alastair leaped into the box, turning only for a second to haul Oonagh up with him, and then shouted wildly to urge the horses into flight again.

Monk swore with breathless venom and skidded to a halt at the crossroads, looking to the left and right for any kind of a vehicle.

Hester caught up with him, and then Hector.

"God damn them!" Monk choked with rage. "God damn her above all!"

"Where can they go?" Hector coughed, gasping to regain his breath. "The police will catch them. . . ."

"We've got to get back and find the police." Monk's voice was rising in an anguish of rage. "And by the time we've explained Quinlan's death, and persuaded them we didn't do it . . . and shown them the room with the forgery equipment, Oonagh and Alastair will have got to the docks, and could even have set sail across towards Holland."

"Can't we get them back?" Hester demanded, even as she said it realizing how hard that would be; with the whole of Europe beyond, and perhaps friends to help them, they might succeed in disappearing.

"Brewery!" Hector said suddenly, jerking his arm to point across the road.

Monk fixed him with a glare that should have withered him to dry bones.

"Horses!" Hector began to shamble across the street.

"We can't chase that in a dray!" Monk bellowed after him, but he began to follow him all the same.

But Hector emerged only a few moments later with not a brewer's dray but a very handsome single-horse gig, and pulled up only long enough for Monk to heave Hester up and then follow after her at a clumsy swing, almost landing on top of her.

"Whose gig have you stolen?" he yelled, not that he cared in the slightest.

"Brewmaster, I expect," Hector yelled back, and then bent his attention to controlling the startled horse and urging it at an unnerving speed along the road after the vanished carriage.

Monk crouched forward, clinging to the side, white-faced. Hester sat back, trying to wedge herself into the seat, while the gig lurched and bucketed all over the road, going faster and faster. Hector was oblivious of everything except his son and daughter ahead.

Hester knew why Monk was so ashen. She imagined the chaos of memories which must be knotting his body and bringing the sweat to his skin, even if his mind only half recalled a haze of sensation, that other carriage careering through the night to end in a heap of splintered wood and spinning wheels, the driver killed and himself lying injured and senseless beneath it, all his life to that moment blotted out and lost forever.

But there was nothing she could do except cling on for dear life. She could not let him know she understood.

Another crossroads loomed ahead and the carriage was already out of sight. It could have gone any of three ways. Presumably straight ahead?

But the gig horse was at a gallop now, and Hector reined it in, almost throwing the beast to the ground, and then urged it to the right, the gig riding on two wheels. Monk was hurled against Hester and the two of them all but fell out. Only Monk's weight, bringing Hester to the floor, saved them.

Monk swore luridly and furiously as the gig righted itself and plunged along Great Junction Street, and then almost immediately turned again towards the sea, sending them pell-mell to the other side.

"What the hell are you doing, you damned lunatic?" Monk made a lunge to grab at Hector, and missed.

Hector was oblivious of him. The carriage was ahead of them again. They could see Alastair's fair hair flying and Oonagh close to him, almost as if he were holding her with his other arm.

The street veered again, and they were beside the narrow, deep river leading to the sea. There were barges moored in it, and fishing smacks. A man leaped out of the way, shouting abuse. A child let out a wail and fled.

A fishwife screamed a string of curses and threw her empty basket at the carriage. One horse reared up and overbalanced onto the other, and in almost dreamlike motion they skewed crazily over to the harbor wall and the sheer drop to the water. The carriage swung around and the shafts snapped. The carriage balanced for a split second, then toppled over into the river, taking Oonagh and Alastair with it. The horses were left shivering on the edge, eyes rolling, squealing with terror, held by the chains and harness.

Hector reined in, throwing his considerable weight backwards to check his own horse, and slamming on the brake with his other hand.

Monk leaped onto the ground and ran to the edge.

Hester scrambled behind him, ripping her skirt where it caught, and almost spraining her ankle on the rough cobbles.

The carriage was already sinking, exquisitely slowly, sucked and held fast in centuries-deep mud beneath the surge of incoming tide. Oonagh and Alastair were both in the water, clear of all tackle and harness, struggling to stay afloat.

The next few moments were imprinted on Hester's heart forever. Alastair gained his breath and swam strongly over to Oonagh, a mere stroke or two away, and for an instant they were face-to-face in filthy water, then slowly and with great care he reached out and grasped her heavy hair and pushed her head under. He held it while she flailed and thrashed. The tide caught him and he ignored it, allowing it to take him rather than let go of his dreadful burden.

Monk looked on in paralyzed horror.

Hester let out a scream. It was the only time she could remember screaming in her life.

"God help you!" Hector said thickly.

There was no more commotion in the water. Oonagh's hair floated pale on the surface and her skirts billowed around her. She did not move at all.

"Sweet Mary mother of God!" the fishwife said from behind Monk, crossing herself again and again.

At last Alastair looked up, his face smeared with mud and his own hair. He was exhausted; the tide had him and he knew it.

As if woken from a dream, Monk turned to the fishwife. "Have you got a rope?" he demanded.

"Holy Virgin!" she said in horrified awe. "You're never going to hang 'im!"

"Of course not, you fool! I'm going to get him out!"

And with that he lashed the rope to the stanchion, the other end around his waist, and leaped into the water and was immediately carried by the current away from the wall and the still-visible floating roof of the carriage.

Others had gathered around. A man in a heavy knitted sweater and sea boots took the weight of the rope, and another went to the edge with a rope ladder.

It was ten minutes before Monk was hauled back and helped in. The fishermen took the bodies from him, and lastly eased him, shivering, streaming water, onto the quayside. He clambered to his feet slowly, his clothes weighing him down.

A little bunch of people stood around, pale-faced, fascinated and flustered as they laid Oonagh on the stones, her skin marble gray, her eyes wide open, and then Alastair beside her, calmer, ice-cold and beyond her reach.

Monk looked down at her, then at Hester, instinctively as he always did, and in that moment he realized the enormity of what lay between them now. He would never seek to put from his mind the night in the secret room, even if he could, nor would he have undone it, but it created new emotions in him he did not want. It opened up vulnerabilities, left him wide open to wounds he could not cope with.

He saw in her face that she understood, that she too was uncertain and afraid; but she was also in that instant certain beyond anything and everything else that there was a trust between them older and stronger than could be broken, something that was not love, although it encompassed it and anger, and differences: true friendship.

He was afraid that she had already seen that it was the most precious thing in the world to him. He looked away quickly, down at the dead face of Oonagh. He reached out a hand and closed her eyes, not out of pity, just a sense of decency.

"The sins of the wolf have come home," he said quietly. "Corruption, deceit, and last of all, betrayal."

ABOUT THE AUTHOR

ANNE PERRY's other William Monk novels include *Defend and Betray*, *A Sudden, Fearful Death*, *A Dangerous Mourning*, and *The Face of a Stranger*. She is also the author of another acclaimed Victorian mystery series, featuring Inspector Thomas Pitt and his wife, Charlotte, which includes *The Hyde Park Headsman*, *Farriers' Lane*, *Silence in Hanover Close*, *Cardington Crescent*, *Highgate Rise*, and others.

Anne Perry lives in Portmahomack in the Scottish Highlands.